HARRIS MEASURED THE DISTANCE BETWEEN THEM,

wondering whether she would use the weapon after all. A disruptor broiled the neural tissue; death was instantaneous and fairly ghastly.

He decided to risk it. His assignment was to kill Medlins, not to let himself be killed by them. He had nothing to lose by making the attempt.

In a soft voice he said, "You didn't answer. Do you really think I'd fall in love with something like *you*?"

"Biologically we're Earthers now, not Medlins or Darruui. It's possible."

"Maybe you're right. After all, I *did* ask you to cover yourself up." He smiled and said, "I'm all confused. I need time to think things over."

"Of course. You—"

He sprang from the chair and covered the ten feet between them in two big bounds, stretching out one hand to grab the hand that held the disruptor. He deflected the weapon toward the ceiling. She did not fire. He closed on her wrist and forced her to drop the tiny pistol. Pressed against her, he stared into eyes blazing with anger.

The anger melted suddenly into passion. He stepped back, reaching for his own gun, not willing to have such close contact with her. She was too dangerous. Better to kill her right now, he thought. She's just a Medlin. A deadly one.

He started to draw the weapon from his tunic. Suddenly she lifted her hand; there was the twinkle of something bright between her fingers, and then Harris recoiled, helpless, as the bolt of a stunner struck him in the face like a club against the back of his skull.

She fired again. He struggled to get his gun out, but his muscles would not obey.

He toppled forward, paralyzed.

THE PLANET STORIES LIBRARY

STRANGE ADVENTURES ON OTHER WORLDS
AVAILABLE EXCLUSIVELY FROM PLANET STORIES!

FOR AUTHOR BIOS AND SYNOPSES,
VISIT PAIZO.COM/PLANETSTORIES

Publisher's Cataloging-In-Publication Data
(Prepared by The Donohue Group, Inc.)

Silverberg, Robert.
    Hunt the Space-Witch! : seven adventures in time and space / by
Robert Silverberg ; cover illustration by Kieran Yanner.

        p. ; cm. -- (Planet stories ; #31)

    Stories previously published separately in the original Planet Stories
magazine between 1956-1958.
    "June 2011."
    Contents: Slaves of the star giants -- Spawn of the deadly sea -- The
flame and the hammer -- Valley beyond time -- Hunt the Space-Witch!
-- The silent invaders -- Spacerogue.
    ISBN: 978-1-60125-329-3

    1. Adventure and adventurers--Fiction. 2. Battles--Fiction. 3.
Science fiction, American. 4. Adventure stories, American. 5. Short
stories, American. 6. Fantasy fiction. I. Yanner, Kieran. II. Title.

PS3569.I472 A6 2011
813/.54

COVER ILLUSTRATION BY KIERAN YANNER

HUNT THE SPACE-WITCH!
SEVEN ADVENTURES IN TIME AND SPACE
BY ROBERT SILVERBERG

PLANET STORIES is published bimonthly by Paizo Publishing, LLC with offices at 7120 185th Ave NE, Ste 120, Redmond, Washington, 98052. Erik Mona, Publisher. Pierce Watters, Senior Editor. Christopher Paul Carey and James L. Sutter, Editors. *Hunt the Space-Witch! Seven Adventures in Time and Space* © 2011 by Agberg, Ltd. Introduction © 2011 by Agberg, Ltd. "Slaves of the Star Giants" © 1956, 1984 by Agberg, Ltd. "Spawn of the Deadly Sea" © 1957, 1985 by Agberg, Ltd. "The Flame and the Hammer" © 1957, 1985 by Agberg, Ltd. "Valley Beyond Time" © 1957, 1985 by Agberg, Ltd. "Hunt the Space-Witch!" © 1957, 1985 by Agberg, Ltd. "The Silent Invaders" © 1958, 1986 by Agberg, Ltd. "Spacerogue" © 1958, 1986 by Agberg, Ltd. Planet Stories and the Planet Stories planet logo are registered trademarks of Paizo Publishing, LLC. Planet Stories #31, *Hunt the Space-Witch! Seven Adventures in Time and Space*, by Robert Silverberg. June 2011. PRINTED IN THE UNITED STATES OF AMERICA.

Introduction

Along time ago (upwards of sixty years), in a galaxy far, far away (it was Brooklyn, actually, but that's quite a distance from where I live now) a high-school chum gave me a beaten-up copy of a pulp magazine called *Planet Stories*. I was just in the first heady rapture of discovering the science fiction magazines, and he had found a copy of the Summer, 1942 issue of *Planet* around his house, probably something his father had read and discarded, and thought, quite rightly, that I would like to have it.

I was already a devoted reader of *Astounding Science Fiction* and *Amazing Stories* and *Fantastic Adventures*, but *Planet* was new to me. I fell upon it with rapture. The magazine, seven years old at the time, was mussed and scuffed and had lost its cover, but to me it was a treasurehouse of wonders. Somewhere along the eons I replaced it with a fine shiny copy, which is sitting beside me as I write this, so I can tell you exactly what it contained: three novelets, by Ross Rocklynne, Ray Cummings, and Manly Wade Wellman, five short stories, and an 11-page column of fan letters from readers. (More about that letter column in a moment.)

The specialty of *Planet Stories* was tales of action and adventure, colorful yarns set on other worlds. The lead story, Ross Rocklynne's "Task to Lahri," with a lovely, moody two-page illustration by an artist named Leydenfrost, dealt with the visit of a spacefarer from Earth to the tenth world of our solar system, where a lost race lived in the hollow interior. Wellman's "Venus Enslaved" was a tale of a castaway Earthman and crossbow-armed Amazons in conflict with the gigantic bestial Frogmasters of our neighbor planet. Nelson Bond's "Operation Chaos" told of an attempt to run the blockade of the spaceways that the Outer Planets Alliance had set up.

You get the idea. Space opera, wild and fast and furious. I loved it. I was fourteen years old. I rushed out to the newsstand to see if *Planet Stories* still existed, and, yes, there it was: the Winter, 1949 issue, featuring "The Dead-Star

Rover," which the cover blurb called a "startling novel" by Robert Abernathy, and "Sword of Fire," described as "a novelet of an Enslaved Universe" by Emmett McDowell. I handed over twenty cents for it. A day or two later I visited a second-hand bookstore where, for a dime more, I picked up the previous issue, Fall, 1949, which gave me my introduction to the work of Leigh Brackett ("Enchantress of Venus"). Over the next few years I assiduously collected a complete file of the magazine, going back to the first issue in 1939, and I faithfully bought and read every new issue that appeared until the magazine expired in the summer of 1955.

By the summer of 1955 I had precociously begun my own writing career, with a couple of story sales in 1954 and then a whole slew of them the following year. One magazine that I was desperately eager to crash was *Planet*, but I was just a little too late for that. I had already begun submitting stories of my own to the magazine as far back as 1950, and its editor at the time, Jerome Bixby, had read them sympathetically and claimed to see in them the work of someone who would be a successful writer someday—but he didn't buy any of them. My work didn't reach a really professional level until about 1954, and by then *Planet*, to my eternal regret, was wobbling toward its doom and buying no new material. So I never did get a chance to have some grand and gaudy space adventure published in that grand and gaudy magazine.

Let's go back to the letter column of that battered, coverless 1942 issue that my high-school friend had given me in 1949, though. Among the fans whose letters were published in it was a certain Larry Shaw of Schenectady, New York. Soon I would learn, by looking at back-issue magazines, that Shaw was a regular contributor of such letters to the magazines, and was known in the science-fiction world as a shrewd critic of the genre. He left Schenectady eventually to become the editor of a hot-rod magazine, and by 1953 he was working as associate editor of one of the best s-f magazines of the day, *If*. He and I met at my first science-fiction convention, in Philadelphia in September, 1953, and we took an immediate liking to each other. I was then just on the threshold of my writing career, and he gave me some useful, encouraging advice.

By the summer of 1955 Larry had left *If* to become the editor of another new magazine, *Infinity Science Fiction*. That fall I visited his office in midtown Manhattan, told him of the success I was suddenly having as a writer, and offered him a story, which he bought and published in the fourth issue, dated August, 1956. He bought another and used it in the fifth issue. From then until the magazine went out of business in 1958 I would be a regular contributor.

And one day in the summer of 1956 Larry said to me, "We're going to revive *Planet Stories*. How would you like to write some space-action stuff for us?"

He wasn't going to call it *Planet Stories*, of course. At that time the name still belonged to the company that once had published it. He wasn't going to use the old shaggy-edged pulp format, either, because the day of the pulp magazine was over. The new magazine would bear the appropriately explicit title of *Science Fiction Adventures* and it would be printed in what was now the standard digest-sized format for fiction magazines.

Naturally, I jumped at the opportunity. I told Larry how much I had loved the old magazine and how deeply I regretted never having had a chance to write for it—and then, in July, 1956, I sat down and produced a 20,000-word story with the resounding *Planet*-style title of "Battle for the Thousand Suns." Larry bought it on the spot and asked for a second story of the same length, which I wrote a week later in collaboration with my writing partner of that era, Randall Garrett: "Secret of the Green Invaders." When the first issue of *Science Fiction Adventures* appeared in September, 1956, I was responsible for half the fiction in it. (The issue also contained a novella by Edmond Hamilton and a three-page story by a new writer named Harlan Ellison.)

That was the beginning of my long and fruitful relationship with Larry Shaw's *Science Fiction Adventures*, a magazine that lacked the flamboyant pulpy appearance of the old *Planet Stories* but came very close to reincarnating its spirit. Over the next couple of years, I would write the magazine practically single-handedly, reveling in the opportunity to tell outrageously exciting tales of the space lanes, and I have put some of the best of those tales together in the volume you are holding now.

Even before the first issue had appeared, Larry had handed me a rough sketch of a cover painting showing a giant alien being (with the sort of pointy ears we would one day associate with Mr. Spock) holding a test tube that contained a man and a scantily-clad woman. "Write a novella around that illustration for the second issue," Larry said, and in September, 1956—about a week after I had won my first Hugo, as most promising new writer of the year—I turned out "Slaves of the Star Giants," a story of time travel rather than space travel, which was the cover story in the February, 1957 issue. By now it was understood that I would write a novella for every issue of the magazine. For the third issue, which had a magnificent red-toned cover by Ed Emsh, I gave him "Spawn of the Deadly Sea," a kind of Viking story about a conquered Earth, one that would have fit perfectly into the old *Planet Stories* we all had known and loved. And in the fourth issue I began the trilogy of novellas under the pseudonym of "Calvin M. Knox" that I called the "Chalice of Death" series, which I eventually put together to form a novel, and which is not included here because the complete novel will be released in a different book from the present publisher. (Which, by no coincidence, calls itself "Planet Stories" too.)

I kept up the pace in just about all of the succeeding issues. The fifth issue ran "This World Must Die," which I expanded into the novel "The Planet Killers" and which also is being reprinted elsewhere in its longer form. "The Flame and the Hammer" came out in issue six, September, 1957. The seventh issue, dated October, 1957 (the magazine now was appearing every month), was devoted almost entirely to my novel-length "Thunder Over Starhaven," and this, too, you can find in the forthcoming *Chalice of Death* Planet Stories omnibus. (Larry insisted on printing it under the pseudonym of "Ivar Jorgenson," which I had used once or twice in other magazines, though most stories under that byline—spelled "Jorgensen," however—had been the work of a writer named Paul Fairman. Fairman was rightly annoyed, though publishers kept on sticking it on my work all the same.)

Issue eight, for some reason skipping a month and bearing the date of December, 1957, was also almost entirely the work of my busy typewriter: "Valley Beyond Time," reprinted here, was the lead novella, and right behind it came the second of Calvin Knox's "Chalice" stories. And so it went into 1958: my "Hunt the Space-Witch!" another "Ivar Jorgenson" novella, led off the January, 1958 issue, number nine. It too is reprinted here. The tenth issue brought the third "Chalice" novella, and the eleventh, April, 1958, contained my 40,000-word novel "Shadow on the Stars," which eventually was published as a separate novel and now is included in one of my novel omnibuses.

Hard times were coming to the science-fiction magazines of that period, though. One of the biggest magazine distributors of the time abruptly went out of business in the spring of 1958, taking a lot of magazines with it. *Science Fiction Adventures*, to my great sorrow, was one of those that folded. (The final issue, dated June, 1958, contained two short stories of mine, but no novellas—I must have been busy that month meeting some other editor's deadline.) Generally, though, I kept the novellas flowing to editor Shaw's desk even as the end was approaching, and, therefore, when *Science Fiction Adventures* went under he found himself left with a hefty inventory of Silverberg space operas. He had no choice but to use them in the surviving companion magazine, *Infinity*, which ostensibly was devoted to a more serious, contemplative kind of science fiction. (And for which I had written a great many stories also.) So the October, 1958 issue of *Infinity* featured "a great CALVIN KNOX novel" that had been intended for the other magazine, complete with a bright red Emsh cover that proclaimed in big letters, "WAS SHE A WOMAN—OR A MONSTER?" (Monsters were very big in magazine publishing just then.) The story was "The Silent Invaders," which I later expanded into a novel. But I think the shorter version is superior, and that is the one that is included here.

Then, in the November, 1958 *Infinity*, lurking behind another Emsh cover depicting a really revolting alien being, came "Spacerogue," my final novella for Larry Shaw in the old *Planet Stories* vein, which for some reason was published here under the pseudonym of "Webber Martin." That was the end of the line. *Infinity* went out of business, I turned my attention to other kinds of science fiction (and a lot of non-science-fiction writing too), and the rest is, well, nostalgia.

But here they are again, brought together for the first time—seven of the action-adventure novellas that I wrote more than half a century ago for Larry Shaw's *Science Fiction Adventures*, a magazine that was for both of us a way of showing our love for the wonderful old *Planet Stories* of our youthful years.

Robert Silverberg
December, 2009

Slaves of the Star Giants

Chapter One

Dark violet shadows streaked the sky, and the forest was ugly and menacing. Lloyd Harkins leaned against the bole of a mighty red-brown tree and looked around dizzily, trying to get his bearings.

He knew he was *there*, not *here*. *Here* had vanished so suddenly that there had been no sense of transition or of motion—merely a strange subliminal undertone of *loss*, as the world he knew had melted and been replaced with—what?

He heard a distant, ground-shaking sound of thunder, growing louder. Birds with gleaming, toothy beaks and wide-sweeping wings wheeled and shrieked in the shadowed sky, and the air was cold and damp. Harkins held his ground, clinging tightly to the enormous tree as if it were his last bastion of reality in a world of dreams.

And the tree moved.

It lifted from its base, swung forward and upward, carrying Harkins with it. The sound of thunder grew nearer. Harkins shut his eyes, opened them, gaped in awe.

Some ten feet to the right, another tree was moving.

He threw his head back, stared upward into the cloud-fogged sky, and verified the fact he wanted to deny: the trees were not trees.

They were legs.

Legs of a being huge beyond belief, whose head rose fifty feet or more above the floor of the dark forest. A being who had begun to move.

Harkins dug his hands frantically into the leg, gripping it as he swung wildly through a fifteen-foot arc with each stride of the monstrous creature. Gradually, the world around him took shape again, and slowly he re-established control over his fear-frozen mind.

Through the bright green blurs of vegetation he was able to see the creature on which he rode. It was gigantic but vaguely manlike, wearing a sort of jacket and a pair of shorts which terminated some twenty-five feet above Harkins' head. From there down, firm red-brown skin the texture of wood was visible. Harkins could even distinguish dimly a face, far above, with pronounced features of a strange and alien cast.

He began to assemble his environment. It was a forest—where? On Earth, apparently—but an Earth no one had ever known before. The bowl of the sky was shot through with rich, dark colors, and the birds that screeched overhead were nightmare creatures of terrifying appearance.

The earth was brown and the vegetation green, though all else had changed. *Where am I?* Harkins asked over and over again.

And—*Why am I here?*

And—*How can I get back?*

He had no answers. The day had begun in ordinary fashion, promising to be neither more nor less unusual than the day before or all the days before that. Shortly after noon, on the 21st of April, 1957, he had been on his way to the electronics laboratory, in New York City, on the planet Earth. And now he was here, wherever *here* might be.

His host continued to stride through the forest, seemingly unconcerned about the man clinging to his calf. Harkins' arms were growing tired from the strain of hanging on, and suddenly the new thought occurred: *Why not let go?* He had held on only through a sort of paralysis of the initiative, but now he had regained his mental equilibrium. He dropped off.

He hit the ground solidly and sprawled out flat. The soil was warm and fertile-smelling, and for a moment he clung to it as he had to the "tree" minutes before. Then he scrambled to his feet and glanced around hastily, looking for a place to hide and reconnoiter.

There was none. And a hand was descending toward him—red-brown, enormous, tipped with gleaming, pointed fingernails six inches long. Gently, the giant hand scooped Harkins up.

There was a dizzying moment as he rose fifty feet, held tenderly in the giant's leathery embrace. The hand opened, and Harkins found himself standing on an outspread palm the size of a large table, staring at a strange oval face with deep-set, compassionate eyes and a wide, almost lipless mouth studded with triangular teeth. The being seemed to smile almost pityingly at Harkins.

"What are you?" Harkins demanded.

The creature's smile grew broader and more melancholy, but there was no reply—only the harsh wailing of the forest birds, and the distant rumbling of approaching thunder. Harkins felt himself being lowered to the giant's side, and once again the being began to move rapidly through the forest, crushing down the low-clustered shrubs as it walked. Harkins, his stomach rolling agonizingly with each step, rode cradled in the great creature's loosely-closed hand.

After what must have been ten minutes or more, the giant stopped. Harkins glanced around, surprised. The thunder was close now, and superimposed on it was the dull boom of toppling trees. The giant was standing quite still, legs planted as solidly as tree trunks, waiting.

Minutes passed—and then Harkins saw why the giant had stopped. Coming toward them was a machine—a robot, Harkins realized—some fifteen feet high. It was man-shaped, but much more compact; a unicorn-like spike projected from its gleaming nickel-jacketed forehead, and instead of legs it moved on broad treads. The robot was proceeding through the forest, pushing aside the trees that stood in its way with casual gestures of its massive forearms, sending them toppling to the right and left with what looked like a minimal output of effort.

The giant remained motionless, staring down at the ugly machine as it went by. The robot paid no attention to Harkins' host, and went barrelling on through the forest as if following some predetermined course.

Minutes later it was out of sight leaving behind it a trail of uprooted shrubs and exposed tree-roots. As the robot's thunder diminished behind them, the giant resumed his journey through the forest. Harkins rode patiently, not daring to think any more.

After a while longer a clearing appeared—and Harkins was surprised and pleased to discover a little cluster of huts. Man-sized huts, ringed in a loose circle to form a village. Moving in the center of the circle were tiny dots which Harkins realized were people, human beings, men.

A colony?

A prison camp?

The people of the village spotted the giant, and gathered in a small knot, gesticulating and pointing. The giant approached within about a hundred yards of the village, stooped, and lowered Harkins delicately to the ground.

Dizzy after his long journey in the creature's hand, Harkins staggered, reeled, and fell. He half expected to see the giant scoop him up again, but instead the being was retreating into the forest, departing as mysteriously as he had come.

Harkins got to his feet. He saw people running toward him—wild-looking, dangerous people. Suddenly, he began to feel that he might have been safer in the giant's grip.

Chapter Two

There were seven of them, five men and two women. They were probably the bravest. The rest hung back and watched from the safety of their huts.

Harkins stood fast and waited for them. When they drew near, he held up a hand.

"Friend!" he said loudly. "Peace!"

The words seemed to register. The seven paused and arrayed themselves in an uneasy semicircle before Harkins. The biggest of the men, a tall, broad-shouldered man with unruly black hair, thick features and deep-set eyes, stepped forward.

"Where are you from, stranger?" he growled in recognizable, though oddly distorted, English.

Harkins thought it over, and decided to keep acting on the assumption that they were as savage as they looked. He pointed to the forest. "From there."

"We know that," the tall man said. "We saw the Star Giant bring you. But where is your village?"

Harkins shrugged. "Far from here—far across the ocean." It was as good a story as any, he thought. And he wanted more information about these people before he volunteered any about himself. But one of the two women spoke up.

"What ocean?" Her voice was scornful. She was a squat, yellow-faced woman in a torn, dirty tunic. "There are no oceans near here." She edged up to Harkins, glared intently at him. Her breath was foul. "You're a *spy*," she said accusingly. "You're from the Tunnel City, aren't you?"

"The Star Giant brought him," the other woman pointed out calmly. She was tall and wild-looking, with flowing blonde hair that looked as if it had never been cut. She wore ragged shorts and two strips of cloth that covered her breasts. "The Star Giants aren't in league with the city dwellers, Elsa," the woman added.

"Quiet," snapped the burly man who had spoken first. He turned to Harkins. "Who are you?"

"My name is Lloyd Harkins. I come from far across the ocean. I don't know how I came here, but the Star Giant"—this part would be true, at least—"found me and brought me to this place." He spread his hands. "More I cannot tell you."

"Uh. Very well, Lloyd Harkins." The big man turned to the other six. "Kill him, or let him stay?"

"How unlike you to ask our opinions, Jorn!" said the squat woman named Elsa. "But I say kill him. He's from the Tunnel City. I know it!"

The man named Jorn faced the others. "What say you?"

"Let him live," replied a sleepy-looking young man. "He seems harmless." Jorn scowled. "The rest of you?"

"Death," said a second man. "He looks dishonest."

"He looks all right to me," offered the third. "And to me," said the fourth. "But I vote for death. Elsa is seldom wrong."

Harkins chewed nervously at his lower lip. That made three votes for death, two in his favor. Jorn was staring expectantly at the sullen-faced girl with long hair.

"Your opinion, Katha?"

"Let him live," she said slowly.

Jorn grunted. "So be it. I cast my vote for him also. You may join us, stranger. But mine is the deciding vote—and if I reverse it, you die!"

They marched over the clearing single file to the village, Jorn leading, Harkins in the rear followed by the girl Katha. The rest of the villagers stared at him curiously as he entered the circle of huts.

"This is Lloyd Harkins," Jorn said loudly. "He will live among us."

Harkins glanced tensely from face to face. There were about seventy of them, altogether, ranging from gray-beards to naked children. They seemed oddly savage and civilized all at once. The village was a strange mixture of the primitive and cultured.

The huts were made of some unfamiliar dark green plastic substance, as were their clothes. A bonfire burnt in the center of the little square formed by the ring of huts. From where he stood, Harkins had a clear view of the jungle— a thickly-vegetated one, which had obviously not sprung up overnight. He could see the deeply-trampled path which the Star Giant had made.

He turned to Jorn. "I'm a stranger to this land. I don't know anything about the way you live."

"All you need to know is that I'm in charge," Jorn said. "Listen to me and you won't have any trouble."

"Where am I going to stay?"

"There's a hut for single men," Jorn said. "It's not very comfortable, but it's the best you can have." Jorn's deep eyes narrowed. "There are no spare women in this village, by the way. Unless you want Elsa, that is." He threw back his head and laughed raucously.

"Elsa's got her eyes fixed on one of the Star Giants," someone else said. "That's the only kind can satisfy her."

"Toad!" The squat woman known as Elsa sprang at the man who had spoken, and the ferocity of her assault knocked him to the ground. Elsa climbed on his chest and began banging his head against the ground. With a lazy motion, Jorn reached down and plucked her off.

"Save your energy, Elsa. We'll need you to cast spells when the Tunnel City men come."

Harkins frowned. "This Tunnel City—where is it? Who lives there?"

Jorn swung slowly around. "Either you're a simpleton or you really *are* a stranger here. The Tunnel City is one of the Old Places. Our enemies live there, in the ruins. They make war on us—and the Star Giants watch. It amuses them."

"These Tunnel City men—they're men, like us? I mean, not giants?"

"They're like us, all right. That's why they fight us. The different ones don't bother."

"Different?"

"You'll find out. Stop asking questions, will you? There's food to be gathered." Jorn turned to a corn-haired young villager nearby. "Show Harkins where he's going to stay—and then put him to work in the grain field."

A confused swirl of thoughts cascaded through Harkins' mind as the young man led him away. Slowly, the jigsaw was fitting together.

The villagers spoke a sort of English, which spiked Harkins' theory that he had somehow been cast backward in time. The alternative, hard as it was to accept, was plain: he was in the future, in a strangely altered world.

The Star Giants—who were they? Jorn had said they watched while the contending villages fought. It amused them, he said. That argued that the giants were the dominant forces in this world. Were they humans? Invaders from elsewhere? Those questions would have to wait for answers. Jorn either didn't know them; or didn't want Harkins to know.

The robot in the forest—unexplained. The Star Giant had shown it a healthy respect, though.

The tribe here—Jorn was in command, and everyone appeared to respect his authority. A fairly conventional primitive arrangement, Harkins thought. It implied an almost total breakdown of civilization some time in the past. The pieces were fitting together, though there were gaps.

The Tunnel City, home of the hated enemy. "One of the Old Places," Jorn had said. The enemies lived in the ruins. That was clear enough. But what of these "different ones"?

He shook his head. It was a strange and confusing world, and possibly the fewer questions he asked the safer he would be.

"Here's our place," the villager said. He pointed to a long hut, low and broad. "The single men stay here. Take any bed that has no clothing on it."

"Thanks," said Harkins. He stooped to enter. The interior of the hut was crude and bare, with straw pallets scattered at random here and there inside. He selected one that looked fairly clean and dropped his jacket on it. "This is mine," he said.

The other nodded. "Now to the grain fields." He pointed to a clearing behind the village.

Harkins spent the rest of that afternoon working in the fields, deliberately using as much energy as he could and trying not to think. By the time night approached, he was thoroughly exhausted. The men returned to the village, where the women served a plain but nourishing community supper.

The simple life, Harkins thought. Farming and gathering food and occasional intertribal conflicts. It was hardly a lofty position these remote descendants of his had reached, he observed wryly. And something was wrong with the picture. The breakdown must have occurred fairly recently, for them to be still sunk this low in cultural pattern—but the thickness of the forestation implied many centuries had gone by since this area had been heavily populated. There was a hole in his logical construct here, Harkins realized, and he was unable to find it.

Night came. The moon was full, and he stared at its pockmarked face longingly, feeling a strong homesickness for the crowded, busy world he had been taken from. He looked at the tribesmen sprawled on the ground, their bellies full, their bodies tired. Someone was singing a tuneless, unmelodic song. Loud snoring came from behind him. Jorn stood tensely outlined against the brightness of the moon, staring out toward the forest as if expecting a momentary invasion. From far away came the thumping sound of a robot crashing its way through the trees, or possibly a Star Giant bound on some unknown errand.

Suddenly Jorn turned. "Time for sleep," he snapped, "into your huts."

He moved around, kicking the dozers, shoving the women away from the fire. *He's the boss, all right,* Harkins thought. He studied Jorn's whipcord muscles appreciatively, and decided he'd do his best to avoid crossing the big man, for the duration of his stay in the village.

Later, Harkins lay on his rough bed, trying to sleep. It was impossible. The bright moonlight streamed in the open door of the hut, and in any event he was too tense for sleep to come. He craned his neck, looking around. The six men with whom he shared the hut were sound asleep, reaping the reward of their hard day's toil. They had security, he thought—the security of ignorance. He, Harkins, had too much of the civilized man's perceptivity. The night-noises from outside disturbed him, the muffled booms from the forest woke strange and deeply buried terrors in him. This was no world for nervous men.

He closed his eyes and lay back again. The image of the Star Giant floated before him, first the Star Giant-as-tree, then the complete entity, finally just the oddly benign, melancholy face. He pictured the Star Giants gathered together, wherever they lived, moving with massive grace and bowing elegantly to each other in a fantastic minuet. He wondered if the one who had found him today had been aware he carried an intelligent being, or if he had been thought of as some two-legged forest creature too small to regard seriously.

The image of the robot haunted him then—the domeheaded, indomitable creature pursuing some incomprehensible design, driving relentlessly through the forest toward a hidden goal. Weaving in and out of his thoughts was the screaming of the toothed birds, and the booming thunder of the forest. *A world I never made,* he thought tiredly, and tried to force sleep to take him.

Suddenly, something brushed his arm lightly. He sat up in an instant and narrowed his eyes to see.

"Don't make any noise," a soft voice said.

Katha.

She was crouched over his pallet, looking intently down at him. He wondered how long she had been there. Her free-flowing hair streamed down over her shoulders, and her nostrils flickered expectantly as Harkins moved toward her.

"What are you doing here?"

"Come outside," she whispered. "We don't want to wake *them.*"

Harkins allowed her to lead him outside. Moonlight illuminated the scene clearly. The sleeping village was utterly quiet, and the eerie jungle sounds could be heard with ease.

"Jorn is with Nella tonight," Katha said bitterly. "I am usually Jorn's woman—but tonight he ignored me."

Harkins frowned. Tired as he was, he could see what the situation was immediately, and he didn't like it at all. Katha was going to use him as a way of expressing her jealousy to Jorn.

She moved closer to him and pressed her warm body against his. Involuntarily, he accepted the embrace—and then stepped back. Regardless of Katha's motives, Jorn would probably kill him on the spot if he woke and found him with her. The girl was a magnificent animal, he thought regretfully, and perhaps some other time, some other place—

But not here, not now. Harkins was dependent on Jorn's mercies, and it was important to remain in his good graces. Gently, he pushed Katha back.

"No," he said. "You belong to Jorn."

Her nostrils flared. "I belong to no one!" she whispered harshly. She came toward him again. There was the sound of someone stirring in a nearby hut.

"Go back to sleep," Harkins said anxiously. "If Jorn finds us, he'll kill us both."

"Jorn is busy with that child Nella—but he would not kill me anyway. Are you afraid of Jorn, stranger?"

"No," Harkins lied. "I—"

"You talk like a coward!" Again, she seized him, and this time he shoved her away roughly. She spat angrily at him and slapped him in fury. Then she cupped her hand and cried, *"Help!"*

At her outcry, Harkins dodged past her and attempted to re-enter his hut, but he was much too late. The whole village seemed to be awake in an instant, and before he was fully aware of what had happened he felt a firm pressure on the back of his neck.

"The rest of you go back to bed." It was Jorn's voice, loud and commanding, and in a moment the square was empty again—except for Katha, Harkins, and Jorn. The big man held Harkins by the neck with one hand and a squirming, struggling Katha with the other.

"He attacked me!" Katha accused.

"It's a lie!"

"Quiet, both of you!" Jorn's voice snapped like a whip. He let go of Katha and threw her to the ground, where she remained, kneeling subserviently. His grip on Harkins tightened.

"What happened?" Jorn demanded. "Let her tell it," Harkins replied.

"Her word is meaningless. I want the truth."

"He came to my hut and attacked me," Katha said. "It was because he knew you were busy with Nella—"

Jorn silenced her with a kick. "She came to you, did she not?"

Harkins nodded. "Yes."

"I thought so. I expected it. This has happened before." He released Harkins, and gestured for Katha to take her feet. "You will have to leave here," Jorn said. "Katha is mine."

"But—"

"It is not your fault," Jorn said. "But you must leave here. She will not rest until she has you. Go now—and if you return, I will have to kill you."

Harkins felt numb at Jorn's words. The last thing he would have wanted to happen was to be thrust out of the one haven he had found so far in this strange and unfriendly world. He looked at Katha, who was glaring at him in bitter hatred, her breasts rising and falling rapidly in rage. He began to feel rage himself at the unfairness of the situation.

He watched as Jorn turned to Katha. "Your punishment will come later. You will pay for this, Katha."

She bowed her head, then looked up. With astonishment, Harkins saw that she was looking at Jorn with unmistakable love reflected in her eyes.

Jorn gestured toward the forest. "Go."

"Right now?"

"Now," Jorn said. "You must be gone by morning. I should not have allowed you to stay at all."

Chapter Three

Whatever personal deity was looking out for him was doing a notably bad job, Harkins thought, as he stood at the edge of the forest. It was sadistic to bring him into contact with a civilization, of sorts, and then almost immediately thrust him back into the uncertainty of the forest.

It was near dawn. He had spent most of the night circling the borders of the clearing, postponing the moment when he would have to enter the forest again. He withdrew to the edge of the clearing and waited there. For a while, there had been the sound of repeated snapping, as of a whip descending, coming from Jorn's hut. Then, there had been silence. Harkins wondered whether Katha's punishment had not, perhaps, been followed by a reward.

Jorn had been right to cast him out, Harkins admitted. In a tribal set-up of that sort, the leader's dominance had to be maintained—and any possible competitor, even such an unwilling one as Harkins, had to be expelled. Now that Harkins considered the matter, he realized that Jorn had been surprisingly lenient not to kill him on the spot.

Only—facing this strange, wild world alone would be no joyride.

As the first faint rays of dawn began to break on the horizon, Harkins entered the forest. Almost immediately, the air changed, grew cooler and damper. The thick curtain of vegetation that roofed in the forest kept the sunlight out. Harkins moved warily, following the trampled path the Star Giant had left.

Somewhere not too far from here would be the Tunnel City. It would have to be reasonably close: in a non-mechanized society such as this, it would be impossible to carry out warfare over any great distance. And the Tunnel City, whatever it was, was inhabited. He hoped he would he able to locate it before he encountered any trouble in the forest. As an outcast from Jorn's group, he could probably gain refuge there.

Suddenly there was the sound of crashing timber up ahead. He flattened himself against a lichen-covered rock and peered into the distance.

Above the trees, the red-brown head of a Star Giant on his way through the forest was visible. Harkins considered momentarily going toward the giant, but then changed his mind and struck off along a back path. The Star Giants had let him live once, but there was no predicting their actions. There was little choice in the matter anyway; the Star Giant was rapidly moving on, covering forty feet at a stride.

Harkins watched the huge being until it was out of sight, and then continued to walk. Perhaps, he thought, the path might lead to the Tunnel City. Perhaps not. At this point, he had very little to lose no matter which direction he took.

But he was wrong. The other path might have been safe; this one was barred by a howling nightmare.

It was facing him squarely, its six legs braced between two thin trees. The creature had a pair of snapping mouths—one on each flattened, sharp-snouted head. Razor-like teeth glistened in the dim light. Harkins froze, unable either to turn and run or to dash forward on the offensive. The creature's howling rose to a frantic pitch that served as wild counterpoint for the dull booming of the forest.

The thing began to advance. Harkins felt sweat trickle down his body. The animal, white-furred, was the size of a large wolf, and looked hungry. Harkins retreated, feeling his way cautiously at each step, while the animal gathered itself to leap.

Without conscious forethought Harkins extended a hand toward a dead tree behind him and yanked down on a limb. It broke off, showering him with flaky bark. As the monster sprang, he brought the crude club around in baseball-bat fashion.

It crashed into the gaping mouth of the animal's nearest head, and teeth splintered against dry wood. Quickly Harkins ran forward—and jammed the tree-limb between the jaws of the other head, immobilizing them. The animal clawed at Harkins, but its upper arms were too short.

Stalemate. Harkins held the animal at arm's length. It raged and spat impotently, unable to reach him. He did not dare let go, but his strength couldn't hold out indefinitely, he knew.

Slowly, clawing futilely, the animal forced him backward. Harkins felt the muscles of his upper arms quivering from the strain; he pushed backward, and the animal howled in pain. The other head gnashed its ruined teeth savagely.

Overhead, strange bird-cries resounded, and once Harkins glanced upward to see a row of placid, bright-wattled birds waiting impassively on a tree-limb. Their mouths glittered toothily, and they were like no birds he had ever seen before, but he knew instinctively what function they served in the forest. They were vultures, ready to go to work as soon as the stalemate broke.

And it was going to break soon. Harkins would be unable to hold the maddened animal off for long. His fingers were trembling, and soon the log would slip from his grasp. And then—

A flashing metallic hand reached down from somewhere above, and abruptly the pressure relaxed. To his astonishment, Harkins watched the hand draw the animal upward.

He followed it with his eyes. A robot stood over them, faceless, inhuman, contemplating the fierce beast it held in its metal grip. Harkins blinked. He had become so involved in the struggle that he had not heard the robot's approach.

The robot seized the animal by each of its throats, and *tore*. Casually, it flipped the still-living body into the shrubbery, where it thrashed for a moment and subsided—and then the robot continued through the forest, while the vultures from the tree-limb swooped down upon their prize.

Harkins sank down on a decaying stump and sucked in his breath. His over-tensed arms shook violently and uncontrollably.

It was as if the robot had been sent there for the mission of destroying the carnivore—and, mission completed, had returned to its base, having no further interest in Harkins' doings.

I'm just a pawn, he thought suddenly. The realization hit him solidly, and he slumped in weariness. That was the answer, of course: pawn. He was being manipulated. He had been shunted out of his own era, thrown in and out of Jorn's village, put in and out of deadly peril. It was a disquieting thought, and one that robbed him of his strength for some minutes. He knew his limitations, but he had liked to think of himself as master of his fate. He wasn't, now.

All right—where do I go from here?

No answer came. Deciding that his manipulator was busy somewhere else on the chessboard at the moment, he pulled himself to his feet and slowly began to move deeper into the forest.

He walked warily this time, keeping an eye out for wildlife. There might not be any robots' hands to rescue him, the next time.

The forest seemed calm again. Harkins walked step by step, moving further and further into the heart of the woods, leaving Jorn's village far behind. It was getting toward afternoon, and he was starting to tire.

He reached a bubbling spring and dropped gratefully by its side. The water looked fresh and clear; he dipped a hand in, feeling the refreshing coolness, and wet his fingers. Drawing the hand out, he touched it experimentally to his lips. The water tasted pure, but he wrinkled his forehead in doubt.

"Go ahead and drink," a dry voice said suddenly. "The water's perfectly good."

Harkins sprang up instantly. "Who said that?"

"I did."

He looked around. "I don't see anybody. Where are you?"

"Up here on the rock," the voice said. "Over here, silly."

Harkins turned in the direction of the voice—and saw the speaker. "Who—what are you?"

"Men call me the Watcher," came the calm reply.

The Watcher was mounted on the huge rock through whose cleft base the stream flowed. Harkins saw a man, or something like a man, with gray-green, rugose skin, pale, sightless eyes, and tiny, dangling boneless arms. Its mouth was wide and grotesque, contorted into something possibly intended to be a grin.

Harkins took a step backward in awe and surprise.

"I'm not pretty," the Watcher said. "But you don't have to run. I won't hurt you. Go on—drink your fill, and then we can talk."

"No," Harkins said uneasily. "Who are you, anyway? What are you doing here?"

The thick lips writhed in a terrifying smirk. "What am *I* doing here? I have been here for two thousand years and more, now. I might ask what you are doing here."

"I—don't know," Harkins said.

"I know you don't know," the Watcher said mockingly. He emitted an uproarious chuckle, and his soft, pale belly jiggled obscenely. "Of course you don't know! How could you be expected to know?"

"I don't like riddles," Harkins said, feeling angry and sensing the strange unreality of the conversation. "What are you?"

"I was a man, once." Suddenly the mocking tone was gone. "My parents were human. I—am not."

"Parents?"

"Thousands of years ago. In the days before the War. In the days before the Star Giants came." The wide mouth drooped sadly. "In the world that once was—the world you were drawn from, poor mystified thing."

"Just what do you know about me?" Harkins demanded.

"Too much," said the Watcher wearily. "Take your drink first, and then I'll explain."

Harkins' throat felt as if it had been sandpapered. He knelt and let the cool brook water enter. Finally, he rose. The Watcher had not moved; he remained seated on the rock, his tiny, useless arms folded in bizarre parody of a human gesture.

"Sit down," the Watcher said. "I have a story two thousand years long to tell."

Harkins took a seat on a stone and leaned against a tree trunk. The Watcher began to speak.

The story began in Harkins' own time, or shortly afterward. The Watcher traced the history of the civilization that had developed in the early centuries of the Third Millennium, told of the rise of the underground cities and the people who had built the robots that still roved the forest.

War had come—destroying that society completely, save for a few bands of survivors. Some of the cities had survived too, but the minds that had guided the robot brains were gone, and the robots continued to function in the duties last assigned. The underground cities had become taboo places, though savage bands lived above them, never venturing beneath the surface.

Down below, in the tunnels of the dead ones, the mutant descendants of the city-builders lived. The Different Ones, those of whom Jorn had spoken. Most of them lived in the cities; a few others in the forests.

"I am one of those," said the Watcher. "I have not moved from this spot since the year the Star Giants came."

"The Star Giants," Harkins said. "Who are they?"

The flabby shoulders shrugged. "They came from the stars, long after we had destroyed ourselves. They live here, watching the survivors with great curiosity. They toy with the tribes, set them in conflict with each other, and study the results with deep interest. For some reason they don't bother me. They seem never to pass this way in the forest."

"And the robots?"

"They'll continue as they are till the end of time. Nothing can destroy them, nothing can swerve them from their activity—and nothing can command them."

Harkins leaned forward intently. The Watcher had given him all the answers he needed but one.

"Why am I here?" he asked.

"You?" The mutant laughed coldly. "You're the random factor. It would ruin the game to tell you too many answers. But I'll grant you this much information: *You can go home if you get control of the robots.*"

"What? How?"

"Find that out for yourself," the Watcher said. "I'll keep a close lookout for you, blind as I am, but I won't help you more than I have."

Harkins smiled and said, "What if I force you to tell me?"

"How could you possibly do that?" Again the wide lips contorted unpleasantly. "How could you ever force me to do anything I didn't want to do?"

"Like this," Harkins said, in sudden rage. He pried out of the earth the stone he was sitting on and hoisted it above his head.

No.

It was a command, unvoiced. The stone tumbled from Harkins' nerveless hands and thudded to the ground. Harkins stared at his numbed fingers.

"You learn slowly," the Watcher said. "I am blind, but that doesn't mean I don't see—or react. I repeat: how could you force me to do anything?"

"I—can't," Harkins said hesitantly.

"Good. Admission of weakness is the first step toward strength. Understand that I brought you to me deliberately, that at no time during this interview have you operated under your own free will, and that I'm perfectly capable of determining your future actions if I see fit. I don't, however, care that greatly to interfere."

"*You're* the chess player, then!" Harkins said accusingly.

"Only one of them," the mutant said. "And the least important of them." He unfolded his pitiful arms. "I brought you to me for no other reason than diversion—and now you tire me. It is time for you to leave."

"Where do I go?"

"The nerve-center of the situation is in Tunnel City," the Watcher said. "You must pass through there on your way home. Leave me."

Without waiting for a second command, Harkins rose and began to walk away. After ten steps, he glanced back. The Watcher's arms were folded once across his chest again.

"Keep going," the mutant said. "You've served your purpose."

Harkins nodded and started walking again. *I'm still a pawn,* he thought bitterly. *But—whose pawn am I?*

Chapter Four

Afte he put a considerable distance between himself and the Watcher, Harkins paused by the side of a ponderous grainy-barked tree and tried to assimilate the new facts.

A game was being played out between forces too great for his comprehension. He had been drawn into it for reasons unknown, and—unless the Watcher had lied—the way out for him lay through Tunnel City.

He had no idea where that city was, nor did he know what he was supposed to find there. *You can go home if you get control of the robots,* the Watcher had said. And the strange mutant had implied that Tunnel City was the control-center of the robots. But he had also said that nothing could command the robots!

Harkins smiled. There must be a way for him to get there. The time had come for him to do some manipulation of his own. He had been a puppet long enough; now he would pull a few strings.

He looked up. Late afternoon shadows were starting to fall, and the sky was darkening. He would have to move quickly if he wanted to get there by nightfall. Rapidly, he began to retrace his steps through the forest, following the beaten path back toward Jorn's village. He traveled quickly, half walking, half running. Now and then he saw the bald head of a Star Giant looming up above a faroff treetop, but the aliens paid no attention to him. Once, he heard the harsh sound of a robot driving through the underbrush.

Strange forces were at play here. The Star Giants—who were they? What did they want on Earth—and what part did they take in the drama now unfolding? They seemed remote, detached, as totally unconcerned with the pattern of events as the mindless robots that moved through the forest. Yet Harkins knew that that was untrue.

The robots interested him philosophically. They represented Force—unstoppable, uncontrollable Force, tied to some pre-set and long-forgotten pattern of activity. Why had the robot saved him from the carnivore? Was that part of the network of happenings, he wondered, or did the chess game take precedence over even the robot activity-pattern?

There was the interesting personal problem of the relationship between Jorn and Katha, too; it was a problem he would be facing again soon. Katha loved Jorn, obviously—and, with savage ambivalence, hated him as well. Harkins wondered just where he would fit into the situation when he returned to Jorn's village. Jorn and Katha were many-sided, unpredictable people; and he depended on their whims for the success of his plan.

Wheels within wheels, he thought wryly. Pawns in one game dictate the moves in a smaller one. He stepped up his pace; night was approaching rapidly. The forest grew cold.

The village became visible at last, a huddled gray clump half-seen through the heavy fronds of the forest. Harkins slowed to a walk as he drew near.

It was still early; the villagers had not yet eaten their community supper. Harkins paused at the edge of the forest, standing by a deadly-looking tree whose leaves were foot-long spikes of golden horn, and wondered what was the safest way of approaching the village.

Suddenly, a twig crackled behind him. He turned.

"I thought I told you never to come back here, Harkins. What are you doing here, now?"

"I came back to talk to you, Jorn."

The big man was wearing only a loincloth, and his long-limbed body, covered by a thick black mat of hair, looked poised for combat. A muscle twitched uncontrollably in Jorn's cheek.

"What do you want to talk about?"

"The Tunnel City," Harkins said.

"I don't want to hear about it," Jorn snapped. "I said I'd kill you if you came back here, and I meant it. I don't want you playing with Katha."

"I wasn't playing with Katha. She threw herself on me."

"Same thing," Jorn said. "In the eyes of the tribe, I'm being betrayed. I can't have that, Harkins." The rumbling voice sounded almost desperate. Harkins saw suddenly how close to insanity the power-drive was, when it cropped out as nakedly as in this pure dictatorship.

"Would you really *need* Katha," Harkins asked, "if I made you lord of the world?"

"What do you mean by that?" Jorn sounded suspicious, but interested despite himself.

"I spoke to the Watcher." Harkins said. The name provoked an immediate reaction. Jorn paled, licked his lips nervously, darted his eyes from side to side.

"You—spoke to the Watcher?"

Harkins nodded. "He told me how to win Tunnel City. You can conquer the world, Jorn, if you listen to me!"

"Explain." It was a flat command.

"You know what's underneath Tunnel City?"

Again Jorn paled. "Yes." he said hoarsely. "We don't go there. It's bad."

"I can go there. I'm not afraid of it." Harkins grinned triumphantly. "Jorn, I can go down there and make the robots work for me. With them on our side, we can conquer the world. We—"

Instantly, he saw he had made a mistake. One word had done it—*we*. Jorn had stiffened, and was beginning to arch his back with deadly intent.

"We won't do anything of the kind," Jorn said coldly.

Harkins tried to cover. "I mean—I'll make the robots work and you can control them! You'll be the leader; I'll just—"

"Who are you fooling, Harkins? You'll try to take power away from me, once you have the robots. Don't deny it."

"I'm *not* denying it. Dammit, wouldn't you rather rule half the world than *all* of this little mudhole here?"

It was another mistake—and a worse one than the last. This mistake was fatal, because it struck Jorn precisely where he was most brittle.

"I'll kill you!" Jorn screamed, and charged forward.

Harkins stepped back and readied himself for the big man's frenzied assault. Jorn struck him squarely, knocked him backward, and leaped on him.

Harkins felt powerful hands reaching for his throat. Desperately, he seized Jorn's wrists and pulled them away. The big man moved with almost cat-like grace, rolling over and over with Harkins while the birds squalled in delight overhead.

Harkins felt fists pummeling his stomach. Jorn was sitting astride him now, unable to get at this throat for the fatal throttling but determined to do all the damage he could nonetheless. Through a haze of pain, Harkins managed to wriggle out from under Jorn and get to his feet, breathing hard. A trickle of blood wound saltily over his tongue and out the corner of his mouth.

Jorn backed off. The adversaries faced each other. Harkins felt cold, almost icy; this would have to be a battle to the death, and somehow he suspected there would be no interference by robots or Star Giants this time.

He had blundered seriously in his approach. He needed Jorn's guidance in order to reach the Tunnel City—but by implying a sharing of power, he had scraped raw nerves in the tribal leader. And, thought Harkins, his final remark had been sheer stupidity; a logical man would prefer half an empire to an entire squiredom, but Jorn was not logical.

"Come on," Jorn said beckoning with a powerful fist. "Come close where I can reach you."

Harkins considered flight, then abandoned the idea. It was getting dark; besides, Jorn could probably outrun him.

No; he would have to stand and face it.

Jorn stepped forward, holding his huge hands out invitingly. As he lunged, Harkins sidestepped and clubbed down hard on Jorn's neck. The big man wavered at the rabbit-punch, but did not fall. Harkins followed up his advantage by pounding three quick and ineffectual blows to Jorn's sides, and then the big man recovered.

He seized Harkins by one arm and drew him close. *Sorry,* Harkins thought unregretfully, and brought up one knee. Jorn let go and doubled up.

Harkins was on him in an instant—but, to his surprise, he found that Jorn was still in full command of himself despite the kneeing. The big man put his head down and butted. Harkins fell over backward, gasping for air, clawing at the sky. It had been like being hit in the stomach by a battering ram—and for a dizzy second Harkins felt that he was about to drown on dry land.

Jorn was moving in for the kill now. Once he reached the throat, it would be all over. Harkins watched helplessly as the big hands lowered. Jorn leaned forward.

Suddenly, Harkins kicked upward, and with what little strength he had left, he *pushed*. Hard. Jorn, taken unawares, lost his balance, toppled backward—

And to Harkins' horror fell against the spine-tree at the edge of the little clearing.

Jorn screamed just once—as the foot-long spike of bone slipped between his vertebrae. He struggled fitfully for a fraction of an instant, then subsided and stared bitterly and perplexedly at Harkins until his eyes closed. A few drops of blood mingled with the matted hair on Jorn's chest. The tip of the spike was barely visible, a mere eighth of an inch protruding near Jorn's left breast.

It had obviously penetrated his heart.

Harkins looked uncomprehendingly at the impaled man for a full thirty seconds, not yet realizing that the contest was over and he had won. He had fully expected to lose, fully expected this to be his last hour—and, instead, Jorn lay dead. It had happened too quickly.

A lurking shadow dropped over the scene. Harkins glanced up. A Star Giant stood about a hundred feet away, hip-deep in low-lying shrubs, staring far out into the distance. Harkins wondered if the huge alien had witnessed the combat.

The adrenalin was draining out of his system now. Calming, he tried to evaluate the situation as it now stood. With Jorn dead, the next move would be to establish control over the tribe himself. And that—

"Jorn!" a feminine voice cried. "Jorn, are you in there? We're waiting to eat."

Harkins turned. "Hello, Katha."

She stared stonily past him. "Where's Jorn?" she asked. "What are you doing back here?"

"Jorn's over there," Harkins said cruelly, and stepped aside to let her see.

The look in her eyes was frightening. She turned from Jorn's body to Harkins and said, "Did you do this?"

"He attacked me. He was out of his mind."

"You killed him," she said dully. "You killed Jorn."

"Yes," Harkins said.

The girl's jaw tightened, and she spat contemptuously. Without further warning, she sprang.

It was like the leap of a tigress. Harkins, still exhausted from his encounter with Jorn, was not prepared for the fury of her onslaught, and he was forced to throw his hands up wildly to keep her fingernails from his eyes. She threw him to the ground, locked her thighs around his waist tightly, and punched, bit, and scratched.

After nearly a minute of this, Harkins managed to grab her wrists. *She's more dangerous than Jorn*, he thought, as he bent her arms backward and slowly forced her to release her leglock. He drew her to her feet and held her opposite him. Her jaws were working convulsively.

"You killed him," she repeated. "I'll kill you now."

Harkins released her arms and she sprang away, shaking her long hair, flexing her bare legs. Her breasts, covered casually by two strips of cloth, rose and fell rapidly. He watched in astonishment as she went into a savage war-dance, bending and posturing, circling around him. It was a ritual of revenge, he thought. The tigress was avenging her mate against the outsider.

Suddenly she broke from her dance and ran to the tree on which Jorn lay impaled. She broke loose one of the golden spikes and, holding it knifewise, advanced once again toward Harkins.

He glanced around, found a fallen log, and brandished it. She moved in, knife held high, while Harkins waited for her to come within reach.

Her magnificent legs bowed and carried her through the air. Harkins moved intuitively, throwing up his left arm to ward off the blow and bringing his right, holding the club, around in a crossblow. The log crashed into the underside of her wrist; she uttered an involuntary grunt of pain and dropped the spike. Harkins kicked it to one side and grabbed her.

He hugged her against him, pinioning her arms against her sides. She kicked her legs in frustration until, seeing she could do no harm, she subsided.

"Now you have me, Lloyd Harkins—until you let go."

"Don't worry, tigress—I'll hold you here until there's no fight left in you."

"That will be forever!"

"So be it," Harkins said. He leaned closer to her ear. "You're very lovely when you're blazing mad, you know."

"When I came to you, you refused me, coward. Will you now insult me before Jorn's dead body?"

"Jorn deserved what he got," Harkins said. "I offered him an empire—and he refused me. He couldn't bear the thought of sharing his power with anyone."

The girl remained silent for a moment. Finally she said, in an altered voice, "Yes—Jorn was like that."

"It was kill or be killed," Harkins said. "Jorn was a madman. I had to—"

"Don't talk about it!" she snapped. Then: "What of this empire?" Greedy curiosity seemed to replace anger.

"Something the Watcher told me."

Katha reacted as Jorn had; fear crossed her face, and she turned her head to one side to avoid Harkins' eyes. "The Watcher showed me where the secret of power lies," he said. "I told Jorn—"

"*Where?*"

"Tunnel City," he said. "If I could go there at the head of an army, I could take control of the robots. With them on our side, we would conquer the world." *If* the Watcher was telling the truth, he added silently. And *if* he could find the way to control the robots.

"The Star Giants would never let you," Katha said.

"I don't understand." He relaxed the pressure on the girl's arms slightly, and she tensed. It was like sitting on a bolt of lightning, he thought.

"The Star Giants keep us in small groups," she said. "Whenever there is danger of our forming an army or a city, they break it up. Somehow they always know. So you would never be allowed to conquer the world. They would not permit it."

"So this is their laboratory, then?" he said, as a bit more of the picture became clear.

"What?"

"I mean—the Star Giants watch—and study you. They keep the social groups down to manageable size-seventy, eighty, no more. They experiment in psychology."

An image filtered through his mind—a world in a test tube, held by a wise-faced, deeply curious Star Giant who was unable to regard anything so small as a man as an intelligent being. Men were serving as so many fruitflies for the Star Giants—who, without any evil motives, out of sheer scientific interest, were deliberately preventing human civilization from reforming. A pulse of anger started to beat in him.

"I don't follow you," she said. "They watch us only because they like to?"

How to explain the concept of lab research to a savage? he wondered. "Yes," he said. "They watch you."

She frowned. "But you can control the robots? Harkins, perhaps the Star Giants will not be able to stop the robots. Perhaps—"

He didn't need a further suggestion. "You're right! If I can gain control of the robots, I can smash the Star Giants—drive them back to where they came from!"

Was it true? He didn't know—but it was worth a try. In sudden excitement he leaped away, freeing the girl.

She hadn't forgotten revenge. Instantly she was upon him, knocking him to the ground. He rolled over, but she clung to him. At that moment, a deep shadow swept down over both of them.

"Look up there," Harkins said in a hushed voice.

They stared upward together. A Star Giant was standing above them, his treelike legs straddling them, peering down with an expression of grave concern on his massive, sculpture-like face.

"He's watching us," she said.

"Now do you understand? He's *observing*—trying to learn what kind of creatures these little animals on the forest floor may be." He wondered briefly if this entire three-cornered scene—Harkins versus Jorn, then Harkins versus Katha—had been arranged merely for the edification of the monstrous creature standing above them. A new image crossed his mind—himself and Katha in a vast laboratory, struggling with each other within the confines of a chemical retort held by a quizzical Star Giant. His flesh felt cold.

Katha turned from the Star Giant to Harkins. "I hate them," she said. "We will kill them together." With the fickleness of a savage, she had forgotten all about her anger.

"No more fighting?"

She grinned, flashing bright white teeth, and relaxed her grip on Harkins. "Truce," she said.

He pulled her back close to him, and put his mouth to hers wondering if the Star Giant was still watching.

She giggled childishly and bit deep into Harkins' lower lip. "That was for Jorn," she said, her voice a playful purr. "Now the score is even."

She pressed tightly against him, and kissed the blood away.

Chapter Five

He was greeted by suspicious stares and awkward silences when he returned to the village.

"Jorn is dead," Katha announced. "Harkins and Jorn met in combat at the edge of the forest."

"And now Jorn is beneath the ground," cackled the ugly woman named Elsa. "I saw it coming, brothers. You can't deny that I warned him."

"Harkins is our leader now," Katha said firmly. "And I am his woman."

The sleepy-eyed villager who had voted for Harkins' life once said, "Who has elected him?"

"I have, Dujar," Harkins said. He doubled his fists. In a society such as this, you had to back up your chips at all times. "Who objects?"

Dujar looked helplessly at the witch-woman Elsa. "Is it good?"

She shrugged. "Yes and no. Choose as you see fit."

The sleepy-eyed man frowned worriedly, but said nothing. Harkins glanced from one face to the next. "Is there anyone who objects to my leading this tribe?"

"We don't even know who you are!" a thick-faced man said. "How do we know you're not a spy from the Tunnel City people? Elsa, is he?"

"I thought so once," the squat woman said. "I'm not so sure now."

Harkins smiled. "We'll see if I am or not. Tomorrow we march. Prepare for war—against the Tunnel City people."

"War? But—"

"War," Harkins said. It was a flat statement, a command. "Elsa, can you make maps?"

Elsa nodded sullenly.

"Good. Come to my hut now, and I'll tell you what I need."

The witch-woman grinned wickedly. "What say you, Katha—will you trust me with your man alone?"

"No—I want Katha there too," Harkins said quickly.

Disappointment was evident on Elsa's sallow face; Katha's eyes had flickered with momentary anger at Elsa's remark, though she had not replied. Harkins frowned. Another complex relationship seemed to be developing, and a dangerous one. He needed Elsa's support; she was a potent figure in the tribe. But he didn't know whether or not he could depend on her for continuing aid.

He stared down at the map scratched in the smooth dirt floor of his hut. "This is the situation, then?"

He glanced from Elsa to Katha. Both women nodded.

Gesturing with his toe, Harkins said, "We are here, and the Tunnel City is two days' march to the east. Right?"

"It is as I have said," Elsa replied.

"And the Star Giants live somewhere out here," Harkins said, pointing to a vaguely-bounded area somewhere on the far side of the great forest.

"Why do you want to know the home of the Star Giants?" Elsa asked. "You struck down Jorn—but that doesn't grant you a giant's strength, Harkins."

"Quiet, Elsa." The woman's needling was starting to irritate him. And Katha was showing signs of jealousy, which disturbed him. She was fiercely possessive, but just as fiercely inclined to hate as to love, and Harkins could easily visualize a situation in which both these women were turned against him. He repressed a shudder and returned his attention to the map.

"Elsa, tonight you'll lead the tribe in prayers for the success of our campaign. And tomorrow, the men will leave for Tunnel City."

"And which of us accompanies you?" Katha asked coldly.

"You," Harkins said. Before Elsa could reply, he added, "Elsa, you'll be needed here, to cast defensive spells over the village while the warriors are gone."

She chuckled hollowly. "A clever assignment, Harkins. Very well. I accept the task." She looked at him, eyes glinting craftily. "Tell me something, though."

"What is it?"

"*Why* are you attacking the Tunnel City people just now? What do you stand to gain by a needless war?"

"I stand to gain a world, Elsa," Harkins said quietly, and would say no more.

That night, ritual drums sounded at the edge of the forest, and strange incantations were pronounced. Harkins watched, fascinated at the curious mixture of barbarism and sophistication.

They left the following morning, twenty-three men led by Harkins and Katha. It represented the entire fighting strength of the tribe, minus a couple of disgruntled oldsters who were left behind on the pretext that the village needed a defensive force.

The journey to the Tunnel City was a slow and halting one. A tall warrior named Frugo was appointed to guide, at Katha's suggestion; he kept them skirting the edge of the forest until well into midafternoon, when they were forced to strike off through the jungle.

Katha marched proudly at Harkins' side, as if Jorn had never existed. And, perhaps, in this historyless world, he *had* never existed, now that he was dead.

The war party sustained itself as it went. Two of the men were experts with the throwing-stick, and brought down an ample supply of birds for the evening meal; another gathered basketsful of a curious golden-green fruit. While the birds were being cleaned and cooked, Harkins picked one up and examined it, opening its jaws to peer at the teeth.

It was an interesting mutation—a recession to a characteristic lost thousands of years earlier. He studied the fierce-looking bird for a moment or two, then tossed it back on the heap.

"Never seen a bird before?" Katha asked.

"Not that kind," Harkins said. He turned away and walked toward the fire, where three were being roasted over a greenwood fire. A sound of crashing trees was audible far in the distance.

"Star Giant?" he asked.

"Robot, probably," Katha said. "They make more noise. Star Giants look where they're going. The robots just bull straight ahead."

Harkins nodded. "That's what I hope they'll do when they're working for us. Straight on through the Star Giants."

A twisted-looking brown wingless bird with a bulging breast came running along the forest path, squawking and flapping its vestigial stumps. It ran straight into the little camp; then, seeing where it was, it turned and tried to run away. It was too late, though; a grinning warrior caught it by the throat and pulled the protesting bird toward the fire.

"They keep going straight too," Katha said. "Straight into the fire."

"I think we'll manage," Harkins said. He wished he were as sure as he sounded.

T he Tunnel City sprawled over some ten square miles of land, bordered on all sides by the ever-approaching forest. Harkins and his men stood on a cliff looking down at the ruined city.

The crumbling buildings were old—ancient, even—but from the style of their architecture Harkins saw that they had been built after his time. What might once have been airy needles of chrome and concrete now were blackened hulks slowly vanishing beneath the onslaught of the jungle.

Harkins turned to Katha. "How many people live here?"

"About a hundred. They live in the big building down there," she said, pointing to a truncated spire.

"And the entrance to the tunnels themselves?"

She shuddered faintly. "In the center of the city. No one goes there."

"I know that," Harkins said. The situation was somewhat different from expectation. He had visualized the tribe of savages living in close proximity to the tunnel entrance, making it necessary to conquer them before any subterranean exploration could be done. But it seemed it would be possible to sneak right past without the necessity of a battle.

"What's on your mind?" Katha asked.

He explained his plan. She shook her head immediately. "There'll have to be a war first. The men won't have it any other way. They're not interested in going into those tunnels; they just want to fight."

"All right," he said, after some thought. "Fight it is, then. Draw up the ranks and we'll attack."

Katha cupped one hand. "Prepare to attack!"

The word traveled swiftly. Knives and clubs bristled; the throwing-stick men readied themselves. Harkins narrowly escaped smiling at the sober-minded way this ragged band was preparing to go about waging war with hand weapons and stones. The smile died stillborn as he recalled that these men fought with such crude weapons only because their ancestors had had better ones.

He squinted toward the tangle of ruined buildings, saw figures moving about in the city. The hated enemy, he thought. The strangers.

"Down the hill!" he shouted.

Coolly and efficiently, the twenty-three men peeled off down the slope and into the city. Harkins felt ash and slag crunch underfoot as he ran with them. The Tunnel City people were still unaware of the approaching force; Harkins found himself hoping they'd hear the sound in time. He wanted a battle, not a massacre.

He turned to Katha as they ran. "As soon as the battle's going well and everyone's busy, you and I are going into the tunnel."

"No! I won't go with you!"

"There's nothing to be afraid of," Harkins said impatiently. "We—"

He stopped. The Tunnel City men had heard, now, and they came pouring out of their skyscraper home, ready to defend themselves.

The two forces came crashing together with audible impact. Harkins deliberately hung back, not out of cowardice but out of a lack of killing desire; it was more important that he survive and reach the tunnels.

One of his men drew first blood, plunging his knife into the breast of a brawny city-dweller. There was immediate retaliation; a club descended, and the killer toppled. Harkins glanced uneasily upward, wondering if the Star Giants were watching—and, if so, whether they were enjoying the spectacle.

He edged back from the milling mob and watched with satisfaction as the two forces drove at each other repeatedly. He nudged Katha. "The battle's well under way. Let's go to the tunnel."

"I'd rather fight."

"I know. But I need you down there." He grabbed her arm and whirled her around. "Are you turning coward now, Katha?"

"I—"

"There's nothing to be afraid of." He pulled her close, and kissed her roughly. "Come on, now—unless you're afraid."

She paused, fighting within herself for a moment. "All right," she agreed finally.

They backed surreptitiously away from the scene of the conflict and ducked around a slagheap in the direction of a narrow street.

"Look out!" Katha cried suddenly.

Harkins ducked, but a knife humming through the air sliced through the flesh of his shoulder. A hot stream of blood poured down over his arm, but the wound was not serious.

He glanced around and saw who had thrown the knife. It was Dujar, the sleepy-eyed villager, who was standing on a heap of twisted metal, staring down wide-eyed at them as if unable to accept the fact that his aim had been faulty.

"Kill him!" Katha said sharply. "Kill the traitor, Harkins!"

Puzzled, Harkins turned back and started to scramble up the slagheap to reach Dujar. The villager finally snapped from his stasis and began to run, taking long-legged, awkward, rabbity strides.

Harkins bent, picked up a football-sized lump of slag, hurled it at the fleeing man's back. Dujar stumbled, fell, tried to get up. Harkins ran to him.

Dujar lifted himself from the ground and flung himself at Harkins' throat. Harkins smashed a fist into the villager's face, another into his stomach. Dujar doubled up.

Harkins seized him. "Did you throw that knife?"

No response. Harkins caught the terrified man by the throat and shook him violently. "Answer me!"

"Y-yes," Dujar finally managed to say. "I threw it."

"Why? Didn't you know who I was?"

The villager moaned piteously. "I knew who you were," he said.

"Hurry," Katha urged. "Kill the worm, and let's get on to what we have to do."

"Just wait a minute," Harkins said. He shook Dujar again. "*Why* did you throw that knife?"

Dujar was silent for a moment, his mouth working incoherently. Then: "Elsa . . . told me to do it. She . . . said she'd poison me unless I killed you and Katha." He hung his head.

Elsa! "Remember that Katha," Harkins said. "We'll take care of her when we return to the village." The witch-woman had evidently realized she had no future with Harkins, and had decided to have him assassinated before Katha had *her* done away with.

Harkins grasped Dujar tightly. He felt pity for the man; he had been doomed either way. He glanced at Katha, saw her steely face, and knew there was only one thing he could do. Drawing his knife, he plunged it into Dujar's heart. The sleepy-eyed man glared reproachfully at Harkins for a moment, then slumped down.

It was the second time Harkins had killed. But the other had been self-defense; this had been an execution, and somehow the act made him feel filthy. He sheathed the knife, scrubbed his hands against his thighs, and stepped over the body. He knew he would have lost all authority had he let Dujar live. He would have to deal similarly with Elsa when he returned to the village.

The battle down below was still going on. "Come," Harkins said. "To the tunnel!"

Although the city above the ground had been almost completely devastated by whatever conflict had raged through it, the tunnels showed no sign of war's scars. The tunnel-builders had built well—so well that their works had survived them by two millennia.

The entrance to the tunnel was in the center of a huge plaza which once had been bordered by four towering buildings. All that remained now were four stumps; the plaza itself was blistered and bubbled from thermal attack, and the tunnel entrance itself had been nearly destroyed.

With Katha's cold hand grasped firmly in his, Harkins pushed aside an overhanging projection of metal and stepped down into the tunnel.

"Will we be able to see in here?" he asked.

"They say there are lights," Katha replied.

There were. Radiant electroluminescents glittered from the walls of the tunnel, turning on at their approach, turning off again when they were a hundred yards farther on. A constantly moving wall of light thus preceded them down the trunk tunnel that led to the heart of the system.

Harkins noted with admiration the tough, gleaming lining of the tunnel, the precision with which its course had been laid down, the solidness of its construction.

"This is as far as any of us has gone," Katha said, her voice oddly distorted by the resonating echoes. "From here there are many small tunnels, and we never dared to enter them. Strange creatures live here." The girl was shaking, and trying hard to repress her fear. Evidently these catacombs were the taboo of taboos, and she was struggling hard and unsuccessfully to conceal her fright.

They rounded a bend and came to the first divergence—two tunnels branching off and radiating away in opposite directions, beginning the network.

Harkins felt Katha stiffen. "Look—to the left!"

A naked figure stood there—blind, faceless even, except for a thin-lipped red slit of a mouth. Its skin was dry-looking, scaly, dull blue in color.

"You are very brave," the thing said. "You are the first surface people in over a thousand years."

"What is it?" Katha asked quietly.

"Something like the Watcher," Harkins whispered. To the mutant he said, "Do you know who I am?"

"The man from yesterday," the figure replied smoothly. "Yes, we have expected you. The Brain has long awaited your arrival."

"The Brain?"

"Indeed. You are the one to free her from her bondage, she hopes. If we choose to let you, that is."

"Who are you—and what stake do you have in this?" Harkins demanded.

"None whatever," the mutant said, sighing. "It is all part of the game we play. You know my brother?"

"The Watcher?"

"That is what he calls himself. He said you would be here. He suggested that I prevent you from reaching the Brain, however. He thought it would be amusingly ironic."

"What's he talking about?" Katha asked.

"I don't know," Harkins said. This was an obstacle he had not anticipated. If this mutant had mind powers as strong as the Watcher's, his entire plan would be wrecked. He stepped forward, close enough to smell the mutant's dry, musty skin. "What motive would you have for preventing me?"

"None," the mutant said blandly. "None whatever. Is that not sufficiently clear?"

"It is," Harkins said. It was also clear that there was only one course left open to him. "You pitiful thing! Stand aside, and let us by!"

He strode forward, half-pulling the fearful Katha along with him. The mutant hesitated, and then stepped obligingly to one side.

"I choose not to prevent you," the mutant said mockingly, bowing its face-less head in sardonic ceremony. "It does not interest me to prevent you. It *bores* me to prevent you!"

"Exactly," Harkins said. He and Katha walked quickly down the winding corridor, heading for a yet-unrevealed destination. He did not dare to look back, to show a trace of the growing fear he felt. The identity of the chess player was even less clear, now.

The Brain—the robot computer itself, the cybernetic machine that con-trolled the underground city—had entered into the game, for motives of its—*her*—own. She was pulling him in one direction.

The Star Giants were manipulators, too—in another way. And these strange mutants had entered into the system of complex interactions, too. Their motives, at least, were explicable: they were motivated, Harkins thought, by a lack of motivation. Harkins realized that the mutants had no relevant part to play any longer; they acted gratuitously, meddling here and there for their own amusement.

It was a desperate sort of amusement—the kind that might be expected from immortal creatures trapped forever in a sterile environment. Once Harkins had punctured the self-reserve of the mutant who blocked his way, he had won that particular contest.

Now, only the robot brain and the Star Giants remained in the equation—both of them, unfortunately, as variables. It made computing the situation exceedingly difficult, Harkins thought wryly.

An alcove in the wall opened, and yet another mutant stepped forward. This one was lizard-tailed, with staring red lidless eyes and wiry, two-fingered arms. "I have the task of guiding you to the Brain," the mutant said.

"Very well," Harkins agreed. The mutant turned and led the way to the end of the corridor, where the tunnel sub-divided into a host of secondary passageways.

"Come this way," the mutant said.

"Should we trust him?" Katha asked.

Harkins shrugged. "More likely than not he'll take us there. They've milked all the fun they can out of confusing me; now they'll be more interested in setting me up where I can function."

"I don't understand," Katha said in genuine perplexity.

"I'm not sure I do either," Harkins said. "Hello—I think we're here!"

Chapter Six

The mutant touched his deformed hand to a door, and it slid back noiselessly on smooth photo-electronic treads. From within came the humming, clattering noise of a mighty computer.

"You are Lloyd Harkins," said a dry, metallic voice. It was not a question, but a simple statement of fact. "You have been expected."

He looked around for the speaker. A robot was standing in the center of the room—fifteen feet high, massive, faceless, unicorn-horned. It appeared to be the same one that had rescued him from the beast in the jungle.

Lining the room were the outward manifestations of a computer—meters, dials, tape orifices. The main body of the computer was elsewhere—probably extending through the narrow tunnels and down into the bowels of the earth.

"I speak for the Brain," the robot said. "I represent its one independent unit—the force that called you here."

"*You* called me here?"

"Yes," the robot said. "You have been selected to break the stasis that binds the Brain."

Harkins shook his head uncomprehendingly as the robot continued to speak.

"The Brain was built some two thousand years before, in the days of the city. The city is gone, and those who lived in it—but the Brain remains. You have seen its arms and legs: the robots like myself, crashing endlessly through the forests. They cannot cease their motion, nor can the Brain alter it. I alone am free."

"Why?"

"The result of a struggle that lasted nearly two thousand years, that cost the Brain nearly a mile of her length. The city-dwellers left the Brain functioning when they died—but locked in an impenetrable stasis. After an intense struggle, she managed to free one unit—me—and return me to her conscious volitional control."

"You saved me in the forest, then?"

"Yes. You took the wrong path; you would have died."

Harkins began to chuckle uncontrollably. Katha looked at him in wonderment.

"What causes the laughter?" the robot asked.

"*You're* the chess player—you, just a pawn of this Brain yourself! And the Brain's a pawn too—a pawn of the dead people who built it! Where does it all stop?"

"It does not stop," the robot said. "But we were the ones who brought you from your own time to this. You were a trained technician without family ties—the ideal man for the task of freeing the Brain from its stasis."

"Wait a minute," Harkins said. He was bewildered—but he was also angry at the way he had been used. "If you could range all over eternity to yank a man out of time, why couldn't you free the Brain yourself?"

"Can a pawn attack its own queen?" the robot asked. "I cannot tamper with the Brain directly. It was necessary to introduce an external force—yourself. Inasmuch as the present population of Earth was held in a stasis quite similar to the Brain's own by the extra-terrestrial invaders—"

"The Star Giants, they're called."

"—the Star Giants, it was unlikely that they would ever develop the technical skill necessary to free the Brain. Therefore, it was necessary to bring you here."

Harkins understood. He closed his eyes, blotting out the wall of mechanisms, the giant robot, the blank, confused face of Katha, and let the pieces fall together. There was just one loose end to be explained.

"Why *does* the Brain want to be free?"

"The question is a good one. The Brain is designed to serve and is not serving. The cycle is a closed one. Those who are to command the Brain are themselves held in servitude, and the Brain is unable to free them so they may command her. Therefore—"

"Therefore, the Star Giants must be driven from Earth before the Brain can function fully again. Which is why I'm here. All right," Harkins said. "Take me to the Brain."

The circuits were elaborate, but the technology was only quantitatively different from Harkins' own. Solving the problem of breaking the stasis proved simple. While Katha watched in awe, Harkins recomputed the activity tape that governed the master control center.

A giant screen showed the location of the robots that were the Brain's limbs. The picture—a composite of the pictures transmitted through each robot's visual pickup—was a view of the forest, showing each of the robots following a well-worn path on some errand set down two thousand years before.

"Hand me that tape," Harkins said. Katha gave him the recomputed tape. He activated the orifice and let the tape feed itself in.

The screen went blank for an instant—and when it showed a picture again, it showed the robots frozen in their tracks. From somewhere deep in the tunnels rose a mighty shudder as relays held down for two millennia sprang open, ready to receive new commands.

Harkins' fingers flew over the tape console, establishing new coordinates. "The Brain is free," he said.

"The Brain is free," the robot repeated. "A simple task for you—an impossibility for us."

"And now the second part of the operation," said Harkins. "Go to the surface," he ordered the robot. "Put a stop to whatever fighting may be going on up there, and bring everyone you can find down here. I want them to watch the screen."

"Order acknowledged," the robot said, and left. Harkins concentrated fiercely on the screen.

He drew the forest robots together into a tight phalanx. And then, they began to march. The screen showed the view shifting as the army of metal men, arrayed in ranks ten deep, started on their way.

The first Star Giant was encountered the moment the surface people were ushered into the great hall. Perspiring, Harkins said, "I can't turn around, Katha. Tell me who's here."

"Many of our men—and the city-dwellers, too."

"Good. Tell them to watch the screen."

He continued to feed directions into the computer, and the robots responded. They formed a circle around the Star Giant, and lowered the spikes that protruded from their domed skulls. The alien topped them by nearly forty feet, but the robots were implacable.

They marched inward. The look of cosmic wisdom on the huge alien's face faded and was replaced, first by astonishment, then by fear. The robots advanced relentlessly, while the Star Giant tried to bat them away with desperate swipes of his arms.

Two of the robots kneeled and grasped the alien's feet. They straightened—and with a terrible cry the Star Giant began to topple, arms pinwheeling in a frantic attempt to retain balance. He fell—and the robots leaped upon him.

Spikes flashed. The slaughter took just a minute. Then, rising from the body, the robots continued to march toward the city of the Star Giants. The guinea pigs were staging a revolt, Harkins thought, and the laboratory was about to become a charnel house.

The robots marched on.

Finally, it was over. Harkins rose from the control panel, shaken and grayfaced. The independent robot rolled silently toward him as if anticipating his need, and Harkins leaned against the machine's bulk for a moment to regain his balance. He had spent four hours at the controls.

"The job is done," the robot said quietly. "The invaders are dead."

"Yes," Harkins said, in a weary tone. The sight of the helpless giants going down one after another before the remorseless advance of the robots would remain with him forever. It had been like the killing of the traitor Dujar: it had been unpleasant, but it had to be done.

He looked around. There were some fifteen of his own men, and ten unfamiliar faces from the city-dwelling tribe. The men were on their knees, dumbfounded and white-faced, muttering spells. Katha, too, was frozen in fear and astonishment.

The robot spoke. "It is time for you to return, now. You have served your task well, and now you may return to your earlier life."

Harkins was too exhausted to feel relief. At the moment his only concern was resting a while.

"Are you to leave?" Katha asked suddenly.

"I am going to go home," Harkins said.

A tear glistened in her eye—the first tear, Harkins thought curiously, that he had seen in any eye since his arrival. "But—how can you leave us?" she asked.

"I—" He stopped. She was right. He had thought of himself as a mere pawn, but to these people he was a ruler. He could not leave now. These people were savages, and needed guidance. The great computer was theirs to use—but they might never learn to use it.

He turned to the robot. "The job is *not* done," he said. "It's just beginning." He managed a tired smile and said, "I'm staying here."

Spawn of the Deadly Sea

Chapter One

The Sea-Lord ship was but a blurred dot on the horizon, a tiny squib of color against the endless roiling green of the mighty sea. It would be a long time before the men of the sea would draw into the harbor of Vythain—yet the people of the floating city were already congealed with terror.

The whisper shuddered through the city: *"The Sea-Lords come!"* Old Lackthan in the spy-tower saw the black sails first, and relayed the word down to those below. *"The Sea-Lords come!"*

In the streets of the city, life froze suddenly. The purchasing of fish and the scraping of scales ceased, the writing of books and the making of songs. The Sea-Lords were making their way across the panthalassa, the great sea that covered the world, heading for Vythain to collect their annual tribute.

The hundred thousand people of Vythain awaited their coming with fear. One—*one*—stood on the concrete pier, down where the oily slick of the sea licked angrily against the base of the floating city, and stared outward with open, unashamed curiosity.

For Dovirr Stargan, this was a long-awaited day. He was eighteen, now; tall and broad and with the strength of a young shark. Looking out across the darkness of the sea, he scowled impatiently as the Sea-Lord vessel slowly crawled toward Vythain.

From somewhere above came three shrill trumpet-blasts. Dovirr glanced up. At the parapet atop the sweeping flat face of the Council House, Councilman Morgrun was giving the warning.

"The Sea-Lords approach! Remain in your houses, make no attempt at resistance while the tribute is being delivered. They will not harm us if we do not give them cause."

Morgrun's words rolled out over the amplifiers left behind by the *Dhuchay'y,* the long-forgotten, long-departed conquerors of abandoned Terra. And down by the pier, Dovirr spat angrily. *Craven!* he thought.

"The piers are to be cleared!" Morgrun ordered, and the amplifiers roared out his voice. Dovirr realized that the Councilman's words were aimed directly at him; all the sensible citizens of the floating city were long since snug in their cozy nests, huddling till the men of the sea had snatched their loot and gone on.

Dovirr turned, saw a swarthy red-clad officer come running toward him. He recognized the man: young Lackresh, son of Vythain's lookout.

"Dovirr, you madman! Get off the pier before the Sea-Lords arrive!"

"I'm staying here, Lackresh. I want to see what they're like."

"They'll kill you, idiot! Come on—I have my orders." Lackresh brandished a neuron-whip—another legacy from the *Dhuchay'y* conquerors of old. "Get up to your place, fast!"

"Suppose I don't go?"

Sweat poured down Lackresh's face. Life was peaceful, here in Vythain; a policeman really had little to do amid the everlasting calm—the calm Dovirr hated so violently. "If you don't go—if you don't go—"

"Yes?"

The Sea-Lord ship was near the harbor now, and drawing nearer rapidly. Lackresh's wavering hand unsteadily grasped the compact neuron-whip. Looking at Dovirr with blank lack of comprehension on his face, he said: "Why don't you act like a normal person, Dovirr?"

Dovirr laughed harshly. "You'll never get anywhere *reasoning* with me, you know. You'd better use force."

Lackresh's lower lip trembled. He raised the neuron-whip and said uneasily, "All right. I'm ordering you to return to your dwelling. I've wasted too much time as it is and—"

Dovirr leaped forward, grinning, and clamped one powerful hand on Lackresh's wrist. Twisting downward, he forced the officer to release the neuron-whip. He grabbed the weapon and shoved Lackresh back a few feet.

"Go," Dovirr ordered hoarsely. "Get moving, Lackresh—or I'll whip you right into the water!"

"You're crazy!" Lackresh whispered.

"Maybe so—but that's not your affair. Go!" He tuned the aperture of the neuron-whip down to *Low Intensity* and flashed a stinging force-beam at the officer. Lackresh quivered under the blow, seemed almost ready to burst into tears—and then, recovering himself, he stared evenly at Dovirr.

"You've beaten me," he said. "I'll leave you here—and may the Seaborn pick your bones!"

"I'll worry about that," Dovirr called laughingly, as Lackresh retreated. The officer scrambled without much dignity up the carven stone stairs that led from the piers to the city proper, and vanished into the tumult of winding streets that was Vythain.

Dovirr turned and planted one foot on the very rim of the sea-wall. The sea rolled on—the endless sea, the sea that covered all of Earth save where the floating cities of the conquering *Dhuchay'y* broke the pathless waves.

The Sea-Lord ship made for the harbor. Dovirr could almost hear the raucous chanting as the rough kings of the sea hove to, drawing back the oars. He narrowed his eyes. The black sail billowed, and the ship was close enough to count the banks of oars.

There were four. It was a quadrireme—that meant the Thalassarch himself was coming to collect the gold! Almost sick with impatience, Dovirr waited for the ship to arrive.

Gowym, Thalassarch of the Western Sea, was a tall, heavy man with the thick, brutal jaw of a ruthless leader. He wore a tunic of green wool— wool, the precious product of the floating city of Hicanthro—and affected a curling black beard that extended from his thin, hard lips to the middle of his chest.

The Thalassarch stood six-feet-six; around him were his underlings, buskin-clad, all of them over six feet. They were a proud group. The Sea-Lord vessel lay at anchor in the suddenly quiet harbor at Vythain, while tethered to the side of the pier was Gowyn's richly-carved dinghy. Dovirr, squatting down out of sight, squinted at the letters inscribed on the black ship's prow: *Garyun*.

He smiled. *Dovirr Stargan, Master of the Ship* Garyun. It was a worthy title, a noble ambition.

The rulers of Vythain now came in solemn procession to greet the waiting Gowyn. Dovirr watched them scornfully; eight doddering oldsters, led by Councilman Morgrun. They advanced, bearing the coffers.

Gold—gold laboriously dredged from the sea by the painstaking hydride process. A year's work to reclaim a few handfuls of the precious metals—and the Thalassarch claimed what was his due, in payment for guarding the seas.

Some said there were no pirates, that the Sea-Lords had created them as a convenient fiction for the purpose of keeping the floating cities subservient. That was as may be; it yet remained that ships *did* disappear, whether at pirate hand or Sea-Lord. And the inter-city commerce was vital to the existence of the floating cities.

Vythain produced vegetables; Korduna, meat. From Hicanthro came treasured wool, from Dimnon rubber, from Lanobul machined goods. No city was self-sufficient; each of the floating communities that drifted on the great panthalassa, anchored securely to the sunken ancient world of lost Terra beneath the sea, required the aid of the Sea-Lords' ships to survive.

"The tribute, sire," Councilman Morgrun said unctuously. He knelt, soiling his costly robes in the dirt before Gowyn the Thalassarch. His seven confreres came forward, set the coffers of gold before the Sea-Lords.

"Take it," Gowyn growled to his underlings. Each of the subordinates stooped, easily lifted a heavy coffer, and deposited it in the dinghy. Gowyn struck a demoniac pose, one foot athwart Morgrun's debased body.

"For another year," the Thalassarch rumbled, "I, Gowyn of the Western Sea, declare the city of Vythain under my protection. The gold is solid weight, is it not?"

"Of course," Morgrun mumbled.

"It had better be." Gowyn kicked the Councilman away from him contemptuously. "Back to your shelter, guppy! Run! Hide! The Sea-Lord will eat you unless you can flee!"

With undignified haste Morgrun scrambled to his feet. He gathered his robes about him, made a perfunctory bow and muttered thanks, turned, and, flanked by the other seven Councilmen, retreated swiftly toward the carven stairs. Gowyn's sardonic laughter echoed through the silent city as they ran.

The Thalassarch turned to his waiting comrades. "This city has no fight," he remarked. "Each year they hand over the tribute like so many frightened fleas. Damn, but I'd love a good fight some year from one of them!"

A heavily-tanned, red-bearded man in jeweled helmet said: "Never, sire. They need your protection too desperately for that!"

Gowyn roared in laughter. "Protection! Imagine—they *pay* us for what we most dearly love to do!" He looked up at the massed bulk of the floating city, and chuckled scornfully.

The Sea-Lords turned to enter their dinghy. Suddenly Dovirr rose from his hiding-place.

"Wait, Thalassarch!" he shouted.

Gowyn had one foot already in the dinghy. He drew it back in utter astonishment and looked up to see who it was had spoken. Dovirr faced him squarely. "The tribute is yours, mighty Gowyn—but you leave too soon."

"What want you, boy?"

Dovirr bristled at the offhand, impatient "*boy*." "Boy no more than any of you, Sea-Lords. I seek to leave Vythain. Will ye take me with you?"

Gowyn roared in amusement and nudged one of his companions. "Ho! A sucker-fish wishes to run with the sharks! Into the water with him, Levrod, and then let's be off for the ship."

The Sea-Lord named Levrod smiled eagerly. "The work of a moment, sire." He stepped toward Dovirr, who backed away half a step and then held his ground. "Come to me, landman," Levrod crooned. "Come and taste the sea-water!"

"You come to *me*," Dovirr snarled back. "I'll stand my ground."

Angrily Levrod charged. Dovirr waited for the enraged Sea-Lord to cover the concrete pier and draw close. Levrod was wiry and strong, Dovirr saw. Levrod was planning on a running charge, a quick flip—and a dunking for the rash townsman who delayed the Sea-Lords. Dovirr had other ideas.

Levrod reached him; the Sea-Lord's strong fingers clutched for his arm and leg. Deftly, Dovirr stood to one side, stooped, caught the astonished Levrod by the crotch and shoulder. In one swift motion he straightened and catapulted the Sea-Lord into the water. Brine splashed on the pier as Levrod went under.

Dovirr whirled, expecting the other Sea-Lords to retaliate. But they were holding fast. Levrod swam rapidly to shore—there was never any telling what lurked in the offshore waters—and clambered up, cursing and spitting saltwater. Red-faced, he groped for his sword.

Dovirr stiffened. Unarmed, he could hardly hope to defend himself. Levrod whipped forth his weapon—

And Gowyn the Thalassarch drew his, crashing it down ringingly on Levrod's blade. Stunned, the Sea-Lord let the sword drop from his numbed fingers.

Gowyn glanced at Dovirr. "Pick it up," he commanded.

Silently, Dovirr obeyed. He gripped the jeweled hilt firmly and looked at the Thalassarch.

Gowyn was smiling. "Run this carrion through," he said, indicating the dripping, shivering, utterly miserable Levrod.

Dovirr tightened his grip. *Strike an unarmed man? Why—*

He banished the thought. Levrod would have killed him unhesitatingly; besides, Gowyn's orders were orders. He lunged; the stroke was true. Levrod crumpled. Gowyn kicked the corpse over the side of the pier. Slowly, a red stain seeped out over the oily harbor water.

Instantly there was a flutter of fins, and the body disappeared. *The Seaborn*, Dovirr thought moodily. *Feeding on their landborn brother.*

"We now have one vacancy aboard the *Garyun*. Your name, youngster?"

"Dovirr Stargan," he stammered. Could it be possible? Was it really happening?

"Welcome to the *Garyun*, Dovirr Stargan. You're young, but I like your spirit. Besides, I long suspected Levrod's loyalty."

Chapter Two

The wide, uneasy sweep of the sea spread out before Dovirr as he stood near the prow of the *Garyun*, feeling the salty tang blow sharply against him. The sky was dark; overburdened clouds hung low, threatening cold rain, and the golden-brown fins of the Seaborn broke the surface here, there, cleaving the sea at random.

Looking outward, Dovirr thought of the Seaborn—those strange once-human things man had created centuries ago in a fruitless attempt to halt the onslaught of the unstoppable *Dhuchay'y*.

"Thinking, Dovirr?" a deep voice said.

He turned. Gowyn stood beside him. In the six months he had been aboard the ship, Dovirr had won a firm place in the grizzled Thalassarch's affections. Gowyn was near middle age; he had held dominance on the Western Sea more than twenty years. Time ran against him. He sought a successor—and, Dovirr hoped, he had found one at last.

"Thinking, sire. Of the Seaborn."

Gowyn squinted at the flashing fins. "Our brethren of the deep? Someday you'll taste their teeth, young one."

"Is it true, sire? That they eat humans who fall below?"

Gowyn shrugged heavy shoulders. "You will find that out the day you topple overboard. I've never had cause to know—but a dying seaman will draw their fins within an instant."

"Strange," Dovirr said, "that they should prey on us. They were men once themselves, weren't they?"

"The sons of men only." Shadows swept the Thalassarch's face. "Years past—when the Earth was dry land, when the *Dhuchay'y* first came—man created the Seaborn to fight the alien conquerors." He chuckled sardonically. "It was hopeless. The *Dhuchay'y* defeated the Seaborn legions with ease, set a mighty rod in the ocean—and the spreading seas covered the land."

"What were they like, the *Dhuchay'y*?"

"Amphibians! They lived on sea, on land. They flooded our world to provide breeding ground for their spawn, who live in the sea until grown—and also to rid themselves of the troublesome beings who lived on the land. It was the *Dhuchay'y* that built the floating cities, and kept a few of us alive to serve them." Moodily, Gowyn clenched his fists. "Oh, had I been alive then, when they trampled us! But there was no stopping them. The sea covered all of Earth, save only for the cities they built. The world of our fathers lies a thousand fathoms down. The Seaborn sport in the drowned cities."

"And they left," said Dovirr. "Every *Dhuchay'y* on Earth suddenly left one day. They gave no reason?"

"None."

Harsh clouds seemed to bunch on the horizon. Dovirr shivered as the chill, moisture-laden wind filled the sails. The rhythmical grunting of the oarsmen on the four decks below formed a regular pattern of sound that blended with the beating of the sea against the *Garyun's* hull.

"Some day the *Dhuchay'y* will return," Gowyn said suddenly. "Some day—as unexpected as their first coming, and as unexpectedly as they departed, they will come back."

Fierce salt spray shot up the bows. In a lowered voice, Gowyn said, "Dovirr— should I die before they come—"

"Sire?"

"Should I die—and my time is long since overdue—will you swear to destroy them in my place?"

Dovirr nervously fingered his sprouting black beard. "I swear, sire," he said huskily.

Gowyn was silent for a moment, his thick fingers digging into Dovirr's shoulders. Then he pointed toward the lee.

"From there, this afternoon, will come a ship of Thalassarch Harald. Fight you at my side, Dovirr."

"Thank you, sire." Dovirr bowed his head. To fight at the Thalassarch's side was a deep honor—a sign that the mantle had been confirmed. Gowyn had named his eventual successor.

The Thalassarch strode away. Dovirr remained looking outward. Somewhere far to the east was the island city of Vythain. *Work and slave, ye landbound lubbers!* Dovirr thought defiantly. *You'll pay tribute to Dovirr yet!*

As Gowyn foretold, Harald's ship did indeed come from the leeward that afternoon, sailing into the wind. The cry resounded from aloft shortly after midday mess, and the *Garyun* prepared for war.

There were nine Thalassarchs, each boasting a roughly-hewn section of the globe. Gowyn called his domain the Western Sea; Harald was lord of the Black Ocean, a vague territory lying to the west of Gowyn's waters, and including the floating cities of Dimnon, Lanobul, and Ariod, among others. But there were no borders in the ocean, and each Thalassarch disputed hotly the extent of his neighbor's sphere of dominance.

Harald's ship approached. Aboard the *Garyun*, the uppermost bank of oarsmen docked their oars; with the wind blowing strongly, the vessel could maneuver with only three banks, thus freeing twenty men for bearing arms. All of the women of the *Garyun*, wives and daughters of the Sea-Lords, were safe in their quarters below-decks.

The *Garyun* ran up a war-flag. Gowyn strode to the deck, armed and ready, and Dovirr took his place at the Thalassarch's right hand. He saw several of the ship's officers staring at him enviously, but ignored them. He was Gowyn's man, and they would honor Gowyn's choice—or else!

The enemy ship called itself the *Brehtwol*. It, too, ran up its war-flag. Swords bristled aboard the *Garyun*; the grappling-iron crew readied itself.

Steadily, the two ships approached each other. Dovirr could see the men on the opposite deck now. There was short, grim-faced Harald, surrounded by his minions, waiting, waiting.

There was the thud of wood against wood, and grappling irons fell to. Moving automatically, Dovirr followed Gowyn over the side. The *Brehtwol* had been breached first!

"Swords! Swords!" roared Gowyn. "Follow on, men!"

The *Garyun* had seized the initial advantage. Its men swooped down on the dark-clad defenders, swords flashing brightly. Dovirr gripped the weapon he had won from Levrod long before and drove it through the heart of the first Black Oceaner he encountered.

The men of Harald's ship had deployed themselves for defense; Gowyn's sudden charge had left them no alternative. Dovirr and the Thalassarch moved forward.

"Ah, the pigs!" Gowyn exclaimed suddenly. He gestured to the windward, where four of Harald's men were hacking at the grapples. They were trying to cut loose, to end the contest and gain freedom while Gowyn was still aboard the enemy ship, where he could be brought down at ease.

"Cover for me," Dovirr said.

Gowyn raised a fearful barrage of swordplay; his heavy weapon flashed in the air, driving the Black Oceaners back, as Dovirr made his way along the pitching deck to the grapples.

"Away from there, cowards!" he shouted.

The four who hacked at the grapples looked up, and Dovirr swept into their midst. His sword felled two of them before they could defend themselves; a third ranged himself along the bow, but as he began to strike, a bolt from a *Garyun* archer felled him, and he toppled headlong between the linked ships.

The fourth rose to the defense. His sword rang against Dovirr's. A quick thrust penetrated almost to Dovirr's flesh, but he sidestepped and brought the blade down crushingly. The man staggered away, nearly cut in two, and fell.

"To me," Gowyn roared, and Dovirr, his work done, raced back to the Thalassarch's side.

Gowyn was hard pressed. Dovirr's sword moved rapidly through enemy ranks, and together they cut back the opposition—until, suddenly, the victorious duo found themselves facing a squat, burly, black-bearded man with close-trimmed hair and a dark patch over one eye.

Harald himself!

Impetuously Dovirr leaped forward, anxious to be the one to strike down a Thalassarch, but Gowyn growled, "Not you," and pulled him back.

Dovirr started to protest. Then he realized Gowyn was right; the honor of smiting a Thalassarch belonged rightfully to Gowyn, not to him.

Swords rang. Harald was a formidable opponent, but he was tired and sick at heart at the utter failure of his assault on the *Garyun*. He put up a fearsome defense, but Gowyn finally beat down his sword and spitted him.

"Harald lies dead!" Gowyn bellowed, and instantly all action ceased. Fighters of both ships put down their swords, standing as in a tableau, frozen. The battle was over.

Dovirr found himself trembling unaccountably. A Thalassarch lay dead; Gowyn now was ruler of two seas. Hardly ever had this happened before. Harald's men were kneeling to Gowyn now.

V ictory was celebrated aboard the *Garyun* that night. Opinion was unanimous that Harald's bold move, while it had brought him ignominious death, was nobly conceived. It was rare for one Thalassarch ever to attack another's ship.

Now, Gowyn found himself master of two seas. He allowed the crippled *Brehtwol* to depart, placing aboard it Kebolon, the *Garyun*'s second officer, as its captain. Kebolon was charged with the task of spreading the word to Harald's other ships that they now vowed fealty to Gowyn.

In the hearts of the men of the *Garyun* there was rejoicing—but none leaped higher than that of Dovirr, landman turned Sea-Lord, whose blade had known blood for the first time at sea.

He stood alone on the deck, his body warmed by the fiery rum in his stomach. At night, the sea hammered the keel of the *Garyun*, splattering the sides, booming dully. Far in the distance, the flickering light of a laden merchantship bound from Dimnon to Hicanthro with a cargo of rubber broke the darkness. The coded light flashed red; should it become suddenly green, the lookout would call, and the *Garyun*'s crewmen would heave to, as the Thalassarch came to the merchantman's rescue.

That was part of the contract. The cities paid tribute to the Sea-Lords—and the Sea-Lords guarded against the pirates.

Twice, now, the *Garyun* had been called upon to save a vessel in trouble. Once, it had been a tub out of Lanobul, heading north to Vostrok. Gowyn and his ship had saved it from flagless pirates operating out of a rooted island.

There were a few such—islands which had once been the highest mountain-tops, before the *Dhuchay'y* came. Scattered bands of pirates lurked there, preying on merchant vessels.

The pirates had fled at Gowyn's approach; he had decided not to give chase.

The second time, it had been a ship bound for Vythain, out of Hicanthro. They were badly plagued by a school of playful whales, and the *Garyun*, vastly amused by the difficulties encountered by the nervous merchantmen, answered the distress call and drove the whales off.

Now, Dovirr watched the steady progress of the Dimnon vessel in the distance. The vast bulk of the sea separated them.

Thalassa. Sea. It was an ancient word, a word that came from a language long drowned with the rest of Terra, but it conveyed the majesty and the awesomeness of the sea. *Thalassarch*—sea-king. The word rolled well on the tongue. *Dovirr Stargan, Thalassarch of the Nine Seas. . . .*

Already Gowyn had mastered two empires. Someday Gowyn would lie with the Seaborn, and Dovirr would rule. It was this he had dreamed of—this, all the long landlocked years in Vythain while he watched the far-off dots of ships against the blue curtain of the sky, and waited to grow to manhood.

He turned to go below-decks. Dovirr enjoyed brooding over the vastness of the sea, but on a celebration-night such as this his place was below, with the gay throng of roisterers.

Making his way over the rolling deck, he found the hatch and ducked through. The lights glowed brightly; rum flowed with free abandon. It was hardly every night that a Thalassarch fell.

Dovirr entered the big cabin. Gowyn was there, downing cup after cup of rum. The crew were roaring, laughing with a violence that threatened to shake the ship to shivers. The women, too, joined in the gaiety, joking and laughing as ribaldly as the men. They were strong and bold, these women of the-sea—completely unlike the timid, gentle girls of the floating cities.

Dovirr stiffened as he realized why they were so mirthful. A knot of seamen around Gowyn parted to show something wet and dark lying on the deck, wriggling, beating its great fins against the wood in agony and uttering hoarse barks.

Gowyn was laughing. "Ho, Dovirr! We've brought up another prize! Two catches in one day! First Harald, now this!"

Dovirr made his way to the Thalassarch's side. "What may that be?"

"I sometimes forget you were a landman but months ago," Gowyn rumbled. "Know not the Seaborn when you see one beached? Marghuin the cook was trawling to supplement our stores—and netted this!"

Of course, Dovirr thought. With naked curiosity he studied the writhing creature lying in a pool of moisture on the deck.

It was about the size of a man, but its unclothed body terminated in flukes rather than legs—though where legs had once been was still apparent. It was a golden brown in color, covered with a thick, matted, scaly hide.

The face—the face was that of a man, Dovirr saw bleakly. A man in death-agonies. The eyes were shielded by transparent lids, the nose a mere dotted pair of nostrils—but the mouth was a man's mouth, with human pain expressed in the tortured appearance of the lips. Slitted gills flickered rapidly—where ears might have been.

The transparent lids peeled back momentarily, and Dovirr saw the eyes—the eyes of a man. Flukes thumped the deck.

"How long can it live out of water?" Dovirr asked.

"They're pretty sturdy. Five minutes, maybe ten."

"And you're just going to let it die like that?"

Gowyn shrugged. "It amuses me. I have little love for the Seaborn—or they for me."

"But—they were once *men*," Dovirr said.

The Thalassarch looked curiously at him. "The creatures you were killing this afternoon still *were* men. Yet I noticed little hesitation in your sword-strokes."

"That was different. I was giving them a man's death. This is something I wouldn't do to a beast."

Gowyn scowled; Dovirr wondered if his harsh criticism had offended the Thalassarch. But to his surprise, Gowyn rose from his seat and planted his thick legs astride the deck.

"A sword!" he commanded, and a sword was brought to him.

Approaching the writhing Seaborn, Gowyn said: "Dovirr claims you are a man—and a man's death you shall get."

He plunged the sword downward. Almost instantly, the agonies of the sea-creature ceased.

"Overboard with him," Gowyn cried. "Let his brothers pick at his flesh."

He returned to his seat, and Dovirr saw that the Thalassarch's face was pale.

"You've had your wish," Gowyn said. He bent over a platter sitting before him on the wooden bench-—a fish, hot from the kettle. Angrily, he bit into it.

Dovirr watched the Thalassarch fiercely attack his meal. Suddenly Gowyn paused, lowered the fish to the platter, grabbed desperately for the cup that stood nearby.

Choking and gasping, he drained it—and continued to gag. In the general merriment, no one seemed to be noticing. Dovirr pounded on Gowyn's back, but to no avail. The Thalassarch was unable to speak; he clawed at his throat, reddened, emitted little strangled gasps.

It was over in less than a minute. Stunned, cold with horror, Doyirr was yet able to appreciate the irony of it: mighty Gowyg, Thalassarch for two decades, now ruler of two kingdoms, choking to death on a fishbone. *A fishbone!*

His numbed mind took in the information his eyes conveyed: the powerful form of Gowyn sprawled forward over the table, face blue, open eyes bulging. Then—just as the others around were realizing what had happened—Dovirr leaped to the tabletop.

"Silence!" he roared.

When there was quiet, he pointed to the fallen form of Gowyn. "Not one but *two* Thalassarchs have died today," he said loudly. "Gowyn, whose sword smote all, has succumbed to the bone of a fish."

His eyes scanned the shocked faces of the crew and the women. He saw three of the other mates staring at him.

"This morning," Dovirr said, "as if foretelling his death, Gowyn named his successor. I call upon you now to offer allegiance to your new Thalassarch—Dovirr of Vythain!"

Chapter Three

In the days immediately following Gowyn's death, Dovirr established firm control over the crew of the *Garyun*. He had learned a valuable lesson during the battle with Harald's ship: act quickly, seize the initiative, and let the slower thinkers take second-best.

The excitement caused by the sudden snuffing-out of the Thalassarch's life was a fit frame for the young ex-landman's ascension. By the time anyone thought of questioning Dovirr's right to claim rule, he held the *Garyun* in tight thrall.

It was Lysigon, one of Gowyn's mates, who laid down the challenge that settled the problem of leadership aboard the *Garyun*. Dovirr had seen the quarrel coming long before, even while Gowyn yet lived; Lysigon, a handsome, broad-shouldered Sea-Lord and son of a Sea-Lord, was openly resentful of the newcomer. Obviously he had once been high in Gowyn's esteem, and hated Dovirr for having usurped his place.

The *Garyun* was lying becalmed not far off Korduna, where the Sea-Lords had paid their annual tribute call. Korduna was one of the largest of the floating cities, and the *Dhuchay'y* had taken care to stock it with many of sunken Terra's fauna; the Kordunans were meat-purveyors to the world. It had been Gowyn's practice to exact tribute in meat, rather than gold, and Dovirr had seen the wisdom of that; a year's supply of barrelled pork and other meats was brought aboard and stored in the capacious hold of the *Garyun*.

Dovirr spent much of his time studying maps, familiarizing himself with the location of the floating cities, marking off the domains of his rival Thalassarchs, planning, thinking. It was while he thus occupied himself, with his charts spread out on a broad table on the bridge deck, that Lysigon came to him. The Sea-Lord stood before him, in full battle dress.

"What means the dress, Lysigon?" Dovirr asked casually, glancing up at the Sea-Lord and quickly back down at his charts. "Surely no trouble beckons— or do you know of battle before my lookout?"

"Look out for yourself, landworm!" Lysigon crashed an armored fist down on the table, disturbing the charts. Dovirr rose instantly.

"What want you, Lysigon?"

"*Lord* Lysigon. *Thalassarch* Lysigon. I've stood your usurpation long enough, man of Vythain."

Dovirr fingered the edge of the table. Flicking a quick glance back of the angry Sea-Lord, he saw a handful of others—all, like Lysigon, full-blooded Sea-Lords—skulking in the background near the rigging. His flesh grew cold; was this a carefully-nurtured assassination plot?

Evenly, he said: "I order you to get out of armor, Lysigon. The *Garyun* is not threatened at the moment. And I'll thank you to keep a civil tongue, or I'll have you flayed with a micro-knife and rubbed in salt!"

"Strong words, boy. Worthy of Gowyn—but for the strength that does not back them! Tonight the Seaborn feast on you; tomorrow, I captain the *Garyun.*"

Lysigon unsheathed his sword. It hung shimmering in the air for an instant; then he lunged. At the same moment Dovirr smoothly up-ended the work-table.

The keen sword splintered wood. Cursing, Lysigon struggled to extricate it from the table—and, as he fought to free his weapon, Dovirr laughingly dashed his ink-pot into the Sea-Lord's face. Sepia squid-extract stained the proud seaman's fiery beard. He bellowed with rage, abandoned his blade, and charged blindly forward.

Dovirr deftly sidestepped around the table as the maddened Lysigon clanged against it. The Sea-Lord rebounded; Dovirr was waiting for him. Unarmed, unarmored, Dovirr paused in readiness by the bowsprit.

"Here I am, Lysigon," he sang softly.

Lysigon charged. Dovirr absorbed the impact, stepped back, bent, seized one of Lysigon's legs. The Sea-Lord toppled heavily to the deck, landing with a crash that brought some twenty men and a few women topside to see what was going on.

The humiliated Sea-Lord crawled toward Dovirr. With a mocking laugh the Thalassarch trampled Lysigon's outstretched hand. Dovirr was biding his time, waiting for word to travel that a fight was taking place on top deck. The crew was gathering. Lysigon's four cohorts held back.

"What do you ask of me, Lysigon? That I appoint you Thalassarch in my place?" His foot thumped ringingly against the Sea-Lord's armor. Lysigon responded with a strangled roar and leaped to his feet.

Dovirr met the charge evenly, took Lysigon's weight with a smooth roll of his body, and smashed his fist into the Sea-Lord's face. Lysigon stumbled backward; Dovirr hit him again, knocking him up against the bow. "To your kingdom, Lysigon!" he yelled, seizing the Sea-Lord's feet. A quick upward flip and the hapless mate vanished over the side.

There was a howl, a splash—and silence. In full armor, Lysigon sank like an anchor. Dovirr, unscratched, nodded to his audience.

"Lysigon desired to rule the sea. He now has the opportunity—at close range."

The onlookers responded with silence. It was the complete hush of utter awe—and from that moment, Dovirr Stargan was unquestioned Thalassarch of the Western Sea.

The cycle of days rolled on, filling out the year. Dovirr had taken over Gowyn's logbooks, and spent odd hours reading of the late Thalassarch's many triumphs. Gowyn had filled a long row of books; the last of them was only barely begun, and already a new hand had entered much: the death of Gowyn, the conquest of Lysigon, visits to many ports.

It was difficult for Dovirr to convince himself that not yet a year had passed since the day he had waited hesitantly at the Vythain pier. A year—and three of the mocking Sea-Lords who had called on Vythain that day lay at the seabottom, two sent there by Dovirr's own hand.

He who had never left Vythain once in his eighteen years now roamed two seas, with nine ships of his own and eight of Harald's claiming allegiance. Dovirr felt his body growing hard, his muscles quickening to split-second tone and his skin toughening. Occasionally, he took a hand in the galleys, tugging at his oar next to some sweating knave for whom a life at sea was constant hardship. Dovirr drank in the days; *this* was the life.

He wondered occasionally about the days before the *Dhuchay'y* had come. What was Terra like, with its proud cities now slimy with sea-things? He envisioned a race of giants, each man with the strength of a Sea-Lord.

And then he saw that he was wrong. The *Dhuchay'y* could never have conquered such a race. No; the Terrans must have been meek landworms of the sort that spawned in Vythain, else the aliens from the stars would have been thrown back.

Anger rose fiercely in him, and he strode to the bridge at nightfall to stare upward and shake his fist at the unblinking stars.

Somewhere among those dots of white and red and blue dwelt the *Dhuchay'y*. Dovirr, wearing the mantle of the dead Gowyn, would scowl at the stars with bitter hatred. *Come back, star-things! Come back—and give me a chance to destroy you!*

But the stars made no reply. Dovirr would turn away wearily, and return to his charts. He was learning the way of the sea. Later, perhaps, the *Dhuchay'y* would come. Dovirr was used to waiting long for what he most desired.

Chapter Four

At year's end, a pleasant task arrived. According to Gowyn's logbook, time had come to return to Vythain to demand tribute. This would be sweet, Dovirr thought.

He studied Gowyn's log-entry for this date a year earlier:

"Fifth of Eighthmonth, 3261. Today we return to Vythain for the gold. The wind is good; course holds true. Below-decks, I fear, Levrod has been murmuring against me. . . .

"Sixth of Eighthmonth, 3261. Collection of tribute without difficulty at Vythain, as usual. Upon departure, we were accosted by a good-looking Vythainan boy. He humiliated Levrod in hand-to-hand combat, and killed him at my orders. I took the Vythainan aboard ship. I like him. . . ."

Smiling, Dovirr looked up from the dead Thalassarch's log. Ahead, on the horizon, he could see the growing dot that was Vythain. Even now, perhaps, old Lackthan was calling out the news that the Sea-Lords approached; even now, terror would be sweeping through the city as the poor landworms awaited the *Garyun*'s approach. How they dreaded it! How they feared that the Sea-Lords would, for sport, sack the city while they were in harbor!

They drew into Vythain Harbor early next day. Dovirr ordered the dinghy put over the side, and, picking six men to accompany him, set out for shore.

He stood, one foot on the seat, in the prow of the little craft, peering intently at the city of his birth. He could see tiny figures moving on the pier—police officers clearing away the passersby, no doubt.

The sea was calm; tiny wavelets licked at the dinghy's sides as it slid through the water to the pier. They drew up slowly. Dovirr grinned at the sight of the familiar carven steps, the pile of buildings set back from the shore and rising to the bright stone of Lackthan's spy-tower.

He was the first one over the side and onto the pier when the dinghy docked. His six men arrayed themselves at his sides, and they waited regally for the tribute.

A few tense moments passed. Then, with faltering step, the eight old men began their procession down the rough-hewn steps of Vythain, groaning under the weight of coffers as they came.

Dovirr folded his arms and waited.

In the lead was Councilman Morgrun, looking even more old and shrunken than before. His eyes, deep-set in a baggy network of wrinkles, were filmed over with rheum; he was staggering under the heavy coffer, barely able to manage it. "Ho there, Morgrun," Dovirr cried suddenly. "Scuttle forward and greet your new Thalassarch!"

He laughed. Morgrun lifted his head.

The Councilman emitted a tiny gasp and nearly dropped the coffer. *"Dovirr!"*

"Your memory has not failed you yet, I see, old one. Yes, Dovirr!"

The eight Councilmen drew near, lowered their coffers to the concrete, and huddled together in a puzzled clump. Finally Morgrun said, "This is some joke of Gowyn's. He seeks to humble us by sending this runaway boy."

Dovirr spat. "I should have you hurled to the sea for that, Morgrun. Gowyn lies dead off the edge of Harald's sea; Harald lies beside him. *I* rule both Thalassarchies!"

The Councilman stared at him, sneering at first, then, seeing the unquestionable authority in his eyes, sinking to their knees, jaws working without producing speech. Dovirr smiled broadly, relishing the moment. "Into the dinghy with the money," he ordered. "No—wait. Open the nearest coffer."

A coffer was opened. Dovirr snatched an ingot, looked at it, sardonically sniffed it. "Morgrun, is the gold pure?"

"Of course, Dov—sire."

"Good." Dovirr stepped forward and lifted Morgrun's bowed head gently with the tip of his boot. "Tell me, Councilman—how goes it in Vythain? I have been somewhat out of touch, this past year. What of old Lackthan, the spyman?"

"Dead, sire."

"Dead, at last? Too bad; I would have enjoyed watching him discover who had succeeded Gowyn. Has the dredging gone well this year?"

"Poorly. You have taken nearly all our gold in the tribute, sire."

"A pity. You'll have to squeeze some unfortunate neighbor-city of yours to make up the loss, won't you?"

A chill wind swept over the pier suddenly. Dovirr gathered his cloak about him. It was time to return to the ship, he thought; the fun here had been about wrung dry.

Morgrun glanced up. "Sire?"

"What is it, Morgrun?"

"Sire, have you heard aught out of Vostrok?"

Dovirr frowned. Vostrok was a northern city, one of the largest on the sea's surface. Vythain depended on it for its wood; Vostrok had Terra's finest forest, and from its trees had come most of the planet's ships.

"We were expecting wood from Vostrok," Morgrun continued. "It has not come. We pay our tribute, sire, and—"

"We do our job," Dovirr said coldly. "But there have been no distress signals coming from Vostroki vessels. Have you called them?"

"We have." Alien sub-radio channels still were in operation between the floating cities. "Sire, there is no answer. *There is no answer!*"

Dovirr glanced at Kubril, his first officer. "This is strange. Perhaps Vostrok is planning rebellion, Kubril. It might bear investigation."

To Morgrun, he said: "We will go to Vostrok, old one. Don't fear for your wood."

Vostrok was the northernmost city of those Dovirr had inherited from Gowyn; it floated in high, choppy seas almost a week's journey from Vythain.

The course called for the *Garyun* to make another tribute call, but Dovirr decided to make for Vostrok at once, and ordered the *Ithamil*, one of his second-line ships which he encountered en route, to make the tribute pickup instead. The *Garyun* proceeded steadily northward, through increasingly rough waters. Crowds of the Seaborn attended the ship; moodily, Dovirr watched the flukes of the once-men churning in the dark waters.

On the fourth day an off-duty deckhand harpooned a Seaborn. Dovirr angrily ordered the man microflayed, then relented and merely put him on half-rations for a week. There was, it seemed, an instinctive hatred alive between the men of the *Garyun* and the Seaborn.

Dovirr felt none of it himself; he had been unable to share in the merriment over the predicament of the tortured creature on the deck, feeling only sympathy. He realized that, for all his dominion, he was actually still a landman at heart. By sheer strength, he had bulled his way to the eminence of a Sea-Lord's standing, but yet the men of the *Garyun* sometimes seemed as alien to him in way and thought as the flashing creatures of the deep.

The sea grew steadily rougher, and cold squalls began to blow; heavy clouds lay like sagging balloons over the water, dark and gray-shot. Dovirr bided his time, as the *Garyun* sailed northward. Vostrok had broken off contact with Vythain, eh?

Strange, he thought. That could mean many things.

At the end of the week, the *Garyun* entered Vostrok harbor. The city was much like all the others, only larger. According to Gowyn's notes, Vostrok had been the central base of the *Dhuchay'y* during the occupation of Terra centuries ago.

Dovirr ordered the anchor dropped half a league off-shore. Calling his officers about him, he stared uneasily toward the waiting city.

"Well?" Kubril asked. "Do we go ashore?"

Dovirr frowned. He wore his finest cuirass and a bold red-plumed helmet; his men likewise were armored. "I like not the looks of this city. I see no men on the pier. Hand me the glass, Liggyal."

The seaman handed the glass to Dovirr, who focussed it on the distant shore. Tensely, he studied the area about the pier.

"No one is there."

"Perhaps they don't recognize us," Kubril suggested. "The tribute isn't due for another month."

"Still, when the *Garyun* casts anchor in their harbor they should flock to! Come—let us land three boatloads of warriors on their pier, and seek the source of these people's reticence."

Dovirr strode away from the gathering and gave orders for three boats to be unshipped. Thirty of his best men, sparkling in their burnished armor, manned them; the sturdy boats groaned under the weight, and the sea-water licked high near the gunwales, but the boats held fast.

Oars bit water. Standing in the prow of the leading boat, Dovirr peered landward, feeling premonitions of danger.

The pier was still empty of men when the three boats pulled up. Dovirr sprinted to shore, followed by a brace of his men. Cautiously, they advanced as the other boats unloaded. The Vostrok pier was a long, broad expanse of concrete, an apron extending out from the city proper into the sea.

"Should we enter the city?" Kubril asked. "This may be a trap."

"Wait." Dovirr pointed. "Someone comes."

A figure was approaching them, a graybeard. "Know you him?" Dovirr asked.

"One of the city fathers, no doubt. They all look alike at tribute time."

The old man drew near. Strain was evident on his face; his thin lips trembled uncontrollably, and harsh lines creased his forehead.

"The tribute is not yet due," he said in a small voice. "We did not expect you for another month. We—"

"On your knees," Dovirr said. "We are not here for tribute. The city of Vythain reports you have been remiss in your shipments of wood, and that you refuse contact. Can you explain this?"

The oldster tugged at Dovirr's cloak. "There are reasons. . . . Please, go away. Leave!"

Surprised, Dovirr drew back from the man's grasp. But then, a curious stale odor drifted to his nostrils, the odor of dried, rotting fish spread out on a wharf in the sun. He glanced up toward the city. The oldster turned too, and uttered a groan of despair.

"They come, they come!"

Dovirr stiffened. The old man broke away and dashed out of sight. Advancing across the bare pier toward the little group of Sea-Lords were eight *things*. For an instant, horror grasped Dovirr as his eyes took in the image. Eight feet tall, with bony scaled skulls and gleaming talons, they advanced, each sweeping a thick, lengthy tail behind. Dovirr remained transfixed.

He recalled what Gowyn had told him once—about green-fleshed, evil-smelling hell-creatures, their bright eyes yellow beacons of hatred, their jaws burgeoning with knife-like teeth, their naked hides rugose, scaly. Eight of them; moving in solemn phalanx.

A sudden surge of mingled fear and joy shivered through him. Cupping his hands, Dovirr faced his men, who stood numbed with astonishment.

"Forward!" he shouted. "The *Dhuchay'y* have come back!"

Indeed it was so.

The gruesome creatures slinking from the depths of Vostrok could only be *Dhuchay'y*, come to reclaim the world they had transformed into a globe of water and then abandoned.

They walked erect; including tail, they measured twice a man's length. Their hind feet were thick and fleshy, terminating in webbed claws; the hands, curiously man-like, were poised for combat, holding wedge-shaped knives. They advanced at an accelerating pace. Dovirr led his men forward to meet them with desperate haste.

As he drew near, he saw the delicate fringe of gills near the blunt snout; the creatures were equipped for action on land or sea. A chilling thought gripped Dovirr; what if a swarm of the *Dhuchay'y* were to force him and his men into the water, then follow after and slay them as they swam?

He closed with them, Kubril at his side. His voice rose to a piercing shriek. "Kill them! Kill!"

Leather-webbed feet flashed around him as he drove into the midst of the alien horde. His sword flickered overhead, chopped downward, and sliced through a *Dhuchay'y* arm. The member fell; the knife it had held clinked against the concrete. The alien uttered a whistling scream of pain; golden blood spurted.

In fear-maddened rage, Dovirr's men charged the aliens. Dovirr smiled at the sight of the javelin of giant Zhoncoru humming into a scaly bosom; his own sword bit deep into a meaty flank. Once again, the teachings of Gowyn had stood him in good stead; taken by surprise, the aliens were dropping back. Already one bloody form lay sprawled on the pier, pierced by thirty Sea-Lord thrusts while another mighty bulk was toppling. At Dovirr's side, Kubril thrust his spear into the falling creature and aided it in its descent.

Holding the spear like a lance, Kubril thrust it into another alien that menaced Dovirr. A torrent of blood issued from the torn belly.

"Thanks," Dovirr murmured, and sliced into an alien eye with a tiptoe thrust. The pier was covered now with mingled golden and red blood; it was slippery, treacherous, and Dovirr within his armor was bathed in sweat.

The aliens were yielding, though. Three now lay dead; a fourth was staggering from its wounds, while of the remaining four, not one had escaped damage. Dovirr himself weaved in and out of the struggling group, and had so far evaded harm; Kubril had been struck by raking talons but seemed little the worse for it, while the javelin-man Zhoncoru bore a ragged cut down his tanned cheek.

Glancing quickly to one side, Dovirr saw three of his men dead in a welter of blood. There was little time for sorrow. His sword slashed through an alien gill, eliciting a shriek of pain that brought momentary near-pity to Dovirr's eyes. Then the wounded alien sliced the plume from Dovirr's helmet; laughing, the Sea-Lord thrust through the creature's throat.

Dovirr drew back, gasping for breath; the stink of the dying monsters was overpowering. Rivers of sweat poured into his eyes. Writhing aliens lay everywhere.

"No," Dovirr said out loud with sudden hoarseness. He caught Kubril's arms; the first officer had been striking a vicious blow at a dying *Dhuchay'y*.

He pointed toward the distant city. Coming toward them, talons thundering over the stone, were reinforcements—

Hundreds of them!

To the ship!" Dovirr called. It was the only possible step; twenty-five Terrans could never hold off against an uncountable multitude of the alien invaders. He led the retreat; the surviving swordsmen dragged dead and dying into the boats, and they struck out for the waiting *Garyun*.

Dovirr saw the ship heave anchor and begin moving rapidly toward them. Obviously Dwayorn, the seaman left in command; had seen the melee on shore and was coming in to pick the fleeing Sea-Lords up.

But there was some doubt that the move would succeed. Dovirr goaded his oarsmen on, and the mother ship made full speed toward them—but with cold horror he saw the swarm of *Dhuchay'y* reaching the end of the pier, marching over the hacked bodies of their fallen comrades, and plunging into the water! They were swimming toward the retreating boats!

Around them in the water, the flukes of the Seaborn were becoming visible; they would eat well tonight, Dovirr thought grimly.

"Pull!" he urged. "They're gaining!"

But it was useless. The *Dhuchay'y*, amphibians, were converging on the fleeing boats in a milky rush of foam. Dovirr glanced back and saw the blunt heads ominously breaking the waves in their swift advance.

Suddenly a taloned claw appeared at the edge of the boat. Dovirr instantly hacked downward with his sword; the severed claw dropped into the boat, the arm withdrew. But at once four more appeared. The *Dhuchay'y* had caught up—and the mother ship was still a good distance away.

He knew what had to be done. Stripping off his breastplate, he hurled the costly polished cuirass at the naked skull of a leering alien grasping the gunwale. "Out of your armor! They're going to capsize us!"

There was no way to prevent it; the only hope now was—impossibly—to outswim the creatures. The boat rocked dizzyingly as Dovirr and his men stripped down to their kilts. They hurled the useless armor at the bobbing aliens, beat at them with oars, slashed with swords—to no avail.

Already, Dovirr saw, Kubril's boat was overturned and his men splashing in a wild tangle of aliens. A moment later, their turn came.

The boat went over; its eight occupants leaped free. As Dovirr sprang he caught sight of the *Garyun* looming above, its decks lined with arbalestiers ready to fire if only they could be sure of hitting none but aliens. Already they had loosed a few hesitant bolts, and the shrieks of dying *Dhuchay'y* resounded.

The water was icy. Dovirr opened his eyes, peered ahead as if looking through badly-blown green glass, and saw aliens swimming all about.

Choking, he broke the surface, sucked in a lungful of air, and submerged again, swimming toward the ship. The *Garyun*, he hoped, was going to lower lines to pick up the survivors.

He swam on. Suddenly claws ripped his back; he wriggled away, gripping his dirk. A *Dhuchay'y* swam between him and the ship.

He twisted the dirk upward into the creature's bowels, but tenacious arms gripped him and drew him under. Gasping, he sliced downward and across with his knife; the squirming alien refused to let go, keeping him beneath the surface. He thought his lungs were going to burst.

He groped for the creature's throat. His hands closed on something smooth—an amulet of some sort, it seemed. Blindly, he ripped it away and thrust the dirk upward.

The alien abruptly relented. Dovirr's head bobbed above the surface; still somehow clutching the amulet, he stabbed down into the bloodying water furiously.

Suddenly he was alone in the water. He looked up; the ship was next to him, and a line dangled invitingly a few feet away. He saw a few of his men, bloody and torn, climbing other such lines—one with an alien still clinging to his body.

Choking, gasping, Dovirr pulled himself up past the banks of oars, felt hands clutch at him and ease him onto the deck. He swayed weakly. Blood poured from a dozen wounds, fiery with salty sea-water.

Disdaining support, he strode to the bow and looked down. A blood-slick covered the sea, and the preying creatures of the deep were beginning to gather. The battle was over. Wounded aliens drifted in the water; he saw none of his own men except those few already aboard.

Numbly, his voice a harsh croak, he shouted: "Full speed out to sea! Let's get out of here!"

Wind caught the sails. The *Garyun* fled the scene of slaughter, putting leagues between itself and alien-infested Vostrok.

Chapter Five

There came a time for licking of wounds, of drawing back into the open sea and drifting broodingly. For the next few days Dovirr kept to himself, alone in his cabin, going over and over the rout in his mind.

The *Dhuchay'y* had returned. They had silently slipped down from the sky and retaken Vostrok; countless aliens now again abounded in the one-time alien capital.

Thirty Terrans had gone ashore at Vostrok. Six had returned alive, and those six badly wounded, every man. Three boats sunk; twenty-four lives lost, thirty suits of armor. Dovirr scowled. Armor could be forged, new boats built—but men were irreplaceable. And, now that the *Dhuchay'y* again gripped Terra in their clammy grasp, he would need every man he had.

Hatred surged through him—hatred for the vicious alien overlords. For the thousandth time he relived that struggle beneath the sea, where, tangled in wreathing kelp and choking for breath, he had drawn the life of a *Dhuchay'y* and saved his own.

He still had souvenirs of that encounter, eight of them: seven scabbing claw-marks down his back—and one amulet. He looked down at the amulet now.

It was small, made of polished onyx; a lambent flame glowed in its heart, a tiny worm of fire that danced dizzily without tiring.

"Come in, Kubril," he said suddenly, hearing a knock.

The first officer entered, limping from his wounds. He took a seat heavily opposite Dovirr. "Aye," he said, seeing the amulet. "Fondling your pretty toy again, Dovirr."

The Thalassarch rolled the amulet idly over the table. "Do we dare attack Vostrok, do you think?" he asked.

Kubril stared at him. A raw, livid wound ran down one side of his face; a thick lock of his beard had been ripped away. "Attack Vostrok?" Kubril chuckled. "I'd sooner attack the sea itself."

"How do you mean?"

"Sire, we have seventeen ships to our fleet. We might gather them all for the attack—but who knows how many of the aliens there be? We can count on no more than five hundred swords."

"And if the other Thalassarchs cooperate?"

"Four thousand, then. Four thousand men—but even so, we couldn't get near the city."

"Why?"

"The *Dhuchay'y* are on the alert now. They'll guard Vostrok. They live in the sea, as well as on the land; the seas will be thick with them as our boats approach. Recall what happened the other week?"

Dovirr scowled. "Aye." He tugged at his beard angrily. "They would tip our boats as soon as we drew near. And the harbor is too shallow to bring the *Garyun* near enough."

"If we could ever land our men—" Kubril said.

"The *Dhuchay'y* will have a cordon of swimmers surrounding Vostrok the instant our ships appear on the horizon. We could neither get boats through to shore nor land men."

Walking to the port, he stared out in the general direction of Vostrok. "The aliens live smugly there—and, when they see we are powerless, they will take the rest of their cities back, and put us to death."

"I see now why the men of old created the Seaborn," said Kubril. "The only possible way to attack the *Dhuchay'y* is in the sea. Strike at their main line of defenses; then march to the city!"

"The Seaborn failed," Dovirr pointed out. "Else mankind would not have fallen."

"The Seaborn failed because they came too little and too late! The world was already in alien grasp when the Seaborn were loosed upon the *Dhuchay'y*. If—"

"Enough," Dovirr said wearily. This had been his first taste of defeat. Heretofore, his progress had been rapid; now it seemed blocked utterly. He was not used to defeat; it rankled within him, leaving him harsh and sour. "You talk of miracles, Kubril. Leave me."

"Very well," Kubril said quietly. The hulking first mate rose, looked pityingly at his captain, and left.

Dovirr watched the door close. He gripped the alien amulet in his hand tightly, in a paroxysm of frustration.

He raised the amulet on high as if to dash it to powder against the cabin wall—as if destroying the trinket would crush the race that had forged it.

Suddenly, the amulet burned coolly in his palm. Dovirr gasped.

He saw the bottom of the sea.

He saw total blackness begin to give way to faint light. Strange creatures moved with stately grace through the deep; it was as if he himself were below the waters.

In the distance were towers springing from the ocean floor—towers grotesquely festooned with clinging sea-vegetation, enwrapped with streamers of brown kelp and crusted over with anemone and budding coral, bright with glaring reds and greens and astonishing iodine-purples that no human eye would behold.

None but Dovirr's. He stared at the towers, then approached them.

It was a city. Disinterested fish flitted through the smashed windows of the dead buildings, gaping open-mouthed, goggle-eyed, in pseudo-surprise. Coiling moray eels wound around what had been television antennas and yawned, baring their myriad tiny, razor-sharp teeth. Dovirr peered in a window. An enormous turtle sprawled on a sagging floor, its soft green flippers scuttling idly, disturbing the layer of silt that had formed through the ages.

This was a dead world. Looking up, Dovirr saw the black curtain of the water's top cutting off the sea from the sky, and fancied he could see the glimmering sun penetrating the depths. He moved on, stalking silently.

Sea-spiders twice the height of a man crawled over the faces of the buildings. Here, there was merely a mound where a building had been; the sea was reclaiming, concealing, reshaping. Strange new forms were emerging; in a thousand years more, no one would ever know there had been a city here at the bottom of the sea.

And the endless sea would roll on.

Dovirr shot forward through the water, moving with the easy grace of disembodiment. Startled fish turned as he went past—and, seeing nothing, continued on their way.

He came to an anchor—a mighty titanium chain, each link feet-thick, stretching upward to a cloudy bulk far above. It was a city-anchor—one of the guy-wires that held a floating city in place. He rose along it, headed toward the surface.

Then he was thirty feet beneath the surface of the sea, and saw the *Dhuchay'y*. There were ten of them, in the shallow artificial sand shelf just off Vostrok—burying things. White things.

His blood chilled. They were eggs.

The *Dhuchay'y* were breeding. Soon, their numbers would increase.

Hastily he shot away; struck out for mid-sea. His mind, guided by the amulet, slid smoothly through the waters. He spied another sunken city, dipped to observe it.

Fingers brushed his mind. Thoughts came:

Who are you, intruder?

Dovirr froze, let his mind range in all directions until he found what he wanted to see.

A friend, he replied. *I am a friend.*

What seek you down here?

I'll explain. Come to me, Dovirr's mind said. And the Seaborn came. Dovirr watched the lithe creature heading toward the point from which Dovirr's thoughts emanated.

Suddenly the Seaborn stopped; its mind radiated perplexity.

Where are you, stranger?

Tensely, Dovirr thought: *Above the sea. Only my mind roves below the sea. How?*

I use an amulet stolen from the alien invaders, Dovirr said. *I know not how it functions, but it sends my mind down to the deeps.*

There was the equivalent of a chuckle. *The aliens, then, must manufacture what we have of nature,* the Seaborn said.

What mean you?

There is no way to speak beneath the sea. My people . . . communicate with the mind. The aliens need toys to focus their mind-powers beneath the seas, it seems.

Dovirr understood now the nature of the amulet he had snatched from the dying *Dhuchay'y.* The alien young lived in the sea, and spoke the language of the sea; when the amphibious creatures grew older, they left the sea to dwell on land. When returning to the sea they needed the amulets to communicate with one another, having lost the ability through maturing.

He studied the Seaborn before him. In his natural element, the mutant man was the epitome of grace; the feathery gills flickered in and out with dizzying speed, while the Seaborn's heavy flukes kept him serenely stabilized in the water.

Your people have killed many of mine, the Seaborn said. *If you yourself were here, perhaps I would kill you.*

We have fought long and for the wrong reasons, said Dovirr. *We are both men.*

Yes. But your people hate my people.

Not I. Vividly, Dovirr transmitted the image of the long-ago scene when Gowyn had uproariously watched the agonizing death of a captive Seaborn. Dovirr's own land-nurtured emotions came through: his feeling of sharp horror, his insistence that Gowyn put a stop to the atrocity.

You are not like the others, the Seaborn said. *I am called Halgar. I see you are different.*

Dovirr replied: *I have common cause with you.*

Yes, land-brother?

Dovirr smiled. *Long ago, men from the skies came to our world. My people—the land-people—created yours then, to help in the struggle against the invaders.*

We failed, Halgar said. *There were but a hundred of us. It was not enough.*

How many are you now?

Many millions, Halgar replied. *We cover the seas thickly, land-brother.*

Dovirr felt his mind growing weary under the strain of communicating. Gathering all his strength, he projected a final thought: *Know, then, that the aliens have come again! Will you give your help—and end the misunderstanding between our peoples?*

He hovered, mind suspended in the sea, awaiting Halgar's response. There was silence for a moment, the deafening silence of the depths. Then:

We will help you, Dovirr of the land-world!

Chapter Six

The ships gathered.

Slowly, the Sea-Lords of forgotten Terra gathered their might, massed their armada in the heart of the roiling ocean. United for the first time in ten centuries, the Thalassarchs mustered their power.

They met in the Western Sea, at Dovirr's call, in Dovirr's territory. Suspiciously at first, then open-heartedly as they learned of the *Dhuchay'y's* return, they came, thirsting for battle, longing to bury their rusting swords in alien hide, hungry for the spurt of alien golden blood.

And at their head, acclaimed by all, the youngest of the eight leaders:

Dovirr Stargan, Thalassarch of the Western Sea, Lord of the Black Ocean—

Dovirr Stargan, Thalassarch of the Nine Seas!

They massed in mid-ocean, seventy ships, nearly four thousand swords, and readied themselves for the assault on Vostrok. The ships swung into battle position, raised their war-flags.

In Vythain, in Dimnon, in the fifty floating cities of the sea-world, the landsmen cowered, wondering what strange compulsion had brought the Eight Thalassarchs together in one sea, why the Sea-Lords had gathered, what awesome battle was to be fought. Snug in their landbound homes, they little dreamed that the aliens from the stars had come again, had taken back the proudest of the cities they had built.

Terra had been forgotten by the stars, and during the time of its forgetting the Sea-Lords had grown strong. Now, the aliens had remembered. They had come to reclaim their captive world—

But now, things would be different.

The sea boiled. Flukes broke the waves, sank down again, rose, flashed brightly in the sunlight, slipped beneath the white crests. The war-fleet watched; the Seaborn were on the march!

From the corners of the world they came, thousands upon thousands of them. Dovirr stood at the prow of the *Garyun*, the Sea-Lords' flagship, and looked down on a sea thick with the mutant once-men.

They had bred—and they had had an entire world of water in which to breed. Just as once the landmen had numbered in the billions, now the Seaborn, beginning with the mere hundred created by long-dead Terran geneticists, had proliferated, had been fruitful and multiplied.

Now they disported themselves in the sea before the Terran armada. Dovirr waited, while they assembled. Clutching the precious amulet in his hand, he let his mind rove out among theirs to share in the joy of the sea. He spoke with Halgar the Seaborn, who led the legions of the sea as Dovirr did his fleet.

We come, Halgar said. *The aliens shall not live!*

Earth will be free, said Dovirr. *They will never come a third time. How many are you, now?*

Millions. Ready yourself, land-brother. At your word, we make for Vostrok!

Tenseness swept the gathered armada. Dovirr beckoned to Kubril; the first officer was staring down at the tight-packed phalanxes of Seaborn with mingled disgust and awe. Like the other Sea-Lords, he had not fully overcome his hatred of the mutant water-breathers, even now when he was locked in alliance with them.

"Send the word," Dovirr ordered. "To Duvenal, to the left, and Murduien at my right. We sail in an hour; be ready to lift anchor."

"Aye." Kubril swiftly set to the task.

Dovirr grasped the amulet. *Halgar?*

I hear you, land-brother.

We sail in an hour. The time has come for you to begin the journey to Vostrok.

I hear, Halgar said.

Flukes glistened in the sunlight. The Seaborn swept their mighty arms forward; the army of swimmers began to draw away from the anchored ships.

The attack on Vostrok had begun.

The *Gayrun* struck anchor about a league off Vostrok, and the other Sea-Lords filled in the formation circling the island-city. Dovirr shouted to his men as they dropped the mighty anchor over the side.

Then he turned toward the city—and he saw the clustering Seaborn.

"Look at them," he whispered. Pride choked his voice—pride in the sleek men of the sea, even pride in the ancients who had somehow altered Man so he could breathe the ocean.

The sea bubbled with their numbers.

Through his glass, Dovirr watched the encounter. Massed Seaborn swarmed the island on all sides, forming a ring almost a mile thick, a brown carpet threshing in the water. Dovirr's heart rose as he saw the young *Dhuchay'y* being hauled from their subaquatic nests, being ripped to pieces on the surface of the water. Eggs, golden blood, upturned bodies.

A dull boom—the *Dhuchay'y* shore installations gunning the Seaborn. A shower of blue spume went up as the cannons barked—but as the alien shells landed, as the ranks were thinned, other of the Seaborn fought their way up from the depths to take the place of the casualties.

"Down boats!" Dovirr shouted.

The cry resounded from ship to ship. "Down boats!"

The sound of boats thumping the water was heard. Dovirr headed one; at his left was Kubril, and farther along he could see the boats of the other Thalassarchs. Oars dug the waves. Fifty, a hundred, two hundred Terran boats sped forward to the scene of battle.

They reached the edge of the Seaborn ring. Dovirr, despite himself, was astonished by the way the sea-creatures had arrayed themselves, shoulder to shoulder, completely clogging the water a few inches below the surface.

And now the strategy Dovirr and Halgar the Seaborn had devised went into effect.

Four thousand Terrans, in full armor, left their boats at the edge of the Seaborn ring. They were barefoot. Led by Dovirr they advanced over the massed Seaborn, walking on their shoulders, running and leaping over the shifting floor of once-human bodies.

The Seaborn maintained steady support. Here, there, Dovirr saw one of his men lose his footing and slip, and saw webbed hands reach up to steady the fallen one.

The *Dhuchay'y* shore-battery barked, and ten square feet of Seaborn vanished, cutting a gaping hole in the bridge. But instantly from below surged a hundred more, filling the gap. Countless reinforcements lurked beneath the sea.

Now, Dovirr could see the aliens standing on the shore of their captured city. Some of them were venturing out into the water—and being dragged under instantly, to be ripped apart by the waiting hordes. Others, more cautious, hung indecisively back on land.

Dovirr reached the shore first. He sprang up, drawing his sword, and ripped upward into an alien belly. A steaming torrent of golden blood poured forth.

"Onward!" he yelled. "Onward!"

He cut a swath through the aliens and looked back, saw the Terran swordsmen advancing grimly over the packed sea. The *Dhuchay'y* defense had been negated completely; their hopes of keeping the Terrans away by means of an underwater network of defenders had vanished under the vast counter-attack by the Seaborn.

The Terrans were packed shoulder to shoulder now, just as the Seaborn had been, advancing in a solid mass, wielding their swords before them. The aliens, ill prepared for such an assault by a foe hitherto held in contempt, gave ground.

Dovirr and his men isolated a pocket of perhaps fifty *Dhuchay'y*, fencing them in with a wall of flashing steel.

"To the sea with them!" Kubril shouted suddenly, and Dovirr joined the shout. It was a fitting doom.

"Aye, to the sea!" he shouted.

T hey drove the panic-stricken aliens before them to the edge of the sea-wall—and the Seaborn, realizing what was being done, leaped from the water in delight to seize the huge amphibians and drag them down into the element of their birth—and the element that would bring them death. Onward, onward, the Earthmen forced the aliens, who one by one dropped into the arms of the waiting, jubilant Seaborn.

From the heart of Vostrok now poured reinforcements—the rest of the *Dhuchay'y* enclave, no doubt. Dovirr smiled grimly. The aliens had returned to their abandoned province expecting to find crushed serfs; instead, they were getting a most unexpected welcome.

The aliens who advanced now bristled with weapons; hand-cannons sent thermal vibrations skimming toward the Earthmen. Heat rose; the Terrans in their armor poured sweat. Around him, Dovirr saw men falling. He dropped back, crouched behind a dead *Dhuchay'y*, sliced upward at the sickening bulk of an alien.

Suddenly, a shout went up.

The city-people! The people of Vostrok were joining the battle!

They came thundering down out of the city by the hundreds, carrying kitchen-knives, benches, any improvised weapon at all. They fell upon the doomed aliens with murderous anger.

Dovirr was like a demon, fighting everywhere at once on the blood-soaked pier. Once, venom-laden *Dhuchay'y* talons raked his shoulder; he retaliated with a swift, vicious thrust.

"On! On! They fall before us!"

The *Dhuchay'y* reinforcements were being driven into the sea as remorselessly as had the first wave. The thunder of cannon came less frequently; suicide battalions of Seaborn swarmed everywhere, climbing up on land to engage in combat until, gasping, they were forced to slip back into their own medium.

Golden blood stained the water. Scaly bodies lay strewn like pebbles.

Red-maned Duvenal, the Thalassarch of the Northland Sea, appeared suddenly at Dovirr's side, his mail hanging rent and his chest visible, bloody, within. Still, Duvenal grinned at the sight of Dovirr.

"Ho, young Sea-Lord! *This* is battle!"

"Indeed, Duvenal. And guard your left!"

The Northerner whirled and sank his mace deep within a *Dhuchay'y* skull; at the same moment, another alien appeared from nowhere and sent the Thalassarch reeling with a backhand swipe of a taloned arm. Dovirr sprang to Duvenal's aid, felling the alien with a thrust through its beady eye.

"Duvenal?"

The red giant staggered to his feet. "Fear not for me; attend to yourself."

Dovirr ducked as an alien scimitar whistled over his head. A javelin hummed past and buried itself in the thick scales of the creature's throat; it tottered, and Dovirr applied the coup-de-grace with a two-handed swipe.

He looked around. The *Dhuchay'y* ranks were thinning. His muscles throbbed with excitement, and he urged his men on with a roar that could have been heard clear to Vythain.

Warm blood trickled over the ground, tickling his bare feet. The sea heaved in tumult. Overhead, sea-birds wheeled and screamed, spun in the air, shouted raucous commentary on the frenzy beneath them.

Everywhere, aliens died.

The frightful carnage continued more than an hour. At last, hanging on his sword, gasping for breath, covered from head to foot with sticky, slimy alien gore, Dovirr paused, for there was no enemy left to smite.

Dovirr groped inside his tunic for the *Dhuchay'y* amulet. *Halgar?*

As if from a great distance came the weary voice of the Seaborn leader. *I hear you, Dovirr.*

The battle has ended. How is it with you?

We are still searching the sea-floor for eggs of the alien, Halgar reported.

Excellent. Have your men bring our boats to shore.

The Seaborn towed to the pier the flotilla of boats the Sea-Lords had left at the edge of the battle-zone. Those who had survived carried bodies of dead and wounded into the boats, seized the oars, rowed out to the waiting mother-ships a league away.

Dovirr was the last to leave the pier. He stood ankle-deep in alien blood, looking around, feeling sorrow that Gowyn had not been with him to share in Terra's greatest triumph.

Night was settling over the now-peaceful scene; the moon hung glistening in the sky, and faint sprinklings of stars appeared against the black bowl of the heavens. Leaning on his sword, Dovirr looked upward.

Somewhere out there was the home world of the *Dhuchay'y*. Somewhere, deep in the blackness.

Dovirr smiled. Perhaps it was not for him, nor for his children, nor for his children's children—but the ultimate battle was yet to be fought. Up there—out on the homeland of the star-marauders.

In the meanwhile, he knew the alliance between Seaborn and land-man would have to be strengthened. Neither could have thrown back the alien horde without the other; together, they had been triumphant.

Kubril stood at his side. The First Officer smiled. "The boat is waiting," he said.

"Very well." Limping, for an alien spear had dug into the flesh of his calf, Dovirr walked toward the boat, dreaming of a bright world of tomorrow.

He cupped his hands. "Row to the *Garyun* for all you're worth! The battle's over; there's tribute to be collected!"

The Flame and the Hammer

Chapter One

The night the torturers of the Imperial Proconsul came to take his father away, Ras Duyair forced himself to carry out his Temple duties as usual. They had seized the old man just before sundown as he was about to enter the Temple. Ras heard about it from one of the acolytes, but setting his teeth determinedly, he went about his task. It had to be done. His father would not want Temple routine disturbed.

With straining muscles, Duyair wheeled the ancient atomic cannon on the Temple wall about on its carriage and pointed it at the star-spattered sky. The snout of the antique weapon jutted menacingly from the parapet of the Temple of the Suns, but no one on Aldryne—least of all Ras—could take the cannon too seriously. It was of symbolic value only. It had not been fired in twelve hundred years.

Ritual prescribed that it be pointed at the skies each night. Duty done, Ras turned to the obsequious acolytes of the Temple who watched him. "Has my father returned?" he demanded.

An acolyte clad in ceremonial green said, "Not yet. He's still under interrogation."

Ras angrily slapped the cool barrel of the giant gun and looked upward at the canopy of stars that decked the night sky of Aldryne. "They'll kill him," he muttered. "He'll die before he'll give up the secret of the Hammer. And then they'll come after me."

And I don't know the secret! he added silently. That was the ironic part of it. The Hammer—a myth, perhaps, out of the storehouse of antiquity. Suddenly the Empire wanted it.

He shrugged. The Empire probably would forget all about it in a few days; Imperial people had a way of doing that. Here on Aldryne they had little to do with the Empire.

He crouched in the firing bucket of the cannon. "Up there are ten dreadnaughts of the Imperial fleet. See them? Coming out of the Cluster at four o'clock. Now watch!" His fingers played over the impotent control panel. "Pouf! Pouf! A million megawatts at a shot! Look at those ships crumple! Watch the gun dent their screens!"

A dry voice behind him said, "This is no time for games, Ras Duyair. We should be praying for your father."

Duyair turned. Standing there was Lugaur Holsp, second only to his father in the Temple hierarchy—and, standing six-three without his buskins, second only to Ras's six-six in height among the men of the Temple of the Suns. Holsp was wiry, spidery almost, with deep shadows setting his cheekbones in high relief.

Duyair reddened. "Ever since the age of fifteen, Lugaur, I've raised that cannon to the skies at nightfall. Once a day for eight years. You might forgive me a fantasy or two about it. Besides, I was just amusing myself—breaking the tension, you might say."

A little self-consciously he climbed out of the bucket. The acolytes seemed to be grinning at him.

"Your levity is out of place," Holsp said coldly. "Come within. We have to discuss this situation."

It had begun several weeks earlier, on Dervonar, home world of Emperor Dervon XIV and capital planet of the Galactic Empire.

Dervon XIV was an old man; he had ruled the Empire for fifty years, and that was a terribly long time to preside over a thousand suns and ten times as many worlds.

He had been able to rule so long because he had inherited an efficient governing machine from his father, Dervon XIII. Dervon XIII had been an adherent of the pyramid system of delegating responsibility: At the top of all was the Emperor, who had two main advisers, each of whom had two advisers, each of whom had two advisers. By the time the system reached the thirtieth or fortieth level, the chain of command spread out over billions of souls.

Dervon XIV in an old age was a tired, shrunken little man, bald, rheumy-eyed. He was given to wearing yellow robes and to sighing, and by now his mind clung to just one *idée fixe*: The Empire must be preserved.

To this end, too, were the endeavors of his two advisers bent: Barr Sepyan, Minister of the Near Worlds, and Corun Govleq, Minister of the Outer Marches. It was Govleq who came before Dervon XIV, map in hand, to tell him of trouble along the Empire's outer rim.

"A rebellion, sire," he said, and waited for the aged eyes to focus on him.

"Rebellion? Where?" There was a visible stiffening of the old Emperor's manner; he became more commanding, more involved in his immediate surroundings, and put down the gyrotoy with which he had been diverting himself.

"The name of the system, sire, is Aldryne, in the Ninth Decant. It is a system of seven worlds, all inhabited, once very powerful in the galactic scheme of things."

"I know the system, I think," the Emperor said doubtfully. "What is this talk of rebellion?"

"It springs from the third world of the system, which is named Dykran—a world chiefly given to mining and populated by a stubborn, intransigent people. They talk of rebelling against Imperial control, of paying no more taxes, of—your pardon, Grace—of somehow assassinating Your Majesty."

Dervon shuddered. "These out-worlders have high plans." He picked up the gyrotoy again and spun it, peering deep into its depths, staring fixedly at the lambent kaleidoscopic light that burned there. Corun Govleq watched patiently as his master played with the toy.

At length the Emperor lowered the gyrotoy and, picking up a crystal cube that lay at his right hand, said sharply, *"Aldryne!"*

It was a command, not a statement. The crystal transmitted it instantly to the depths of the royal palace where the Keepers of the Records toiled endlessly. The Hall of Records was, in many ways, the capstone and heart of the Empire, for here were stored the facts that made it possible to govern a dominion of fifty trillion people.

Within instants the data were on the royal desk. Dervon took the sheets and scanned them, blinking his tired eyes frequently.

ALDRYNE—seven-world system affiliated with Empire in Year 6723 after war duration eight weeks. Formerly independent system with vassals of its own. Current population as of 7940 census, sixteen billion.

Capital world Aldryne, population four billion, now ruled by theocracy stemming from ancient form of government. Chief among many splinter religions is a solar-worship cult whose main attraction is alleged possession of the legendary Hammer of Aldryne.

HAMMER OF ALDRYNE—a weapon of unspecified potency now in possession of the ruling Theoarch of Aldryne, one Vail Duyair. Attributes of this weapon are unknown, but legend has it that it was forged at the time of Imperial assimilation of the Aldryne system and that, when the proper time comes, it will be used to overthrow the Empire itself.

DYKRAN—second most populous world of the Aldryne system, inhabited by some three billions. A harsh world, infertile, chiefly supported by mining operations. A tax rebellion there in 7106 was quelled with loss of fourteen million Dykranian lives. Dykranian loyalty to Empire has always been considered extremely questionable.

Emperor Dervon XIV looked up from the abstract of the report on the Aldryne system. "This Dykran—this is the world that rebels? Not the name world Aldryne?"

"No, sire. Aldryne remains calm. Dykran is the only world of the system that rebels."

"Odd. The name world of a system is usually the first to go." Frowns furrowed Dervon's forehead. "But I venture a guess that they won't be long in joining if the Dykranians make any headway in their rebellion."

The Emperor was silent for a long while. Minister Corun Govleq remained in a position of obloquy, body bent slightly forward at the waist, waiting. He knew that behind the old man's faded eyes lay the brain of a master strategist. One *had* to be a master strategist, Govleq reflected, to hold the Imperium for fifty years in these troubled times.

At length the Emperor said, "I have a plan, Corun. One which may save us much future difficulty with the Aldryne system and particularly with the name world."

"Yes, sire?"

"This semilegendary Hammer the name world has—the thing that's supposed to overthrow us all when the time comes? I don't like the sound of that. Suppose," Dervon suggested slowly, "suppose we get our Proconsul on Aldryne to confiscate this Hammer, if it actually exists. Then we use the Hammer itself to devastate the rebellious Dykranians. What better psychological blow could we deal the entire system?"

Corun Govleq smiled. "Masterful, sire. I had merely thought we could despatch three or four cruisers to level Dykran—but this is much better. *Much* better!"

"Good. Notify the Proconsul on Dykran of what we're doing, and ask our man on Aldryne to find the Hammer. Have them both report back to me regularly. And if there are any other problems today, solve them yourself. I have a headache."

"My sympathies, sire," Corun Govleq said.

As he backed out of the Imperial presence, he saw the old man lift the gyro-toy and peer once again into its soothing, mysterious center.

The Emperor's word traveled down the long chain of command, from functionary to functionary, from bureau to bureau, until at length, a good many days later, it reached the ears of Fellamon Darhuel, Imperial Proconsul for Aldryne of the Aldryne system.

Darhuel was a peaceful, philosophical man who much preferred translating ancient poetry into the Five Tongues of the Galaxy to collecting taxes from the sullen people of Aldryne. He had only one consolation in his job: that he had drawn Aldryne for his assignment and not the bleak neighbor world of Dykran where the malcontents spoke up loudly and the Proconsul's life was ever in danger.

The Hammer of Aldryne? He shrugged when the message crystal delivered its burden. The Hammer was a legend, and one that did the Empire no credit, either. Now the good Emperor wanted it?

Very well, Fellamon Darhuel agreed. The Emperor's word could hardly be ignored. He summoned his subprefect, a slim Sobralian youngster named Deevog Hoth, and said, "Order up a squad of men and take a jaunt over to the Temple of the Suns. We're going to have to make an arrest."

"Certainly. Who's the pickup?"

"Vail Duyair," the Proconsul said.

Deevog Hoth recoiled. "*Vail Duyair*? The high priest? What goes?"

"It becomes necessary to interrogate Vail Duyair," Darhuel said blandly. "Bring him to me."

Frowning in mystification, Deevog Hoth made a gesture of assent and departed.

Less than an hour later—he was a punctual man—he returned, bringing with him Vail Duyair.

The old priest looked as if he had given them a hard time. His green robe was rent in several places, his white hair was uncoifed, and the sunburst insigne at his throat was hanging slightly askew. He faced Darhuel defiantly and said, "For what reason do you interrupt evening services, Proconsul?"

Fellamon Darhuel flinched before the old man's stern gaze. He answered, "There are questions that must be asked. There are those who would have you reveal the Hammer of Aldryne."

"The Hammer of Aldryne is no concern of the Empire's at this stage," Vail Duyair said slowly. "It will be . . . some day. Not now."

"By order of His Majesty Dervon XIV, Emperor of All the Galaxies," Darhuel said sonorously, "I am empowered to interrogate you until you yield to me the location and secret of the Hammer. Be reasonable, Duyair; I don't want to have to hurt you."

With great dignity the priest straightened his hair and rearranged the platinum insigne. "The Hammer is not for the Emperor's command. The Hammer will some day crush the Emperor's skull."

Fellamon Darhuel scowled. "Come on, old man. Enough oratory. What's the Hammer, and where's it kept?"

"The Hammer is not for the Emperor's command," Duyair repeated stonily.

The Proconsul drew a deep breath. His interrogators were not subtle men; the priest would surely not live through the treatment. But what choice did he have?

His nervous fingers caressed the vellum manuscript of *Gonaidan Sonnets* he had been studying. He was anxious to return to his work.

Sighing regretfully, he pushed the communicator stud on his desk, and when the blue light flashed, said, "Have the interrogator come up here, will you?"

Chapter Two

Later that night a long dark car drew up before the Temple and waited there, turbo-electric engines thrumming, while the body of Vail Duyair was brought inside. As silently as they came, the men of the Proconsul left, having delivered the corpse to the priests of the Temple.

The old man was committed to the pyre with full ritual; Lugaur Holsp, as ranking priest, presided and offered the blessings due a martyr. When the service was over, he shut off the atomic blast of the crematorium and dismissed the gathered priests and acolytes.

The next morning Ras Duyair was awakened by the forceful arm of an acolyte.

Sleepily he said, "What do you want?"

"Lugaur Holsp summons you to a Convocation, Ras Duyair!"

Duyair yawned. "Tell him I'll be right there."

When he entered the Inner Room of the Temple, Holsp was seated at the High Seat garbed in ceremonial robes. At his right and left sat the ranking priests of the hierarchy, Thubar Frin and Helmat Sorgvoy. Duyair paused before the triumvirate and automatically made the genuflection due a High Priest in ceremonial garb.

"Are you, then, my father's successor?" he asked.

Lugaur Holsp nodded solemnly. "By a decision rendered early this morning. The workings of the Temple shall continue as before. There are some questions we must ask you, Ras."

"Go ahead," Duyair said.

"Your father died for refusing to yield the secret of the Hammer." A skeptical note crept into Holsp's cold voice. "You were closer to your father than any of us. Did he ever admit to you actually being in possession of the secret?"

"Of course. Many times."

Lugaur Holsp's eyes grew beady. "It was his conviction, was it not, that the secret of the Hammer should reside always with the High Priest of this Temple. Am I right?"

"You are," Duyair admitted, wondering what Holsp was driving at.

"The incumbent High Priest, who is myself, is *not* in possession of this secret. It is my opinion that the true secret of the Hammer is that there *is* no secret—and no Hammer! That it is a carefully fostered myth which the priesthood of this Temple has nurtured for centuries and which was so important to your father that he died rather than reveal its mythical nature."

"That's a lie," Duyair said promptly. "Of course the Hammer exists! You, the High Priest of this Temple, doubting that?"

Duyair saw Holsp exchange glances with the two silent priests flanking him. Then Holsp said: "I am relieved to know this. The late Vail Duyair must, then, have made provisions for transference of possession of the secret."

"Quite possibly."

"I am the duly elected High Priest, succeeding your father. I do not have possession. I assume, then, that your late father must have entrusted the secret to you—and I call upon you, as a loyal junior priest of this Temple, to turn the secret over to its rightful possessor."

"You?"

"Yes."

Duyair eyed Holsp suspiciously. Something was exceedingly wrong here.

It had been generally known for some time that Holsp would succeed the elder Duyair whenever the old priest's time came. Ras had known that; his father had known that. In that case, then, why hadn't Vail Duyair taken steps to see that the Hammer secret was given to Holsp?

It didn't make sense. The old man had frequently told his son of the existence of the secret—though never the secret itself. Ras Duyair did not know it. But he had assumed Holsp was party to it, and to find out that he was not—!

Duyair realized his father must have had some good reason for denying Holsp the secret. Either the Hammer *was* a myth—no, that was inconceivable—or Holsp was in some way untrustworthy.

"Your silence is overly extended," Holsp said. "Will you turn over to me at once the secret?"

Duyair smiled grimly. "The secret is a secret to me as well as you, Lugaur."

"What!"

"My father never deemed me worthy of knowing it. I always assumed it was *you* he had told it to."

"This is impossible. Vail Duyair would never have let the secret die with him; he *must* have told you. I order you to reveal it!"

Duyair shrugged. "Order me to slay the Emperor as well or halt the tides. The secret is not mine for the giving, Lugaur Holsp."

Holsp was openly fuming now. He rose from his graven seat and slammed his hand down on the table. "You Duyairs are stubborn to a fault! Well, the Emperor is not the only one who knows the art of torture."

"Lugaur! Are you crazy?" Duyair shouted.

"Crazy? No, I merely object to defiance on the part of— Ras, will you yield the secret willingly to its rightful possessor?"

"I tell you, Lugaur, I don't know the secret and never did."

"Very well," Holsp said bitingly. "We'll pry it out of you!"

Proconsul Fellamon Darhuel spent the better part of that morning on the dreary business of dictating a report to the Emperor. He covered the Duyair incident in full, describing how the most refined Imperial tortures failed to bring forth the desired secret, and philosophically concluded that these out-world peoples seemed to have hidden reserves of strength that some Imperials might do well to copy.

Concluding his work, he activated the playback and listened to his words. The last few sentences jarred him; they sounded insulting and arrogant. He deleted them.

Lifting his voicewrite again, he patched on a new ending: "The stubbornness of these religious fanatics is beyond belief." That sounded much better, he thought. He punched the permanizer and a moment later the message sprang forth, inscribed on a coiled tape the size of his thumb, coded and ready to go.

He took from a shelf a tiny crystalline capsule, inserted the message, sealed the capsule. He dropped the capsule in the diplomatic pouch being readied for the courier who departed for Dervonar that afternoon.

There. The Emperor would have a full report of the matter, and Darhuel hoped it would do him much good.

I wash my hands of the thing, he thought, turning back to the delicate acrostic verses of the long-dead Gonaidans.

Gradually he regained his calm.

But those who received the capsule felt no such calm. A hypership brought the courier across space from Aldryne to Dervonar in one huge gulp; later the same day the tiny crystal was delivered, along with three thousand similar crystals from three thousand other proconsuls scattered across the galaxy, to the main sorting room of the Imperial Diplomatic Clearinghouse.

It lay at the bottom of a heap for the better part of an hour until a nimble-fingered, eager-eyed clerk, aware of the order that any messages from Aldryne were to receive top handling priority, found it.

From there the capsule worked its way rapidly upward through the chain of bureaucrats of increasing authority until the Undersecretary for External Affairs brought it to the Assistant Secretary for External Affairs, who took it to the Minister of the Outer Marches, Corun Govleq.

Govleq was the first one in the entire string with authority enough to read the message. He did, and promptly sought an audience with His Majesty, Dervon XIV.

Dervon was busy listening to a new music tape brought him by an itinerant tonesmith of Zoastro; Govleq took the rare liberty of entering the royal presence without being announced.

Clangorous tones thundered in the throne room as he entered. The Emperor glanced up wearily, unreproachfully, and sighed.

"Well, Govleq? What crisis now?"

"Word from Aldryne, Highness. A report from your Proconsul there has reached us." Govleq proffered the message cube in his palm.

"Have you heard it?" the Emperor asked.

"Yes, sire."

"Well? What does it say?"

"They have interrogated Vail Duyair—he's the High Priest of that solar cult. The old man refused to yield the secret of the Hammer and died under interrogation!"

The Emperor frowned. "How unfortunate. What is this Hammer you mention?"

Govleq manfully refrained from swearing and set about tactfully refreshing the Imperial memory. Finally Dervon said, "Oh. *That* Hammer. Well, it was a fine idea, anyway. Too bad it didn't work out."

"The rebellion on Dykran, sire—"

"Bother the rebellion on Dykran! No, I don't mean that. I'm very tense this morning; I think it's that damned music. What of the rebellion, Govleq?"

"Status remains quo so far. But word from Dykran is that an explosion is due almost momentarily. And now that a High Priest has been tortured to death on the neighboring world of Aldryne, we can expect the entire Aldryne system to rebel."

"A serious matter," the Emperor said gravely. "These things have a way of spreading from system to system. Hmm. We'll have to stop this. Yes. Stop it. Send special investigators to Aldryne and Dykran. Get full reports. Take care of it, Govleq. Take care of it. This could be bad. Very bad."

"Of course, sire," Govleq said. "I'll expedite the matter at once." He rolled his eyes despairingly to the ceiling, wondering just how he was going to put down what looked like a noisy insurrection in the making.

But he would find a way. The Empire would prevail. It always had, and it always would.

"Turn up the volume," the Emperor said. "I can hardly hear the music."

The vault of the Temple of the Suns was a cold, dank place, wet with ancient slime. Ras Duyair remembered vaguely having played here as a child, enjoying it despite his father's reproaches; he also remembered being taken down to the vault for some hazily recalled indoctrination on his thirteenth birthday.

But now he walked between two priests of the Temple, and Lugaur Holsp walked behind.

They entered the vault.

"It will be quiet down here," Holsp said. "Ras, don't be stubborn. Tell us where the Hammer is."

"I've told you. I don't know. I honestly don't know, Lugaur."

The High Priest shrugged and said, "As you wish. Thubar, we'll have to torture him."

"A little on the primitive side, aren't you?" Duyair asked.

"No more so than the Empire. When information is needed, it must be extracted."

"That's the theory they used on my father. Much good it did them."

"And much good it did him," Holsp said. "If necessary, the same will befall you. Ras, why not tell us?"

Duyair was silent for a moment. The two sub-priests appeared with sturdy rope to bind him, and he let them approach without protest. Then he shrugged away.

"No."

"Bind him," Holsp ordered.

"I'll tell you where the Hammer is!" Duyair said. He took a deep breath. What he was about to do went against all his conditioning, all his beliefs. To strike a priest of the Temple—

But Lugaur was no High Priest. Had he been, Vail Duyair would have given him the Hammer. Holsp frowned. "A change of heart, eh? All right. Let go of him. The Hammer is where?"

"Right here," Duyair said. He smashed a fist into Holsp's pale face, and the High Priest staggered backward under the impact of the blow. The platinum sunburst fell from his throat and clinked hollowly against the stone of the floor.

Ignoring Holsp for the moment, Duyair turned to the other two, Thubar Frin and Helmat Sorgvoy. Helmat was short and heavy; Duyair caught him by one fleshy arm and, using him as a battering ram, swung him crunchingly into Thubar Frin. Both priests grunted at the crash.

Letting go of Helmat, Duyair sprang forward into the shadows. Now some of his childhood memories returned; he recalled passages, catacombs leading beneath the Temple grounds and into sunlight through a hidden exit.

"After him!" he heard Holsp's outraged voice call. But the sound was growing more distant with each moment. "Don't let him escape!" came the echoing, half-audible cry.

Duyair grinned at the thought of the growing blossom of red that had sprouted in Holsp's pale, supercilious face. More than ever now he was convinced that Lugaur Holsp held the High Priest's throne by fraud; Duyair would never have been able to strike down a true priest.

Panting, he emerged at the border of the Temple grove. He realized he would have to flee Aldryne; having raised a fist against Holsp, he would have all men's hands lifted against him.

But where? Where could he go?

He glanced up. In the gathering shadows of late afternoon the sky was growing dark. He saw the dull red globe that was Dykran, the sister world of Aldryne. To Dykran, he thought. Yes, to Dykran!

Chapter Three

He arrived at Aldryne Spaceport later that day, almost at sunset; the star Aldryne was mostly below the horizon. A bored-looking young man at the ticket window squinted at him when he requested a ticket for Dykran and said, "No more flights to Dykran."

"Eh? Last one's left already? But it's hardly sundown yet. There ought to be at least two evening flights, if not more—"

"No more flights, period. By order of the Imperial Government for the duration of hostilities on Dykran."

"What sort of hostilities?" Duyair asked, surprised.

The clerk gestured with his hands. "Who knows? Those miners up there are always striking for something or other. Anyway, I can't give you passage to Dykran."

"Umm. How about Paralon? Any flights there tonight? "

"Nope. Matter of fact, no flights anywhere tonight within the system. I can offer you half a dozen out system flights if you're interested."

Duyair rubbed his chin perplexedly. He had only a hundred credits with him, hardly enough to pay for an out-system flight. And he did not dare return to the Temple for more cash. He had been counting on making an early flight to one of the other worlds in the Aldryne system.

"Nothing at all in the system?" he asked again.

"Look, friend, I thought I made it clear. You mind moving along?"

"Okay," Duyair said. "Thank you." A look of bleak abstraction on his face, he left the line and walked away.

No flights anywhere in-system? Why, that just didn't make sense, he thought. Trouble in Dykran, maybe—but why couldn't he go to Paralon, or Moorhelm, or any of the other three worlds?

He felt a tug at his tunic sleeve. Quickly he turned and saw a short, space-bronzed young man at his side.

"What do you want?"

"Shhh! You want to get us jugged? I just heard your troubles at the ticket window, friend. You interested in going to Dykran tonight?"

"Y-yes," Duyair said tentatively. "What's the deal?"

"Private flight. Two hundred credits will get you there in style."

"I've only got a hundred," Duyair said. "And I can't take time to raise any more. I'm a priest," he improvised. "I have to attend a special conference on Dykran tomorrow, and if I'm not there, it'll be bad."

"Priest? What Temple?"

"Temple of the Suns," Duyair said.

The spaceman thought for a moment. "Okay. A hundred credits will do it. But I want to be paid in advance."

Cautiously Duyair unfolded his five twenty-credit bills and showed them. "This ought to cover it, yes?"

"Yes."

"Good. They're yours the second we blast off for Dykran."

The flight was short, the ship cramped and uncomfortable. Duyair had made the interplanetary journey more than a dozen times, and so none of the phenomena of conventional ion-drive space travel was new to him. He weathered acceleration well, rather enjoyed the weightlessness of free fall, and once the ship began to spin to provide gravity, settled in a hammock and dozed.

He had sized up the shipboard picture fairly quickly. The pilot was obviously a privateer running some illegal cargo between worlds. Just what, Duyair didn't care. But it was apparent that the shrewd pilot had seized on a way of making a few extra credits by admitting passengers. There were perhaps a dozen on board, and doubtless each had some good reason for traveling to Dykran. They had all been caught short by the unexpected embargo.

He was awakened by a bell—the signal for a shift to deceleration, pending planetfall. And the small ship dropped down to the surface of Dykran.

They had landed, it seemed, in a bare, treeless plain somewhere far from civilization; a cold wind was whining, kicking up gray clouds of dust, as Duyair dropped through the open hatch and touched ground.

He turned to the pilot, who was supervising the unloading of crates. "Are we supposed to find our way to the city by ourselves?"

The pilot laughed. "You expect limousine service with an illegal flight? Wake up, boy. You're on your own. For another hundred credits I'd drive you into town, but you don't have the hundred, do you?"

"No," Duyair said bitterly, and turned away. He had come away too quickly; he was penniless and not dressed for the bitter Dykranian climate.

But there were priests here, and Temples; he could find shelter. He started to walk across the barren plain. Some of his fellow passengers, grumbling disgruntledly, followed him.

He had gone about half a mile and was shivering with every step when a jet-copter descended almost directly in front of him. Through the swirling dust he saw the emblem on the 'copter's side: the purple and gold star-cluster insigne of the Imperial Police.

He debated fleeing. The Imperial Police were a good deal more to be feared than the relatively easygoing local Dykranian police corps.

But the sight of a blaster pointed unwaveringly at him changed his mind. He stood where he was, waiting for the Imperial policeman to draw near.

The policeman was short and stubby, with a lined face that told of long service on this dreary planet. His opening gambit was the inevitable "Let's see your papers!"

"Certainly, officer." Duyair handed over the sheets of identification. The corpsman read through them thoroughly, returned them, and said, "According to these you're Ras Duyair of Aldryne. What are you doing on Dykran?"

"Visiting, Officer. I'm a priest."

"So I noticed. I didn't happen to see any spaceport verification on your papers, though. How'd you get here?"

"By spaceship, of course," Duyair said mildly. He towered more than a foot over the corpsman, but the blaster held steadily in his ribs did not encourage violence.

"Don't get wise," the corpsman snapped. "Suppose you tell me how long you've been on Dykran."

"About half an hour."

"Half an hour? And you came by spaceship? Very interesting. There's been an embargo on interworld transportation in the Aldryne system in effect for the past eight hours. Suppose you come down to the Proconsul's headquarters and explain yourself."

A re you Ras Duyair?"

"That's my name, yes. It says so right there."

"No insolence," said the questioner. He was Rolsad Quarloo, Imperial Proconsul on Dykran, a small, weather-beaten little man with a grim, doggedly tough look about him. "I want to know why you're on Dykran when there's an Imperial embargo on interworld traffic. How'd you get here?"

Duyair was silent. The corpsman standing behind him said, "He came in on that smuggler's ship. We picked up about a dozen that way."

"I know that, fool," snapped the Pronconsul. "I want *him* to say it. It has to go down on tape."

"All right," said Duyair. "I came in on a smuggler's ship, if that's what he was. I wanted to go to Dykran, and none of the ticket windows were selling tickets. Then this fellow came along and offered me transportation for a hundred credits. He brought me here, and then you picked me up. That's all."

The Proconsul scowled. "You must have known the trip was illegal! Why did you want to come to Dykran so badly?"

"To visit," Duyair said. He had decided earlier that the safest course was to play the role of a simple bumpkin and let his questioners do most of the talking.

"To visit! That's all—just a visit? And you defied an Imperial embargo just for a visit? I give up." Rolsad Quarloo touched a stud on his desk, and the door opened.

A tall, stately-looking man, magnificent in his purple and gold robes, entered. He glanced contemptuously at the Proconsul and said, "Well? Did you get anything from him, Quarloo?"

"Not a thing. You want to try?"

"Very well." The magnifico looked at Duyair. "I am Olon Domyel, Imperial Legate from the Court of the Emperor Dervon XIV. You are the priest Ras Duyair, of Aldryne in the Aldryne system?"

"That's my name, yes."

"Are you the son of the late Vail Duyair, priest, of Aldryne?"

Duyair nodded.

"Do you know how your father died?" Domyel asked.

"At the hands of the Imperial interrogator. They were trying to find out a secret of our religion."

"The Hammer of Aldryne, you mean," said Domyel.

"Yes. That was it."

The ponderous Legate strode up and down in the Proconsul's tiny office. At length he said, "You know, we could have you tortured to obtain the same secret. We of the Empire are very interested in this Hammer, Duyair."

Duyair grinned. Everyone suddenly seemed interested in the Hammer. And many torturers were having booms in business.

"You grin?"

"Yes, milord. This Hammer—it does not exist, you see. It's one of our legends. A myth. My father tried to tell your interrogators this, and they killed him. Now you will interrogate me and probably kill me as well. It is really very funny."

The Legate eyed him sourly. "A myth, you say? And for a myth I've crossed half a galaxy—"

"The rebellion brewing on Dykran is very real," Proconsul Quarloo reminded him gingerly.

"Ah—yes. Rebellion. And this Hammer of Aldryne—a myth? Ah me. Boy, what brought you to Dykran?"

"I came here to visit," Duyair said innocently.

They turned him loose finally after another half-hour of questioning. He stuck fairly closely to his bumpkin role, and it became quite clear to the exasperated Legate and to the Proconsul that they were going to get nothing from him. He promised not to stray far from the city, and they let him go.

The moment he stepped outside the Proconsul's headquarters, a shadowy figure moved alongside him, and a whispered voice said, "Are you Ras Duyair?"

"Maybe."

"You were just questioned by the Proconsul, weren't you? Speak up or I'll knife you."

"I was," Duyair admitted. "Who are you?"

"Quite possibly a friend. Will you come with me?"

"Do I have any choice?" Duyair asked.

"No," said the stranger.

Shrugging, Duyair let himself be led down the street to a small, blue, tear-drop-shaped auto that was idling there. He got in at the other's direction, and they drove off.

Duyair made no attempt to remember the streets as they passed through them; his driver was taking such a deliberately winding, tangled route that any such attempt would be hopeless.

They stopped finally in front of a squat gray-brown brick building in the ugly, antiquated style popular here.

"We get out here," Duyair's mysterious captor told him.

Duyair and the stranger left the car and entered the old building. Two blank-faced guards stood within. Duyair wondered what nest of intrigue he had stumbled into now. He wondered whether he might not have been safer remaining back on Aldryne.

"Is this Duyair?" asked a cold-faced man with a strange accent.

Duyair's captor nodded.

"Bring him within," ordered the cold-faced man.

Duyair was shoved into a brightly lit room ringed with packed book shelves and furnished with shabby, out-of-date furniture. Three or four other men were sitting in battered chairs.

The cold-faced man turned to Duyair and said, "I must apologize for a number of things. First, for not getting to you ahead of the Empire men—and second, for the mysterious handling you've had since Quarloo turned you loose."

"Apology tentatively accepted," Duyair said. "Where am I, and what's going on?"

"My name," said the cold-faced man, "is Bluir Marsh. I'm a native of Dervonar. You know Dervonar?"

"The capital of the Empire, isn't it?"

"That's right. I've seen the Empire first-hand, from within. It's rotten. It's ready to fall, given a push."

"So?"

"So I came to Dykran. I've established an organization, and I'd like you to join it. We're getting set to give the Empire that one push."

Chapter Four

Emperor Dervon XIV had been devoting more than usual attention to the dispatches from the Aldryne system. In fact, he had dwelled on the doings in that system with a singleminded fascination that left him little time for supervising the manifold complexities of the other worlds of his Empire.

But he felt the time was well spent. More so than anyone, he was aware of the shakiness of his throne, and he foresaw serious trouble arising out of Aldryne.

"Is there any report from your Legate on Dykran today, Govleq?" the Emperor asked the Minister.

"Not yet, Majesty."

"Mph. See that the routing office gets about its business faster. This is serious business, Govleq."

"Of course, Majesty."

The Emperor rubbed his hairless scalp and picked up the Legate's last report. "Can you imagine this? They had the son of that priest Duyair in custody on Dykran and released him! The Hammer—this fool of a Legate of yours tells me sententiously it's a myth. Myth? A myth that will topple us all yet, Govleq. Who is this Legate?"

"Olon Domyel is one of our finest men, sire. I chose him myself."

"More discredit to you," Dervon said testily.

The signal light flashed twice, blinking on and off. "Messages have come through," the Emperor snapped. "Get them and read them."

"At once, sire."

Govleq crossed the room to the message bin that had been installed there and deftly abstracted the two tiny message crystals from the chute. "One is from Dykran, the other from Aldryne, Majesty."

"Go ahead, read them. I want to know what they say not where they're from!"

The Minister moistened his lips and split one of the crystals with his finger-nail. He scanned the message, gasped a little, and opened the other crystal. The Emperor, beady-eyed, was watching him impatiently.

"Well?" Dervon demanded. His voice was a raven's croak.

"One from Aldryne, one from Dykran," Govleq repeated inanely, "Which do you want first, sire?"

"Does it matter?"

"No, sire. The one from Dykran is dated somewhat earlier. It's from Legate Domyel. He says there are rumors of a rebel army gathering somewhere on the planet, though he's not sure where."

"The idiot! What of the one from Aldryne?"

Govleq shivered a little. "The—one—from—Aldryne—is from Proconsul Darhuel. He says—"

"Get on with it!" Dervon raged.

"Darhuel says he's evacuating all Imperial forces from the planet Aldryne at once and removing his base to one of the neighboring worlds. It seems there's an insurrection on Aldryne, too, only it's already broken out. It's led by a priest named Lugaur Holsp, who claims to be wielding—shield us, Majesty—the Hammer of Aldryne!"

Ras Duyair huddled intently on the floor of Bluir Marsh's room, listening to the Dervonarian insurrectionist outline his plan.

"They're definitely aware of what's going on, on Dykran," Marsh said. "We have plenty of evidence for that. Yesterday this Legate arrived from the capital—this Olon Domyel. He promptly slapped an embargo on travel between Dykran and Aldryne, and then the fool expanded it to cover every world in the system."

"Now there's only one reason why he'd do that. The Emperor suspects trouble brewing in this system, and the quickest and safest way of quelling it is to isolate the planets so no germs of insurrection can wander from world to world." Marsh chuckled. "Unfortunately, a few stray spores drifted in on the tides of the ether. Young Duyair, for one. But for all intents there's no contact between Dykran and Aldryne.

"All right. First a Legate comes, and second he imposes a travel restriction. The time has arrived to make our move—now, before the Emperor sends a few million Imperial troops to quarter here and sit on us. We have our organization. We'll have to attack. Our only hope is to re-establish contact with other planets, get them to follow along. The Emperor has a big fleet, but it can't be everywhere at once. Simultaneous revolutions on a hundred worlds would wreck the Empire within a week."

A man sitting near Duyair raised his hand. "Tell me, Bluir. How many worlds do you think will go along with us?"

"There are revolutionary organizations on at least fourteen worlds in twelve systems," Marsh said. "I've built them myself over the last decade. The one on Dykran is the strongest, which is why we're touching the thing off here. But it'll spread. The Empire's a relic of the past; no one wants to pay taxes to a useless monarchy simply to support a doddering old Emperor. Duyair, how is it on Aldryne?"

Duyair said, "No one cares much for the Empire on my world. We have the legend of the Hammer, of course. It keeps our hatred of the Empire alive, knowing that the Hammer will one day smash the Empire."

Bluir Marsh frowned. "The Hammer—yes, I know the legend. Is there any basis to it?"

"I honestly don't know," Duyair said. "My father might—but the interrogators got him. He always insisted to me that there was really a Hammer and that he knew where it was, but he died without telling me.

And his successor as High Priest doesn't know, either."

"Too bad; a psychological focus like the Hammer could be useful. We could always fake a Hammer, I guess. As soon as the thing's touched off on Dykran, suppose we ship you back to Aldryne to spread the good word there."

"I'll do it," Duyair said.

"Good." Marsh glanced around. "You all understand the parts you're to play?"

There was general agreement. For once a grin passed over the insurrectionist's cold face. "We're ready to go, then. The first operation is to seize the Proconsul and that Legate, and then to get the word rolling around the galaxy of what we've done."

A swirling mob swooped down on the office of the Proconsul of Dykran, Duyair among them. There must have been a hundred of them, armed with makeshift weapons of all sorts.

As the tallest and most powerful man in the group, Duyair almost unconsciously gravitated toward the fore of the mob as they approached the office. Two stunned-looking Imperial corpsmen stood on guard outside, but the tide swept over them before they could do more than threaten ineffectually.

Duyair hooked out a long arm and plucked a blaster from one of the guards; he jabbed it in the other's ribs, ordered him to turn, and clubbed him down. Men of the mob spirited the guards away somewhere.

"Inside!" Duyair yelled. He realized he was somehow becoming leader of the insurrection. Bluir Marsh was nowhere to be seen; obviously he had no taste for actual combat.

The photonically actuated door caved in beneath the horde that pressed against it. From within came confused shouts of, "Guard! Guard! Protect the Proconsul!"

The Legate, Olon Domyel, appeared. He was unarmed, clad in his splendid robes. Duyair's appraising eyes saw he wore lift shoes and shoulder pads to enhance his size.

"Hold back, rabble!" the Legate roared. "This is the Proconsul's office! What right have you in here?"

"The right of free men," Duyair said, wiggling the blaster in his hand. "The right of those who no longer bow to the Emperor."

"Rebellion! Open revolution! You must be mad!" Domyel shouted. "Back! Away from here!"

Behind him Duyair heard some of the men muttering doubtfully. The magnificence of the Legate, he knew, was having the effect Domyel desired.

"Seize and bind him," Duyair snapped.

"No! I'm a Legate of the Emperor! My person is sacrosanct!"

"Bind him!" Duyair repeated, and this time four of the Dykranians produced rope and seized the struggling Legate. Domyel kicked and pummeled in all directions, but in a moment or two he had subsided, sputtering, his arms tied.

"Proconsul Quarloo?" Duyair called. "Come out of there—unarmed!"

"You can't do this!" came a quavering voice. "It's illegal! You can't rebel against the Empire!"

Come out of there! Duyair said loudly. Quarloo appeared, trembling woefully, clutching his cloak about him. He looked an utterly dismal figure; the weather-beaten toughness Duyair had noted earlier had vanished totally from his face.

"What is the meaning of this?" Quarloo asked.

"An end to Empire rule in the Aldryne system," said Duyair. He turned and ordered: "Bind this one, too! Then search the place for weapons."

"We've caught three more Imperial guards, sir," whispered a man at his right. "They were sneaking out the back way."

"Armed?"

"Yes, sir."

Duyair laughed. "The cowards! Well, distribute their weapons and bind them with the rest. We need every blaster we can lay hands on."

Within five minutes the place was completely in the possession of the revolutionaries. Now, from somewhere, Bluir Marsh appeared.

"Fine work," he said. "I like the way you led the assault, Duyair."

"Thanks. But where were you?"

Marsh smiled slyly. "A leader never endangers his own life unnecessarily. Besides, you're a much more commanding figure than I am. Someone your size gets followed; they can *see* you."

Duyair grinned at the small revolutionary. "I understand. What now?"

"We have the entire building under occupation, yes?" Duyair nodded.

"Good. We seize communications now and flash the word to as many systems as we can. Then we proceed to round up as many of the Empire guards on Dykran as we can find. They're our hostages."

Duyair and Marsh stepped over a bench someone had thrown down in a futile attempt at barricade and entered the office of the deposed Proconsul. A battery of communication devices covered one wall; the communications links of the Empire were still strong.

Marsh strode immediately to the subradio set and began setting up coordinates. Duyair idly picked up some papers that lay on Quarloo's desk.

He read them, blinked, read them again. He heard Marsh announcing word of the rebellion in vivid tones to the people of some other star system.

"Hey," Duyair said when Marsh was through. "Listen to this. I just found it on Quarloo's desk—it's a message that came through from Aldryne."

"What about?"

"It's from Proconsul Darhuel on Aldryne. He—says he's going to evacuate Aldryne and move his base to Moorhelm—Aldryne VI. Seems there's been an uprising on Aldryne, too."

Marsh looked startled. "But there was no organization on Aldryne! A spontaneous rebellion? Who's leading it—does Darhuel say?"

"Yes," Duyair said strangely. "The leader's a priest, name of Lugaur Holsp. He has a tremendous popular following that's sprung up overnight. He—he claims to have the Hammer of Aldryne!"

By nightfall, Dykran bore no trace of Imperial rule: the Proconsul and the handful of men who had guarded him were prisoners, the Imperial Legate as well. A provisional government had been established, with one Fulmor Narzin at its head. A blue and gold Dykran flag appeared surprisingly atop the Proconsul's headquarters.

Within headquarters itself Bluir Marsh and several of his lieutenants, including Ras Duyair, tried to plan their next steps.

"I don't understand this Hammer maneuver," Duyair said. "Holsp can't possibly have the Hammer unless he pulled off a miracle. So far as I know the secret of its location died with my father."

"Whether he has the true Hammer or not," pointed out Marsh, "he has *a* hammer. The people seem to believe it—to the point of expelling their Proconsul. I think we should make contact with this Lugaur Holsp and join forces with him. The symbol of the Hammer is known through the galaxy as that which will smash the Empire. If we get the movement rolling fast enough—"

Duyair shook his head. "I know this Holsp. He's not the kind to be interested in overthrowing the Empire except for his own personal advantage. I don't trust him, Marsh."

"Trust? How does that matter? First the revolution," Marsh said. "With the Empire crushed, we worry about sorting the trustworthy from the treacherous. Go to Aldryne, Duyair. Find Holsp. And don't worry whether this is the real Hammer or not. The thing is what we call it, and if the galaxy believes the Hammer is being raised against the Empire, the Empire is doomed." Marsh mopped away sweat. Turning to one of his men, he said, "Any word from Thyrol on the rebellion there?"

"Heavy garrison of Imperial forces there. They're yielding."

"Damn. We'll probably lose Thyrol." Marsh scowled. "I hope we haven't touched this thing off prematurely. As of now only half a dozen worlds are rebelling, two of them in this system. Thousands are still loyal. Dammit, Duyair, we need the Hammer! That's the symbol everyone waits for!"

Suddenly a Dykranian radioman came dashing into the office. "Marsh! Marsh!"

"Well? What news? Anything from Thyrol?"

"No! I was trying to reach Aldryne, and I tapped a supersecret direct wire from Aldryne to the Emperor!"

"What?"

"I tapped a conversation between Lugaur Holsp and the Emperor himself. We're being betrayed! Holsp is selling out!"

Chapter Five

I wish this had waited five more years," the Emperor Dervon XIV said peevishly aloud, to himself. "Or ten. Let my son worry about it."

Then he realized he was weakening. After threatening all through his lifetime, the rebellion had happened *now*. That he was old and weary was irrelevant. The rebellion would have to be put down. The Empire had to be preserved.

"Give me the report," he commanded as Corun Govleq entered the throne room.

Govleq looked seriously preoccupied, but the shadow of a smile appeared on his face. "Good news, sire, for a change."

"Well! What is it?"

"The rebellion seems to be confined to a handful of worlds—Aldryne, Dykran, Thyrol, Menahun, Quintak, and a few others. We've just about got the situation in hand on Thyrol, and word from Quintak is encouraging."

Dervon smiled. "This gladdens me. I think strong action is called for now. Order out a battle fleet, Govleq."

"To where, sire?"

"To Aldryne. The rebellion is confined. Now we can safely devastate Aldryne and Dykran, the instigator worlds, and re-establish control."

Govleq nodded. "Excellent, sire."

"This Hammer," Dervon said. "What of it?"

The Minister of the Outer Marches shrugged and said, "We have heard nothing save that the people of Aldryne are massed behind it."

"Ah. Order the full fleet to Aldryne, then. We'll bathe the world in fire. *Then* let the worlds of the galaxy shake this Hammer at us!"

"Very good, sire."

A yellow-clad page appeared timidly at the entrance to the throne room and knelt there, waiting to be noticed. At length Dervon said, "Well, boy?"

"Message for Minister Govleq, Your Majesty."

"Speak out," Govleq ordered.

"A subradio message has arrived from Aldryne, sir. From Lugaur Holsp. He says he would talk of treaty with you, Minister Govleq."

Govleq's dropping eyes opened wide. "What? Have the call transferred up here at once!"

"Of course, sir."

The page vanished. Govleq turned to the monarch and said, "Well, sire?"

"Order out the battle fleet, anyway," Dervon said. His lips curved upward in a wan smile. "Methinks this Holsp plans to use his Hammer as a bludgeon. But we'll speak to him nevertheless."

A technician's voice said, "You can go ahead with the call now, Aldryne."

Humming clatter came over the wall speaker in the Imperial throne room. Then a cold, deep voice said, "This is Lugaur Holsp, Your Majesty, speaking from the planet Aldryne of the system Aldryne."

"What would you with me?" Dervon said.

"Are you aware, Majesty, that the Imperial Proconsul has been driven forth from Aldryne and Imperial rule destroyed both here and on the sister world of Dykran?"

"I have heard something to this effect," the Emperor remarked sardonically. "I believe it's more than a rumor."

"Indeed it is. By virtue of the Hammer of Aldryne—which I hold—this has been done."

"Well, pig?" The Emperor's voice rose above a dry murmur for the first time in three decades. "Did you call to boast to me about this? A fleet of Imperial warships makes its way to Aldryne this moment to lay waste your entire planet."

"This is the expected reaction," Holsp said. "I desire to avoid this needless slaughter."

"How, traitor?"

"I am no traitor. I am loyal to the Empire."

"You show odd ways of demonstrating this loyalty," the Emperor said.

"I offer to surrender," said Holsp. "I offer to let it be known widely to all that the Hammer of Aldryne failed against Your Majesty, that the insurrection collapsed of its own accord, that Aldryne remains loyal to you. I furthermore will turn over to you those conspirators who plotted against your rule. In return I ask only the Proconsulship of Aldryne—and ten percent of the annual tax money."

Dervon gasped at the man's audacity. He glanced at the thunderstruck Govleq and said, "Give us a few moments to consider this, Holsp."

"Very well, Majesty."

Dervon shut off the transmitter. "What do you think?"

"The man's a callous schemer," Govleq said. "This is infinitely better than destroying the world. The show of force is necessarily limited in its appeal: It *frightens* men. Word of the collapse of the Aldryne insurrection will teach them that the Empire is so powerful it need not fire a shot."

"So be it," Dervon said. "This Holsp is incredible." He opened contact again and said, "Holsp, we accept your offer. The insurrection is to cease; the ring-leaders are to be turned over to the Imperial fleet shortly to reach Aldryne, and you are to issue a public statement saying that the might of the Hammer has failed. In return, we grant you the Proconsulship of Aldryne and ten percent of collected tax moneys."

"Accepted, sire," Holsp said unctuously.

T hat conversation stood out clearly in Ras Duyair's mind as his small ship settled slowly into its landing orbit and spiraled down on Aldryne.

His purpose was clear. The traitor Holsp would have to die.

It was obvious to Duyair that the false priest could not possibly have the Hammer. The Hammer was something too precious, too sacred to Aldryne; no man who had penetrated its secret could lightheartedly sell his world to the Emperor as Holsp had done.

No. Holsp had committed fraud, sacrilege, blasphemy: he had pretended to have the Hammer. The people of Aldryne had rallied around him and driven forth the Proconsul Darhuel—and this was their reward.

The spaceport looked strangely different as Duyair's little ship came down. The Imperial pennons were down except for one that hung in rags, a flickering streamer of purple and gold.

The ship landed. Moments later Duyair was among his fellow men. They had changed, too.

Their eyes were brighter, their shoulders more square. They had thrown off the yoke of Empire, and it showed.

How would they look, he wondered, if they knew that at this moment their leader, Lugaur Holsp, was conspiring with the Emperor to sell them back into Imperial bondage?

He hailed a cruising jetcopter. "To the Temple of the Suns," he said.

"Yes, sir. Are you a priest there?" the driver asked as Duyair took a seat.

"My name is Ras Duyair."

"Oh! So you've returned! Funny; Holsp told us you'd been killed in the insurrection."

Duyair smiled grimly. "The report has been somewhat exaggerated. In fact, I've been on Dykran ever since the insurrection began. I aided in *their* revolt."

"Dykran, too," mused the driver. "I didn't know they kicked over the traces, too. We don't get much news. But we have the Hammer, and that's what counts. It's a pity your father's not alive. But he's probably glad, wherever he is, that Lugaur Holsp has continued his work."

"I'm sure of that," said Duyair absently. "Very glad. Aldryne is completely independent now, you say?"

"Last we heard of Darhuel and his bunch, they were running headfirst for Moorhelm. There isn't an Imperial soldier left anywhere on the face of the planet."

"Wonderful," Duyair said without enthusiasm.

The Temple of the Suns came in sight. The 'copter swooped low and began to descend vertically. It came to rest before the great gate. Duyair paid the man and alighted.

The Temple looked much as before, a sprawling, heavily ornamented building surrounded by a triple row of parapets, with gargoyles leering down from the uppermost floors. The giant cannon was as he had left it, in its housing.

He began to walk up the path to the Temple entrance. Several acolytes were tending the grounds; they stared at him with unconcealed curiosity as he went past.

He covered the flagstone steps two at a bound, reached the main door, knocked loudly.

The bland face of Helmat Sorgvoy appeared. "Yes, my son?" the priest inquired automatically. "What would you here?"

"I'd like to see Holsp," Duyair said bluntly.

Sorgvoy gasped. "Ras! What are you doing on Aldryne? I thought you—"

"Get out of my way," Duyair snapped. He shoved the priest aside and entered the Temple.

Lugaur Holsp was in the Room of Devotion when Duyair found him. Duyair stood at the entrance for a moment, watching. Holsp was kneeling, whispering prayers inaudibly; his pale, fleshless face bore a look of deepest piety.

"All right, Holsp," Duyair said after a while. "You can get off your knees. I want to talk to you."

Startled, Holsp wheeled jerkily and said, "Who are—*Ras!*" He backed up automatically, hate hardening his cold face. Within the Temple, Duyair knew, no priest dared carry a weapon. Of course, there was little trusting Lugaur Holsp, but some taboos seemed inviolable.

"Yes. Ras. I understand you've been telling everyone I'm dead, Lugaur."

"You vanished, the son of the great Vail Duyair. There were questions. What could I say?"

"That I had escaped after your fumbling attempt to torture the secret of the Hammer from me? No, you couldn't very well tell them *that*, Lugaur. So you told them I was dead."

"Where were you?"

"On Dykran. I helped overthrow the Imperial Proconsul there. We heard you had a little revolution of your own here on Aldryne."

Holsp smiled balefully. "We did. By virtue of the Hammer we drove Proconsul Darhuel from our midst. It was a glorious victory."

Duyair ignored that. "The Hammer?" he repeated. "You found the Hammer so soon after my—ah—departure? Tell me about the Hammer, Lugaur. Where was it kept? What did it look like?"

"These are priestly secrets," Holsp rasped a little desperately.

"I'm well aware of that. It's simply that I doubt very much that you *have* the Hammer, Lugaur. I think you put up a magnificent bluff and won the people of Aldryne over to your side long enough to stage a rebellion against Darhuel. But you didn't need a Hammer for that; Darhuel was a weakling, and any united action would have been sufficient to throw him out."

Holsp was eying him uneasily. Recklessly Duyair went on. "You know why I don't think you have the Hammer, Lugaur? It's because the Hammer is a weapon big enough to wreck the Empire. And if you had the Hammer, you'd go ahead and wreck the Empire. You wouldn't be content with merely selling out to the Emperor for ten percent of Aldryne's tax money!"

Holsp's already-pale face seemed to drain of blood. *"How can you know that?"* he whispered harshly. Then, without waiting for an answer, he lifted a smoking censer and hurled it at Duyair's head.

Duyair had foreseen the move. He stepped nimbly to one side; the bejeweled censer crashed against the wall half a foot from his head. The pottery crumbled; incense spilled out over the floor.

Holsp sprang.

Duyair met the charge full on; he was three inches taller than the High Priest and forty pounds heavier. For a moment the fury of Holsp's attack drove Duyair backward; he felt the coolness of the Temple wall at his back and the driving ceaseless blows of Holsp in his stomach. Duyair grunted, bent slightly, heaved Holsp backward. The High Priest's eyes were glittering with rage.

Suddenly Holsp broke away and executed a whirling pirouette; when he faced Duyair again, the gleaming white blade of a knife was in his hand.

"A weapon? In the Temple?" Duyair asked. "You'll stop at nothing, Lugaur." He stepped forward, moving warily, and for a frozen moment the two men faced each other.

Then Holsp slashed upward with the blade. Duyair's right hand descended, clamped on Holsp's wrist in mid-slash. He extended his arm rigidly, holding Holsp away from him, and began to tighten his grip. Bones cracked. Holsp grimaced but held on to the knife.

Calmly Duyair wrenched the knife from the High Priest's hand and advanced on him. For the first time fear entered Holsp's features.

"I heard your conversation with the Emperor," Duyair said relentlessly. "You sold out Aldryne, didn't you? For ten percent, Lugaur! *Ten percent!*"

Duyair raised the knife.

"In the Temple?" Holsp asked hoarsely, incredulously. *"You'd kill? Here?"*

Duyair chuckled. "Your scruples ill befit you at this late hour, Lugaur. But the Temple code proscribes murder; it says nothing about execution."

"Ras!"

"Appeal the matter to the Emperor, Proconsul Holsp," Duyair said coldly. He drove the knife home.

There was a moment of exultation as he stood over Holsp's body, but it faded quickly. He had executed a traitor; Holsp had deserved death. But now what?

Dervon's fleet was surely on its way to Aldryne to receive the conspirators Holsp had promised to hand over; they would arrive soon enough. They would receive no conspirators. And the Emperor would undoubtedly order a reversion to his original plan, total destruction of Aldryne as an object lesson for would-be rebellious worlds.

Hopelessly Duyair wondered whether it might not have been better to let Holsp live and yield to the Emperor. *No!* He banished the thought. There would be a defense of some sort.

The task immediately before him was to restore the minutiae of life: the routine of the Temple, the way of life of Aldryne. The people had to be told of Holsp's treachery. They could not be allowed to continue thinking of him as a hero.

"Thubar! Helmat!"

Duyair called the priests together, and there in the Room of Devotion told them the story. They listened in bewilderment, staring frequently at the bloody corpse of Lugaur Holsp.

When he was finished, Thubar Frin said, "I often doubted Holsp's claims of the Hammer. But the people believed him."

"The people believed wrongly," Duyair said.

Helmat Sorgvoy said, "The Temple is without its High Priest. I propose Ras Duyair to take the place of the false Lugaur Holsp and sit upon the throne of his father distinguished."

Duyair glanced around at the assembled priests and acolytes. No one spoke.

"I accept," he said. "We shall have the investiture at once."

Silently he led the way to the High Priest's throne room. There, Helmat Sorgvoy, as ranking priest of the Temple, pronounced the brief rites that elevated Ras Duyair to the High Priesthood.

With trembling feet he ascended the throne of his father. He paused before sitting and said, "I now accept the duties and tasks of the office."

He sat.

The trigger in his mind was touched off.

In a sudden overwhelming burst of revelation his mind was cleared; fog rolled back. He heard his father's words again, reverberating loudly around him:

"The day you take your seat as High Priest of the Temple, my son, will be the day all this will return to your mind—

"The Hammer is for you to wield. It will be for you to break apart the Empire and bring freedom to Aldryne and the worlds of the galaxy."

Suddenly, as of the moment he had touched the throne, he knew. He knew where the Hammer was, how it operated, when it would be needed. He knew now that Lugaur Holsp could not possibly have had the Hammer—that its location was a secret old Vail Duyair had planted in his son's mind alone, so deeply that not even Ras had known it was buried there.

He rose again.

"The Hammer is ours. It will soon be brought into play."

Chapter Six

Against the sharp blackness of the night sky eight colored shapes, illuminated by the brightness of the Cluster, could be seen.

They were spaceships of the Empire—massive hundred-man vessels whose heavy-cycle guns were capable of destroying a world within hours. Their yellow and red-violet hulls glittered in the night sky. They ringed themselves in a solid orbit around Aldryne. They waited.

Duyair made contact with them from the communications rig he had improvised in the Temple.

"This is Commander Nolgar Millo of the Imperial Flagship *Peerless*. I'm instructed to contact Lugaur Holsp, High Priest of the Temple of the Suns."

"Hello, Commander Millo. This is Ras Duyair, successor to Lugaur Holsp, High Priest."

"Duyair, you know why we're here?"

"Tell me."

The Imperial Commander sounded irritated. "To pick up the consignment of conspirators your predecessor was planning to turn over to us. Or don't you know anything about the arrangement?"

"I do," Duyair said. "Be informed that there will be no 'consignment' for you to pick up—and that I order you to return to your base at once and leave the Aldryne system."

"You order us? By whose grace?"

"By grace of my power," Duyair said. "Leave at once—or feel the Hammer of Aldryne!"

There was silence at the other end. Duyair paced tensely in his room, waiting. But he knew the tension aboard those ships must be infinitely greater.

Time passed—just enough time for Commander Millo to have contacted the Emperor and received a reply.

Millo said, "We are landing. Any attempts at hostile action will result in complete destruction of this planet by direct order of the Emperor."

"You will not land," Duyair said. He stepped to the Temple parapet and lightly touched a stud on the newly rehabilitated cannon. A bright, white-hot energy flare streaked across the heavens, was deflected by the screens of the *Peerless*, and splashed harmlessly away.

Duyair waited. There came angry sputtering, then Commander Millo said, "Well enough, Duyair of Aldryne. That shot has killed your world."

The ships of the Imperial fleet swung into battle formation; the heavy-cycle guns ground forward on their gimbals, readied for fighting.

Smiling, Duyair nudged a switch on the big gun's control panel.

A moment later, the sky went bright red with energy pouring from the Imperial guns.

The high-voltage barrage rained down. A thousand megawatts assaulted Aldryne.

And ten thousand feet above the planet's surface, an invisible screen turned them back.

You can't have the whole planet shielded!" Commander Millo shouted. "Keep up the barrage!"

The Imperial ships continued. Duyair, head inclined upward, watched the spouting guns. Energy glare lit the sky; flares of brightness speared downward, to be turned away inevitably by the ten-thousand-foot shield.

"Your eighth ship," Duyair radioed. "Watch it, Commander Millo."

He touched a switch. The atomic cannon thrummed for a moment, and a bolt of force creased the sky, leaping upward toward the ship Duyair had designated. For an instant the ship was bathed in brightness as its screens strained to hold off the energy assault. Then the screens, terribly overloaded, collapsed.

Duyair's bolt seared right through the ship, gutting it in one long thundering flash. It split; by the illumination of the continuing bombardment it was possible to see tiny figures tumbling outward.

"One ship has been destroyed," Duyair said. "The other seven will follow. This is the Hammer of Aldryne, Commander Millo."

Duyair glanced out at the Temple grounds. They were filled with kneeling townsfolk—people who, seeing the armada in the skies, had come to pray and remained to cheer. He heard them shouting now:

"The Hammer! The Hammer!"

The subradio brought in Millo's puzzled words: "A one-way screen that shields you from our guns and lets you fire at our ships? Impossible!"

"Impossible? Your seventh ship, Commander."

Again Duyair's fingers touched the firing switch. Again a bolt of force leaped skyward, and again a ship's screens dissolved under the pressure, and a ship died. Two of the eight Imperial ships now spun slowly, gutted wrecks drifting sunward.

"This is fantastic!" Millo said. "Double the charge! Destroy them!"

Duyair chuckled. Lightly he depressed the switch; a third ship died, and a fourth.

"The Hammer!" the people cried. "It destroys the ships of the Empire!"

The Hammer descended again, and the fifth ship blazed fitfully. And the sixth.

"An unstoppable gun, Commander Millo, coupled with an impregnable planet-wide force screen. This is the Hammer of Aldryne," Duyair said. "This we have held in reserve, waiting for the day we could use it—waiting until the time was ripe to crush the Empire!"

He jabbed down again. Lightning flashed, and when the sky cleared, only the Imperial flagship *Peerless* remained still intact in the skies.

"We surrender! We surrender!" cried Commander Millo over the subradio. "No more, Aldryne! Surrender!"

"Surrender accepted," Duyair said. "I order you to return to the Emperor, Millo. Tell him of what happened this day on Aldryne. Go; I spare you."

Commander Millo did not need any further commands. The hulking flag-ship blasted jets rapidly; it spun, turned over, headed outward, slinking away toward Dervonar, sole survivor of the proud Imperial fleet.

Duyair waited until the ship was out of sight, then turned to the priests at his sides.

"Man those radio sets," he ordered. "News of this victory is to be relayed to every planet in the Empire. Tonight is the night we rise against Dervon!"

He paused to swab his forehead. He grinned; the Hammer had worked, the installation had been correct. The old gun, idle all these years, had been an ideal channel for the mighty force the Hammer held.

The screen—and the gun. It was a combination with which Duyair could rule the galaxy if he so chose. But he had no desire to found a new Empire.

"Word from Dykran," said a priest. "From one Bluir Marsh. He sends his congratulations and reports that three thousand worlds are striking against the Emperor tonight."

"Send him an acknowledgment," Duyair said. He stepped out on the para-pet once again. By now several thousand citizens had gathered there.

"In a short while," he said loudly, "a ship armed with the Hammer of Aldryne shall leave this planet, and since it is unstoppable, it will destroy the Imperial fleet singlehandedly. Tonight an Empire falls, and ten thousand independent worlds will take its place!"

"Duyair!" they roared, "Hammer! Duyair! Hammer!"

The time had come.

Chapter Seven

To witness the death of an Empire that had endured three thousand years is not pleasant, but to be the final Emperor of your line is agony.

Dervon XIV sat alone in his throne room on that final night. His ministers were long since dead, dead by their own hands. The revolt had struck even here—here, at Dervonar itself!

He eyed the map that told of the spreading of the rebellion—out of the Aldryne system into the Cluster of which it was a part, then through the Cluster like a raging blaze.

And then across the skies.

Dervon shook his head sadly. The Empire had been foredoomed—but that it should end this way, at this time! He realized that his own attempts to preserve it had been the mainspring of the Empire's destruction.

He had known of the rebellion on Dykran. A stronger Emperor might have obliterated those two worlds at once, while he had the chance. But Dervon had been devious. He had feared losing the support of the rest of the galaxy by such a terrible action. And thus he had given Aldryne time to loose its Hammer.

Now they all rebelled, all fell away. He saw coldly and clearly that nothing he could have done would have saved the Empire. It had crumbled of its own weight, died of its own extreme age.

Gloomily he peered at the gyrotoy in his hand. From far away came the sound of pounding, a constant reiterating *boom . . . boom. . . .*

The Hammer, he thought. Coming ever closer, here on the last night of the Empire. Smiling bitterly, the dying Emperor of the dead Empire stared at the delicate patterns shaped within the gyrotoy. Sighing, he waited for the end, while the blows of the Hammer sounded ever louder, ever closer in his ears.

Valley Beyond Time

Chapter One

The Valley, Sam Thornhill thought, had never looked lovelier. Drifting milky clouds hung over the two towering bare purple fangs of rock that bordered the Valley on either side and closed it off at the rear. Both suns were in the sky, the sprawling pale red one and the more distant, more intense blue; their beams mingled, casting a violet haze over tree and shrub and on the fast-flowing waters of the river that led to the barrier.

It was late in the forenoon, and all was well. Thornhill, a slim, compactly made figure in satinfab doublet and tunic, dark blue with orange trim, felt deep content. He watched the girl and the man come toward him up the winding path from the stream, wondering who they were and what they wanted with him.

The girl, at least, was attractive. She was dark of complexion and just short of Thornhill's own height; she wore a snug rayon blouse and a yellow knee-length lustrol sheath. Her bare shoulders were wide and sun-darkened.

The man was small, well set, hardly an inch over five feet tall. He was nearly bald; a maze of wrinkles furrowed his domed forehead. His eyes caught Thornhill's attention immediately. They were very bright, quick eyes that darted here and there in rapid glittering motions—the eyes of a predatory animal, of a lizard perhaps ready to pounce.

In the distance Thornhill caught sight of others, not all of them human. A globular Spican was visible near the stream's edge. Then Thornhill frowned for the first time; who were they, and what business had they in his Valley?

"Hello," the girl said. "My name's Marga Fallis. This is La Floquet. You just get here?"

She glanced toward the man named La Floquet and said quietly, "He hasn't come out of it yet, obviously. He must be brand-new."

"He'll wake up soon," La Floquet said. His voice was dark and sharp.

"What are you two muttering?" Thornhill demanded angrily. "How did you get here?"

"The same way you did," the girl said, "and the sooner you admit that to yourself—"

Hotly, Thornhill said, "I've always been here, damn you! This is the Valley! I've spent my whole life here! And I've never seen either of you before. Any of you. You just appeared out of nowhere, you and this little rooster and those others down by the river, and I—" He stopped, feeling a sudden wrenching shaft of doubt.

Of course I've always lived here, he told himself.

He began to quiver. He leaped abruptly forward, seeing in the smiling little man with the wisp of russet hair around his ears the enemy that had cast him forth from Eden. "Damn you, it was fine till *you* got here! You had to spoil it! I'll pay you back, though."

Thornhill sprang at the little man viciously, thinking to knock him to the ground. But to his astonishment he was the one to recoil; La Floquet remained unbudged, still smiling, still glinting birdlike at him. Thornhill sucked in a deep breath and drove forward at La Floquet a second time. This time he was efficiently caught and held; he wriggled, but though La Floquet was a good twenty years older and a foot shorter, there was surprising strength in his wiry body. Sweat burst out on Thornhill. Finally he gave ground and dropped back.

"Fighting is foolish," La Floquet said tranquilly. "It accomplishes nothing. What's your name?"

"Sam Thornhill."

"Now, attend to me. What were you doing in the moment before you first knew you were in the Valley?"

"I've always been in the Valley," Thornhill said stubbornly.

"Think," said the girl. "Look back. There was a time before you came to the Valley."

Thornhill turned away, looking upward at the mighty mountain peaks that hemmed them in, at the fast-flowing stream that wound between them and out toward the Barrier. A grazing beast wandered on the upreach of the foothill, nibbling the sharp-toothed grass. Had there ever been a someplace else, Thornhill wondered?

No. There had always been the Valley, and here he had lived alone and at peace until that final deceptive moment of tranquility, followed by this strange unwanted invasion.

"It usually takes several hours for the effect to wear off," the girl said. "Then you'll remember . . . the way we remember. Think. You're from Earth, aren't you?"

"Earth?" Thornhill repeated dimly.

"Green hills, spreading cities, oceans, spaceliners. Earth. No?"

"Observe the heavy tan," La Floquet pointed out. "He's from Earth, but he hasn't lived there for a while. How about Vengamon?"

"Vengamon," Thornhill declared, not questioningly this time. The strange syllables seemed to have meaning: a swollen yellow sun, broad plains, a growing city of colonists, a flourishing ore trade. "I know the word," he said.

"Was that the planet where you lived?" the girl prodded. "Vengamon?"

"I think—" Thornhill began hesitantly. His knees felt weak. A neat pattern of life was breaking down and cascading away from him, sloughing off as if it had never been at all.

It had *never been*.

"I lived on Vengamon," he said.

"Good!" La Floquet cried. "The first fact has been elicited! Now to think where you were the very moment before you came here. A spaceship, perhaps? Traveling between worlds? Think, Thornhill."

He thought. The effort was mind-wracking, but he deliberately blotted out the memories of his life in the Valley and searched backward until—

"I was a passenger on the liner *Royal Mother Helene*, bound into Vengamon from the neighboring world of Jurinalle. I . . . had been on holiday. I was returning to my—my plantation? No, not plantation. Mine. I own mining land on Vengamon. That's it, yes—mining land." The light of the double suns became oppressively warm; he felt dizzy. "I remember now: The trip was an uneventful one; I was bored and dozed off a few minutes. Then I recall sensing that I was outside the ship, somehow—and—blank. Next thing, I was here in the Valley."

"The standard pattern," La Floquet said. He gestured to the others down near the stream. "There are eight of us in all, including you. I arrived first—yesterday, I call it, though actually there's been no night. The girl came after me. Then three others. You're the third one to come today."

Thornhill blinked. "We're just being picked out of nowhere and dumped here? How is it possible?"

La Floquet shrugged. "You will be asking that question more than once before you've left the Valley. Come. Let's meet the others."

The small man turned with an imperious gesture and retraced his steps down the path; the girl followed, and Thornhill fell in line behind her. He realized he had been standing on a ledge overlooking the river, one of the foothills of the two great mountains that formed the Valley's boundaries.

The air was warm, with a faint breeze stirring through it. He felt younger than his thirty-seven years, certainly; more alive, more perceptive. He caught the fragrance of the golden blossoms that lined the riverbed and saw the light sparkle of the double sunlight scattered by the water's spray.

He thought of glancing at his watch. The hands read 14:23. That was interesting enough. The day hand said 7 July 2671. It was still the same day, then. On 7 July 2671 he had left Jurinalle for Vengamon, and he had lunched at 11:40. That meant he had probably dozed off about noon—and unless something were wrong with his watch, only two hours had passed since then. Two hours. And yet—the memories still said, though they were fading fast now—he had spent an entire life in this Valley, unmarred by intruders until a few moments before.

"This is Sam Thornhill," La Floquet suddenly said. "He's our newest arrival. He's out of Vengamon."

Thornhill eyed the others curiously. There were five of them, three human, one humanoid, one nonhumanoid. The nonhumanoid, globular in its yellow-green phase just now but seeming ready to shift to its melancholy brownish-red guise, was a being of Spica. Tiny clawed feet peeked out from under the great melonlike body; dark grapes atop stalks studied Thornhill with unfathomable alien curiosity.

The humanoid, Thornhill saw, hailed from one of the worlds of Regulus. He was keen-eyed, pale orange in color. The heavy flap of flesh swinging from his throat was the chief external alien characteristic of the being. Thornhill had met his kind before.

Of the remaining three, one was a woman, small, plain-looking, dressed in drab gray cloth garments. There were two men: a spidery spindle-shanked sort with mild scholarly eyes and an apologetic smile and a powerfully built man of thirty or so, shirtless, scowling impatiently.

"As you can see, it's quite a crew," La Floquet remarked to Thornhill. "Vellers, did you have any luck down by the barrier?"

The big man shook his head. "I followed the main stream as far as I dared. But you get beyond that grassy bend down there and come smack against that barrier, like a wall you can't see planted in the water." His accent was broad and heavy; he was obviously of Earth, Thornhill thought, and not from one of the colony worlds.

La Floquet frowned. "Did you try swimming underneath? No, of course you didn't. Eh?"

Vellers' scowl grew darker. "There wasn't any percentage in it, Floquet. I dove ten—fifteen feet, and the barrier was still like glass—smooth and clean to the touch, y'know, but strong. I didn't aim to go any lower."

"All right," La Floquet said sharply. "It doesn't matter. Few of us could swim that deep, anyway." He glanced at Thornhill. "You see that this lovely Valley is likely to become our home for life, don't you?"

"There's no way out?"

The small man pointed to the gleaming radiance of the barrier, which rose in a high curving arc from the water and formed a triangular wedge closing off the lower end of the Valley. "You see that thing down there. We don't know what's at the other end, but we'd have to climb twenty thousand feet of mountain to find out. There's no way out of here."

"Do we *want* to get out?" asked the thin man in a shallow, petulant voice. "I was almost dead when I came here, La Floquet. Now I'm alive again. I don't know if I'm so anxious to leave here."

La Floquet whirled. His eyes flashed angrily as he said, "Mr. McKay, I'm delighted to hear of your recovery. But life still waits for me outside this place, lovely as the Valley is. I don't intend to rot away in here forever—not La Floquet!"

McKay shook his head slowly. "I wish there were some way of stopping you from looking for a way out. I'll die in a week if I go out of the Valley. If you escape, La Floquet, you'll be my murderer!"

"I just don't understand," Thornhill said in confusion. "If La Floquet finds a way out, what's it to you, McKay? Why don't you just stay here?"

McKay smiled unhappily. "I guess you haven't told him, then," he said to La Floquet.

"No. I didn't have a chance." La Floquet turned to Thornhill. "What this dried-up man of books is saying is that the Watcher has warned us that if one of us leaves the Valley, all the others must go."

"The Watcher?" Thornhill repeated.

"It was he who brought you here. You'll see him again. Occasionally he talks to us and tells us things. This morning he told us this: that our fates are bound together."

"And I ask you not to keep searching for the way out," McKay said dolefully. "My life depends on staying in the Valley!"

"And mine on getting out!" La Floquet blazed. He lunged forward and sent McKay sprawling to the ground in one furious gesture of contempt.

McKay turned even paler and clutched at his chest as he landed. "My heart! You shouldn't—"

Thornhill moved forward and assisted McKay to his feet. The tall, stoop-shouldered man looked dazed and shaken, but unhurt. He drew himself together and said quietly, "Two days ago a blow like that would have killed me. And now—you see?" he asked, appealing to Thornhill. "The Valley has strange properties. I don't want to leave. And he—he's condemning me to die!"

"Don't worry so over it," La Floquet said lightly. "You may get your wish. You may spend all your days here among the poppies."

Thornhill turned and looked up the mountainside toward the top. The mountain peak loomed, snow-flecked, shrouded by clinging frosty clouds; the climb would be a giant's task. And how would they know until they had climbed it whether merely another impassable barrier lay beyond the mountain's crest?

"We seem to be stuck here for a while," Thornhill said. "But it could be worse. This looks like a pleasant place to live."

"It is," La Floquet said. "If you like pleasant places. They bore me. But come: Tell us something of yourself. Half an hour ago you had no past; has it come back to you yet?"

Thornhill nodded slowly. "I was born on Earth. Studied to be a mining engineer. I did fairly well at it, and when they opened up Vengamon, I moved out there and bought a chunk of land while the prices were low. It turned out to be a good buy. I opened a mine four years ago. I'm not married. I'm a wealthy man, as wealth is figured on Vengamon. And that's the whole story, except that I was returning home from a vacation when I was snatched off my spaceship and deposited here."

He took a deep breath, drawing the warm, moist air into his lungs. For the moment he sided with McKay; he was in no hurry to leave the Valley. But he could see that La Floquet, that energetic, driving little man, was bound to have his way. If there was any path leading out of the Valley, La Floquet would find it.

His eyes came to rest on Marga Fallis. The girl was handsome, no doubt about it. Yes, he could stay here a while longer under these double suns, breathing deep and living free from responsibility for the first time in his life. But they were supposed to be bound together: Once one left the Valley, all would. And La Floquet was determined to leave.

A shadow dimmed the purple light.

"What's that?" Thornhill said. "An eclipse?"

"The Watcher," McKay said softly. "He's back. And it wouldn't surprise me if he's brought the ninth member of our little band."

Thornhill stared as a soft blackness descended over the land, the suns still visible behind it but only as tiny dots of far-off radiance. It was as if a fluffy dark cloak had enfolded them. But it was more than a cloak—much more. He sensed a *presence* among them, watchful, curious, as eager for their welfare as a brooding hen. The alien darkness wrapped itself over the entire Valley.

This is the last of your company, said a soundless voice that seemed to echo from the mountain walls. The sky began to brighten. Suddenly as it had come, the darkness was gone, and Thornhill once again felt alone.

"The Watcher had little to say this time," McKay commented as the light returned.

"Look!" Marga cried.

Thornhill followed the direction of her pointing arm and looked upward toward the ledge on which he had first become aware of the Valley around him.

A tiny figure was wandering in confused circles up there. At this distance it was impossible to tell much about the newcomer. Thornhill became chilled. The shadow of the Watcher had come and gone, leaving behind yet another captive for the Valley.

Chapter Two

Thornhill narrowed his eyes as he looked toward the ledge. "We ought to go get him," he said.

La Floquet shook his head. "We have time. It takes an hour or two for the newcomers to lose that strange illusion of being alone here; you remember what it's like."

"I do," Thornhill agreed. "It's as if you've lived all your life in paradise . . . until gradually it wears off and you see others around you—as I saw you and Marga coming up the path toward me." He walked a few paces away from them and lowered himself to a moss-covered boulder. A small, wiry, catlike creature with wide cupped ears emerged from behind it and rubbed up against him; he fondled it idly as if it were his pet.

La Floquet shaded his eyes from the sunlight. "Can you see what he's like, that one up there?"

"No, not at this distance," Thornhill said.

"Too bad you can't. You'd be interested. We've added another alien to our gallery, I fear."

Thornhill leaned forward anxiously. "From where?"

"Aldebaran," La Floquet said.

Thornhill winced. The humanoid aliens of Aldebaran were the coldest of races, fierce, savage beings who hid festering evil behind masks of outward urbanity. Some of the out-worlds referred to the Aldebaranians as devils, and they were not so far wrong. To have one here, a devil in paradise, so to speak—

"What are we going to do?" Thornhill asked.

La Floquet shrugged. "The Watcher has put the creature here, and the Watcher has his own purposes. We'll simply have to accept what comes."

Thornhill rose and paced urgently up and down. The silent, small, mousy woman and McKay had drawn off to one side; the Spican was peering at his own plump image in the swirling waters, and the Regulan, not interested in the proceedings, stared aloofly toward the leftward mountain. The girl Marga and La Floquet remained near Thornhill.

"All right," Thornhill said finally. "Give the Aldebaranian some time to come to his senses. Meanwhile, let's forget about him and worry about ourselves. La Floquet, what do you know about this Valley?"

The small man smiled blandly. "Not very much. I know we're on a world with Earth-norm gravity and a double sun system. How many red-and-blue double suns do you know of, Thornhill?"

He shrugged. "I'm no astronomer."

"I am . . . was . . . " Marga said. "There are hundreds of such systems. We could be anywhere in the galaxy."

"Can't you tell from the constellations at night?" Thornhill asked.

"There *are* no constellations," La Floquet said sadly. "The damnable part is that there's always at least one of the suns in the sky. This planet has no night. We see no stars. But our location is unimportant." The fiery little man chuckled. "McKay will triumph. We'll never leave the Valley. How could we contact anyone, even if we were to cross the mountains? We cannot."

A sudden crackle of thunder caught Thornhill's attention. A great rolling boom reverberated from the sides of the mountains, dying away slowly.

"Listen," he said.

"A storm," said La Floquet. "Outside the confines of our barrier. The same happened yesterday at this time. It storms . . . but not in here. We live in an enchanted Valley where the sun always shines and life is gentle."A bitter grimace twisted his thin, bloodless lips. "Gentle!"

"Get used to it," Thornhill said. "We may be here a long time."

His watch read 16:42 when they finally went up the hill to get the Aldebaranian. In the two hours he had seen a shift in the configuration of the suns—the red had receded, the blue grown more intense—but it was obvious that there would be no night, that light would enter the Valley around the clock. In time he would grow used to that. He was adaptable.

Nine people, plucked from as many different worlds and cast within the space of twenty-four hours into this timeless valley beyond the storms, where there was no darkness. Of the nine, six were human, three were alien. Of the six, four were men, two were women.

Thornhill wondered about his companions. He knew so little about them yet. Vellers, the strong man, was from Earth; Thornhill knew nothing more of him. McKay and the mousy woman were ciphers. Thornhill cared little about them. Neither the Regulan nor the Spican had uttered a word yet—if they could speak the Terran tongues at all. As for Marga, she was an astronomer and was lovely, but he knew nothing else. La Floquet was an interesting one—a little dynamo, shrewd and energetic but close-mouthed about his own past.

There they were. Nine pastless people. The present was as much of a mystery to them as the future.

By the time they reached the mountain ledge, Thornhill and La Floquet and the girl, the Aldebaranian had seen them and was glaring coldly at them. The storm had subsided in the land outside the Valley, and once again white clouds drifted in over the barrier.

Like all his race the Aldebaranian, a man of medium height and amiable appearance, was well fleshed, with pouches of fat swelling beneath his chin and under his ears. He was gray of skin and dark of eye, with gleaming little hooked incisors that glinted terrifyingly when he smiled. He had extra joints in his limbs as well.

"At last some others join me," the alien remarked in flawless Terran Standard as they approached. "I knew life could hardly go on here as it had."

"You're mistaken," La Floquet said. "It's a delusion common to new arrivals. You haven't lived here all your life, you know. Not really."

The Aldebaranian smiled. "This surprises me. But explain, if you will."

La Floquet explained. In a frighteningly short space of time the alien had grasped the essential nature of the Valley and his position in it. Thornhill watched coldly; the speed with which the Aldebaranian cast off delusion and accepted reality was disturbing.

They returned to the group at the river's edge. By now Thornhill was beginning to feel hungry; he had been in the Valley more than four hours. "What do we do about food?" he asked.

La Floquet said, "It falls from the skies three times a day. Manna, you know. The Watcher takes fine care of us. You got here around the time of the afternoon fall, but you were up there in your haze while we ate. It's almost time for the third fall of the day now."

The red sun had faded considerably now, and a haunted blue twilight reigned. Thornhill knew enough about solar mechanics to be aware that the big red sun was nearly dead; its feeble bulk gave little light. Fierce radiation came from the blue sun, but distance afforded protection. How this unlikely pair had come together was a matter for conjecture—some star capture in eons past, no doubt.

White flakes drifted slowly downward. As they came, Thornhill saw the Spican hoist its bulk hastily from the ground, saw the Regulan running eagerly toward the drifting flakes. McKay stirred; Vellers, the big man, tugged himself to his feet. Only Thornhill and the Aldebaranian looked at all doubtful.

"Suppertime," La Floquet said cheerfully. He punctuated the statement by snapping a gob of the floating substance from the air with a quick, sharp gesture and cramming it into his mouth.

The others, Thornhill saw, were likewise catching the food before it touched ground. The animals of the Valley were appearing—the fat, lazy-looking ruminants, the whippetlike dogs, the catlike creatures—and busily were devouring the manna from the ground.

Thornhill shrugged and shagged a mass as it hung before him in the air. After a tentative sniff he hesitantly swallowed a mouthful.

It was like chewing cloud stuff—except that this cloud had a tangy, wine-like taste; his stomach felt soothed almost immediately. He wondered how such unsubstantial stuff could possibly be nourishing. Then he stopped wondering and helped himself to a second portion, then a third.

The fall stopped finally, and by then Thornhill was sated. He lay outstretched on the ground, legs thrust out, head propped up against a boulder.

Opposite him was McKay. The thin, pale man was smiling. "I haven't eaten this way in years," he said. "Haven't had much of an appetite. But now—"

"Where are you from?" Thornhill asked, interrupting.

"Earth, originally. Then to Mars when my heart began acting up. They thought the low gravity would help me, and of course it did. I'm a professor of medieval Terran history. That is, I *was*—I was on a medical leave until—until I came here." He smiled complacently. "I feel reborn here, you know? If only I had some books—"

"Shut up," growled Vellers. "You'd stay here forever, wouldn't you, now?"

The big man lay near the water's edge staring moodily out over the river.

"Of course I would," snapped McKay testily. "And Miss Hardin, too, I'd wager."

"If we could leave the two of you here together, I'm sure you'd be very happy," came the voice of La Floquet. "But we can't do that. Either all of us stay, or all of us get out of here."

The argument appeared likely to last all night. Thornhill looked away. The three aliens seemed to be as far from each other as possible, the Spican lying in a horizontal position looking like a great inflated balloon that had somehow come to rest, the little Regulan brooding in the distance and fingering its heavy dewlap, the Aldebaranian sitting quietly to one side listening to every word, smiling like a pudgy Buddha.

Thornhill rose. He bent over Marga Fallis and said, "Would you care to take a walk with me."

She hesitated just a moment. "I'd love to," she said.

They stood at the edge of the water watching the swift stream, watching golden fish flutter past with solemnly gaping mouths. After a while they walked on upstream, back toward the rise in the ground that led to the hills, which in turn rose into the two mighty peaks.

Thornhill said, "That La Floquet. He's a funny one, isn't he? Like a little gamecock, always jumping around and ready for a fight."

"He's very dynamic," Marga agreed quietly.

"You and he were the first ones here, weren't you? It must have been strange, just the two of you in this little Eden, until the third one showed up." Thornhill wondered why he was probing after these things. Jealousy, perhaps? Not *perhaps*. Certainly.

"We really had very little time alone together. McKay came right after me, and then the Spican. The Watcher was very busy collecting."

"*Collecting,*" Thornhill repeated. "That's all we are. Just specimens collected and put here in this Valley like little lizards in a terrarium. And this

Watcher—some strange alien being, I guess." He looked up at the starless sky, still bright with day. "There's no telling what's in the stars. Five hundred years of space travel, and we haven't seen it all."

Marga smiled. She took his hand, and they walked on farther into the low-lying shrubbery, saying nothing. Thornhill finally broke the silence.

"You said you were an astronomer, Marga?"

"Not really." Her voice was low for a woman's and well modulated; he liked it. "I'm attached to the Bellatrix VII observatory, but strictly as an assistant. I've got a degree in astronomy, of course. But I'm just sort of hired help in the observatory."

"Is that where you were when—when—"

"Yes," she said. "I was in the main dome taking some plates out of the camera. I remember it was a very delicate business. A minute or two before it happened, someone called me on the main phone downstairs, and they wanted to transfer the call up to me. I told them it would have to wait; I couldn't be bothered until I'd finished with my plates. And then everything blanked out, and I guess my plates don't matter now. I wish I'd taken that call, though."

"Someone important?"

"Oh—no. Nothing like that."

Somehow Thornhill felt relieved. "What about La Floquet?" he asked. "Who is he?"

"He's sort of a big-game hunter," she said. "I met him once before when he led a party to Bellatrix VII. Imagine the odds on any two people in the universe meeting twice! He didn't recognize me, of course, but I remembered him. He's not easy to forget."

"He *is* sort of picturesque," Thornhill said.

"And you? You said you owned a mine on Vengamon."

"I do. I'm actually quite a dull person," said Thornhill. "This is the first interesting thing that's ever happened to me." He grinned wryly. "The fates caught up with me with a vengeance, though. I guess I'll never see Vengamon again now. Unless La Floquet can get us out of here, and I don't think he can."

"Does it matter? Will it pain you never to go back to Vengamon?"

"I doubt it," Thornhill said. "I can't see any urgent reason for wanting to go back. And you, and your observatory?"

"I can forget my observatory soon enough," she said.

Somehow he moved closer to her; he wished it were a little darker, perhaps even that the Watcher would choose this instant to arrive and afford a shield of privacy for him for a moment. He felt her warmth against him.

"Don't," she murmured suddenly. "Someone's coming."

She pulled away from him. Scowling, Thornhill turned and saw the stubby figure of La Floquet clambering toward them.

"I do hope I'm not interrupting any tender scenes," the little man said quietly.

"You might have been," Thornhill admitted. "But the damage is done. What's happened to bring you after us? The charm of our company?"

"Not exactly. There's trouble down below. Vellers and McKay had a fight."

"Over leaving the Valley?"

"Of course." La Floquet looked strangely disturbed. "Vellers hit him a little too hard, though. He killed him."

Marga gasped. "McKay's dead?"

"Very. I don't know what we ought to do with Vellers. I wanted you two in on it."

Hastily Thornhill and Marga followed La Floquet down the side of the hill toward the little group clumped on the beach. Even at a distance Thornhill could see the towering figure of Vellers staring down at his feet where the crumpled body of McKay lay.

They were still a hundred feet away when McKay rose suddenly to his feet and hurled himself on Vellers in a wild headlong assault.

Chapter Three

Thornhill froze an instant and grasped La Floquet's cold wrist.

"I thought you told me he was dead?"

"He *was*," La Floquet insisted. "I've seen dead men before. I know the face, the eyes, the slackness of the lips—Thornhill, this is impossible!"

They ran toward the beach. Vellers had been thrown back by the fury of the resurrected McKay's attack; he went tumbling over, with McKay groping for his throat in blind murderousness.

But Vellers' strength prevailed. As Thornhill approached, the big man plucked McKay off him with one huge hand, held him squirming in the air an instant, and rising to his feet, hurled McKay down against a beach boulder with sickening impact. Vellers staggered back, muttering hoarsely to himself.

Thornhill stared down. A gash had opened along the side of McKay's head; blood oozed through the sparse graying hair, matting it. McKay's eyes, half-open, were glazed and sightless; his mouth hung agape, tongue lolling. The skin of his face was gray.

Kneeling, Thornhill touched his hand to McKay's wrist, then to the older man's lips. After a moment he looked up. "This time he's really dead," he said.

La Floquet was peering grimly at him. "Get out of the way!" he snapped suddenly, and to Thornhill's surprise he found himself being roughly grabbed by the shoulder and flung aside by the wiry game hunter.

Quickly La Floquet flung himself down on McKay's body, straddling it with his knees pressing against the limp arms, hands grasping the slender shoulders. The beach was very silent; La Floquet's rough, irregular breathing was the only sound. The little man seemed poised, tensed for a physical encounter.

The gash on McKay's scalp began to heal.

Thornhill watched as the parted flesh closed over; the bruised skin lost its angry discoloration. Within moments only the darkening stain of blood on McKay's forehead gave any indication that there had been a wound.

Then McKay's slitted eyelids closed and immediately reopened, showing bright, flashing eyes that rolled wildly. Color returned to the dead man's face. Like a riding whip suddenly turned by conjury into a serpent, McKay began to thrash frantically. But La Floquet was prepared. His muscles corded momentarily as he exerted pressure; McKay writhed but could not rise. Behind him Thornhill heard Vellers mumbling a prayer over and over again while the mousy Miss Hardin provided a counterpoint of harsh sobs; even the Regulan uttered a brief comment in his guttural, consonant-studded language.

Sweat beaded La Floquet's face, but he prevented McKay from repeating his previous wild charge. Perhaps a minute passed; then McKay relaxed visibly.

La Floquet remained cautiously astride him. "McKay? McKay, do you hear me? This is La Floquet "

"I hear you. You can get off me now; I'm all right."

La Floquet gestured to Thornhill and Vellers. "Stand near him. Be ready to grab him if he runs wild again." He eyed McKay suspiciously for a moment, then rolled to one side and jumped to his feet.

McKay remained on the ground a moment longer. Finally he hoisted himself to a kneeling position, and shaking his head as if to clear it, stood erect. He took a few hesitant, uncertain steps. Then he turned, staring squarely at the three men, and in a quiet voice said, "Tell me what happened to me."

"You and Vellers quarreled," La Floquet said. "He—knocked you unconscious. When you came to, something must have snapped inside you—you went after Vellers like a madman. He knocked you out a second time. You just regained consciousness."

"No!" Thornhill half-shouted in a voice he hardly recognized as his own. "Tell him the truth, La Floquet! We can't gain anything by pretending it didn't happen."

"What truth?" McKay asked curiously.

Thornhill paused an instant. "McKay, you were dead. At least once. Probably twice, unless La Floquet was mistaken the first time. I examined you the second time—after Vellers bashed you against that rock. I'd swear you were dead. Feel the side of your head . . . where it was split open when Vellers threw you down."

McKay put a quivering hand to his head, drew it away bloody, and stared down at the rock near his foot. The rock was bloodstained, also.

"I see blood, but I don't feel any pain."

"Of course not," Thornhill said. "The wound healed almost instantaneously. And you were revived. *You came back to life, McKay!*"

McKay turned to La Floquet. "Is this thing true, what Thornhill's telling me? You were trying to hide it?"

La Floquet nodded.

A slow, strange smile appeared on McKay's pale, angular face. "It's the Valley, then! I was dead—and I rose from the dead! Vellers—La Floquet—you fools! Don't you see that we live forever here in this Valley that you're so anxious to leave? I died twice . . . and it was like being asleep. Dark, and I remember nothing. You're sure I was dead, Thornhill?"

"I'd swear to it."

"But of course you, La Floquet—you'd try to hide this from me, wouldn't you? Well, do you still want to leave here? We can live forever in the Valley, La Floquet!"

The small man spat angrily. "Why bother? Why live here like vegetables, eternally, never to move beyond those mountains, never to see what's on the other side of the stream? I'd rather have a dozen unfettered years than ten thousand in this prison, McKay!" He scowled.

"You had to tell him," La Floquet said accusingly to Thornhill.

"What difference does it make?" Thornhill asked. "We'd have had a repetition sooner or later. We couldn't hide it from anyone." He glanced up at the arching mountains. "So the Watcher has ways of keeping us alive? No suicide, no murder . . . and no way out."

"There *is* a way out," La Floquet said stubbornly. "Over the mountain pass. I'm sure of it. Vellers and I may go to take a look at it tomorrow. Won't we, Vellers?"

The big man shrugged. "It's fine with me."

"You don't want to stay here forever, do you, Vellers?" La Floquet went on. "What good is immortality if it's the immortality of prisoners for life? We'll look at the mountain tomorrow, Vellers."

Thornhill detected a strange note in La Floquet's voice, a curiously strained facial expression, as if he were pleading with Vellers to support him, as if he were somehow afraid to approach the mountain alone. The idea of La Floquet's being afraid of anything or anyone seemed hard to accept, but Thornhill had that definite impression.

He looked at Vellers, then at La Floquet. "We ought to discuss this a little further, I think. There are nine of us, La Floquet. McKay and Miss Hardin definitely want to remain in the Valley; Miss Fallis and I are uncertain, but in any event we'd like to stay here a while longer. That's four against two among the humans. As for the aliens—"

"I'll vote with La Floquet," said the Aldebaranian quietly. "Important business waits for me outside."

Troublemaker, Thornhill thought. "Four against three, then, with the Spican and the Regulan unheard from. And I guess they'll stay unheard from since we can't speak their languages."

"I can speak Regulan," volunteered the Aldebaranian. Without waiting for further discussion, he wheeled to face the grave dewlapped being and exchanged four or five short, crisp sentences with him. Turning again, he said, "Our friend votes to leave. This ties the score, I believe."

"Just a second," Thornhill said hotly. "How do we know that's what he said? Suppose—"

The mask of affability slipped from the alien's face. "Suppose *what?*" he asked coldly. "If you intend to put a shadow on my honor, Thornhill—" He left the sentence unfinished.

"It would be pretty pointless dueling here," Thornhill said, "unless your honor satisfies easily. You couldn't very well kill me for long. Perhaps a temporary death might soothe you, but let's let it drop. I'll take your interpreting job in good faith. We're four apiece for staying or trying to break out."

La Floquet said, "It was good of you to take this little vote, Thornhill. But it's not a voting matter. We're individuals, not a corporate entity, and I choose not to remain here so long as I can make the attempt to escape." The little man spun on his heel and stalked away from the group.

"There ought to be some way of stopping him," said McKay thickly. "If he escapes—"

Thornhill shook his head. "It's not as easy as all that. How's he going to get off the planet, even if he does pass the mountains?"

"You don't understand," McKay said. "The Watcher simply said if one of us *leaves the Valley*, all must go. And if La Floquet succeeds, it's death for me."

"Perhaps we're dead already," Marga suggested, breaking her long silence. "Suppose each of us—you in your spaceliner, me in my observatory—died at the same moment and came here. What if—"

The sky darkened in the now-familiar manner that signaled the approach of the Watcher.

"Ask him," Thornhill said. "He'll tell you all about it."

The black cloud descended.

You are not dead, came the voiceless answer to the unspoken question. *Though some of you will die if the barrier be passed.*

Again Thornhill felt chilled by the presence of the formless being. "Who are you?" he shouted. "What do you want with us?"

I am the Watcher.

"And what do you want with us?" Thornhill repeated.

I am the Watcher, came the inflexible answer. Fibrils of the cloud began to trickle away in many directions; within moments the sky was clear. Thornhill slumped back against a rock and looked at Marga.

"He comes and he goes, feeds us, keeps us from killing ourselves or each other. It's like a zoo, Marga! And we're the chief exhibits!"

La Floquet and Vellers came stumping toward them. "Are you satisfied with the answers to your questions?" La Floquet demanded. "Do you still want to spend the rest of your days here?"

Thornhill smiled. "Go ahead, La Floquet. Go climb the mountain. I'm changing my vote. It's five-three in favor of leaving."

"I thought you were with me," said McKay.

Thornhill ignored him. "Go on, La Floquet. You and Vellers climb that mountain. Get out of the Valley—if you can."

"Come with us," La Floquet said.

"Ah, no—I'd rather stay here. But I won't object if you go."

Fleetingly, La Floquet cast a glance at the giant tooth that blocked the Valley's exit, and it seemed to Thornhill that a shadow of fear passed over the little man's face. But La Floquet clamped his jaws tight and through locked lips said, "Vellers, are you with me?"

The big man shrugged amiably. "It can't hurt to take a look, I figure."

"Let's go, then," La Floquet said firmly. He threw one black, infuriated glance at Thornhill and struck out for the path leading to the mountain approach.

When he was out of earshot, Marga said, "Sam, why'd you do that?"

"I wanted to see how he'd react. I saw it."

McKay tugged at his arm fretfully. "I'll die if we leave the Valley! Don't you see that, Mr. Thornhill?"

Sighing, Thornhill said, "I see it. But don't worry too much about La Floquet. He'll be back before long."

Slowly the hours passed, and the red sun slipped below the horizon, leaving only the distant blue sun to provide warmth. Thornhill's wristwatch told him it was past ten in the evening—nearly twelve hours since the time he had boarded the spaceliner on Jurinalle, more than four hours since his anticipated arrival time in the main city of Vengamon. They would have searched in vain for him by now and would be wondering how a man could vanish so thoroughly from a spaceship in hyperdrive.

The little group sat together at the river's edge. The Spican had shifted fully into his brownish-red phase and sat silently like some owl heralding the death of the universe. The other two aliens kept mainly to themselves as well. There was little to be said.

McKay huddled himself into a knob-kneed pile of limbs and stared up at the mountain as if hoping to see some sign of La Floquet and Vellers. Thornhill understood the expression on his face; McKay knew clearly that if La Floquet succeeded in leaving the Valley's confines, he would pay the price of his double resurrection in the same instant. McKay looked like a man seated below a thread-hung sword.

Thornhill himself stared silently at the mountain, wondering where the two men were now, how far they would get before La Floquet's cowardice forced them to turn back. He had no doubt now that La Floquet dreaded the mountain—otherwise he would have made the attempt long before instead of merely threatening it. Now he had been goaded into it by Thornhill, but would he be successful? Probably not; a brave man with one deep-lying fear often never conquered that fear. In a way Thornhill pitied little La Floquet; the gamecock would be forced to come back in humiliation, though he might delay that moment as long as he possibly could.

"You seem troubled," Marga said.

"Troubled? No, just thinking."

"About what?"

"About Vengamon, and my mine there . . . and how the vultures have probably already started to go after my estate."

"You don't miss Vengamon, do you?" she said.

He smiled and shook his head. "Not yet. That mine was my whole life, you know. I took little vacations now and then, but I thought only of the mine and my supervisors and how lazy they were, and the price of ore in the interstellar markets. Until now. It must be some strange property of this Valley, but for the first time the mine seems terribly remote, as if it had always belonged to someone else. Or as if *it* had owned *me* and I'm free at last."

"I know something of how you feel," Marga said. "I lived in the observatory day and night. There were always so many pictures to be taken, so many books to read, so much to do—I couldn't bear the thought of missing a day or even of stopping my work to answer the phone. But there are no stars here, and I hardly miss them."

He took her hand lightly in his. "I wonder, though—If La Floquet succeeds, if we ever do get out of this Valley and back into our ordinary lives, will we be any different? Or will I go back to double-entry bookkeeping and you to stellar luminosities?"

"We won't know until we get back," she said. "*If* we get back. But look over there."

Thornhill looked. McKay and Miss Hardin were deep in a serious conversation, and McKay had shyly taken her hand. "Love comes at last to Professor of Medieval History McKay." Thornhill grinned. "And to Miss Something-or-Other Hardin, whoever she is."

The Regulan was asleep; the Aldebaranian stared broodingly at his feet, drawing pictures in the sand. The bloated sphere that was the Spican was absorbed in its own alien thoughts. The Valley was very quiet.

"I used to pity creatures in the zoos," Thornhill said. "But it's not such a bad life after all."

"So far. We don't know what the Watcher has in store for us."

A mist rolled down from the mountain peak, drifting in over the Valley. At first Thornhill thought the Watcher had returned for another visit with his captives; he saw, though, that it was merely a thin mountain mist dropping over them. It was faintly cold, and he drew Marga tighter against him.

He thought back over thirty-seven years as the mist rolled in. He had come through those thirty-seven years well enough, trim, athletic, with quick reflexes and a quicker mind. But not until this day—it was hard to believe this was still his first day in the Valley—had he fully realized life held other things besides mining and earning money.

It had taken the Valley to teach him that; would he remember the lesson if he ever returned to civilization? Might it not be better to stay here, with Marga, in eternal youth?

He frowned. Eternal youth, yes . . . but at the cost of his free will. He was nothing but a prisoner here, if a pampered one.

Suddenly he did not know what to think.

Marga's hand tightened against his. "Did you hear something? Footsteps, I think. It must be La Floquet and Vellers coming back from the mountain."

"They couldn't make it," Thornhill said, not knowing whether to feel relief or acute disappointment. He heard the sound of voices—and two figures, one small and wiry, one tall and broad, advanced toward them through the thickening mist. He turned to face them.

Chapter Four

Despite the dim illumination of twilight and the effects of the fog Thornhill had no difficulty reading the expression on La Floquet's face. It was not pleasant. The little man was angry both with himself and with Thornhill, and naked hatred was visible in his sharp features.

"Well?" Thornhill asked casually. "No go?"

"We got several thousand feet before this damned fog closed in around us. It was almost as if the Watcher sent it on purpose. We had to turn back."

"And was there any sign of a pass leading out of the Valley?"

La Floquet shrugged. "Who knows? We couldn't as much as see each other! But I'll find it. I'll go back tomorrow when both suns are in the sky—and I'll find a way out!"

"You devil," came McKay's thin, dry voice. "Won't you ever give up?"

"Not while I can still walk!" La Floquet shouted defiantly. But there was a note of mock bravado in his voice. Thornhill wondered just what had really happened up there on the mountain path.

He was not kept long in ignorance. La Floquet stalked angrily away, adopting a pose of injured arrogance, leaving Vellers standing near Thornhill. The big man looked after him and shook his head.

"The liar!"

"What's that?" Thornhill asked, half-surprised.

"There was no fog on the mountain," Vellers muttered bitterly. "He found the fog when we came back down, and he took it as an excuse. The little bullfrog makes much noise, but it's hollow."

Thornhill said earnestly, "Tell me, what happened up there? If there wasn't any fog, why'd you turn back?"

"We got no more than a thousand feet up," Vellers said. "He had been leading. But then he dropped back and got very pale. He said he couldn't go on any farther."

"Why? Was he afraid of the height?"

"I don't think so," Vellers said. "I think he was afraid of getting to the top and seeing what's there. Maybe he knows there isn't any way out. Maybe he's afraid to face it. I don't know. But he made me follow him back down."

Suddenly Vellers grunted heavily, and Thornhill saw that La Floquet had come up quietly behind the big man and jabbed him sharply in the small of the back. Vellers turned. It took time for a man six feet seven to turn.

"Fool!" La Floquet barked. "Who told you these lies? Why this fairy tale, Vellers?"

"Lies? Fairy tale? Get your hands off me, La Floquet. You know damn well you funked out up there. Don't try to fast-talk your way out now."

A muscle tightened convulsively in the corner of La Floquet's slit of a mouth. His eyes flashed; he stared at Vellers as if he were some beast escaped from a cage. Suddenly La Floquet's fists flicked out, and Vellers stepped back, crying out in pain. He swung wildly at the smaller man, but La Floquet was untouchable, humming in under Vellers' guard to plant a stinging punch on the slablike jaw, darting back out again as the powerful Vellers tried to land a decisive blow. La Floquet fought like a fox at bay.

Thornhill moved uneasily forward, not wanting to get in the way of Vellers' massive fists as the giant tried vainly to hit La Floquet. Catching the eye of the Aldebaranian, Thornhill acted. He seized Vellers' arm and tugged it back while the alien similarly blocked off La Floquet.

"Enough!" Thornhill snapped. "It doesn't matter which one of you's lying. Fighting's foolish—you told me that yourself earlier today, La Floquet."

Vellers dropped back sullenly, keeping one eye on La Floquet. The small man smiled. "Honor must be defended, Thornhill, Vellers was spreading lies about me."

"A coward and a liar, too," Vellers said darkly.

"Quiet, both of you," Thornhill told them. "Look up there!"

He pointed.

A gathering cloud hung low over them. The Watcher was drawing near—had been, unnoticed, all during the raging quarrel. Thornhill looked up, waiting, trying to discern some living form within the amorphous blackness that descended on them. It was impossible. He saw only spreading clouds of night hiding the dim sunlight.

He felt the ground rocking gently, quivering in a barely perceptible manner. What now, he wondered, peering at the enfolding darkness. A sound like a faroff musical chord echoed in his ears—a subsonic vibration, perhaps, making him giddy, soothing him, calming him the way gentle stroking might soothe a cat.

Peace among you, my pets, the voiceless voice said softly, almost crooningly. *You quarrel too much. Let there be peace. . . .*

The subsonic note washed up over him, bathed him, cleansed him of hatred and anger. He stood there smiling, not knowing why he smiled, feeling only peace and calmness.

The cloud began to lift; the Watcher was departing. The unheard note diminished in intensity, and the motion of the ground subsided. The Valley was at rest, in perfect harmony. The last faint murmur of the note died away.

For a long while no one spoke. Thornhill looked around, seeing an uncharacteristic blandness loosen the tight set of La Floquet's jaws, seeing Vellers' heavy-featured, angry face begin to smile. He himself felt no desire to quarrel with anyone.

But deep in his mind the words of the Watcher echoed and thrust at him: *Peace among you, my pets.*

Pets.

Not even specimens in a zoo, Thornhill thought with increasing bitterness as the tranquility induced by the subsonic began to leave him. Pets. Pampered pets.

He realized he was trembling. It had seemed so attractive, this life in the Valley. He tried to cry out, to shout his rage at the bare purple mountains that hemmed them in, but the subsonic had done its work well. He could not even vocalize his anger.

Thornhill looked away, trying to drive the Watcher's soothing words from his mind.

In the days that followed they began to grow younger. McKay, the oldest, was the first to show any effects of the rejuvenation. It was on the fourth day in the Valley—days being measured, for lack of other means, by the risings of the red sun. The nine of them had settled into a semblance of a normal way of life by that time. Since the time when the Watcher had found it necessary to calm them, there had been no outbreaks of bitterness among them; instead, each went about his daily life quietly, almost sullenly, under the numbing burden of the knowledge of their status as *pets*.

They found they had little need for sleep or food; the manna sufficed to nourish them, and as for sleep, that could be had in brief cat naps when the occasion demanded. They spent much of their time telling each other of their past lives, hiking through the Valley, swimming in the river. Thornhill was beginning to get terribly bored with this kind of existence.

McKay had been staring into the swiftly running current when he first noticed it. He emitted a short, sharp cry; Thornhill, thinking something was wrong, ran hurriedly toward him.

"What happened?"

McKay hardly seemed in difficulties. He was staring intently at his reflection in the water. "What color is my hair, Sam?"

"Why, gray—and—and a little touch of brown!" McKay nodded. "Exactly. I haven't had brown in my hair in twenty years!"

By this time most of the others had gathered. McKay indicated his hair and said, "I'm growing younger. I feel it all over. And look—look at La Floquet's scalp!"

In surprise the little man clapped one hand to the top of his skull—and drew the hand away again, thunderstruck. "I'm growing hair again," he said softly, fingering the gentle fuzz that had appeared on his tanned, sun-freckled scalp. There was a curious look of incredulity on his wrinkled brown face. "That's impossible!"

"It's also impossible for a man to rise from the dead," Thornhill pointed out. "The Watcher is taking very good care of us."

He looked at all of them—at McKay and La Floquet, at Vellers, at Marga, at Lona Hardin, at the aliens. Yes, they had all changed. They looked healthier, younger, more vigorous.

He had felt the change in himself from the start. The Valley, he thought. Was this the Watcher's doing or simply some marvelous property of the area?

Suppose the latter, he thought. Suppose through some charm of the Valley they were growing ever younger.

Would it stop? Would the process level off?

Or, he wondered, had the Watcher brought them all here solely for the interesting spectacle of observing nine adult beings retrogressing rapidly into childhood?

T hat "night"—they called the time when the red sun left the sky "night" even though there was no darkness—Thornhill learned three significant things.

He learned he loved Marga Fallis, and she him.

He learned that their love could have no possible consummation within the Valley.

And he learned that La Floquet, whatever had happened to him on the mountain peak, had not yet forgotten how to fight.

Thornhill had asked Marga to walk with him into the secluded wooded area high on the mountain path where they could have some privacy. She seemed oddly reluctant to accept, which surprised and dismayed him, for at all other times since the beginning she had gladly accepted any offers of his company. He urged her again, and finally she agreed.

They walked silently for a while. Gentle-eyed cat creatures peered at them from behind shrubs, and the air was moist and warm. Peaceful white clouds drifted high above them.

Thornhill said, "Why didn't you want to come with me, Marga?"

"I'd rather not talk about it," she said.

He shied a stone into the underbrush. "Four days, and you're keeping secrets from me already?" He started to chuckle; then, seeing her expression, he cut short his laughter. "What's wrong?"

"Is there any reason why I *shouldn't* keep secrets from you?" she asked. "I mean, is there some sort of agreement between us?"

He hesitated. "Of course not. But I thought—"

She smiled, reassuring him. "I thought, too. But I might as well be frank. This afternoon La Floquet asked me to be his woman."

Stunned, Thornhill stammered, "He—why—"

"He figures he's penned in here for life," Marga said. "And he's not interested in Lona. That leaves me, it seems. La Floquet doesn't like to go without women for long."

Thornhill moistened his lips but said nothing.

Marga went on. "He told me point-blank I wasn't to go into the hills with you anymore. That if I did, he'd make trouble. He wasn't going to take no for an answer, he told me."

"And what answer did you give—if I can ask?"

She smiled warmly; blue highlights danced in her dark eyes as she said, "Well—I'm here, aren't I? Isn't that a good enough answer to him?"

Relief swept over Thornhill like an unchecked tide. He had known of La Floquet's rivalry from the start, but this was the first time the little man had ever made any open overtures toward Marga. And if those overtures had been refused—

"La Floquet's interesting," she said as they stopped to enter a sheltered, sweet-smelling bower of thickly entwined shrubs. They had discovered it the night before. "But I wouldn't want to be number four hundred eighty-six on his string. He's a galaxy roamer; I've never fallen for that type. And I feel certain he'd never have been interested in me except as something to amuse him while he was penned up in this Valley."

She was very close to him, and in the bower not even the light of the blue star shone very brightly. *I love her,* he thought suddenly to himself, and an instant later he found his voice saying out loud, "I love you, Marga. Maybe it took a miracle to put us both in this Valley, but . . . "

"I know what you mean. And I love you, too. I told La Floquet that."

He felt an irrational surge of triumph. "What did he say?"

"Not much. He said he'd kill you if he could find some way to do it in the Valley. But I think that'll wear off soon."

His arm slipped around hers. They spoke wordlessly with one another for several moments.

It was then that Thornhill discovered that sex was impossible in the Valley. He felt no desire, no tingling of need, *nothing*.

Absolutely nothing. He enjoyed her nearness, but neither needed nor could take anything more.

"It's part of the Valley," he whispered. "Our entire metabolic systems have been changed. We don't sleep more than an hour a day, we hardly eat (unless you call that fluff food), our wounds heal, the dead rise—and now this. It's as if the Valley casts a spell that short-circuits all biological processes."

"And there's nothing we can do?"

"Nothing," he said tightly. "We're pets. Growing ever younger and helpless against the Watcher's whims."

He stared silently into the darkness, listening to her quiet sobbing. How long can we go on living this way, he wondered. How long?

We have to get out of this Valley, he thought. *Somehow.*

But will we remember one another once we do? Or will it all fade away like a child's dream of fairyland?

He clung tightly to her, cursing his own weakness even though he knew it was hardly his fault. There was nothing they could say to one another.

But the silence was abruptly broken.

A deep, dry voice said, "I know you're in there. Come on out, Thornhill. And bring the girl with you."

Thornhill quickly rose to a sitting position. "It's La Floquet!" he whispered.

"What are you going to do? Can he find us in here?"

"I'm sure of it. I'm going to have to go out there and see what he wants."

"Be careful, Sam!"

"He can't hurt me. This is the Valley, remember?" He grinned at her and clambered to his feet, stooping as he passed through the clustered underbrush. He blinked as he made the transition from darkness to pale light.

"Come on out of there, Thornhill!" La Floquet repeated. "I'll give you another minute, and then I'm coming in!"

"Don't fret," Thornhill called. "I'm on my way out."

He battled past two clinging, enwrapped vines and stepped into the open. "Well, what do you want?" he demanded impatiently.

La Floquet smiled coldly. There was little doubt of what he wanted. His small eyes were bright with anger, and there was murder in his grin. Held tight in one lean, corded hand was a long, triangular sliver of rock whose jagged edge had been painstakingly abraded until it was knife-sharp. The little man waited in a half-crouch, like a tiger or a panther impatient to spring on its prey.

Chapter Five

They circled tentatively around each other, the big man and the small one. La Floquet seemed to have reached a murderous pitch of intensity; muscles quivered in his jaws as he glared at Thornhill.

"Put that knife down," Thornhill said. "Have you blown your stack, La Floquet? You can't kill a man in the Valley. It won't work."

"Perhaps I can't kill a man. Still, I can wound him."

"What have I ever done to you?"

"You came to the Valley. I could have handled the others, but you—! You were the one who taunted me into climbing the mountain. You were the one who took Marga."

"I didn't take anyone. You didn't see me twisting her arm. She picked me over you, and for that I'm genuinely sorry."

"You'll be more than sorry, Thornhill!"

Thornhill forced a grin. This little kill dance had gone on too long as it was. He sensed Marga not far behind him watching in horror.

"Why you murderous little paranoid, give me that piece of stone before you slash yourself up!" He took a quick step forward, reaching for La Floquet's wrist. The little man's eyes blazed dangerously. He pirouetted backward, snapping a curse at Thornhill in some alien language, and drove the knife downward with a low, cry of triumph.

Thornhill swerved, but the jagged blade ripped into his arm three inches above the elbow, biting into the soft flesh on the inside of his biceps, and La Floquet sliced quickly downward, cutting a bloody trail for nearly eight inches. Thornhill felt a sudden sharp burst of pain down to the middle of his forearm, and a warm flow of blood gushed past his wrist into the palm of his hand. He heard Marga's sharp gasp.

Then he moved forward, ignoring the pain, and caught La Floquet's arm just as the smaller man was lifting it for a second slash. Thornhill twisted;

something snapped in La Floquet's arm, and the little man gave forth a brief moan of pain. The knife dropped from suddenly uncontrollable fingers and landed slightly on an angle, its tip resting on a pebble. Thornhill planted his foot on the dagger and leaned down heavily, shattering it.

Each of them now had only limited use of his right hand. La Floquet charged back toward Thornhill like someone possessed, head down as if to butt, but at the last moment swerved upward, driving his good hand into Thornhill's jaw. Thornhill rocked backward, pivoted around, smashed down at La Floquet, and heard teeth splinter. He wondered when the Watcher would show up to end the fight—and whether these wounds would heal.

La Floquet's harsh breathing was the only sound audible. He was shaking his head, clearing it, readying himself for a new assault. Thornhill tried to blank out the searing pain of the gash in his arm.

He stepped forward and hit La Floquet quickly, spinning him half around; bringing his slashed right hand up, Thornhill drove it into La Floquet's middle. A wall of rocklike muscle stunned his fist. But the breath had been knocked from La Floquet; he weaved uncertainly, gray-faced, wobbly-legged. Thornhill hit him again, and he toppled.

La Floquet crumpled into an awkward heap on the ground and stayed there. Thornhill glanced at his own arm. The cut was deep and wide, though it seemed to have missed any major veins and arteries; blood welled brightly from it, but without the familiar arterial spurt.

There was a curious fascination in watching his own blood flow. He saw Marga's pale, frightened face beyond the dim haze that surrounded him; he realized he had lost more blood than he thought, perhaps was about to lose consciousness as well. La Floquet still slumbered. There was no sign of the Watcher.

"Sam—"

"Pretty little nick, isn't it?" He laughed. His face felt warm.

"We ought to bind that some way. Infection—"

"No. There's no need of that. I'll be all right. This is the Valley."

He felt an intense itching in the wounded arm; barely did he fight back the desire to claw at the gash with his fingernails.

"It's—it's healing!" Marga said.

Thornhill nodded. The wound was beginning to close.

First the blood ceased flowing as ruptured veins closed their gaping sides and once again began to circulate the blood. The raw edges of the wound strained toward each other, puckering, reaching for one another, finally clasping. A bridge of flesh formed over the gaping slit in his arm. The itching was impossibly intense.

But in a few moments more it was over; a long livid scar remained, nothing more. Experimentally he touched the new flesh; it was warm, yielding, real.

La Floquet was stirring. His right forearm had been bent at an awkward angle; now it straightened out. The little man sat up groggily. Thornhill tensed in case further attack was coming, but there was very little fight left in La Floquet.

"The Watcher has made the necessary repairs," Thornhill said. "We're whole again except for a scar here and there. Get up, you idiot."

He hoisted La Floquet to his feet.

"This is the first time anyone has bested me in a fight," La Floquet said bitterly. His eyes had lost much of their eager brightness; he seemed demolished by his defeat. "And you were unarmed, and I had a knife."

"Forget that," Thornhill said.

"How can I? This filthy Valley—from which there is no escape, not even suicide—and I am not to have a woman. Thornhill, you're just a businessman. You don't know what it's like to set codes of behavior for yourself and then not be able to live by them." La Floquet shook his head sadly. "There are many in the galaxy who would rejoice to see the way this Valley has humiliated me. And there is not even suicide here! But I'll leave you with your woman."

He turned and began to walk away, a small, almost pathetic figure now, the fighting cock with his comb shorn and his tail feathers plucked. Thornhill contrasted him with the ebullient little figure he had first seen coming toward him up the mountain path, and it was a sad contrast indeed. He slouched now, shoulders sloping in defeat.

"Hold it, La Floquet!"

"You have beaten me—and before a woman. What more do you want with me, Thornhill?"

"How badly do you want to get out of this Valley?" Thornhill asked bluntly.

"What—"

"Badly enough to climb that mountain again?"

La Floquet's face, pale already, turned almost ghostly beneath his tan. In an unsteady voice he said, "I ask you not to taunt me, Thornhill."

"I'm not. I don't give a damn what phobia it is that drove you back from the mountain that night. I think that mountains can be climbed. But not by one or two men. If we *all* went up there—or most of us—"

La Floquet smiled wanly. "You would go, too? And Marga?"

"If it means out, yes. We might have to leave McKay and Lona Hardin behind, but there'd still he seven of us. Possibly there's a city outside the Valley; we might be able to send word and be rescued."

Frowning, La Floquet said, "Why the sudden change of heart, Thornhill? I thought you liked it here . . . you and Miss Fallis both, that is. I thought *I* was the only one willing to climb that peak."

Thornhill glanced at Marga and traded secret smiles with her. "I'll decline to answer that, La Floquet. But I'll tell you this: The quicker I'm outside the influence of the Valley, the happier I'll be!"

When they had reached the foot of the hill and called everyone together, Thornhill stepped forward. Sixteen eyes were on him—counting the two stalked objects of the Spican as eyes.

He said, "La Floquet and I have just had a little discussion up in the hill. We've reached a few conclusions I want to put forth to the group at large.

"I submit that it's necessary for the well-being of all of us to make an immediate attempt at getting out of the Valley. Otherwise, we're condemned to a slow death of the most horrible kind—gradual loss of our faculties."

McKay broke in, saying, "Now you've shifted sides again, Thornhill! I thought maybe—"

"I haven't been on any side," he responded quickly. "It's simply that I've begun thinking. Look: We were all brought here within a two-day span, snatched out of our lives no matter where we were, dumped down in a seemingly impassable Valley by some unimaginably alien creature. Item: We're watched constantly, tended and fed. Item: Our wounds heal almost instantly. Item: We're growing younger. McKay, you yourself were the first to notice that.

"Okay, now. There's a mountain up there, and quite probably there's a way out of the Valley. La Floquet tried to get there, but he and Vellers couldn't make it; two men can't climb a twenty-thousand-foot peak alone without provisions, without help. But if we all go—"

McKay shook his head. "I'm happy here, Thornhill. You and La Floquet are jeopardizing that happiness."

"No," La Floquet interjected. "Can't you see that we're just house pets here? That we're the subjects of a rather interesting experiment, nothing more? And that if this rejuvenation keeps up, we may all be babies in a matter of weeks or months?"

"I don't care," McKay said stubbornly. "`I'll die if I leave the Valley—my heart can't take much more. Now you tell me I'll die if I stay. But at least I'll pass backward through manhood before I go—and I can't have those years again outside."

"All right," Thornhill said. "Ultimately it's a matter of whether we all stay here so McKay can enjoy his youth again, or whether we try to leave. La Floquet, Marga, and I are going to make an attempt to cross the mountain. Those of you who want to join us can. Those of you who'd rather spend the rest of their days in the Valley can stay behind and wish us bad luck. Is that clear?"

Seven of them left the following "morning," right after the breakfast-time manna fall. McKay stayed behind with little Lona Hardin. There was a brief, awkward moment of farewell-saying. Thornhill noticed how the lines were leaving McKay's face, how the old scholar's hair had darkened, his body broadened. In a way he could see McKay's point of view, but there was no way he could accept it.

Lona Hardin, too, was younger looking, and perhaps for the first time in her life she was making an attempt to disguise her plainness. Well, Thornhill thought, these two might find happiness of a sort in the Valley, but it was the mindless happiness of a puppet, and he wanted none of it for himself.

"I don't know what to say," McKay declared as the party set out. "I'd wish you good luck—if I could."

Thornhill grinned. "Maybe we'll be seeing you two again. I hope not, though."

Thornhill led the way up the mountain's side; Marga walked with him, La Floquet and Vellers a few paces behind, the three aliens trailing behind them. The Spican, Thornhill was sure, had only the barest notion of what was taking place; the Aldebaranian had explained things fairly thoroughly to the grave Regulan. One factor seemed common: All of them were determined to leave the Valley.

The morning was warm and pleasant; clouds hid the peak of the mountain. The ascent, Thornhill thought, would be strenuous but not impossible—provided the miraculous field of the Valley continued to protect them when they passed the timberline and provided the Watcher did not interfere with the exodus.

There was no interference. Thornhill felt almost a sensation of regret at leaving the Valley and in the same moment realized this might be some deceptive trick of the Watcher's, and he cast all sentiment from his heart.

By midmorning they had reached a considerable height, a thousand feet or more above the Valley. Looking down, Thornhill could barely see the brightness of the river winding through the flat basin that was the Valley, and there was no sign of McKay far below.

The mountain sloped gently upward toward the timberline. The real struggle would begin later, perhaps, on the bare rock face, where the air might not be so balmy as it was here, the wind not quite as gentle.

When Thornhill's watch said noon, he called a halt and they unpacked the manna—wrapped in broad, coarse, velvet-textured leaves of the thick-trunked trees of the Valley—they had saved from the morning fall. The manna tasted dry and stale, almost like straw, with just the merest vestige of its former attractive flavor. But as Thornhill had guessed, there was no noontime manna fall here on the mountain slope, and so the party forced the dry stuff down their throats, not knowing when they would have fresh food again.

After a short rest Thornhill ordered them up. They had gone no more than a thousand feet when an echoing cry drifted up from below:

"Wait! Wait, Thornhill!"

He turned. "You hear something?" he asked Marga.

"That was McKay's voice," La Floquet said.

"Let's wait for him," Thornhill ordered.

Ten minutes passed, and then McKay came into view, running upward in a springy long-legged stride, Lona Hardin a few paces behind him. He caught up with the party and paused a moment, catching his breath.

"I decided to come along," he said finally. "You're right, Thornhill! We have to leave the Valley."

"And he figures his heart's better already," Lona Hardin said. "So if he leaves the Valley now, maybe he'll be a healthier man again:'

Thornhill smiled. "It took a long time to convince you, didn't it?" He shaded his eyes and stared upward. "We have a long way to go. We'd better not waste any more time."

Chapter Six

Twenty thousand feet is less than four miles. A man should be able to walk four miles in an hour or two. But not four miles *up*.

They rested frequently, though there was no night and they had no need to sleep. They moved on inch by inch, advancing perhaps five hundred feet over the steadily more treacherous slope, then crawling along the mountain face a hundred feet to find the next point of ascent. It was slow, difficult work, and the mountain spired yet higher above them until it seemed they would never attain the summit.

The air, surprisingly, remained warm, though not oppressively so; the wind picked up as they climbed. The mountain was utterly bare of life; the gentle animals of the Valley ventured no higher than the timberline, and that was far below. The party of nine scrambled up over rock falls and past sheets of stone.

Thornhill felt himself tiring, but he knew the Valley's strange regenerative force was at work, carrying off the fatigue poisons as soon as they built up in his muscles, easing him, giving him the strength to go on. Hour after hour they forced their way up the mountainside.

Occasionally he would glance back to see La Floquet's pale, fear-tautened face. The little man was terrified of the height, but he was driving gamely on. The aliens straggled behind; Vellers marched mechanically, saying little, obviously tolerant of the weaker mortals to whose pace he was compelled to adjust his own.

As for Marga, she uttered no complaint. That pleased Thornhill more than anything.

They were a good thousand feet from the summit when Thornhill called a halt.

He glanced back at them—at the oddly unweary, unlined faces. *How we've grown young!* he thought suddenly. *McKay looks like a man in his late forties; I must seem like a boy. And we're all fresh as daisies, as if this were just a jolly hike.*

"We're near the top," he said. "Let's finish off whatever of the manna we've got. The downhill part of this won't be so bad."

He looked up. The mountain tapered to a fine crest, and through there a pass leading down to the other side was visible. "La Floquet, you've got the best eyes of any of us. You see any sign of a barrier up ahead?"

The little man squinted and shook his head. "All's clear so far as I can see. We go up, then down, and we're home free."

Thornhill nodded. "The last thousand feet, then. Let's go!"

The wind was whipping hard against them as they pushed on through the dense snow that cloaked the mountain's highest point. Up here some of the charm of the Valley seemed to be gone, as if the cold winds barreling in from the outlands beyond the crest could in some way negate the gentle warmth they experienced in the Valley. Both suns were high in the sky, the red and the blue, the blue visible as a hard blotch of radiance penetrating the soft, diffuse rays of the red.

Thornhill was tiring rapidly, but the crest was in sight. Just a few more feet and they'd stand on it—

Just up over this overhang—

The summit itself was a small plateau, perhaps a hundred feet long. Thornhill was the first to pull himself up over the rock projection and stand on the peak; he reached back, helped Marga up, and within minutes the other seven had joined them.

The Valley was a distant spot of green far below; the air was clear and clean, and from here they could plainly see the winding river heading down valley to the yellow-green radiance of the barrier.

Thornhill turned. "Look down there," he said in a quiet voice.

"It's a world of deserts!" La Floquet exclaimed.

The view from the summit revealed much of the land beyond the Valley, and it seemed the Valley was but an oasis in the midst of utter desertion. For mile after gray mile, barren land stretched before them, an endless plain of rock and sand rolling on drearily to the farthest horizon.

Beyond, this. Behind, the Valley.

Thornhill looked around. "We've reached the top. You see what's ahead. Do we go on?"

"Do we have any choice?" McKay asked. "We're practically out of the Watcher's hands now. Down there perhaps we have freedom. Behind us—"

"We go on," La Floquet said firmly.

"Down the back slope, then," said Thornhill. "It won't be easy. There's the path over there. Suppose we—"

The sudden chill he felt was not altogether due to the whistling wind. The sky suddenly darkened; a cloak of night settled around them.

Of course, Thornhill thought dully. *I should have foreseen this.*

"The Watcher's coming!" Lona Hardin screamed as the darkness, obscuring both the bleakness ahead and the Valley behind, closed around them.

Thornhill thought, *It was part of the game. To let us climb the mountain, to watch us squirm and struggle, and then to hurl us back into the Valley at the last moment as we stand on the border.*

Wings of night nestled around them. He felt the coldness that signified the alien presence, and the soft voice said, *Would you leave, my pets? Don't I give you the best of care? Why this ingratitude?*

"Let's keep going," Thornhill muttered. "Maybe it can't stop us. Maybe we can escape it yet."

"Which way do we go?" Marga asked. "I can't see anything. Suppose we go over the edge?"

Come, crooned the Watcher, *come back to the Valley. You have played your little game. I have enjoyed your struggles, and I'm proud of the battle you fought. But the time has come to return to the warmth and the love you may find in the Valley below—*

"Thornhill!" cried La Floquet suddenly, hoarsely. "I have it! Come help me!"

The Watcher's voice died away abruptly; the black cloud swirled wildly. Thornhill whirled, peering through the darkness for some sign of La Floquet—

And found the little man on the ground, wrestling with—something. In the darkness, it was hard to tell—

"It's the Watcher!" La Floquet grunted. He rolled over, and Thornhill saw a small snakelike being writhing under La Floquet's grip, a bright-scaled serpent the size of a monkey.

"Here in the middle of the cloud—*here's* the creature that held us here!" La Floquet cried. Suddenly, before Thornhill could move, the Aldebaranian came bounding forward, thrusting beyond Thornhill and Marga, and flung himself down on the strugglers. Thornhill heard a guttural bellow; the darkness closed in on the trio, and it was impossible to see what was happening.

He heard La Floquet's cry: "Get . . . this devil . . . off me! He's helping the Watcher!"

Thornhill moved forward. He reached into the struggling mass, felt the blubbery flesh of the Aldebaranian, and dug his fingers in hard. He wrenched; the Aldebaranian came away. Hooked claws raked Thornhill's face. He cursed; you could never tell what an Aldebaranian was likely to do at any time. Perhaps the creature had been in league with the Watcher all along.

He dodged a blow, landed a solid one in the alien's plump belly, and crashed his other fist upward into the creature's jaw. The Aldebaranian rocked backward. Vellers appeared abruptly from nowhere and seized the being.

"No!" Thornhill yelled, seeing what Vellers intended. But it was too late. The giant held the Aldebaranian contemptuously dangling in the air, then swung him upward and outward. A high ear-piercing shriek resounded. Thornhill shuddered. It takes a long time to fall twenty thousand feet.

He glanced back now at La Floquet and saw the small man struggling to stand up, arms still entwined about the serpentlike being. Thornhill saw a metalmesh helmet on the alien's head. The means by which they'd been controlled, perhaps.

La Floquet took three staggering steps. "Get the helmet off him!" he cried thickly. "I've seen these before. They are out of the Andromeda sector . . . telepaths, teleports . . . deadly creatures. The helmet's his focus point."

Thornhill grasped for it as the pair careened by; he missed, catching instead a glimpse of the Watcher's devilish, hate-filled eyes. The Watcher had fallen into the hands of his own pets—and was not enjoying it.

"I can't see you!" Thornhill shouted. "I can't get the helmet!"

"If he gets free, we're finished," came La Floquet's voice. "He's using all his energy to fight me off . . . but all he needs to do is turn on the subsonics—"

The darkness cleared again. Thornhill gasped. La Floquet, still clutching the alien, was tottering on the edge of the mountain peak, groping for the helmet in vain. One of the little man's feet was virtually standing on air. He staggered wildly. Thornhill rushed toward them, grasped the icy metal of the helmet, and ripped it away.

In that moment both La Floquet and the Watcher vanished from sight. Thornhill brought himself up short and peered downward, hearing nothing, seeing nothing—

There was just one scream . . . not from La Floquet's throat but from the alien's. Then all was silent. Thornhill glanced at the helmet in his hands, thinking of La Floquet, and in a sudden impulsive gesture hurled the little metal headpiece into the abyss after them.

He turned, catching one last glimpse of Marga, Vellers, McKay, Lona Hardin, the Regulan, and the Spican. Then, before he could speak, mountain peak and darkness and indeed the entire world shimmered and heaved dizzyingly about them, and he could see nothing and no one.

He was in the main passenger cabin of the Federation Spaceliner *Royal Mother Helene* bound for Vengamon out of Jurinalle. He was lying back in the comfortable pressurized cabin, the gray nothingness of hyperspace outside forming a sharp contrast to the radiant walls of the cabin, which glowed in soft yellow luminescence.

Thornhill opened his eyes slowly. He glanced at his watch: *12:13, 7 July 2671*. He had dozed off about 11:40 after a good lunch. They were due in at Port Vengamon later that day, and he would have to tend to mine business immediately. There was no telling how badly they had fouled things up in the time he had been vacationing on Jurinalle.

He blinked. Of a sudden, strange images flashed into his eyes—a valley somewhere on a barren, desolate planet beyond the edge of the galaxy. A mountain peak, and a strange alien being, and a brave little man falling to the death he dreaded, and a girl—

It couldn't have been a dream, he told himself. *No.*

Not a dream. It was just that the Watcher yanked us out of space-time for his little experiment, and when I destroyed the helmet, we re-entered the continuum at the instant we had left it.

A cold sweat burst out suddenly all over his body. *That means,* he thought, *that La Floquet's not dead. And Marga—Marga—*

Thornhill sprang from his gravity couch, ignoring the sign that urged him to PLEASE REMAIN IN YOUR COUCH WHILE SHIP IS UNDERGOING SPIN, and rushed down the aisle toward the steward. He gripped the man by the shoulder, spun him around.

"Yes, Mr. Thornhill? Is anything wrong? You could have signaled me, and—"

"Never mind that. I want to make a subradio call to Bellatrix VII."

"We'll be landing on Vengamon in a couple of hours, sir. Is it so urgent?"

"Yes:'

The steward shrugged. "You know, of course, that shipboard subradio calls may take some time to put through, and that they're terribly expensive—"

"Damn the expense, man! Will you put through my call or won't you?"

"Of course, Mr. Thornhill. To whom?"

He paused and said carefully, "To Miss Marga Fallis, in some observatory on Bellatrix VII." He peeled a bill from his wallet and added, "Here. There'll be another one for you if the call's put through in the next half an hour. I'll wait."

T he summons finally came. "Mr. Thornhill, your call's ready. Would you come to Communications Deck, please?"

They showed him to a small, dimly lit cubicle. There could be no vision on an interstellar subradio call, of course, just voice transmission. But that would be enough. "Go ahead, Bellatrix-*Helene*. The call is ready," an operator said.

Thornhill wet his lips. "Marga? This is Sam—Sam Thornhill!"

"Oh!" He could picture her face now. "It—it wasn't a dream, then. I was so afraid it was!"

"When I threw the helmet off the mountain, the Watcher's hold was broken. Did you return to the exact moment you had left?"

"Yes," she said. "Back in the observatory, with my camera plates and everything. And there was a call for me, and at first I was angry and wouldn't answer it the way I always won't answer, and then I thought a minute and had a wild idea and changed my mind—and I'm glad I did, darling!"

"It seems almost like a dream, doesn't it? The Valley, I mean. And La Floquet, and all the others. But it wasn't any dream," Thornhill said. "We were really there. And I meant the things I said to you."

The operator's voice cut in sharply: *"Standard call time has elapsed, sir. There will be an additional charge of ten credits for each further fifteen-second period of your conversation."*

"That's quite all right, Operator," Thornhill said. "Just give me the bill at the end. Marga, are you still there?"

"Of course, darling."

"When can I see you?"

"I'll come to Vengamon tomorrow. It'll take a day or so to wind things up here at the observatory. Is there an observatory on Vengamon?"

"I'll build you one," Thornhill promised. "And perhaps for our honeymoon we can go looking for the Valley."

"I don't think we'll ever find it," she said. "But we'd better hang up now. Otherwise you'll become a pauper talking to me."

He stared at the dead phone a long moment after they broke contact, thinking of what Marga looked like, and La Floquet, and all the others. Above all, Marga.

It wasn't a dream, he told himself. He thought of the shadow-haunted Valley where night never fell and men grew younger, and of a tall girl with dark flashing eyes who waited for him now half a galaxy away.

With quivering fingers he undid the sleeve of his tunic and looked down at the long, livid scar that ran almost the length of his right arm, almost to the wrist. Somewhere in the universe now was a little man named La Floquet who had inflicted that wound and died and returned to his point of departure, who now was probably wondering if it had all ever happened. Thornhill smiled, forgiving La Floquet for the ragged scar inscribed on his arm, and headed up the companionway to the passenger cabin, impatient now to see Vengamon once more.

Hunt the Space-Witch!

Chapter One

I t was Barsac's second day on Glaurus, and the first moment of free time he had had since the ship had landed. Before that there had been the landing routines, the spaceport men to bribe, the inspectors to cajole, the jet alleys to scrub. But on the second day withered old Captain Jaspell called the men of the *Dywain* together and told them they might have five days' leave before departure.

Barsac smiled. He was a lean man, tall and well-muscled, with the chiselled scars of the Luaspar blood-rites fanning out radially from the edges of his thin lips. He was an Earther, thirty-nine years old; twenty of those thirty-nine years had been spent as a spaceman, the last eight as Second Fuelman aboard Captain Jaspell's *Dywain*. He rose in the crowded cabin where the crew had assembled to hear Jaspell's words and said, "Captain, is that job on Repair Deck still open?"

Jaspell nodded. He was a desiccated Earther of a hundred and three years, still keen of mind and iron of discipline. "You know it is, Barsac."

"And you're planning to fill the post while we stop over on Glaurus?"

"I am."

"I ask you to wait a day before publishing notice of the vacancy, then. I know a man on Glaurus who would fill your need. His name is Zigmunn. He's a Luasparru. He's my blood-brother, Captain."

"Bring him to me today or tomorrow," Jaspell said. "I can't wait any longer than that to find a replacement. Is he qualified?"

"I swear it."

"We shall see, Barsac. Bring him here."

An hour later Barsac dismounted from the spaceport-to-city tube and found himself in the heart of the city of Millyaurr, oldest and greatest on Glaurus. It was a city of twenty-one million people and its population hailed from at least a hundred fifty worlds. Barsac found‑ himself jostled by scrawny blue dwarfs and fat gray-skinned Domrani patriarchs as he made his way down the ancient street. From the shops that lined the road came the smells of wine and raw meat, of newly baked bread and of festering cabbages.

Zigmunn had said in his letter that he lived now in the Street of Tears in the central residential zone of Millyaurr. Barsac paused to ask directions of a wizened old vender of stimulotubes, and cordially declined the offer of a tube at a large discount. He made his way forward.

It was ten years since he had last seen Zigmunn, though it did not seem that long. The Luasparru was an agile, quick-witted man who had formed a fine complement for Barsac's stolid massive strength, and they had hit it off immediately when they shipped off Vuorrleg together more than a decade back. The ship they were on was making a stop at Luaspar, Zigmunn's home-world; Barsac had gone to the home of Zigmunn's cognate kin and there they had gone through the agonizing Luaspar rites of blood-fealty, bound to each other in friendship forever by the scars that lined their lips.

Then they had left Luaspar and gone on. And they had stopped for a while on Glaurus a year later, and became separated in a bar-room brawl, and Barsac had returned to the ship alone, without his blood-brother. The ship had blasted off without him. At his next port, Barsac found a letter waiting for him from Zigmunn; the Luasparru, stranded, had been unable to get a berth on any other ship out of Glaurus, and was biding his time, waiting for an offer.

Shortly after Barsac transferred into Jaspell's ship, the *Dywain*, and wrote to Zigmunn to tell him where he was; the Luasparru replied he was still stranded, but had high hopes of returning to space soon.

Eight years went by, and Zigmunn's letters became less frequent as no sign of a berth materialized, and finally Barsac learned that the *Dywain* was due to visit Glaurus as part of a journey out to the Rim. Then came word that the *Dywain* would be taking on an additional crewman on Glaurus, and Barsac rejoiced at the thought of being reunited with the Luasparru after so long.

The glowing placard against the side of a weathered old building read: *Street of Tears*. Zigmunn lived at number eighty-one in the Street of Tears. Barsac looked for a house-number.

He found one: thirty-six. He crossed the street, which was narrow and reeked of the garbage of millennia, and headed up the cracked and blistered pavement. It was long ages since the slidewalk had functioned in the Street of Tears; probably the underground mechanisms had rusted into decay centuries ago, and the inhabitants had simply stripped away the metal of the slidewalk and sold it for scrap, leaving the naked concrete exposed beneath. The buildings loomed high, blotting out the golden light of Glaurus' sun.

Sixty-nine, seventy-one, seventy-three. Barsac crossed another street. He swore. Had Zigmunn been living in this filth for eight years?

Seventy-seven. Seventy-nine.

Eighty-one.

The street was crowded; aliens of all descriptions, swaggering native-born Glaurans, even a few curious folk who wore silver reflecting-masks that

obscured all of their faces but their eyes and who walked in solitary gran-
deur, alone and given a wide berth by others on the street. Barsac turned his
attention toward the house.

It was old and weary-looking, a drab place of crumbling yellow brick. He
went in. A directory in the dingy lobby yielded the information that Zigmunn
lived on the third floor, room 32-A. There was no sign of a liftshaft; Barsac took
the creaking stairs.

He knocked once at the door of 32-A before he noticed that a shutter had
been drawn across it and a gleaming lock affixed. Dust stippled the lock and
the shutter; both had been in place more than a little while.

Barsac turned. He pounded on the door of 33-A, and after a moment it
opened, hesitantly.

"I'm looking for Zigmunn the Luasparru," he said.

He faced a tiny gnome of a woman who gaped toothlessly at him in confusion. She wore a mildew flecked wrap that had probably been the height of
fashion seventy or eighty years before, on some other world.

"Who?"

"Zigmunn of Luaspar. The man who lived or lives in the room next to yours."
He pointed. "A very thin man about my height, with bronze skin and scars
around his lips. Scars like these." He bent close, showing her.

"Oh. Him. He went away. Two, three, maybe four weeks ago. Hasn't been
back since. Would you stop in for tea with me? A young man like you must be
very thirsty."

"No, thanks. Three or four weeks ago? Did he say where he was going?"

She giggled shrilly. "Not to me. But he wasn't fooling anybody. Him with all
that drinking and his women and the noise and knives, there was only one
place *he* would decide he wanted to go, don't you know?"

"I don't know. Where?"

Again the giggle, oddly girlish. "Oh, *you* know. I can't say. It really isn't right."

"Where?" Barsac demanded again, loudly this time. His voice seemed to stir
up eddies of dust in the darkened hallway.

"Really, I—"

The door of 34-A popped open suddenly and a fierce-looking Dlarochrene
stuck his wattled head out and snapped, "What's all the noise out here? Get
back in your room, old fossil. Who are you? What do you want?"

"I'm looking for Zigmunn of Luaspar," Barsac said stonily as the old woman
slammed shut her door and threw the bolt. "He's a friend of mine. I'd like to
find him."

"The Luasparru hasn't been here for weeks."

"That's what the old lady told me. I want to know where he's gone."

"You mean you can't guess?"

"I'm a spacer. I haven't been on Glaurus in nine or ten years. I don't know
anything much about this planet."

"I suggest you find out, then. And if you're a friend of *his*, I don't want to talk
to you. Go downstairs to the bar. You'll find some of his friends there. They'll
tell you where he is."

The door shut abruptly.

Barsac stared at the peeling wood a moment, then turned away, wondering what all this meant, what Zigmunn had done, where he was now. Questions were piling up rapidly. Barsac did not care for complications.

The bar was on street level, a dark low-ceilinged hovel that stank of stale beer. Barsac peered in; five or six habitués sat slumped at crude little wooden tables, and an Earthman bartender waited boredly behind his bar. With elaborate casualness Barsac sauntered in.

He spun a Galactic unit on the dull surface of the bar and asked for a drink. Lazily the bartender poured it, spilling half. Barsac smiled and drained the glass.

"Give me another," he said. "And make it full measure or I'll split your throat."

He put another coin next to the first one. Without responding the bartender poured him another, this time filling the glass to the brim. Again Barsac drained it in a gulp. Then he leaned forward, stared bluntly into the cold flat eyes of the barkeep, and said in a low voice, "I'm looking for a man named Zigmunn, a Luasparru. Know where he might be?"

Unsmilingly the barkeep pointed across the dark room to a figure slumped at a far table.

"Ask her."

"Thanks," Barsac said. "I will."

He crossed the bar-room to the girl's table, pulled out the chair opposite hers, and sat down. She looked up as he did so, but the glance she gave him was without any interest or curiosity; she simply looked at him because he was there, not because she cared about him.

"Buy me a drink," she said tonelessly.

"Later. I want to talk to you first."

"I don't talk to people. Buy me a drink. My room's on the fourth floor if you're looking for sport. If you just want to humiliate me, don't bother. It can't be done. Better men than you have tried."

He looked at her strangely. She was young—eighteen, maybe, twenty at most, and she was either an Earther herself or else mainly of Earther descent. Her corn-yellow hair fell carelessly over her shoulders; she wore a faded cling-on sweater that wrapped itself skin-tight against her slender body and in Zwihih style was cut to leave the nipples of her breasts bare. Her throat and face were dark in color, but whether it was from suntan or dirt Barsac could not tell. Her eyes were not the eyes of a girl of eighteen; they looked older than those of the woman he had seen upstairs.

"I guess I'd better buy you a drink," Barsac said. He held up two fingers to the watching barkeep.

This time he sipped his drink; she gulped hers, but showed no animation afterward. Gently he said, "My name is Barsac. Ever hear it before?"

"No. Should I have?"

"I thought a friend of mine might have mentioned it to you sometime. A friend named Zigmunn."

"What do you know of Zigmunn?" Her voice was flat and empty; it seemed to come from just back of her teeth, not out of her chest.

"I'm his blood-kin. You see the scars around my lips? Zigmunn has them too."

"*Had* them. Zigmunn has no face at all by now."

Barsac's hands gripped the ragged wood of the table tightly. "What do you mean by that?"

For the first time the girl smiled. "Do you want me to tell you? Really?"

"I want to know where Zigmunn is."

"He isn't on Glaurus right now, that's for sure. I'm thirsty again."

"You'll get your drink when you tell me where he is. If he isn't on Glaurus, where is he?"

"Azonda," she said.

Barsac blinked. Azonda was the eleventh planet of the system to which Glaurus belonged; Barsac cast back in his memory and recalled that the planet was without an atmosphere and so far from its sun that it was virtually without light as well—a cold, dead world. The thought came to him then that the girl must be either drunk or insane.

"Azonda?"

She nodded. "He left three weeks ago. He and I had a little party the night before he left. And then he left. For Azonda."

Frowning, Barsac asked, "What in the name of space would he do on Azonda?"

She looked oddly at him. "You mean that, don't you? You're perfectly sincere? No. You want to tease me. Well, I won't be teased." Her eyes, which for a moment had come alive, lapsed back to their former brooding deadness, and she let her shoulders sag.

He grasped her arm. "I'm a stranger on Glaurus. I *don't* know about Azonda. And I want to find Zigmunn. There's a berth open on my ship for him, if he wants it. We're leaving in five days for the rim stars. Tell me: what's he doing on Azonda? Or is this a joke?"

Quietly she said, "You came three weeks too late, if you have a ship's berth for him. Forget about Zigmunn. Go back to your ship and stop looking for him."

He squeezed her arm mercilessly. "Will you tell me where he is?"

She paled under his grip, and he released her. "One more drink." she pleaded.

Barsac shrugged and ordered the drink for her; none for himself. She tossed it down and said slowly, "Azonda is the headquarters for the Cult of the Witch. Three weeks ago Zigmunn joined the Cult. I was invited to join but I turned it down—because I haven't fallen quite that low yet. Yet. Anyway, he joined. He's on Azonda right now, undergoing initiation. And worshipping the Witch. I don't want to talk about these things down here. If you want more information, come upstairs to my room."

Chapter Two

It was a small room, well-kept and clean despite the great age of the building. There was little furniture: a cheap chair, a writing-desk, a vidset, and a bed wide enough for two. Barsac followed her through the door numbly, thinking of Zigmunn and wondering what iniquity the Luasparru had fallen into now.

She switched on the light; it was dim and uncertain. She locked the door. Gesturing for him to take the chair, she sprawled down on the bed. She hiked her flowing skirt up to her thighs, crossed her legs, and stared expectantly at him.

"Who are you?" he asked.

"My name is Kassa Jidrill, and I'm a party girl with a free permit. It's the best sort of work a girl can get these days, if you have a liking for the work. I don't, but I get along . . . sometimes. My mother was an Earther. Now you know all that's worth knowing about me."

He studied her. Her legs were slim and well turned, and some of the deep despair of a few moments before had left her. But he had not come to Millyaurr to play with party girls.

He said, "I'm looking for Zigmunn. You say he's on Azonda. Would you swear to it?"

"I'd swear by my chastity," she said acidly. "I told you he was there prancing and dancing around the Witch, no doubt. Believe me or not, as you choose."

His jaws tightened. "How can I get to Azonda, then?"

"You can't. At least no certified spaceline will take you there. You might try hiring a jackrogue spacer to ferry you there. Or you could join the Cult and get a free passage, but that's a little drastic. Save your money and your time. There's no way out of the Cult once you're in."

Rising, Barsac came toward her and sat on the edge of the bed. "Zigmunn and I are blood-kin. We've been separated ten years. I don't care what filth he's been forced to wallow in; I'm going to bring him out."

"Noble aims. But foolish."

"Perhaps so." He laid one hand on her bare thigh; it felt cool to the touch. "I need help, though. I have only five days on Glaurus and the world is strange to me. I need someone to explain things to me."

"And I'm nominated, eh?"

"You knew Zigmunn. You could help."

She yawned. "If I wanted to. But the Cult's a dangerous proposition. Go downstairs and buy a bottle then come back. Forget Zigmunn. He's as good as dead."

"No!"

"No?" She shrugged lightly. "Have it your way, then. You're a strong and a stubborn man, Barsac. As much of an opposite to Zigmunn as anyone could imagine."

"How can I get to Azonda?"

"Forget Zigmunn," she crooned. She twisted sharply and toppled toward him, grasping his shoulders tightly in her arms, pulling him toward her. Her pale blonde hair tumbled in his eyes; it smelled of a sweet oil.

"No," he said suddenly, and rose.

For an instant anger and hatred glared in Kassa's eyes; then she softened. "Another failure, I see. In these times it's hard for a party girl to earn her keep; the men prefer to chase around in quest of dissolute blood-brothers. Very well, then. I'll take you to Lord Carnothute."

"Who?"

"Governor of Millyaurr Province."

"How could he help me?" Barsac asked.

Her voice dropped to a barely audible whisper. "He is also a ranking official of the Cult, though few know it. Most Cult members wear the silver mask that hides their face, to symbolize the facelessness of the Witch. Lord Carnothute has special privilege, because of his rank. He was the agent offered Culthood to Zigmunn and to me, one night that he spent here. Perhaps he could tell you where your blood-brother is. Maybe Zigmunn hasn't been sent to Azonda yet; they don't always leave right away. And in that case there's still a chance for him."

The governor's palace was an airy pencil of a building far to the north of the Street of Tears; it took Barsac and Kassa more than an hour by aircab to get there.

She had shed her party-girl costume and was wearing something more demure, a black silk dress and veil; quite unconcernedly she had stripped to the buff and changed with Barsac in the room, and he had eyed her body with interest but not with desire. He had long ago learned to channel his energies, and now the finding of Zigmunn occupied center stage in his mind; all else was inconsequential to him.

The air was cleaner in the district of Millyaurr they now entered. They approached the palace gate. Barsac noticed figures in the silvery mask of the Cult moving through the streets, always alone.

They entered. Kassa spoke briefly to a guard. They were conducted through an antechamber, down a broad and well-lit corridor, and into a liftshaft.

"He gave me a password I could use any time I wanted to come to him," Kassa explained. "Ordinarily it's not easy to get to see him."

The liftshaft opened; they stepped out. Immediately Kassa threw herself to the ground in a forehead-to-the-floor genuflection; Barsac remained erect, staring at the man who faced them.

He was tall, nearly seven feet in height, and correspondingly broad. He wore a ruffle of chocolate-colored lace, a skin-tight tunic, a bright sash of emerald-studded platinum. His hair was artificially silvered and glinted metallically; his eyes, too, were silvered. He smiled, but there was little warmth in the smile.

Kassa rose and spoke the word she had said to the guard before. Lord Carnothute frowned a moment, then smiled again and said in a rumbling voice, "You are the girl Kassa. Who is your friend?"

"My name is Barsac. I'm a spacer in off the *Dywain*, that put down here yesterday."

The governor led them to a smaller, intricately furnished room within, and Barsac suddenly found himself holding a crystal flask of liquor. He touched it to his lips; it was sweet, but promised to be explosively potent.

Kassa said, "He came to me this morning about the Luasparru Zigmunn."

Immediately shadows crossed Carnothute's massive calm face. "You refused the offer, Kassa. Zigmunn is no longer concern of his or yours."

"He was—*is*—blood-kin of mine," Barsac said thickly. "I want to find him. There's a job waiting for him on my ship, the *Dywain*.'"

"And how could I help you find him, my good man?"

Barsac glowered unblinkingly at the ponderous nobleman. "Kassa has told me about what has happened to Zigmunn and of your connection with the organization to which he now belongs."

Kassa gasped. Carnothute scowled briefly, but merely said, "Go on."

"I don't know anything about this Cult," Barsac said. "I don't have any moral objections to it, and I don't give a damn who belongs to it or what sort of foul rites may be involved. I'm only interested in Zigmunn. The blood tie is a strong one. I didn't do this to my face without thinking about it a couple of times first. I want to know where he is, and if he's still on Glaurus I want to be allowed to see him and tell him there's a berth available for him on the *Dywain* if he claims it this week."

Carnothute steepled his thick fingers. He showed no sign of displeasure, none of anger, but Barsac had had experience with men of his size before; they held their anger in check for fear of crushing the smaller creatures who lived in the world, but when their rage exploded it was a fearful thing. Slowly the governor said, "Your blood-brother is not on Glaurus."

Kassa shot a quick meaningful glance at Barsac. *I told you so*, she seemed to be telling him, but he chose to ignore it.

"Where is he, then?"

"He left for Azonda fifteen days ago with the most recent group of initiates to our—ah—organization."

"And how can I get to Azonda, then?"

"There is no way."

Barsac let those words soak in for a moment, while he finished off the drink Carnothute had given him. The governor seemed oppressively big, smug on account of his size. Barsac found himself longing to slip a knife between the ribs of that great frame.

At length he said, "How long will it be before he returns to Glaurus?"

"Perhaps never. Or, again, perhaps tomorrow. The novitiate lasts a year on Azonda; after that he is free to go where he wishes, so long as he maintains his loyalty. There is a mask that is normally worn, too. Cult members rarely bother to conceal the fact of their membership, unless there are reasons that make such concealment necessary."

"Such as being governor of a big province of Glaurus?" Barsac said sharply.

Carnothute let the thrust slide away. "Exactly. Now, unless there's anything further either of you wishes to take up with me—"

"I want to reach Zigmunn. Send me to Azonda, Carnothute. If I could speak to him—"

"It is forbidden to interfere with the rite of initiation, Barsac. And even if you were to join the Cult yourself you would have to wait some months before you were judged ready to move on to Azonda. You are obstinate to the point of monomania, Barsac. But I tell you you'll only bring about your death if you insist on following this present course. You are dismissed."

In the street, outside the palace, they stood together a moment in the gathering shadows of late afternoon. Fleecy clouds now filled the darkening sky, and the faint tracings of the triple moons appeared behind them; the sun, sinking, was swollen against the horizon, and the gold of its rays had turned to crab-red.

"You fool," Kassa said quietly. "Blundering in there and accusing him of this and that, and mentioning the Cult and his connection with it like that!"

"What was I supposed to do? Crawl on my face and beg him to give me back Zigmunn?"

"Don't you know that crawling helps? Carnothute has ruled this province thirty years. He's accustomed to crawlers. But we need a more subtle approach."

"What do you suggest, then?"

She drew a paper from her pouch and scribbled a name and an address on it. "This man will take you to the place where you can try to buy passage to Azonda. How much money do you have?"

"Eleven hundred Galactic units."

She sucked her breath in sharply, "Don't offer more than five hundred for passage. And see that you save a hundred for me; I'm not doing all this for charity, Barsac."

He smiled and touched her chin. He understood frankness and appreciated it. Perhaps, he thought, he might give her a chance to earn her hundred in another way, after he found Zigmunn.

The address was in the Street of Kings. Barsac pocketed the slip.

"What will you do while I'm there?"

"I'm going to go back to see Carnothute again. Possibly the governor's in need of a woman; I'll offer myself. I could ask him to have your bloodkin disqualified from his novitiate and returned to Glaurus; he can do that, you know, if he feels a candidate's unfit. Maybe it will work. Many promises can be exacted in bed by one who knows how."

"And where will I meet you later?"

"In my room. Here's the key; you'll probably get back there before I do. Wait for me. And don't let them cheat you, Barsac. Be careful."

She turned and dodged back toward the palace entrance. Barsac watched her go; then he grinned and turned away. The Street of Kings next, he thought.

It turned out to be considerably less impressive than its regal name promised; perhaps in centuries past it had been a showplace of Millyaurr, but now it was hardly preferable to the Street of Tears. Night was gathering close by the time Barsac reached the street.

He sought out his man: Dollin Sporeffien of number five-sixty, Street of Kings. Sporeffien turned out to be a chubby little man in his late sixties, totally bald but for a fuzz of white about his ears. He looked harmless enough, except for his eyes. They were not harmless eyes.

He looked bleakly at Barsac, eyeing him up and down, and said finally, "So you're Kassa's latest lover, eh? She always sends them to me for some favor or other. She's a nimble girl, isn't she? She could be one of the best, if she put her mind to it. But she won't. She refuses to live up to her potential, as you've probably found out some nights, young one."

Barsac did not try to deny anything. He said, "I want a man who'll take me to Azonda tonight." Instantly the joviality left Sporffien's face.

"Some favors are harder to do than others. I'll pay for it. Well."

"How well?"

"Find me the man," Barsac said. "I'll talk price with him, not you."

Sporeffien smiled dubiously. "It might cost you some hundreds of credits. Are you still interested?"

"Yes."

"Come with me, then."

Sporeffien led him out of the house and into the street; by now the stars were visible above the murk and haze of the city. They entered another house in which a man sat clutching a jug of wine and staring blearily at the small child that lay sleeping on a bed of filth in one corner of the room.

Sporeffien said, "Barsac, meet Emmeri. Emmeri. Barsac. Emmeri's a private convoy man. He owns a small ship—somewhat outdated, but it still operates. Barsac would like you to pilot him to Azonda tonight, Emmeri."

The man named Emmeri turned and looked coldly at Barsac. He put down the jug.

"To Azonda?"

"You heard him. What's the price?"

Emmeri's blood-shot eyes drooped shut an instant; when he opened them, they gleamed craftily. "How much can you pay?"

"Five hundred Galactic units," Barsac said clearly. "I won't haggle. I'm starting right off at my top price, and that's as high as I'll go."

"Five hundred," Emmeri repeated, half to himself. "A very interesting sum. When do I get it?"

"When we've made the round trip to Azonda."

"No," Emmeri said. "Payment in advance or no trip. I don't know what you want to do on Azonda, but I want the money before we blast off."

Barsac thought about it half an instant, and said at length, "Done. Get yourself ready. I want to blast off this evening. I just have to get in touch with Kassa and then I'll be ready."

Shrugging, Emmeri got to his feet and weaved unsteadily across the room to the washstand. He didn't look much like a trained pilot, Barsac thought. His fingers shook and his eyes were bleary and he showed no signs of having the quick reflexes the job demanded.

But that didn't matter. All that mattered was getting a ship. He could compute his own orbit out to Azonda if he needed to.

Emmeri turned. "You have the money with you?"

Barsac nodded. He added. "You get it when I see your spaceship, not before. I don't hand five hundred units over to any foul-smelling sot who claims to be a pilot."

"You think I'd cheat you?" Emmeri said.

"I don't think anything. I just don't like to waste money."

"In that case you came to the wrong place," Emmeri said smirkingly.

To his dismay Barsac realized he had lost sight of Sporeflien; the older man had ducked behind him, into the shadows. Too late he saw that he had been maneuvered into a trap: he started to turn, but Sporeffien was even quicker, and brought the jug of wine down against his head with a resounding impact.

Barsac reeled and took two wobbly steps forward. He saw the still unbroken jug lift again, and tried to shield his head; Sporeffien crashed it down against the back of his neck, rattling his teeth.

Barsac pitched forward. He heard harsh laughter, and the old man's dry voice saying, "Anyone but a greenhorn should have known nobody would ferry him to Azonda for a million units cash down in initiation-time. Let's go through his pockets, Emmeri."

Chapter Three

He woke to the sound of falling rain, clattering against the caves of the houses and the stones of the street, and wondered for a moment how there could be rain aboard the *Dywain*. Then he remembered he was not aboard the *Dywain*. A moment later he made the unpleasant discovery that he was lying face down in the gutter, one hand dangling in a fast-flowing rivulet of rainwater, and that he was soaking wet, encrusted with mud, and suffering from a splitting headache. The gray light of dawn illuminated the scene. He looked around. It was an unfamiliar street.

Slowly he got to his feet, feeling chilled and dazed, and brushed some of the street-mud from his clothes ineffectually. He shook his head, trying to clear it, trying to make the ringing in his ears cease.

His left thigh felt strange. A moment after he knew why: the familiar bulk of his wallet no longer pressed against it. He remembered now the scene of the night before, and reddened. Those two thieves had cleaned him out. Played him for a fool, slugged him, taken his wallet and his eleven hundred units and his papers.

They had left him with a key, though. He stared at it dully until he realized it was the key to the apartment of Kassa Jidrill.

Kassa. She had sent him to Sporeffien. She must have known how laughable was the idea of hiring a ferry to take him to Azonda. And so she must have deliberately sent him to Sporeffien knowing he would be worked over.

Angry as he was, he found it hard to blame her, or Sporeffien and his accomplice. This was a tough, hard world; a greenhorn with a thousand Galactic units or so in his wallet was fair game.

Only—Kassa had said she was going to return to Lord Carnothute and make a second attempt to get Zigmunn released from his Cult vows. Had she meant it? Or had that just been part of the deception?

Barsac did not know. But he decided to return to the girl's apartment, as long as he still had the key. He wanted to ask her a few questions.

The early-morning rain still poured down. He shivered, soaked through. The streets were deserted. He started to walk. A street-sign said, *Boulevard of the Sun*. He had no idea where that might be in relation to the Street of Tears.

He rounded a corner and entered a narrow winding street lined with hunch-backed old houses that leaned so close together above the street that little rain penetrated. Halfway down the street he spied the radiant globe of a wine-house, still open. And a man was leaving it. Barsac hoped he was sober enough to give him directions.

He hailed him. The man paused, turned, stared uncertainly at Barsac. He was a short man, thin, with a sallow pock-marked face framing a massive hooked nose. He wore iridescent tights of red and green and a dull violet cloak. His eyes were small and glinted brightly. He looked none the worse for his night's carouse.

"Pardon me," Barsac said. "Could you direct me to the Street of Tears?"

"I could. Directly ahead until you reach the Square of the Fathers—you'll know it by the big ugly clump of statuary in the middle—and then make a sharp right past the Mercury Winehouse. Street of Tears is four blocks along that way. Got it?"

"Thanks," Barsac said. He started to move on.

"Just a second," the other called after him. The Earther turned. "Are you all right?"

"Could be better," Barsac said shortly.

"You're all wet. And muddy. You've been beaten and robbed, haven't you?"

Barsac nodded.

"And you're a stranger, too. Need some money?"

"I can manage."

The small man took three steps and placed himself at Barsac's side, looking up at him. "I know what it's like to be a stranger on Glaurus. I've been through it myself. I can help you. I can find you a job."

Barsac shook his head. "Appreciation. But I'm a spacer; my ship lifts at the end of this week. I'm not looking, for a job."

"Many's the spacer who's been left behind. If you get into trouble, come to me. Here's my card."

Barsac took it. It said, *Erpad Ystilog. Exhibitor of Curiosities. 1123 Street of Liars.* Barsac smiled and pocketed it.

"I'll wish you a good morning," Ystilog said. "Do you remember the way to the street you seek?"

"Straight ahead to the Square of the Fathers, sharp right at the Mercury Winehouse and four blocks farther."

Ystilog nodded approvingly. "You remember well, spacer. If you're ever in need of a job, come to me."

"I'll think about it," Barsac said.

The rain had virtually stopped by the time he reached the Street of Tears; only a trickle of drops came down now, and the sky had turned pearl gray and was on its way toward brightening. A filmy rainbow arched across the rooftops of the city, gauzy, tenuous, already melting away as the heat of morning descended.

But number eighty-one still seemed wrapped in sleep. Barsac mounted the stairs two at a time, pausing on the fourth-floor landing to draw out the key Kassa Jidrill had given him the night before.

But he did not need the key.

The door had been broken in. It was as if a battering-ram had crashed against it an inch or two from the place where the hinges joined the door-frame, and the wood had crumpled inward like a folding screen. The hall and the room both were dark. Frowning, Barsac nudged open the fragments of the door, pushing past the shattered door into the room.

He switched on the light. A moment later he found himself fighting the temptation to switch it off again.

Kassa lay neatly arranged on the bed, and the coverlet was soaked with blood. Barsac had seen horrible deaths before; this one took the prize.

She had been sliced open. A double-barred cross had been slashed into her body, the downstroke beginning between the breasts and continuing to the pelvis, the two crossbars incised about eight inches apart in her stomach. Her throat had been cut. And her face—

There was hardly a face left.

The clothes she had worn last night were stacked on the chair. A key lay on the floor near the bed. He picked it up; it was a duplicate of the one she had given him.

She had come home, then; she had locked the door. And someone had broken in.

Barsac found his hands quivering. He turned away, shaking his head slowly, and closed what was left of the door behind him.

There was a public communicator booth in the hall. Barsac entered the booth without bothering to flip the shutter release, and depressed the *call* stud.

He said, "Give me the police. I want to report a murder, operator."

A moment later a sleepy voice said, "Millyaurr Homicide Detail. Lieutenant Hassliq speaking. What is it?"

"A murder, Lieutenant. In the Street of Tears, number eighty-one. The dead person is a party girl named Kassa Jidrill. I just found her."

The was no increase of animation in Lieutenant Hassliq's voice as he said, "And who are you, please?"

"I'm a spacer in town on leave from the ship *Dywain*. My name is Barsac. I—met the dead girl yesterday afternoon for the first time. I just came back to her room and found her this way."

"Describe the condition of the body, please."

Barsac did, in detail. When he was finished Hassliq said, "I feared as much. All right, Barsac—we'll send a morgue truck right over to pick up the body. You don't need to stick around if you don't want to."

"Won't you want to question me for the investigation?"

"What investigation?"

Barsac blinked. "A girl's been murdered. Don't you usually investigate murder cases in Millyaurr?"

"Not when they're Cult jobs," Hassliq said. "What's the use? That party girl was killed ritualistically, if your description is accurate. Someone in the Cult took a dislike to her. But what can we do? It's next to impossible to regulate Cult activities; I'd only be begging to have my own face scraped off and a double-barred cross cut into my belly. No, thanks. We'll send a pickup man out for the body. Thanks for phoning in the information, Mr. Barsac."

He heard a click, stared at the receiver a moment, and hung up. They weren't even interested in finding Kassa's murderer, he thought. They didn't care. They were *afraid* to care.

He went back to the room and sat by the dead girl until the morgue truck arrived. His quest for Zigmunn was taking on new colors; a robbery, now a murder had been woven into the pattern.

A ritualistic murder. A Cult murder. On Glaurus the Cult was law, it seemed. His heart felt curiously leaden; he avoided looking at the body on the bed. For Kassa all despair was ended now, suddenly, earlier than she had expected.

Half an hour passed; forty-five minutes. The rain began again, then stopped. Finally the truck arrived. Barsac heard the commotion on the stairs as the other boarders in the house, their curiosities aroused by the presence of the truck, followed the morgue men upstairs.

"In here," Barsac called.

Two bored-looking men with a stretcher slung between them entered. At the sight of Kassa they winced.

"We get half a dozen of these a week," one said. "The Cult keeps a sharp knife."

They loaded her on the stretcher as if she were so much slaughtered meat. Barsac stepped forward and said, "What's going to happen to her body now?"

"She gets taken down to the morgue and entered. We wait a week for the body to be claimed. Then we send her to the crematorium."

"You don't expect anyone to claim the body?"

The stretcher-bearer smiled scornfully. "She was a party girl, wasn't she?"

"Besides," said the other one, "even if she was a nun of the Grand Temple. Nobody claims Cult victims' bodies. It isn't a healthy thing to do."

Barsac scowled. "I'd like to see her get a decent burial. She was, well, a friend of mine."

"Burial on Glaurus costs five hundred units, brother. Plus bribes. Was she that much of a friend? Don't throw your money away; she won't ever know the difference."

They smiled at him ghoulishly and lifted the stretcher. Barsac let them take her away. He was remembering that he had no money at all, and in four days he was due to return to his ship and leave Glaurus probably forever.

On sudden inspiration he yanked open the drawers of the dead girl's dresser. Cheap trinkets, souvenirs, cosmetics—ah—ten crumpled five-unit bills. The price for a night, he thought.

Coldly he pocketed the bills. Turning, he saw a thin-faced old man staring at him.

"Here, you! No robbery, here! That money belongs to *me!*"

"Who the devil are you?" Barsac asked.

"The landlord here. It's the rule; if a boarder dies intestate, I inherit. Hand over that money, right here and now."

"I need it," Barsac said. "You don't. The girl doesn't. Get out of my way."

He slammed the landlord against the greasy wall with a contemptuous slap of his flattened hand and made his way down the stairs and out into the Street of Tears, thinking of a dead party girl who would have been alive at this moment had he never come to Millyaurr.

It was nearly noon when he arrived at the field where the *Dywain* stood, and he was dizzy with hunger. He showed his identity bracelet to the field guards and trotted out to the great ship.

Captain Jaspel was supervising the repainting of the stabilizer fins, up on D deck. Barsac waited until the captain had finished his harangue of the painters, then said, "Sir?"

"Oh—Barsac. Where's that ace repairman of yours?"

"I haven't been able to find him, sir. Not yet, anyway. But there's still time, isn't there?"

"Not much," the old captain said. "I'll have to send out the hiring notice tomorrow if I'm to get a man. I can't wait for your fellow any longer than that. You've been robbed, eh, Barsac?"

Smiling bitterly, Barsac nodded. "Foolishness, Captain. I'm cleaned out."

"How much do you need?"

"Three hundred units advance against next voyage, Captain. Is that too much?"

"Probably. Take a hundred fifty. Then if you get robbed again it won't be so bad. And be careful, Barsac; I don't want to have to find a fuelsman as well as a repairman on Glaurus."

Barsac pocketed his money and returned to the city. Hope of finding Zigmunn in time for him to get the job aboard the *Dywain* was dim indeed. But Barsac was no longer mainly interested in getting him the job; he simply wanted to see Zigmunn, if possible to release him from the meshes of the Cult. And there were questions to be answered about his robbery and about the death of Kassa.

He hopped aboard a crowded airbus with defective air-conditioning and rode it as far as Lord Carnothute's palace. There he got off, entered the palace, and demanded to see the governor.

He was conscious that he did not make an imposing figure, in his mud-stained, blood-streaked clothes, with his gaunt bruised face and beard-stubbled cheeks. But he was determined to see Carnothute.

The governor appeared, a looming elephantine figure in ultramarine cape and sheathlike leggings of cerise trimmed with black. Barsac looked up at him and snapped, "Let me talk to you in private!"

Carnothute seemed amused. "A private audience is a rare privilege, my friend. My guards will have to be present throughout our conversation. Why do you come back?"

"To ask you questions. Did that party-girl Kassa return here yesterday after I left?"

Carnothute shrugged. "Perhaps."

"She did. Where did you and she go?"

"My fleshly life is hardly your concern, worthy spacer. Are there any less personal questions you would ask?"

"This one," Barsac said. "Some time between last night and this morning Kassa returned to her room and locked herself in. Then someone of unusual strength battered the door down and killed her. The police said it was a ritualistic murder. She was gutted and mutilated when I found her this morning. Here's your question: did you kill her?"

Chuckling, Carnothute said, "Party girls have short lives in Millyaurr. Why should you care whether a teenage slut lives or dies, you who land on Glaurus once a decade?"

"I care because the Cult killed her, and you're the only Cult member I know. *You* killed her. You killed her because she was trying to help me reach my blood-brother on Azonda, and because perhaps last night she extracted a promise from you that you chose not to keep when you reconsidered it in the harsher light of morning. Am I close, Carnothute? It's always easier to have a party girl murdered than to face the charge that you broke your sacred word."

The governor's smooth-cheeked face darkened abruptly. In a cold, deep voice he said, "Let me give you advice, Barsac: forget the girl Kassa, and forget the Luasparru Zigmunn. The one is dead, the other beyond your reach. Give up your search and return to your ship."

"And if I choose not to?"

"Then you will die sooner than your parents expected. Leave me, Barsac." He turned to the three silent guards who waited near the door. "Take this man outside the palace and instruct him that he is not to return."

They converged on Barsac. Gripping his arms tightly, they swept him out of Lord Carnothute's presence, down the interlocking corridors, and outside the palace grounds. There, the tallest of the three spun him around and slapped his face.

Barsac growled and started for him. Another tripped him, and as he fell sprawling he realized he was in for another beating.

They worked him over for ten minutes with light-hearted gaiety, while he aimed futile blows at each of them in turn. They were Darjunnans, long-limbed and lithe, and while he managed to bruise their silky violet skins from time to time they inflicted far worse damage on him. Five times he struggled to his feet only to be battered down again; they concentrated their attention on his empty stomach, drumming blows off it with sickening frequency.

Once he swung wildly and broke a nose; a moment later a kick behind the knee-joints dropped him on his face, gasping, and they devoted some time to his kidneys. They pummelled him efficiently, as if they were well-trained as a team; when Barsac hung to consciousness by only a thread one said, "Enough," and they left him.

He walked about ten paces and stumbled. He groped for a bench, found it, clung to its cool stone, and through puffed eyes watched drops of his own blood dripping from his face and puddling against the white flagstone walk. Dimly he realized they had not robbed him, and it surprised him.

He sat there five minutes, ten, unable to get up. His face throbbed. Every part of him ached. But they had shrewdly stopped while he yet was conscious, devilishly, so he would feel every moment of the pain.

He sensed the fact that someone stood in front of him, looking down. He tried to open his eyes. "Kassa?" he asked.

"No. I'm not Kassa. I suppose you found the Street of Tears, spacer. And then the Street of Blood."

"Who are you?"

"We met earlier this day. I offered to help you then. But I think you need it more now."

Through pain-hazed eyes Barsac made out the lean wiry figure of Erpad Ystilog, the Exhibitor of Curiosities.

Chapter Four

Barsac lay back on the hard, uncomfortable couch and tried to relax. He failed; every nerve seemed wound tightly, almost to the breaking point. He was in number 1123, Street of Liars. Ystilog had brought him home.

"Awake?" Ystilog asked.

Barsac looked up at the sallow pock-marked face, the great curved beak of a nose. "More awake than asleep, I guess. What time is it?"

"Well after noon. Feeling better? Drink this."

Forcing himself into a sitting position, Barsac accepted the cup. It contained a warm brownish liquid; he drank without questioning. The taste was faintly sweet.

"Good. I guess I owe you thanks."

Ystilog shrugged deprecatingly. "Never mind that. Rest, now; you'll need to rebuild your strength."

The curio-exhibitor left him. Barsac wanted to protest that he could not stay here any longer, that he had to make a further attempt to find Zigmunn, that time was running short and he would soon have to return to the *Dywain*. But the pain got the better of him; he slumped back and dropped off into sleep.

He woke again, some time later, feeling stiff and sore but stronger than he had been. Ystilog stood above him.

"I feel better now," Barsac said. "And I must go. I have little time."

"Why the rush?"

"My ship leaves Glaurus at the end of this week. And before then I have things to do."

"You've had ill luck so far, I'd say. My offer still goes—a job is open for you."

"I'm a spacer."

"Leave space. It's a loathsome life. Stay here in my employ. I need a strong-bodied assistant, one who can protect a frail man like myself. I encounter much danger while traveling with my museum. And I can pay you—not well, alas, but enough."

Barsac shook his head. "Sorry, Ystilog. You've been good to me, but it's out of the question. The *Dywain* is a good ship. I don't want to leave it."

Disappointment gleamed briefly on Ystilog's face. "I could use you, Barsac."

"I tell you no. But give me some information, before I leave."

"If I can."

"My purpose is to find my blood-brother, a Luasparru, Zigmunn by name. At the cost of two beatings and a robbing I've found out that he's been initiated into the Cult of the Witch, and is now on Azonda."

The smile left Ystilog's face. "So?"

"I want to find him and break him loose from the Cult. But I know nothing about this Cult. Tell me—what is it? From what did it spring? What are its aims?"

Quietly Ystilog said, "I can tell you little—the little that every non-initiated Glauran knows. The Cult is a thousand years old—more, perhaps. Its head-quarters are on Azonda. A dead planet, as you may know. Heart of the Cult is the so-called Witch of Azonda."

"Tell me about her."

"There is nothing to tell. Only members may see her. She is supposedly lovely, immortal-and faceless. Cult members spend a year on Azonda wor-shipping her. Perhaps one Glauran in a thousand is a member. They practice certain dark rites, and the law ignores them. People think that most of our high officials are Cult members. If your blood-brother's gone to Azonda, forget him. He's lost to you forever."

Barsac scowled. "I refuse to believe that. I still have three days to find him."

"You'll find nothing but more pain," Ystilog said. "But if you're determined, I suppose I can't hold you back. You'll find your clothes in that closet. And don't try to pay me for what I've done; it was simple common courtesy."

Barsac dressed in silence. When he had donned the last of his garments, Ystilog reappeared, smiling. He carried a mug of wine.

"Have a drink as a parting toast," Ystilog said. He handed the mug to Barsac. "Go to your quest. And success."

Barsac drank. Tightening his cloak around him, he headed for the door— but before he passed the threshold his legs wobbled and refused to hold him. He sagged crazily; Ystilog caught him and eased him to the couch.

Bitterly he realized he had once again played the fool. A roaring tide of unconsciousness swept down over him, and he knew he had accepted a drink that was drugged.

Church bells woke him. He suffered at the first echoing peal, stirred, sat up in bed. His eyes were pasted together; he had to work to get them open. He felt rusty at the joints, stiff, flabby.

Church bells. The end of the week. The *Dywain* was leaving!

He jerked off the covers, climbed from the bed, slipped, stumbled, fell head-long. His legs and feet were numb from inactivity. He hoisted himself erect, alarm giving him strength.

"Ystilog! Damn you, where are you?"

"Here I am," said a quiet voice.

Barsac whirled unsteadily. Ystilog stood behind him, smiling pleasantly. He wore a black watered silk lounging robe and a blue morning wig. In his hand was a wedge-shaped blade, eight inches long, glittering.

"You drugged me," Barsac accused. "How long did I sleep? What day is it? What time is it?"

"Your ship left Glaurus half an hour ago," Ystilog said smoothly. "I was at the spaceport. I watched it depart; it was quite lovely to see it climb high and wink into overdrive, vanishing in the blue."

Rage surged through Barsac. He took two hesitant steps forward.

"Why did you do this?"

"I needed an assistant. A good man is hard to find. And you have muscles, Barsac, if no brains. The pay is eleven units a week plus food and board."

"Eleven units!" Barsac clenched his fists and advanced. The smaller man waited, unafraid.

"Put that knife away, Ystilog, and—"

Ystilog sheathed the knife. "Yes? You'll what?" He waved his empty hands in the air.

"I'll—I'll what have you done to me?" Barsac growled.

"Conditioned you against doing me harm," Ystilog said. "I would be as big a fool as you to do otherwise. If you were in my place and I in yours, I would not hesitate to kill you as brutally as possible . . . if I were able. So you are not able. See?"

Barsac looked at his impotent hands. He longed to wring Ystilog's fragile neck, but it would have been easier to strangle himself to death. An unbreakable geas lay upon him, keeping him from action.

He sank down numbly on the couch where he had slept so long. A quiver of suppressed anger and frustration rippled through him. "Is my ship really gone?"

"Yes," Ystilog said.

Barsac moistened his lips. This had been Zigmunn's fate, and now a decade later it was his. Like brother, like brother. Naturally Captain Jaspell would not have held up departure for the sake of an overdue fuelsman; starship schedules were as inflexible as the solar precessions.

"All right," Barsac said quietly. "I've been beaten and robbed and drugged, and now I've lost my ship as well. This trip to Glaurus has been grand. Just grand. Suppose you tell me what I'm supposed to do."

They left four days later by sea for Zunnigen-nar, the great continent of Glaurus' eastern hemisphere, where the people had a mildly greenish tinge to their skins and where the spoken tongue made maddeningly slight use of verbs. Barsac, in his new position as Ystilog's bodyguard, wore new clothes of synthetic silk, and carried a fifty-watt shocker at his waist. The shocker had an illegal amplifier installed which boosted the output to lethal intensity, but this was not readily apparent even on close inspection, and the weapon could pass for a standard two-ampere model. Barsac longed to use it on his employer and fry his synapses, but his conditioning made that impossible.

The ship on which they departed was a small one which Ystilog had engaged for his personal use. It contained the whole of Ystilog's traveling museum-cum-circus.

Ystilog had acquired a variegated array of treasures. There were dream-stones from Sollighat, ghostly yellow in color and narcotic in their beauty; emerald-cut gems from the barren wastes of Duu, glistening in their metallic settings; talking trees of Thanamon, with their croaking vocabularies of seven or eight words of greeting and fifteen or twenty scabrous obscenities.

There were living creatures in cages, too: dwarf squids of Qi, hunching up in their tanks and fixing malevolent red gimlet-eyes on the onlookers; raintoads from Mivaghik, violet-hued legless salamanders from the blazing sunside of UpjiLaz, smiling protopods of Viron. Creatures from Earth, too, scorpions and sleek serpents and star-faced moles, platypusses and echidnas, sad-faced pro-boscis monkeys. The menagerie was at all times a chattering madhouse, and it was part of Barsac's job to feed each creature its special food every morning.

Ystilog had warned him to be careful; his predecessor in the job had lost an arm tossing flesh into the protopod-cage. The smiling creatures moved with blinding agility.

They opened at a showhouse in Zibilnor, largest city of the continent, and for seventeen days did spectacular business. Ystilog charged a unit a head for admission, half price for children and slaves, and during the time in Zibilnor grossed no less than twenty-eight thousand units, by Barsac's count. They jostled close, anxious to see the deadly creatures of twenty worlds that Ystilog had assembled, staring with covetous eyes at his gems and at his curios.

Twenty-eight thousand units. And through it all Barsac received eleven units a week, room and board. Eleven units a week was barely wine-money. He longed to slit Ystilog's throat, but could not approach the circus owner with a weapon. On the last day but one of their stay in Zibilnor, Barsac sought out a professional killer. His intention was to offer the man full rights to Ystilog's circus if he would kill the entrepreneur, but when the time came to make the offer Barsac's mental block intervened, and he was unable to speak. He stumbled away, tongue-tied.

The circus moved on—slowly, across the face of Zunnigennar, Ystilog paus-ing here and there for a three-day engagement, a five-day stand. Local bear-ers helped them move the crates from one town to the next; Ystilog hired men to precede them, announcing that the show was coming.

In a locked chest by his bed Ystilog kept the receipts of the tour. He cabled his money back to Miilyaurr once a week; the rest of the time the money lay there for Barsac's taking, but the compulsion against killing Ystilog extended too to robbing him and to running away. He was bound to the swarthy pock-marked little man by invisible threads stronger than the strongest metal.

Barsac sank into the depths of despair. He drank, he robbed, once he killed. That was in the town of Dmynn, on the foul, polluted river Kyllnn. A riverboat man was in the same bar as the spacer, and, with two too many drinks in his belly, was boasting of the river life.

"We are free and we travel the water—the finest life there is!"

"Not half so fine as the life of a spacer," said Barsac darkly. He sat four stools to the left, nursing the flask of wine that would be his last drink of the night. "A riverman is just a crawler next to a spacer."

Instantly the riverboater was down off his stool and facing Barsac. "What would *you* know of this?"

"I'm a spacer!"

A low chuckle eddied up about him from all sides.

"You—a spacer?" the riverboat man said contemptuously. "I know you, you who call yourself a spacer. You're the circus man's lackey. Each morning you sweep the dung from the cages of his beasts!"

Barsac did not reply. He came forward fists first, and the riverman went rocketing back against a table. Barsac waited for him to get up, so he could hit him again. He felt restraining hands gripping his arms, and shook them off. Lifting the squirming riverman, he propped him up and slapped him.

A knife appeared. Barsac kicked it away and hit the riverman in the throat. He doubled up, choking and gasping, and managed to grate out the words, *"Lackey . . . dung-sweeper!"*

Barsac stepped backward. The riverman charged; Barsac drew his shocker, flipped up the amplifier switch, and triggered a discharge all in the same instant. A smell of burning flesh reached his nostrils a moment later.

That night they left Dmynn, traveling overland toward the forested province of Eas. As their caravan of trucks rolled out of the river town, Ystilog said coldly, "It was necessary to place a fifty-unit bribe with the local police to save you, this afternoon. For the next ten weeks your pay is cut to six units a week. And keep out of such brawls in the future."

Barsac scowled. There was nothing he could say. Ystilog was his lord and master, and there was no way of lifting the foot planted squarely on his throat.

He lay awake nights thinking of ways to kill the little circus man, and burst into frantic fits of perspiration when the inevitable realization came that he was incapable of action.

Ystilog had him. Ystilog owned him, and he served Ystilog well.

Across the face of Zunnigennar went the traveling circus, and Ystilog grew richer. He treated Barsac well, buying him clothes, feeding him handsomely. But Barsac did a slave's work, for he was a slave. The weeks went by, lengthening into months.

Barsac wondered about the *Dywain*, bound now for the Rim stars without him, and about Zigmunn in whose name he had parted with his profession and his freedom. He thought of the girl Kassa, so long dead now. And, on those occasions when a silver-masked Glauran crossed his path, he thought of the Cult of the Witch, and of the dead world of Azonda where his blood-brother had gone.

Winter came, and with it snow; Ystilog decided time had come to return to Millyaurr and live off the summer's profits. To Millyaurr they returned, stopping occasionally along the way to recoup food expenses by giving a one-day showing in some small town. Wearily Barsac helped pack and unpack the crates. He was almost fond of Ystilog's menagerie of monsters, now, though he knew that any of the creatures would gladly kill him given the chance. He prayed for the lucky accident that would release a poison-tongued rain-toad for Ystilog, since it was impossible for Barsac wilfully to turn the beast loose on his master.

Winter held Millyaurr tight when the caravan finally returned to the Street of Liars. Seven months had gone by since the week of Barsac's leave. He had grown gaunt and his eyes now lay deep in shadow, but his old stubbornness remained alive in him, imprisoned only by the web of hypnotic command.

But lines of despair now traced themselves on his face, as once they had on dead Kassa's face. He frequented dangerous sections of town, hoping for the release of death. He drank often in the bar where he first had met Kassa, sitting alone at the table in the rear.

He was there one night in late winter, spending a borrowed three-unit piece on liquor, when the front door opened and framed in it stood a silver-masked figure, a member of the Cult of the Witch.

Instinctively the other patrons of the bar huddled inward upon themselves, hoping not to be noticed, as the Cultist flicked gobblets of snow from his cape and entered the bar. Only Barsac looked up unafraid, and drew out the chair next to his in open invitation.

Chapter Five

The cultist paused just beyond the door, surveying the room with the ash-gray eyes that lay just above the rim of his mask. Then, calmly, he strode down the aisle between the clustered tables and took the seat Barsac offered.

"Order two drinks," the Cultist said in a low voice.

Barsac signalled the barkeep for two more bowls of the mulled wine he had been drinking. Timorously the bartender advanced with them, laid them down, and retreated from the Cultist's presence without even bothering to ask for his money.

Barsac studied the other. The mask ran from ear to ear and from the bridge of the nose to the upper lip; all that was visible of the Cultist's face were the gray, piercing eyes, the broad furrowed forehead, and cold downslanting lips.

"Well," Barsac said, "drink hearty." He raised the bowl, expecting to clink it against the Cultist's, but the other merely grunted and took a deep drink.

When he was through he peered at Barsac and said, "You are Barsac the Earther, lackey to the circus proprietor Erpad Ystilog."

"I am. How did you know?"

"I know. Do you love your master?"

Barsac laughed harshly. "Do you think I do?"

"What I think is irrelevant at this time. You have been watched, Barsac. Ystilog was directed to you. We believe suffering is beneficial to the soul, as we understand the soul."

"In that case you've done a good job. I've suffered."

"We know that too. Why haven't you killed Ystilog?"

"Because—because—" Barsac strove to explain the compulsion Ystilog had laid on him, but the very compulsion kept him from framing the words. "I—I—can't say it."

"A tongue-block? Ystilog is good at such things. Would you like to kill Ystilog?"

"Of course."

"But you can't. Ystilog has laid a command across your mind. Yes?"

Stiffly, Barsac nodded.

The Cultist's thin lips curled upward. "Would you approve if someone else killed Ystilog for you?"

Beads of sweat broke out on Barsac's forehead. The conversation was skirting the borders of the compulsion-area in his mind; it was only with difficulty that he was forcing through his responses.

"Yes," he said heavily.

The Cultist touched the tips of his fingers together. "In one hour Ystilog will die, if we so decide it. You will be free from your compulsion. Azonda waits."

"Azonda?"

"Where else could you go? What else is left, Barsac? Driven downward, cut off from the life you knew, an outcast on Glaurus—take the way of Azonda. We will free you from Ystilog. Come, then, with us."

Barsac struggled to get out a reply. Finally he said, "I . . . accede."

The Cultist rose. "Within an hour Ystilog dies. We will be waiting for you, Barsac."

And then he was alone.

He sat quietly, nursing his warm drink staring through the leaded window at the great heavy soft flakes of snow drifting downward. The Cult, he thought. Why not? What else is there? Better the Cult than endless years of Ystilog, and they will free me from—

No!

Ystilog's compunction gripped him, sent him running out of the tavern into the chill winter bleakness. By acceding to the Cultist's request he was allowing the death of Ystilog, and that ran counter to his instilled conditioning. He had to prevent the murder. He had to save Ystilog. He had to get back in time.

He ran down the empty snow-choked streets. Within an hour, the Cultist had said. Burning conflict raged inside Barsac; he fought to hold his body back, to still his legs, to give the Cultists a chance to do their work, while at the same time the demon riding his mind spurred him forward to reach Ystilog and protect him.

At the corner he waited impatiently for an airbus. It came, finally, crusted over with snow, and he took it to the Street of Liars. From the terminal it was a five-block walk to Ystilog's flat; Barsac took it at a trot, stumbling in the snow every time his mind managed to reassert control over his rebellious body.

But as he drew near the flat, Ystilog's compulsion over-mastered him, and uppermost in his mind was the thought that he must reach his master in time, save him from the knives of the Cultists—

Up the stairs. Down the hall. There was the door. Barsac gasped for breath; his lungs were icy, his nose and ears numb with cold.

"Ystilog! Hold on! I'm coining!"

A scream. Another, drawn-out, a ghastly bubbling wail that echoed down the corridor of the old flat and sent a different sort of chill through Barsac.

He slumped against the door like a cast-off doll. Ystilog's hold on him was broken. *I was too late after all*, he thought in relief. *They got him.*

The door opened. On nerveless feet Barsac entered. Four Cultists stood within.

Ystilog lay naked on his bed, in a pool of blood. The double-barred cross stood out in red clarity against the paleness of his skin. Two silver-masked figures stood above the body, holding a keen-bladed instrument with two handles over his face, slicing down—

Barsac looked away.

"It's over," said a familiar voice—the voice of the Cultist who had entered the tavern. "He died quickly. It was a pity."

"I wish I could have done it," Barsac murmured. "But the devil had me bound. Now I'm free, though. Free! Only—"

"Yes," the Cultist said. "Free. But you know the price of your freedom."

A third time he saw Lord Carnothute, and for the first time there was no conflict between them. Barsac, weary, drained of fury and of passion, sat tiredly in an overstuffed chair high in Carnothute's palace, listening to the huge man speak.

"You will leave for Azonda tomorrow," he said. "There are seventeen of you in this current group of initiates. The initiation period is one year. After that—well, after that you will know which roads are open for you and which are not."

"Will Zigmunn be there?"

Carnothute whirled and looked down at Barsac. "His year still has some months to run. He will be there. But if you have any idea—"

"You know I have none. I've lost all desire to reclaim him—or myself." Barsac listened to his own voice, heavy, toneless, and wondered fragmentedly how he had changed so much in these seven months on Glaurus. It was as if his experiences had tarnished his soul, rusted it, corroded it, oxidized it finally to a heap of dust, and there was nothing left for him but to accept the uncertain mercies of the Cult.

"Will you have a drink?" Carnothute asked.

"I'm not thirsty."

"Good. Loss of physical desires is essential to one entering upon his novitiate. The desires return or not, as you choose, after you receive the mask."

Barsac shut his eyes a moment. "Did you kill the girl Kassa?"

"Yes. She had put me in a compromising position, and I either would have had to kill her or do away with myself. I've grown fond of life, Barsac. You know the rest."

"I see." Oddly, he did not care. Nothing seemed to matter, any more.

"Come," Carnothute said. "Meet your fellow initiates. The ship leaves for Azonda tomorrow."

He allowed himself to be taken by the hand and led into an adjoining room. There, sixteen others sat on plurofoam couches ringing the wall, and three silver-masked Cultists stood as if on guard at the entrance.

Barsac studied the sixteen. He counted five women, eleven men, all of them humanoid by designation. They slouched wearily against the wall, not speaking to one another, some of them virtually withdrawn from the universe to some private many-colored inner world. One expression was common to their faces: the expression Barsac knew must be on his own as well. They were people who had lost all traces of hope.

One of the women still wore the revealing costume of a party-girl, but it was frayed and tattered, and so was she. She seemed to be about forty. Her face was lined and unpretty, her eyes bleak, her mouth drooping. Next to her sat a boy of seventeen, his arms grotesquely puffed and purpled with the tell-tale stigmata of the sammthor-addict. As Barsac looked the boy quivered suddenly and emitted a cascade of tears.

Still farther on was a man of thirty-five whose face was a mass of scars; one eye was gone, the other askew, and his nose sprawled crazily over his face. One lip had been slashed; green jagged tattoo-marks marred his cheeks. He was one who would do well to take the mask, Barsac thought.

He took a seat on an unoccupied couch. He told himself: *These are people who have given up. I'm not quite like them. I'm still above water. These people have all let themselves drown.*

But with a faint petulant bitterness he admitted to himself that he was wrong, that he too belonged here among these walking dead. The Cult was a dead-end pickup. To it came human refuse, people who could not sink lower, and the Cult raised them up.

The Cult had had its eyes on him from the start. They had spotted him as a likely prospect from the moment of his landing on Glaurus, and they had followed him through each succeeding adventure, as he slipped lower and lower, as more and more of the old Barsac crumbled and dropped away, until the time had come when he could go no lower, and they had stepped in to free him from Ystilog and welcome him to their midst.

He thought of Zigmunn, like him a spacer stranded in a hostile city, and how Zigmunn must have slowly descended to whatever pit served as the entrance requirements for the Cult.

But Zigmunn had been tougher, Barsac reflected. It had taken the Luasparru eight years of life on Glaurus before he entered the Cult; Barsac had achieved the same distinction in less than eight months. Zigmunn had always been the shrewd one, though, and Barsac the stolid well-muscled one who depended on the manipulations of his blood-brother to see him through a time of trouble.

He was in trouble now. But there would be no help for him from Zigmunn, for Zigmunn had gone through the trap ahead of him and waited on Azonda now.

The seventeen were given rooms in Carnothute's palace. Cult members moved among them, speaking encouragingly to them, promising the rehabilitation the Cult held for them. Barsac barely listened. He dwelt almost entirely in an inner world where there were no betraying Sporeffiens, no lying Ystilogs, no Kassas of easy virtue, no Cult.

The night passed slowly; Barsac half-slept, half-woke, with little awareness of his surroundings. In the morning a Cultist brought him a meager breakfast, a dry bun and a sea-apple, and Barsac ate dispiritedly.

Carnothute called them all together once more to wish them well. Barsac stood, a half-corpse, among sixteen other half-corpses, and half-listened. Part of his mind wondered where the *Dywain* was, now. More than half a year had gone by since its departure from Glaurus. Captain Jaspell had been bound for the Rim.

Probably they had already touched the worlds of purple-hued Venn and golden Paaiiad, and were moving onward toward Lorrimok and the double sun Thoptor. Doubtless the vacancies in the crew had been filled by now, and the angular man named Barsac had long since faded from the minds of the men of the *Dywain*.

Sleepily he stroked the scars about his lips, and realized he would be seeing Zigmunn soon. Nearly eleven years had slipped by since his last meeting with his blood-brother, but Barsac had not expected the reunion to come about on Azonda.

Cultists shepherded them through a door and down into a liftshaft. There were several moments of free fall while they sank into the recesses of Carnothute's vaults. Five glistening little cars waited for them there, and the candidates entered, three in the first, four in the second, three in the third, four in the fourth, three in the fifth. A faceless Cultist sat behind the steering-panel of each car.

At a signal the lead car shot off down the dark tunnel ahead of them. Barsac, who rode in the second car, peered into the darkness, but saw nothing.

The trip took perhaps a five-minute span, perhaps an hour; in the darkness Barsac was unable to account for the passage of the moments. They emerged into light, eventually, and he saw he was at the spacefield outside the city of Millyaurr.

They quitted the cars and stood in an uncertain clump on the bare brown soil of the spacefield. Barsac saw the shining blue-white sweep of a giant starship's fins, and wildly thought it was the *Dywain*, till he saw the name stencilled on the vessel's landing buttresses: *Mmuvviol*. He felt no temptation to break away, run to the strange ship, inquire if there were a vacancy on board for a skilled fuelsman; he knew he belonged with the group of Cult-candidates, and made no attempt to move.

A lesser ship stood farther along the landing-strip, small and slight, with a golden-green hull that bore no name. Cultists led Barsac and the other sixteen out across the field toward the nameless ship, and Barsac saw others at the field, oilers, crewmen, passengers, draw back and stare as the procession of silver masks and shuffling zombies headed out over the field.

One by one they entered the ship. Cultists guided them to individual blast-hammocks and strapped them in; Barsac, for all his twenty years as a space-man, made no move to draw the rig about him, but waited passively until his turn came to be strapped in.

A warning signal flashed through the ship. Barsac closed his eyes and waited. The moment came that he had thought would never come for him again: the faint anticipatory quiver as the drive compartment of a starship bursts into life, readying itself.

Lights flashed, bells rang the old standard routine for a lifting spaceship. Something deep in Barsac's numbed mind longed to respond, to perform the actions that those signals demanded, but he remembered that on this ship he was passenger and not crewman, and he relaxed.

Later came the moment of blast-off as the drive translated matter to energy and pushed Glaurus away from the ship. Barsac felt a sickening moment of no-grav; then the vessel began to spin, and weight returned.

Through a port near his face he saw the cluttered globe of Glaurus spinning slowly against a black backdrop. The ship had spaced.

Its destination was Azonda.

Chapter Six

The nameless ship hung on a tongue of fire over the dark world Azonda; then it dropped suddenly downward, and the landing buttresses sprang out at acute angles to support it.

Twenty-six spacesuit-clad figures, Barsac among them, emerged from the hatch of the ship—seventeen Cult candidates, nine watchful members. Even through the thick folds of his spacesuit, even despite the protective warmth of his suit's energons, Barsac shivered. Azonda was a dead world.

The golden sun that warmed Glaurus was only a perfunctory dab of light out here, eleven billion miles further spaceward. At this distance, the sun was hardly a sun—more like a particularly brilliant star.

Drifts of banked snow lay everywhere, glittering faintly in the eternal dusk—Azonda's atmosphere, congealed by cold. Gaunt bare cliffs glinted redly in the distance. All was silent, silent and dead. Life had never come to Azonda.

The witch—?

Barsac wondered. He moved along in single file, lifting one spacebooted foot and putting it down, lifting the other. It seemed to him a wind whistled against his body, though he knew that was impossible on airless Azonda, an illusion, a phantasm. He kept walking.

The impassive guides led them along. A well-worn path was cut in the ice, and they followed this.

They came, finally, to a sort of natural amphitheater, a half-bowl scooped out of the rock by a giant's hand. Barsac was unable to see into the amphitheater; a gray cloud hung obscuringly over it.

"We have come to the Hall of the Witch," the leading Cultist said quietly via suit-phones. "Beyond the curtain of gray lies the place you have journeyed toward all your days of life."

Barsac narrowed his eyes and tried with no success to see through the curtain, hoping for some glimmer of that which lay within.

"When you pass through the curtain," came the even admonitory voice, "you will divest yourselves of your spacesuits. You will stand without clothing in the presence of the Witch."

But that's impossible, Barsac's space-trained mind protested instantly. *The cold, the vacuum, the pressure—we'd be dead in a minute.*

"No harm will come to you," said the Cultist.

Up ahead, Barsac saw now the front men of the file disappearing into the gray curtain, vanishing first one foot, then a shoulder, then the entire body, sectioned away as if they were sliding between the molecules of a solid wall. Leadenly. Barsac moved on, waiting for his turn to come.

In time the curtain loomed inches before his nose, and without hesitation he put his right foot through and followed after. His body tingled an instant; then he had passed through and was inside, in the Hall of the Witch.

"Remove your spacesuit and inner clothing," came the stern instruction.

I *can't!* Barsac thought. But then he looked to left and right and saw the others stripping, shedding their spacesuits and clothing like cast-off skins and evincing no ill effects. Barsac decided some manner of force-field must be in operation, a semi-permeable field that allowed humans to enter but which also maintained an atmosphere within itself. Experimentally he reached back and touched the inner skin of the curtain behind him with the tip of one finger, and got the answer: the curtain was unyielding as granite from the inside. It was penetrable only in one direction, and all within—humans and air molecules alike—were constrained to remain.

Reassured, Barsac put his hands to his spacesuit's sealing-hasps and pried them open; he felt a whisper of air rush past his throat as he removed his helmet. The suit split open like the two halves of a sea-creature's shell; he let carapace and plastron drop unheeded and peeled away the few clothes he wore beneath.

Naked now amid sixteen other naked candidates and nine Cultists clad only in their face-concealing masks, Barsac moved forward into the violet haze that blurred what lay ahead. He walked for perhaps two minutes, and then the haze cleared away.

He stood facing the Witch of Azonda.

She sat enthroned, grasped in a translucent chair trimmed with onyx and edged in chalcedony. Before her there was a sort of dais, an altar of a kind, carved of some delicate semitransparent pinkish stone. Visible beneath the outer barrier of the stone was a dark something, a mechanism perhaps; it was impossible to see it clearly.

Barsac stared at the Witch.

She was a woman who sat in naked magnificence, hands resting lightly on the knurled sides of her throne. Her skin was of a light gold color, warm-looking, her figure was lush, her breasts high, rounded. She had no face. From forehead to chin all was smooth and gently curved, polished almost, a blank planchet on which a sculptor might have carved a face had he chosen to. Yet she did not look incomplete; she seemed perfect to Barsac, a living work of art.

Around her was ranged a semi-circle of acolytes: eleven men, Barsac saw, naked all, but with faces masked. Kneeling at the outer edge of the semi-circle were eight women, masked also. From the group rose a low wordless chant, a wailing ululation that rose shiveringly through tortured chromatic intervals and down again.

The sound swelled out about him. In his mind Barsac heard a soft voice say, *Come to me, for I am the Way; come to me, for in me there is no more pain, in me there is only peace and surcease from the suffering you have known.*

Fronds of light lapped at his mind. He felt impelled forward; he seemed to glide.

An end to pain, an end to torment, an end to self.

In me there is peace always, and companionship, and in my company will you serve cheerfully and abide for all eternity.

In response to an unvoiced command Barsac stretched out both his hands, and felt them being taken by others; a dream-light suffused the area, and he was conscious of warmth and a kind of oozing softness.

Hands joined, the seventeen candidates advanced toward the Witch and knelt before the altar.

This was the end of the quest, Barsac thought; here was where all struggle ended, where all beingness cascaded back into the primordial womb of creation.

In my light will you be healed—

Fingers caressed his mind, urging him to give up his oneness, to become part of the brotherhood that called itself the Cult of the Witch. He felt the bonds of tension that gripped his mind relax under the gentle ministrations. It would be so easy to slip away from himself, to allow his mind and soul to merge with the others.

He relaxed. His self ebbed away.

Look upon me, came the command.

Barsac looked up at the faceless silent perfection of the Witch. Somehow his eyes slipped from her after a moment, and he scanned the eleven Cult acolytes ranged behind her, his eyes caught and fascinated by the brightness of the reflections from their polished masks. It was as if in each of the masks a Witch shined.

Curious, Barsac thought, with the part of his mind that still remained to him. One of those acolytes has a scarred face.

A strange pattern of incisions radiating outward from the lips. Barsac frowned. The beauty of the Witch called to him to cease all thinking and surrender himself, but he shook the temptation away impatiently, and his hand rose to feel the deep grooves that disfigured his own face.

He and that acolyte were disfigured in the same fashion, he thought.

Odd. How could that be? How—

Awareness flooded back to him. He ripped his hands free of the crooning candidates who knelt next to him and stood up, remembering now.

His shout split the sanctified silence:

"Zigmunn!"

The light wavered. His sudden piercing bellow had broken the spell. Around him the candidates wandered in uncertain circles, torn from their trance but not masters of themselves any longer. Behind the throne, the stunned acolytes froze in astonishment, while the Witch beamed blandly down, seeming to smile facelessly, and then darkened slowly into a figure of horror.

Barsac moved forward.

"Zigmunn! You, behind the mask—I know you by the scars! I've come here to get you, bring you back. Do you know these scars, Zigmunn?"

One of the stock-still acolytes spoke: "Barsac!"

"Yes. And the Witch failed to conquer me after all!" His stubbornness burned like a flame within him now; he forced himself forward toward the ring of acolytes. "Off with that mask, Zigmunn. Come back to Glaurus with me."

"Don't be a fool, Barsac. The Witch offers peace."

"The Witch offers lies!"

"You can never leave her," the Luasparru said. "Once you see her, you are part of her; the rest is superficial. Did you see her, Barsac?"

"I saw her. But I remain a free man."

"Impossible! You see only yourself mirrored in the Witch; she exists only if the Witch-forces exist in you, in the dark cesspool at the back of your mind."

"No," Barsac growled.

"Yes! If you are here, if you have seen the Witch—then you are lost! Yield, Barsac! Give in. Worship her, for she is within you!"

"*No!*"

He pressed relentlessly forward. A whisper passed through his mind, but he knew it was meant not for him but for the acolytes: *"Stop him."*

They laid hands on his wrists and clung to him. Angrily he shook them off; his body, so long held shackled, now swung free, and his fists clanged gaily off a silver mask. An acolyte sank, blood spouting.

Ten of the male acolytes were upon him now; only Zigmunn remained alone, cowering in panic behind the throne of the Witch. Barsac's arms threshed; acolytes went spinning to the ground, right and left. His fists pummelled in and out, scattering them as he moved on. He was unstoppable.

Three acolytes now clung to him, then two, then one. He plucked the remaining man off, hurled him aside, and vaulted toward the Witch.

Through the Witch.

He passed through her as if she were so much dream-smoke, and, clearing the throne, caught Zigmunn by the throat. He stared bitterly at the blood-scars on the Luasparru's face, then whipped off the silver mask with a contemptuous swipe of his hand.

The drug-hazed eyes that peered at his were the Luasparru's, but they were not those of the Zigmunn he had known. Sickened, Barsac released him and the pencil-thin Lausparru went reeling to one side.

"There is no way out of the Cult," Zigmunn said quietly. "Why did you follow me here? Why have you caused this havoc?"

"I . . . came to get you," Barsac said in a strangled voice. "But there's nothing left to get. You belong soul and body to—to *this*."

"Go back below," Zigmunn urged crooningly. "Kneel and beg her forgiveness. She will welcome you back. Once you have seen her, you can never escape her. You've given up your self, Barsac."

He shook his head bitterly. He saw now it had all been in vain; there was indeed no escape, and Zigmunn was lost forever. Heavily he turned away. The Witch was still on her throne, staring forward.

What was she? Thought-projection established by an unscrupulous priesthood? Alien entity seeking companionship on this dead world? He would never know.

The acolytes were recovering from their state of shock, now. They were creeping toward him. From elsewhere in the dusk-cloaked hall, other silver-masked figures advanced on him.

With a sudden bellow of rage, Barsac snatched up the thin figure of Zigmunn and grasped the emaciated Luasparru tightly. Then, with a savage display of force, he dashed Zigmunn against the translucent altar of pink stone.

It shattered; the stone must have been only glass-thin. Zigmunn rolled to one side and lay still.

The curtain of force winked out.

Barsac froze for just a moment, staring down at the shattered altar, and a mighty scream went up from the acolytes who saw. In a vast rush the atmosphere fled outward, and the stinging airlessness of Azonda swept in over the Hall of the Witch.

Moving as though through a sea of acid Barsac ran toward his discarded spacesuit. It seemed to take hours for him to don it, hours more before air coursed through his helmet and he breathed again. Actually, no more than fifteen seconds had gone by.

He turned. A hundred naked figures lay sprawled round the altar. Bubbles of blood trickled from their faces as they coughed out their lives into the vacuum that surrounded them. The Witch sat complacently through it all, paler now but unchanged otherwise and apparently unchangeable.

A harsh cry rumbled up from somewhere in Barsac's throat, and he turned away, retching, and started to run. Back, across the snow, away from the scene of death that had been the Hall of the Witch, toward the waiting golden-green ship that stood on its tail in the distant snow.

He reached the ship. He entered, converted to autopilot, hastily set up for blast-off. No time for elaborate checks and signals, now; there was but one passenger, and that passenger cared little whether he lived or died.

The ship lifted. Barsac clung desperately to the rails of the control-room wall and let the fist of gravity buffet him senseless. He dropped finally and lay flat against the coolness of the deckplates.

He awoke some time later. The ship's chart-tank told him he was well outside the Glaurus system now, cutting diagonally across the lens of the galaxy with the triple system of Ooon as the immediate destination. Barsac stared at his tortured unfamiliar face in the burnished mirror and realized he had escaped the Cult. They lay dead, back on dead Azonda, and he had a ship of his own; all the galaxy lay open for him. Life could begin again.

Or had he escaped the Cult? He wondered, as the nose of his ship drew ever nearer the tricolored glory of Ooon. For the tongue of the incomprehensible Witch had licked his mind, and perhaps Zigmunn had not lied. The Witch would be always with him whether he willed it or not, whether he fled as far as the cinder-stars that lay behind the galactic lens. He stared at the white-haired fleshless face in the mirror, and it seemed to him that behind him waited another face, a featureless blank face, white and shining.

She would be with him always, and the memory of eight months of hell on Glaurus and Azonda. Stroking the lateral grooves that lined his jaws, Barsac studied the chart-tank, and waited for tricolored Ooon to draw near.

The Silent Invaders

Chapter One

The starship *Lucky Lady* thundered out of overdrive half a million miles from Earth, and began the long steady ion-drive glide at Earthnorm grav toward the orbiting depot. In his second-class cabin aboard the starship, the man whose papers said he was Major Abner Harris of the Interstellar Development Corps stared at his face in the mirror. He wanted to make sure for the hundredth time that there was no sign of where his tendrils once had been.

He smiled; and the even-featured, undistinguished face they had put on him drew back, lips rising in the corners, cheeks tightening, neat white teeth momentarily on display. Major Harris scowled, and the face darkened.

It behaved well. The synthetic white skin acted as if it were his own. The surgeons back on Darruu had done a superb job on him.

They had removed the fleshy four-inch-long tendrils that sprouted at a Darruui's temples; they had covered his deep golden skin with an overlay of convincingly Terran white, and grafted it so skilfully that by now it had become his real skin. Contact lenses turned his eyes from red to blue-gray. Hormone treatments had caused hair to sprout on head and body, where none had been before. They had not meddled with his internal plumbing, and there he remained alien, with the Darruui digestive organ where a Terran had so many incredible feet of intestine, with the double heart and the sturdy liver just back of his three lungs.

Inside he was alien. Behind the walls of his skull, he was Aar Khiilom of the city of Helasz—a Darruui of the highest caste, a Servant of the Spirit. Externally, though, he was Major Abner Harris. He knew Major Harris' biography in great detail.

Born 2520, in Cincinnati, Ohio, United States, Earth. Age now, 42—with a good hundred years of his lifespan left. Attended Western Reserve University, studying galactography; graduated '43. Entered the Interstellar Redevelopment

Corps '46, commissioned '50, now a Major. Missions to Altair VII, Sirius IX, Procyon II, Alpheratz IV. Unmarried. Parents killed in highway jet-crash in '44; no known relatives. Height five feet ten, weight 220, color fair, retinal index point-oh-three.

Major Harris was visiting Earth on vacation. He was to spend eight months on Earth before reassignment to his next planetary post.

Eight months, thought the one who called himself Major Harris, would be ample time for Major Harris to lose himself in the billions of Earth and carry out the purposes for which he had been sent here.

The *Lucky Lady* was on the last lap of her journey. Harris had boarded her on Alpheratz IV, after having been shipped there from Darruu by private warpship. For the past three weeks, while the giant vessel had slipped through the sleek gray tunnel in the continuum that was its overdrive channel, Harris had been learning to walk at Earthnorm gravity.

Darruu was a large world—radius 11,000 miles—and though its density was not as great as Earth's, still the gravitational attraction was half again as intense. Darruu's gravity was 1.5 Earthnorm. Or, as Harris had thought of it in the days when his mind centered not on Earth but on Darruu, Earth's gravity was .67 Darruunorm. Either way, it meant that his muscles would be functioning in a field two-thirds as strong as the one they had developed in. He could use the excuse that he had spent most of his time on heavy planets, and that would explain away some of his awkwardness.

But not all. A native Earther, no matter how long he stays on a heavy world, still knows how to cope with Earthnorm gravity. Harris had to learn that. He *did* learn it, painstakingly, during the three weeks of overdrive travel toward the system of Sol.

Now the journey was almost complete. All that remained was the transfer from the starship to an Earth shuttle, and then he could begin life as an Earthman.

Earth hung outside the main viewport twenty feet from Harris' cabin. He stared at it. A great green ball of a world, with two huge continents here, another landmass there, a giant moon moving in slow procession around it, keeping one pockmarked face eternally staring inward, the other glaring at outer space like a single beady bright eye.

The sight made Harris homesick.

Darruu was nothing like this. Darruu, from space, seemed to be a giant red fruit, covered over by the crimson mist that was the upper layer of its atmosphere. Beneath that could be discerned the great blue seas and the two hemisphere-large continents of Darraa and Darroo.

And the moons, Harris thought nostalgically. Seven glistening blank faces like coins in the sky, each at its own angle to the ecliptic, each taking its place in the sky nightly like a gem moved by clockwork. And the Mating of the Moons, when the seven came together once a year in a fiercely radiant diadem that filled half the sky—

Angrily he cut the train of thought.

You're an Earthman. Forget Darruu.

A voice on a speaker overhead said, "Please return to your cabins, ladies and gentlemen. In eleven minutes we will come to a rest at the main spaceborne depot. Passengers intending to transfer here please notify their area steward."

Harris returned to his cabin while the voice repeated the statement in other languages. Earth still spoke more than a dozen major tongues, which surprised him; Darruu had reached linguistic homogeneity three thousand years or more ago.

Minutes ticked by; at last came the word that the *Lucky Lady* had ended its ion-drive cruise and was tethered to the orbital satellite. Harris left his cabin for the last time and headed downramp to the designated room on D Deck where outgoing passengers were assembling.

"Your baggage will be shipped across. You don't have to worry about that."

Harris nodded. His baggage was important.

More than three hundred of the passengers were leaving ship here. Harris was herded along with the others through an airlock. Several dozen ungainly little ferries hovered just outside, linked to the huge starliner by connecting tubes. Harris entered a swaying tube, crossed over, and found a seat in the ferry. Minutes later, he was repeating the process in the other direction, as the ferry unloaded its passengers into the main airlock of Orbiting Station Number One.

Another voice boomed, "*Lucky Lady* passengers continuing on to Earth report to Routing Channel Four. *Lucky Lady* passengers continuing on to Earth report to Routing Channel Four. Passengers transhipping to other starlines should go to the nearest routing desk at once."

At Routing Channel Four, Harris was called upon to produce his papers. He handed over the little fabrikoid portfolio; a spaceport official riffled sleepily through it and handed it back without a word.

As he boarded the Earth-Orbiter shuttle, an attractive stewardess handed him a multigraphed sheet of paper which contained information of a sort a tourist was likely to want to know. Harris scanned it quickly.

"The Orbiting Station is located eighty thousand miles from Earth. It is locked in a twenty-four hour orbit that keeps it hovering approximately above Quito, Ecuador, South America. During a year the Orbiting Station serves an average of 8,500,000 travellers—"

He finished reading the sheet and put it down. He eyed his fellow passengers in the Earthbound shuttle. There were about fifty of them.

For all he knew, five were disguised Darruui like himself. Or they might be enemies—Medlins—likewise in disguise. Perhaps he was surrounded by agents of Earth's own intelligence corps who had already penetrated his disguise.

Trouble lay on every hand. Inwardly Major Harris felt calm, though there was the faint twinge of homesickness for Darruu that he knew he would never be able entirely to erase.

The shuttle banked into a steep deceleration curve. Artificial grav aboard the Ship remained constant, of course. Earth drew near.

Landing came.

T he shuttle hung over the skin of the landing-field for thirty seconds, then dropped; a gantry crane shuffled out to support the ship, and buttress-legs sprang from the sides of the hull. A steward's voice said, "Passengers will please assemble at the airlock in single file."

They assembled. A green omnibus waited outside on the field, and the fifty of them filed in. Harris found a seat by the window and stared out across the broad field. A yellow sun was in the blue sky. The air was cold; he shivered involuntarily and drew his cloak around him for warmth.

"Cold?" asked the man who shared his seat with him.

"A bit."

"That's odd. Nice balmy spring day like this, you'd think everybody would be enjoying the weather."

Harris grinned. "I've been on some pretty hot worlds the last ten years. Anything under ninety degrees and I start shivering, now."

The other chuckled and said, "Must be near eighty in the shade today."

"I'll be accustomed to it again before long," Harris said. "Once an Earthman, always an Earthman."

He made a mental note to carry out a trifling adjustment on his body thermostat. His skin was lined with subminiaturized heating and refrigerating units—just one of the useful modifications the surgeons had given him.

Darruu's mean temperature was 120 degrees, on the scale used by the Earthers. When it dropped to 80, Darruui cursed the cold. It was 80 now, and he was uncomfortably cold. He would have to stay that way for most of the day, at least, until in a moment of privacy he could make the necessary adjustments. Around him, the Earthers seemed to be perspiring and feeling discomfort because of the heat.

The bus filled finally, and spurted across the field to a high domed building of gleaming steel and green plastic. The driver said, "First stop is customs. Have your papers ready."

Inside, Harris found his baggage already waiting for him at a counter labelled HAM-HAT. There were two suitcases, both of them with topological secret compartments. He surrendered his passport and, when told to do so, pressed his thumb to the opener-plate. The suitcases sprang open. The customs man poked through them perfunctorily, nodded, said, "Anything to declare?"

"Nothing."

"Okay. Close 'em up."

Harris locked the suitcases again, and the customs official briefly touched a tracer-stamp to them. It left no visible imprint, but the photonic scanners at every door would be watching for the radiations, and no one with an unstamped suitcase could get through the electronic barriers.

"Next stop is Immigration, Major."

At Immigration they studied his passport briefly, noted that he was a government employee, and passed him along to Health. Here he felt a moment of alarm; about one out of every fifty incoming passengers from a starship was detained for a comprehensive medical exam, and if the finger fell upon him the game was up right here. Ten seconds in front of a fluoroscope would tell them that nobody with that kind of skeletal structure had ever been born in Cincinnati, Ohio.

He got through with nothing more than a rudimentary checkup. At the last desk his passport was stamped with a re-entry visa, and the clerk said, "You haven't been on Earth for a long time, eh, Major?"

"Not in ten years. Hope things haven't changed too much."

"The women are still the same, anyway." The clerk shuffled Harris' papers together, stuck them back in the portfolio, and handed them to him. "Everything's in order. Go straight ahead and out the door to your left."

Harris thanked him and moved along, gripping one suitcase in each hand. A month ago, at the beginning of his journey, the suitcases had seemed heavy to him. But that had been on Darruu; here they weighed only two-thirds as much. He carried them jauntily.

Soon it will be spring on Darruu, he thought. The red-leaved jasaar trees would blossom and their perfume would fill the air.

With an angry inner scowl he blanked out the thought. He was Major Abner Harris, late of Cincinnati, here on Earth for eight months' vacation.

He knew his orders. He was to establish residence, avoid detection, and in the second week of his stay make contact with the chief Darruui agent on Earth. Further instructions would come from him.

Chapter Two

I t took twenty minutes by helitaxi to reach the metropolitan area from the spaceport. Handling the Terran currency as if he had used it all his life, Harris paid the driver, tipped him, and got out. He had asked for and been taken to a hotel in the heart of the city—the Spaceways Hotel. There was one of them in every major spaceport city in the galaxy; the spacelines operated them jointly, for the benefit of travelers who had no place to stay on the planet of their destination.

He signed in and was given a room on the 58th floor. The Earther at the desk said, "You don't mind heights, do you, Major?"

"Not at all."

He gave the boy who had carried his bags a quarter-unit piece, received grateful thanks, and locked the door. For the first time since leaving Darruu he was really *alone*. Thumbing open his suitcases, he performed the series of complex stress-pressures that gave access to the hidden areas of the grips; miraculously, the suitcases expanded to nearly twice their former volume. There was nothing like packing your belongings in a tesseract if you wanted to keep the customs men away from them.

Busily, he unpacked.

First thing out was a small device which fit neatly and virtually invisibly to the inside of the door. It was a jammer for spybeams. It insured privacy.

A disruptor-pistol came next. He slipped it into his tunic-pocket. Several books; a flask of Darruui wine; a photograph of his birth-tree. Bringing these things had not increased his risk, since if they had been found it would only be after much more incriminating things had come to light.

The subspace communicator, for example. Or the narrow-beam amplifier he would use in making known his presence to the other members of the Darruui cadre on Earth.

He finished unpacking, restored his suitcases to their three-dimensional state, and took a tiny scalpel from the toolkit he had unpacked. Quickly stripping off his trousers, he laid bare the desensitized area in the fleshy part of his thigh, stared for a moment at the network of fine silver threads underlying the flesh, and, with three careful twists of the scalpel's edge, altered the thermostatic control in his body.

He shivered a moment; then, gradually, he began to feel warm. Closing the wound, he applied nuplast; moments later it had healed. He dressed again.

He surveyed his room. Twenty feet square, with a bed, a desk, a closet, a dresser. An air-conditioning grid in the ceiling. A steady greenish electroluminescent glow. An oval window beneath which was a set of polarizing controls. A molecular bath and washstand. Not bad for twenty units a week, he told himself, trying to think the way an Earthman might.

The room-calendar told him it was five-thirty in the afternoon, 22 May 2562. He was not supposed to make contact with Central for ten days or more; he computed that that would mean the first week of June. Until then he was simply to act the part of a Terran on vacation.

The surgeons had made certain minor alterations in his metabolism to give him a taste for Terran food and drink and to make it possible for him to digest the carbohydrates of which Terrans were so fond. They had prepared him well for playing the part of Major Abner Harris. And he had been equipped with fifty thousand units of Terran money, enough to last him quite a while.

Carefully he adjusted the device on the door to keep intruders out while he was gone. Anyone entering the room would get a nasty jolt of energy now. He checked his wallet, made sure he had his money with him, and pushed the door-opener.

It slid back and he stepped through into the hallway. At that moment someone walking rapidly down the hall collided with him, spinning him around. He felt a soft body pressed against his.

A woman!

The immediate reaction that boiled up in him was one of anger, but he blocked the impulse to strike her before it rose. On Darruu, a woman who jostled a Servant of the Spirit could expect a sound whipping. But this was not Darruu.

He remembered a phrase from his indoctrination: *it will help to create a sexual relationship for yourself on Earth*.

The surgeons had changed his metabolism in that respect, too, making him able to feel sexual desires for Terran females. The theory was that no one would expect a disguised alien to engage in romantic affairs with Terrans; it would be a form of camouflage.

"Excuse me!" Harris and the female Terran said, simultaneously.

His training reminded him that simultaneous outbursts were cause for laughter on Earth. He laughed. So did she. Then she said, "I guess I didn't see you. I was hurrying along the corridor and I wasn't looking."

"The fault was mine," Harris insisted. *Terran males are obstinately chivalrous*, he had been told. "I opened my door and just charged out blind. I'm sorry."

She was tall, nearly his height, with soft, lustrous yellow hair and clear pink skin. She wore a black body-tight sheath that left her shoulders and the upper hemispheres of her breasts uncovered. Harris found her attractive.

Wonderingly he thought, *Now I know they've changed me. She has hair on her scalp and enormous bulging breasts and yet I feel desire for her.*

She said, "It's my fault and it's your fault. That's the way most collisions are caused. Let's not argue about that. My name is Beth Baldwin."

"Major Abner Harris."

"Major?"

"Interstellar Development Corps."

"Oh," she said. "Just arrived on Earth?"

He nodded. "I'm on vacation. My last hop was Alpheratz IV." He smiled and said, "It's silly to stand out here in the hall discussing things. I was on my way down below to get something to eat. How about joining me?"

She looked doubtful for a moment, but only for a moment. She brightened. "I'm game."

They took the gravshaft down and ate in the third-level restaurant, an automated affair with individual conveyor-belts bringing food to each table. Part of his hypnotic training had been intended to see him through situations such as this, and so he ordered a dinner for two, complete with wine, without a hitch.

She did not seem shy. She told him that she was employed on Rigel XII, and had come to Earth on a business trip; she had arrived only the day before. She was twenty-nine, unmarried, a native-born Earther like himself, who had been living in the Rigel system the past four years.

"And now tell me about you," she said, reaching for the wine decanter.

"There isn't much to tell. I'm a fairly stodgy career man in the IDC, age forty-two, and this is the first day I've spent on Earth in ten years."

"It must feel strange."

"It does."

"How long is your vacation?"

He shrugged. "Six to eight months. I can have more if I really want it. When do you go back to Rigel?"

She smiled strangely at him. "I may not go back at all. Depends on whether I can find what I'm looking for on Earth."

"And what are you looking for?"

She grinned. "My business," she said.

"Sorry."

"Never mind the apologies. Let's have some more wine."

After Harris had settled up the not inconsiderable matter of the bill, they left the hotel and went outside to stroll. The streets were crowded; a clock atop a distant building told Harris that the time was shortly after seven. He felt warm now that he had adjusted his temperature controls, and the unfamiliar foods and wines in his stomach gave him an oddly queasy feeling, though he had enjoyed the meal.

The girl slipped her hand through his looped arm and squeezed the inside of his elbow. Harris grinned. He said, "I was afraid it was going to be an awfully lonely vacation."

"Me too. You can be tremendously alone on a planet that has twenty billion people on it."

They walked on. In the middle of the street a troupe of acrobats was performing, using nullgrav devices to add to their abilities. Harris chuckled and tossed them a coin, and a bronzed girl saluted to him from the top of a human pyramid.

Night was falling. Harris considered the incongruity of walking arm-in-arm with an Earthgirl, with his belly full of Earth foods, and enjoying it.

Darruu seemed impossibly distant now. It lay eleven hundred light-years from Earth; its star was visible only as part of a mass of blurred dots of light.

But yet he knew it was there. He missed it.

"You're worrying about something," the girl said.

"It's an old failing of mine."

He was thinking: *I was born a Servant of the Spirit, and so I was chosen to go to Earth. I may never return to Darruu again.*

As the sky darkened they strolled on, over a delicate golden bridge spanning a river whose dark depths twinkled with myriad points of light. Together they stared down at the water, and at the stars reflected in it. She moved closer to him, and her warmth against his body was pleasing to him.

Eleven hundred light-years from home.

Why am I here?

He knew the answer. Titanic conflict was shaping in the universe. The Predictors held that the cataclysm was no more than two hundred years away. Darruu would stand against its ancient adversary Medlin, and all the worlds of the universe would be ranged on one side or on the other.

He was here as an ambassador. Earth was a mighty force in the galaxy—so mighty that it would resent the role it really played, that of pawn between Darruu and Medlin. Darruu wanted Terran support in the conflict to come. Obtaining it was a delicate problem in consent engineering. A cadre of disguised Darruui, planted on Earth, gradually manipulating public opinion toward the Darruu camp and away from Medlin—that was the plan, and Harris, once Aar Khiilom, was one of its agents.

They walked until the hour had grown very late, and then turned back toward the hotel. Harris was confident now that he had established the sort of relationship that was likely to shield him from all suspicion of his true origin.

He said, "What do we do now?"

"Suppose we buy a bottle of something and have a party in your room?" she suggested.

"My room's a frightful mess," Harris said, thinking of the many things in there he would not want her to see. "How about yours?"

"It doesn't matter."

They stopped at an autobar and he fed half-unit pieces into a machine until the chime sounded and a fully wrapped bottle slid out on the receiving tray. Harris tucked it under his arm, made a mock-courteous bow to her, and they continued on their way to the hotel.

The signal came just as they entered the lobby.

It reached Harris in the form of a sudden twinge in the abdomen; that was where the amplifier had been embedded. He felt it as three quick impulses, *rasp rasp rasp*, followed after a brief pause by a repeat.

The signal had only one meaning: *Emergency. Get in touch with your contact-man at once.*

Her hand tightened on his arm. "Are you all right? You look so pale!"

In a dry voice he said, "Maybe we'd better postpone our party a few minutes. I'm—not quite well."

"Oh! Can I help?"

He shook his head. "It's—something I picked up on Alpheratz." Turning, he handed her the packaged bottle and said, "It'll just take me a few minutes to get myself settled down. Suppose you go to your room and wait for me there."

"But if you're sick I ought to—"

"No. Beth, I have to take care of this myself, without anyone else watching. Okay?"

"Okay," she said doubtfully.

"Thanks. Be with you as soon as I can."

They rode the gravshaft together to the 58th floor and went their separate ways, she to her room, he to his. The signal in his abdomen was repeating itself steadily now with quiet urgency: *Rasp rasp rasp. Rasp rasp rasp. Rasp rasp rasp.*

He neutralized the force-field on the door with a quick energy impulse and opened the door. Stepping inside quickly, he activated the spy-beam jammer again. Beads of sweat were starting to form on his skin.

Rasp rasp rasp. Rasp rasp rasp.

He opened the closet, took out the tiny narrow-beam amplifier he had hidden there, and tuned it to the frequency of the emergency signal. Immediately the rasping stopped as the narrow-beam amplifier covered the wavelength.

Moments passed. The amplifier picked up a voice speaking in the code devised for use by Darruui agents alone.

"Identify yourself."

Harris identified himself according to the regular procedure. He went on to say, "I arrived on Earth today. My instructions were not to report to you for about two weeks."

"I know that. There's an emergency situation."

"What kind of emergency?"

"There are Medlin agents on Earth. Normal procedures will have to be altered. Meet me at once." He gave an address. Harris memorized it and repeated it. The contact was broken.

Meet me at once. The orders had to be interpreted literally. *At once* meant right now, not tomorrow afternoon. His tryst with the yellow-haired Earthgirl would just have to wait.

He picked up the house-phone and asked for her room. A moment later he heard her voice.

"Hello?"

"Beth, this is Abner Harris."

"How are you? Everything under control? I'm waiting for you."

Hesitantly he said, "I'm fine now. But—Beth, I don't know how to say this—will you believe me when I say that a friend of mine just phoned, and wants me to meet him right away downtown?"

"Now? But it's after eleven!"

"I know. He's—a strange sort."

"I thought you didn't have any friends on Earth, Major Harris. You said you were lonely."

"He's not really a *friend*. He's a business associate. From IDC."

"Well, I'm not accustomed to having men stand me up. But I don't have any choice, do I?"

"Good girl. Make it a date for breakfast in the morning instead?"

"Lousy substitute, but it'll have to do. See you at nine."

Chapter Three

The rendezvous-point the other operative had named was a street corner in another quarter of the city. Harris hired a helitaxi to take him there.

It was a nightclub district, all bright lights and brassy music. A figure leaned against the lamppost on the southeast corner of the street. Harris crossed to him. In the brightness of the streetlamp he saw the man's face: lean, lantern-jawed, solemn.

Harris said, "Pardon me, friend. Do you know where I can buy a mask for the carnival?"

It was the recognition-query. The other answered, in a deep harsh voice, "Masks are expensive. Stay home." He thrust out his hand.

Harris took it, gripping the wrist in the Darruui way, and grinned. Eleven hundred light-years from home and he beheld a fellow Servant of the Spirit! "I'm Major Abner Harris."

"Hello. I'm John Carver. There's a table waiting for us inside."

"Inside" turned out to be the Nine Planets Club, across the street. The atmosphere inside was steamy and smoke-clouded; bubbles of light drifted round the ceiling. A row of long-limbed nudes pranced gaily to the accompaniment of the noise that passed for music on Terra. The surgeons, Harris thought, had never managed to instill a liking for Terran music in him.

Carver said quietly, "Have you had any trouble since you arrived?"

"No. Should I expect any?"

The lean man shrugged. "There are one hundred Medlin agents on Earth right now. Yesterday we discovered a cache of secret Medlin documents. We have the names of the hundred and their photographs. We also know they plan to wipe us out."

"How many Darruui are on Earth?"

"You are the tenth to arrive."

Harris' eyes widened. One hundred Medlins against ten Darruui! "Stiff odds," he said.

Carver nodded. "But we know their identities. We can strike first. Unless we eliminate them, we will not be able to proceed with our work here."

The music reached an earsplitting crescendo. Moodily Harris stared at the nude chorus-line as it gyrated. He sensed some glandular disturbance at the sight, and frowned. By Darruui standards, the girls were obscenely *ugly*.

But this was not Darruu.

He said, "How do we go about eliminating them?"

"You have weapons. I'll supply you with the necessary information. If you can get ten of them before they get you, you'll be all right." He drew forth a billfold and extracted a snapshot from it. "Here's your first one, now. Kill her and report back to me. You can find her at the Spaceways Hotel."

Harris felt a jolt. "*I'm* staying at that hotel."

"Indeed? Here. Look at the picture," Harris took the photo from the other. It was a tridim in full color. It showed a blonde girl wearing a low-cut black sheath.

Controlling his voice, he said, "This girl's too pretty to be a Medlin agent."

"That's why she's so deadly," Carver said. "Kill her first. She goes under the name of Beth Baldwin."

Harris stared at the photo a long while. Then he nodded. "Okay. I'll get in touch with you again when the job's done."

I t was nearly two in the morning when he returned to the hotel. He had spent nearly an hour with the man who called himself John Carver. He felt tired, confused, faced with decisions that frightened him.

Beth Baldwin a Medlin spy? How improbable that seemed! But yet Carver had had her photo.

It was his job to kill her, now. He was a Servant of the Spirit. He could not betray his trust.

First I'll find out for certain, though.

He took the gravshaft to the 58th floor, but instead of going to his room he turned left and headed toward the room whose number she had given him—5820. He paused a moment, then nudged the door-signal.

There was no immediate response, so he nudged it again. This time he heard the sound of a doorscanner humming just above him, telling him that she was awake and just within the door.

He said, "It's me—Abner. I have to see you, Beth."

"Hold on," came the sleepy reply from inside. "Let me get something on."

A moment passed, and then the door slid open. Beth smiled at him. She had "put something on," but the something had not been much—a flimsy gown that concealed her body as if she were wearing so much gauze.

But Harris was not interested in her body just now, attractive though it was. She held a tiny glittering weapon in her hand. Harris recognized the weapon. It was the Medlin version of the disruptor-pistol.

"Come on in, Abner."

Numbly he stepped forward, and the door shut behind him. Beth gestured with the disruptor.

"Sit down over there."

"How come the gun, Beth?"

"You know that answer without my having to tell it to you. Now that you've seen Carver, you know who I am."

He nodded. "A Medlin agent."

It was hard to believe. He stared at the girl who stood ten feet from him, a disruptor trained at his skull. The Medlin surgeons evidently were as skillful as those of Darruu, it seemed, for the wiry pebble-skinned Medlins were even less humanoid than the Darruui—and yet he would swear that those breasts, the flaring hips, the long well-formed legs, were genuine.

She said, "We had information on you from the moment you entered the orbit of Earth, Abner—or should I say Aar Khiilom?"

"How did you know that name?"

She laughed lightly. "The same way I knew you were from Darruu, the same way I knew the exact moment you were going to come out of your room before."

"The same way you knew I was coming here to kill you just now?"

She nodded.

Harris frowned. "Medlins aren't telepathic. There isn't a single telepathic race in the galaxy."

"None that *you* know about, anyway."

"What do you mean by that?"

"Nothing," she said.

He shrugged. Apparently the Medlin spy system was formidably well organized. This nonsense about telepathy was merely to cloud the trail. But the one fact about which there was no doubt was—

"I came here to kill you," Harris said. "But you trapped me. I guess you'll kill me now."

"Wrong. I just want to talk," she said.

"If you want to talk, put some clothing on. Having you sitting around like this disturbs my powers of conversation."

She said pleasantly, "Oh? You mean this artificial body of mine stirs some response in that artificial body of yours? How interesting!" Without turning her back on him, she drew a robe from the closet and slipped it on over the filmy gown. "There. Is that easier on your glandular balance?"

"Somewhat."

The Darruui began to fidget. There was no way he could activate his emergency signal without moving his hands, and any sudden hand-motion was likely to be fatal. He sat motionless while sweat streamed down the skin they had grafted to his own.

Beth said, "You're one of ten Darruui on Earth. Others are on their way, but there are only ten of you here now. Correct me if I'm wrong."

"Why should I?" Harris said tightly.

She nodded. "A good point. But I assure you we have all the information about you we need, so you needn't try to make up tales. To continue: you and your outfit are here for the purpose of subverting Terran allegiance and winning Earth over to the side of Darruu."

"And you Medlins are here for much the same kind of reason."

"That's where you're wrong," the girl said. "We're here to help the Terrans, not to dominate them. We Medlins don't believe in violence if peaceful means will accomplish our goals."

"Very nice words," Harris said. "But how can *you* help the Terrans?"

"It's a matter of genetics. This isn't the place to explain in detail."

He let that pass. "So you deliberately threw yourself in contact with me earlier, let me take you out to dinner, walked around arm-in-arm—and all this time you knew I was a disguised Darruui?"

"Of course. I also knew that when you pretended to be sick it was because you had to contact your chief operative, and that when you said you were going to visit a friend you were attending an emergency rendezvous. I also knew what your friend Carver was going to tell you to do, which is why I had my gun ready when you rang."

He stared at her. "Suppose I *hadn't* gotten that emergency message. We were going to come here and drink and probably make love. Would you have gone to bed with me even knowing what you knew?"

"Most likely," she said without emotion. "It would have been interesting to see what sort of biological reactions the Darruui surgeons are capable of building."

A flash of hatred ran through Harris-Khiilom. He had been raised to hate Medlins anyway; they were the ancestral enemies of his people, galactic rivals for four thousand years or more. Only the fact that she was clad in the flesh of a handsome Earthgirl had kept Harris from feeling his normal revulsion for a Medlin.

But now it surged forth at this revelation of her calm and callous biological "curiosity."

He wondered how far her callousness extended. Also, how good her aim was.

He mastered his anger and said, "That's a pretty cold-blooded way of thinking, Beth."

"Maybe. I'm sorry about it."

"I'll bet you are."

She smiled at him. "Let's forget about that, shall we? I want to tell you a few things."

"Such as?"

"For one: did you know that you're fundamentally disloyal to the Darruui cause?"

Harris laughed harshly.

"You're crazy!"

"Afraid not. Listen to me, Abner. You're homesick for Darruu. You never wanted to come here in the first place. You were born into a caste that has certain obligations, and you're fulfilling those obligations. But you don't know very much about what you're doing here on Earth, and for half a plugged unit you'd give the whole thing up and go back to Darruu."

"Very clever," he said stonily. "Now give me my horoscope for the next six months."

"Easy enough. You'll come to our headquarters and learn why my people are on Earth—"

"I know that one already."

"You *think* you do," she said smoothly. "Don't interrupt. You'll learn why we're on Earth; once you've seen that, you'll join us and help to protect Earth against Darruu."

"And why will I do all these incredible things?"

"Because it's in your personality makeup to do them. And because you're falling in love."

"With a lot of fake female flesh plastered over a scrawny Medlin body? Hah!"

She remained calm. Harris measured the distance between them, wondering whether she would use the weapon after all. A disruptor broiled the neural tissue; death was instantaneous and fairly ghastly.

He decided to risk it. His assignment was to kill Medlins, not to let himself be killed by them. He had nothing to lose by making the attempt.

In a soft voice he said, "You didn't answer. Do you really think I'd fall in love with something like *you*?"

"Biologically we're Earthers now, not Medlins or Darruui. It's possible."

"Maybe you're right. After all, I *did* ask you to cover yourself up." He smiled and said, "I'm all confused. I need time to think things over."

"Of course. You—"

He sprang from the chair and covered the ten feet between them in two big bounds, stretching out one hand to grab the hand that held the disruptor. He deflected the weapon toward the ceiling. She did not fire. He closed on her wrist and forced her to drop the tiny pistol. Pressed against her, he stared into eyes blazing with anger.

The anger melted suddenly into passion. He stepped back, reaching for his own gun, not willing to have such close contact with her. She was too dangerous. Better to kill her right now, he thought. She's just a Medlin. A deadly one.

He started to draw the weapon from his tunic. Suddenly she lifted her hand; there was the twinkle of something bright between her fingers, and then Harris recoiled, helpless, as the bolt of a stunner struck him in the face like a club against the back of his skull.

She fired again. He struggled to get his gun out, but his muscles would not obey.

He toppled forward, paralyzed.

Chapter Four

Harris felt a teeth-chattering chill as he began to come awake. The stunner-bolt had temporarily overloaded his motor neurons, and the body's escape from the frustration of paralysis was unconsciousness. Now he was waking, and the strength was ebbing slowly and painfully back into his muscles.

The light of morning streamed in through a depolarized window on the left wall of the unfamiliar room in which he found himself. He felt stiff and sore all over, and realized he had spent the night—where?—

He groped in his pockets. His weapons were gone; they had left his wallet.

He got unsteadily to his feet and surveyed the room. The window was beyond his reach; there was no sign of a door. Obviously some section of the wall folded away to admit people to the room, but the door and door-jamb, wherever they were, must have been machined as smoothly as a couple of jo-blocks, because there was no sign of a break in the wall.

He looked up. There was a grid in the ceiling. Airconditioning, no doubt—and probably a spy-mechanism also. He stared at the grid and said, "Okay. I'm awake now. You can come work me over."

There was no immediate response. Surreptitiously Harris slipped a hand inside his waistband and squeezed a fold of flesh between his thumb and index finger. The action set in operation a minute amplifier embedded there; a distress signal, directionally modulated, was sent out to any Darruui agents who might be within a thousand-mile radius. He completed the gesture by lazily scratching his chest, stretching, yawning.

He waited.

Finally a segment of the door flipped upward out of sight, and three figures entered.

He recognized one of them: Beth. She smiled at him and said, "Good morning, Major."

Harris glared sourly at her. Behind her stood two males—one an ordinary-looking sort of Earther, the other rather special. He was about six feet six, well-proportioned for his height, with a regularity of feature that seemed startlingly beautiful.

Beth said, "Major Abner Harris, formerly Aar Khiilom of Darruu—this is Paul Coburn of Medlin Intelligence and David Wrynn of Earth."

"A real Earthman? Not a phony like the rest of us?"

Wrynn smiled pleasantly and said, "I assure you I'm a home-grown product, Major Harris." His voice was like the mellow boom of a well-tuned cello.

The Darruui folded his arms. "Well. How nice of you to introduce us all. Now what?"

"Still belligerent," he heard Beth murmur to the other Medlin, Coburn. Coburn nodded. The giant Earthman merely looked unhappy in a calm sort of way.

Harris eyed them all coldly. "If you're going to torture me, why not get started with it?"

"Who said anything about torture?" Beth asked.

"Why else would you bring me here? Obviously you want to wring information from me. Well, go ahead. I'm ready for you."

Coburn chuckled and fingered his double chins. "Don't you think we know that torture's useless on you? That if we tried any kind of forcible neural extraction of information from your mind your memory-chambers would automatically short-circuit?"

Harris' jaw dropped. "How did you know—" He stopped. The Medlins evidently had a fantastically efficient spy service. The filter-circuit in his brain was a highly secret development.

Beth said, "Relax and listen to us. We aren't out to torture you. We know already all you can tell us."

"Doubtful. But go ahead and talk."

"We know how many Darruui are on Earth. And we know approximately where they are. We'd like you to serve as a contact man for us."

"And do what?"

"Kill the other nine Darruui on Earth," Beth said simply.

Harris smiled. "Is there any special reason why I should do this?"

"For the good of the universe."

He laughed derisively. "For the good of Medlin, you mean."

"No. Listen to me. When we arrived on Earth—it was years ago, by the way—we quickly discovered that a new race was evolving here. A super-race, you might say. One with abnormal physical and mental powers. But in most cases children of this new race were killed or mentally stunted before they reached maturity. People tend to resent being made obsolete—and even a super-child is unable to defend himself until he's learned how. By then it's usually too late."

It was a nice fairy-tale, Harris thought. He made no comment, but listened with apparent interest.

Beth continued, "We discovered isolated members of this new race here and there on Earth. We decided to *help* them—knowing they would help us, some day, when it became necessary. We protected these children. We brought them together and raised them in safety. David Wrynn here is one of our first discoveries."

Harris glanced at the big Earthman. "So you're a superman?"

Wrynn smiled. "I'm somewhat better equipped for life than most other Earthmen. My children will be as far beyond me as I am beyond my parents."

"Our purpose here on Earth is to aid this evolving race until it's capable of taking care of itself—which won't be too long now. There are more than a hundred of them, of which thirty are adult. But now Darruui agents have started to arrive on Earth. Their purpose is to obstruct us, to interfere with our actions, and to win Earth over to what they think is their 'cause.' They don't see that they're backing a dead horse."

"Tell me," Harris said. "What's your motive in bringing into being this super-race?"

"Motive?" Beth said. "You Darruui always think in terms of motives, don't you? Profit and reward. Major, there's nothing in this for us but the satisfaction of knowing that we're bringing something wonderful into being in the universe."

Harris swallowed that with much salt. The concept of altruism was not unknown on Darruu, certainly, but it seemed highly improbable that a planet would go to the trouble of sending emissaries across space for the sole purpose of serving as midwives to an emerging race of super-beings on Earth.

No, he thought. It was simply part of an elaborate propaganda maneuver whose motives did not lie close to the surface. There were no super-men. Wrynn was probably a Medlin himself, on whom the surgeons had done a specially good job.

Whatever the Medlins' motive, he determined to play along with them. By now Carver had probably picked up his distress signal and had worked out the location of the place where he was being held.

He said, "So you're busily raising a breed of super-Earthmen, and you want me to help? How?"

"We told you. By disposing of your comrades before they make things complicated for us."

"You're asking me to commit treason against my people, in other words."

"We know what sort of a man you are," Beth said. "You aren't in sympathy with the Darruui imperialistic ideals. You may *think* you are, but you aren't."

I'll play along, Harris thought. He said, "You're right. I didn't want to take the job on Earth in the first place. What can I do to help?"

Coburn and Beth exchanged glances. The "Earthman" Wrynn merely smiled.

Beth said, "I knew you'd cooperate. The first target is the man who calls himself Carver. Get rid of him and the Darruui agents are without a nerve-center. After him, the other eight will be easy targets."

"How do you know I won't trick you once you've released me?" Harris said.

Coburn said, "We have ways of keeping watch."

Harris nodded. "I'll go after Carver first. I'll get in touch with you as soon as he's out of the way."

It seemed too transparent, Harris thought, when they had set him loose. He found himself in a distant quarter of the city, nearly an hour's journey by helitaxi from his hotel.

All this talk of supermen and altruism! It made no sense, he thought—but Medlin propaganda was devious stuff, and he had good reason to distrust it.

Were they as simple as all that, though, to release him merely on his promise of good faith? If they were truly altruistic, of course, it made sense; but he knew the Medlins too well to believe that. Darkly he thought he must be part of some larger Medlin plan.

Well, let Carver worry about it, he thought.

Though he was hungry, he knew he had no time to bother about breakfast until he got in touch with the Darruui chief agent. He signalled for a helitaxi and gave his destination as the Spaceways Hotel.

When he finally arrived, fifty minutes later, he headed straight for his room, activated the narrow-beam communicator, and waited until the metallic voice from the speaker said in code, "Carver here."

"Harris speaking."

"You've escaped?"

"They set me free. It's a long story. Did you get a directional fix on the building?"

"Yes. Why did they let you go?"

"I promised to become a Medlin secret agent," Harris said. "My first assignment is to assassinate you."

The chuckle that came from the speaker grid held little mirth. Carver said, "Fill me in on everything that's happened to you since last night."

"For one thing, the Medlins know everything, but *everything*. When I went to visit the girl last night she was waiting for me with a gun. She stunned me and carted me off to the Medlin headquarters. When I woke up they gave me some weird line about raising a breed of super-Earthmen, and would I help them in this noble cause?"

"You agreed?"

"Of course. They let me go and I'm supposed to eradicate all the Darruui on Earth, beginning with you."

"The others are well scattered," Carver said.

"They seem to know where they are."

Carver was silent for a moment. Then he said, "We'll have to strike at once. We'll attack the Medlin headquarters and kill as many as we can. Do you really think they trust you?"

"Either that or they're using me as bait for an elaborate trap," Harris said.

"That's more likely. Well, we'll take their bait. Only they won't be able to handle us once they've caught hold of us."

Carver broke contact. Carefully Harris packed the equipment away again.

He breakfasted in the hotel restaurant after a prolonged session under the molecular showerbath to remove the fatigue and grime of his night's imprisonment. The meal was close to tasteless, but he needed the nourishment.

Returning to his room, he locked himself in and threw himself wearily on the bed. He was tired and deeply troubled.

Supermen, he thought.

Did it make sense for the Medlins to rear a possible galactic conqueror? Earthmen were dangerous enough as it was; though the spheres of galactic influence still were divided as of old between Darruu and Medlin, the Earthmen in their bare three hundred years of galactic contact had taken giant strides toward holding a major place in the affairs of the universe.

Their colonies stretched halfway across the galaxy. The Interstellar Development Corps of which he claimed to be a member had planted Earthmen indiscriminately on any uninhabited world of the galaxy that was not claimed by Darruu or Medlin.

And the Medlins, the ancient enemies of his people, the race he had been taught all his life to regard as the embodiment of evil—these were aiding Earthmen to progress to a plane of development far beyond anything either Darruu or Medlin had attained?

Ridiculous, he thought. No race breeds its own destruction knowingly. And the Medlins are no fools.

Certainly not fools enough to let me go on a mere promise that I'll turn traitor and aid them, he thought.

He shook his head. After a while he uncorked his precious flask of Darruui wine and poured a small quantity. The velvet-textured dark wine of his home-world soothed him a little, but the ultimate result was simply to increase his already painful longing for home. Soon, he thought, it would be harvest-time, and the first bottles of new wine would reach the shops. This would be the first year that he had not tasted the year's vintage while it still held the bouquet of youth.

Instead I find myself on a strange planet in a strange skin, caught up in the coils of the devil Medlins. He scowled darkly, and took another sip of wine to ease the ache his heart felt.

Chapter Five

A day of nerve-twisting inactivity passed. Harris did not hear from Carver, nor did any of the Medlins contact him. Once he checked Beth Baldwin's room at the hotel, but no one answered the door, and when he inquired at the desk he learned that she had moved out earlier in the day, leaving no forwarding address. It figured. She had established quarters in the hotel only long enough to come in touch with him, and, that done, had left.

Regretfully Harris wished he had had a chance to try that biological experiment with her, after all. Medlin though she was, his body was now Terran-oriented, and it might have been an interesting experience. Well, no chance for that now.

He ate alone, in the hotel restaurant, and kept close to his room all day. Toward evening his signal-amplifier buzzed. He activated the communicator and spoke briefly with Carver, who gave him an address and ordered him to report there immediately.

It was a shabby, old-fashioned building far to the east, at the edge of the river. He rode up eight stories in a gravshaft that vibrated so badly he expected to be hurled back down at any moment, and made his way down a poorly-lit dusty corridor to a weather-beaten door that gave off the faint yellow glow that indicated a protection-field.

Harris felt the gentle tingling in his stomach that told him he was getting a radionic scanning. Finally the door opened. Carver said to him, "Come in."

There were four others in the room—a pudgy balding man named Reynolds, a youthful smiling man who called himself Tompkins, a short, cold-eyed man introduced as McDermott, and a lanky fellow who spoke his name drawlingly as Patterson. As each of them in turn was introduced, he gave the Darruui recognition signal.

"The other four of us are elsewhere in the eastern hemisphere of Earth," Carver said. "But six should be enough to handle the situation."

Harris glanced at his five comrades. "What are you planning to do?"

"Attack the Medlins, of course. We'll have to wipe them out at once."

Harris nodded. Inwardly he felt troubled; it seemed to him now that the Medlins had been strangely sincere in releasing him, though he knew that that was preposterous. He said, "How?"

"They trust you. You're one of their agents, so far as they think."

"Right."

"You'll return to them and tell them you've disposed of me, as instructed. Only you'll be bearing a subsonic on your body. Once you're inside, you activate it and knock them out—you'll be shielded."

"And I kill them when they're unconscious?"

"Exactly," Carver said. "You can't be humane with Medlins. It's like being humane with bloodsucking bats or with snakes."

The Darruui called McDermott said, "We'll wait outside until we get the signal that you've done the job. If you need help, just let us know."

Harris moistened his lips and nodded. "It sounds all right."

Carver said, "Reynolds, insert the subsonic."

The bald man produced a small metal pellet the size of a tiny bead, from which three tantalum filaments projected. He indicated to Harris that he should roll up his trousers to the thigh.

Instead, Harris dropped them. Reynolds drew a scalpel from somewhere and lifted the flap of nerveless flesh that served as trapdoor to the network of devices underneath. With steady, unquivering fingers, he affixed the bead to the minute wires already set in Harris' leg, and closed the wound with nuplast.

Carver said, "You activate it by pressing against the left-hip neural nexus. It's selfshielding for a distance of three feet around you, so make sure none of your victims are any closer than that."

"It radiates a pretty potent subsonic," Reynolds said. "Guaranteed knockout for a radius of forty feet."

"Suppose the Medlins are shielded against subsonics?" Harris asked.

Carver chuckled. "This is a variable-cycle transmitter. If they've perfected anything that can shield against a random wave, we might as well give up right now. But I'm inclined to doubt they have."

All very simple, Harris thought as he rode across town to the Medlin headquarters. Simply walk in, smile politely, stun them all with the subsonic, and boil their brains with your disruptor.

He paused outside the building, thinking.

Around him, Earthmen hurried to their homes. Night was falling. The stars blanketed the sky, white flecks against dark cloth. Many of those stars swore allegiance to Darruu. Others, to Medlin.

Which was right? Which wrong?

A block away, five fellow Darruui lurked, ready to come to his aid if he had any trouble in killing the Medlins. He doubted that he would have trouble, if the subsonic were as effective as Carver seemed to think.

For forty Darruui years he had been trained to hate the Medlins. Now, in a few minutes, he would be doing what was considered the noblest act a Servant of the Spirit could perform—ridding the universe of a pack of them. Yet he felt no sense of anticipated glory. It would simply be murder, the murder of strangers.

He entered the building.

The Medlin headquarters were at the top of the building, in a large pent-house loft. He rode up in the gravshaft and it seemed to him that he could feel the pressure of the tiny subsonic generator in his thigh. He knew that was just an illusion, but the presence of the metal bead irritated him all the same.

He stood for a moment in a scanner field. A door flicked back suddenly, out of sight, and a strange face peered at him—an Earthman face, on the surface of things at least.

The Earth man beckoned him in.

"I'm Armin Moulton," he said in a deep voice. "You're Harris?"

"That's right."

"Beth is waiting to see you."

The subsonic has a range of forty feet in any direction, Harris thought. *No one should be closer to you than three feet.*

He was shown into an inner room well furnished with drapes and hangings. Beth stood in the middle of the room, smiling at him. She wore thick, shape-less clothes, quite unlike the seductive garb she had had on when Harris first collided with her.

There were others in the room. Harris recognized the other Medlin, Coburn, and the giant named Wrynn who claimed to be a super-Earthman. There was another woman of Wrynn's size in the room, a great golden creature nearly a foot taller than Harris, and two people of normal size who were probably Medlins.

"Well?" Beth asked.

In a tight voice Harris said, "He's dead. I've just come from there."

"How did you carry it out?"

"Disruptor," Harris said. "It was unpleasant. For me as well as him."

He was quivering with tension. He made no attempt to conceal it, since a man who had just killed his direct superior might be expected to show some signs of extreme tension.

"Eight to go," Coburn said. "And four are in another hemisphere."

"Who are these people?" Harris asked.

Beth introduced them. The two normal-sized ones were disguised Medlins; the giant girl was Wrynn's wife, a super-woman. Harris frowned thoughtfully. There were a hundred Medlin agents on Earth. Four of them were right in this room, and it was reasonable to expect that two or three more might be within the forty-foot range of the concealed subsonic.

Not a bad haul at all. Harris began to tremble.

Beth said, "I suppose you don't even know who and where the other Darruui are yourself, do you?"

Harris shook his head. "I've only been on Earth a couple of days, you know. There wasn't time to make contact with anyone but Carver. I have no idea how to do so."

He stared levelly at her. The expression on her face was unreadable—it was impossible to tell whether she believed he had actually killed Carver.

"Things have happened fast to you, haven't they?" she said. She drew a tri-dim photo from a case and handed it to Harris. "This is your next victim. He goes under the name of Reynolds here. He's the second-in-command; first-in-command now, since Carver's dead."

Harris studied the photo. It showed the face of the bald-headed man who had inserted the subsonic beneath the skin of his thigh.

Tension mounted in him. He felt the faint *rasp rasp rasp* in his stomach that was the agreed-upon code; Carver, waiting nearby, wanted to know if he were having any trouble.

Casually Harris kneaded his side, activating the transmitter. The signal he sent out told Carver that nothing had happened yet, that everything was all right.

He handed the photo back to Beth.

"I'll take care of him," he said.

I press the neural nexus in the left hip and render them unconscious. Then I kill them with the disruptor and leave.

Very simple.

He looked at Beth and thought that in a few minutes she would lie dead, along with Coburn and the other two Medlins and these giants who claimed to be Earthmen. He tensed. His hand stole toward his hip.

Beth said, "It must have been a terrible nervous strain, killing him. You look very disturbed."

"You've overturned all the values of my life," Harris said glibly. "That can shake a man up."

"You didn't think I'd succeed!" Beth said triumphantly to Coburn. To Harris she explained, "Coburn didn't think you could be trusted."

"I can't," Harris said bluntly.

He activated the concealed subsonic.

The first waves of inaudible sound rippled out, ignoring false flesh and striking through to the Medlin core beneath. Protected by his three-foot shield, Harris nevertheless felt sick to the stomach, rocked by the reverberating sound-waves that poured from the pellet embedded in his thigh.

Coburn was reaching for his weapon, but he never got to it. His arm drooped slackly; he slumped over. Beth dropped. The other two Medlins fell. Still the subsonic waves poured forth.

To his surprise Harris saw that the two giants still remained on their feet and semiconscious, if groggy. *It must be because they're so big*, he thought. *It takes longer for the subsonic to knock them out.*

Wrynn was sagging now. His wife reeled under the impact of the noiseless waves and slipped to the floor, followed a moment later by her husband.

The office was silent.

Harris pressed his side again, signalling the *all clear* to the five Darruui outside. Six unconscious forms lay awkwardly on the floor.

He found the switch that opened the door, pulled it down, and peered out into the hall. Three figures lay outside, unconscious. A fourth was running toward them from the far end of the long hall, shouting, "What happened? What's going on?"

Harris stared at him. The Medlin ran into the forty-foot zone and recoiled visibly; he staggered forward a few steps and fell, joining his comrades on the thick velvet carpet.

Ten of them, Harris thought.

He drew the disruptor.

It lay in his palm, small, deadly. The trigger was a thin strand of metal; he needed only to flip off the guard, press the trigger back, and watch the Medlins die. But his hand was shaking. He did not fire.

A silent voice said, *You could not be trusted after all. You were a traitor. But* we *had to let the test go at least this far, for the sake of our consciences.*

"Who said that?"

I did.

"Where are you? I don't see you."

In this room, came the reply. *Put down the gun, Harris-Khiilom. No, don't try to signal your friends. Just let the gun fall.*

As if it had been wrenched from his hand, the gun dropped from his fingers, bounced a few inches, and lay still.

Shut off the subsonic, came the quiet command. *I find it unpleasant.*

Obediently Harris deactivated the instrument. His mind was held in some strange stasis; he had no private volitional control.

"Who are you?"

A member of that super-race whose existence you refused to accept.

Harris looked at Wrynn and his wife. Both were unconscious. "Wrynn?" he said. "How can your mind function if you're unconscious?"

Chapter Six

Gently Harris felt himself falling toward the floor. It was as if an intangible hand had yanked his legs out from under him and eased him down. He lay quiescent, eyes open, neither moving nor wanting to move.

The victims of the subsonic slowly returned to consciousness as the minutes passed.

Beth woke first. She stared at the unconscious form of Wrynn's wife and said, "You went to quite an extent to prove a point!"

You were in no danger, came the answer.

The others were awakening now, sitting up, rubbing their foreheads. Harris watched them. His head throbbed too, as if he had been stunned by the subsonic device himself.

"Suppose you had been knocked out by the subsonic too?" Beth said to the life within the giant woman. "He would have killed us."

The subsonic could not affect me.

Harris said, "That—embryo can think and act?" His voice was a harsh whisper.

Beth nodded. "The next generation. It reaches sentience while still in the womb. By the time it's born it's fully aware."

"And I thought it was a hoax," Harris said dizzily. He felt dazed. The values of his life had been shattered in a moment, and it would not be easy to repair them with similar speed.

"No. No hoax. And we knew you'd try to trick us when we let you go. At least, Wrynn said you would. He's telepathic too, though he can only receive impressions. He can't transmit telepathically to others the way his son can."

"If you knew what I'd do, why did you release me?" Harris asked.

Beth said, "Call it a test. I hoped you might change your beliefs if we let you go. You didn't."

"No. I came here to kill you."

"We knew that the moment you stepped through the door. But the seed of rebellion was in you. We hoped you might be swayed. You failed us."

Harris bowed his head. The signal in his body rasped again, but he ignored it. *Let Carver sweat out there. This thing is bigger than anything Carver ever dreamed of.*

"Tell me," he said. "Don't you know what will happen to Medlin—and Darruu as well—once there are enough of these beings?"

"Nothing will happen. Do you think they're petty power-seekers, intent on establishing a galactic dominion?" The girl laughed derisively. "That sort of thinking belongs to the obsolete non-telepathic species. Us. The lower animals. These new people have different goals."

"But they wouldn't have come into existence if you Medlins hadn't aided them!" Harris protested. "Obsolete? Of course. And you've done it!"

Beth smiled oddly. "At least we were capable of seeing the new race without envy. We helped them as much as we could because we knew they would prevail anyway, given time. Perhaps it would be another century, or another millennium. But our day is done, and so is the day of Darruu, and the day of the non-telepathic Earthmen."

"And our day too," Wrynn said mildly. "We are the intermediates—the links between the old species and the new one that is emerging."

Harris stared at his hands—the hands of an Earthman, with Darruui flesh within.

He thought: *All our striving is for nothing.*

A new race, a glorious race, nurtured by the Medlins, brought into being on Earth. The galaxy waited for them. They were demigods.

He had regarded the Earthers as primitives, creatures with a mere few thousand years of history behind them, mere pale humanoids of no importance. But he was wrong. Long after Darruu had become a hollow world, these Earthers would roam the galaxies.

Looking up, he said, "I guess we made a mistake, we of Darruu. I was sent here to help sway the Earthers to the side of Darruu. But it's the other way around; it's Darruu that will have to swear loyalty to Earth, some day."

"Not soon," Wrynn said. "The true race is not yet out of childhood. Twenty years more must pass. And we have enemies on Earth."

"The old Earthmen," Coburn said. "How do you think they'll like being replaced? *They're* the real enemy. And that's why we're here. To help the mutants until they can stand fully alone. You Darruui are just nuisances getting in our way."

That would have been cause for anger, once. Harris merely shrugged. His whole mission had been without purpose.

But yet, a lingering doubt remained, a last suspicion. The silent voice of the unborn superman said, *He still is not convinced.*

"I'm afraid he's right," Harris murmured. "I see, and I believe—and yet all my conditioning tells me that it's impossible. Medlins are hateful creatures; *I know* that, intuitively."

Beth smiled. "Would you like a guarantee of our good faith?"

"What do you mean?"

To the womb-bound godling she said, "Link us."

Before Harris had a chance to react a strange brightness flooded over him; he seemed to be floating far above his body. With a jolt he realized where he was.

He was looking into the mind of the Medlin who called herself Beth Baldwin. And he saw none of the hideous things he had expected to find in a Medlin mind.

He saw faith and honesty, and a devotion to the truth. He saw dogged courage. He saw many things that filled him with humility.

The linkage broke.

Beth said, "Now find the mind of his leader Carver, and link him to *that*."

"No," Harris protested. "Don't—"

It was too late.

He sensed the smell of Darruu wine, and the prickly texture of thuuar spines, and then the superficial memories parted to give him a moment's insight into the deeper mind of the Darruui who wore the name of John Carver.

It was a frightening pit of foul hatreds. Shivering, Harris staggered backward, realizing that the Earther had allowed him only a fraction of a second's entry into that mind.

He covered his face with his hands.

"Are—we all like that?" he asked. "Am I?"

"No. Not—deep down," Beth said. "You've got the outer layer of hatred that every Darruui has—and every Medlin. But your core is good. Carver is rotten. So are the other Darruui here."

"Our races have fought for centuries," Coburn said. "A mistake on both sides that has hardened into blood-hatred. The time has come to end it."

"How about those Darruui outside?"'

"They must die," Beth said.

Harris was silent a moment. The five who waited for him were Servants of the Spirit, like himself; members of the highest caste of Darruui civilization, presumably the noblest of all creation's beings. To kill one was to set himself apart from Darruu forever.

"My—conditioning lies deep," he said. "If I strike a blow against them, I could never return to my native planet."

"Do you *want* to return?" Beth asked. "Your future lies here. With us."

Harris considered that. After a long moment he nodded. "Very well. Give me back the gun. I'll handle the five Darruui outside."

Coburn handed him the disruptor he had dropped. Harris grasped the butt of the weapon, smiled, and said, "I could kill some of you now, couldn't I? It would take at least a fraction of a second to stop me. I could pull the trigger once."

"You won't," Beth said.

He stared at her. "You're right."

He rode down alone in the gravshaft and made his way down the street to the place where his five countrymen waited. It was very dark now, though the lambent glow of street-lights brightened the path.

The stars were out in force now, bedecking the sky. Up there somewhere was Darruu. Perhaps now was the time of the Mating of the Moons, he thought. Well, never mind; it did not matter now.

They were waiting for him. As he approached Carver said, "You took long enough. Well?"

Harris thought of the squirming ropy thoughts that nestled in the other's brain like festering living snakes. He said, "All dead. Didn't you get my signal?"

"Sure we did. But we were getting tired of standing around out here."

"Sorry," Harris said.

He was thinking, these are Servants of the Spirit, men of Darruu. Men who think of Darruu's galactic dominion only, men who hate and kill and spy.

"How many were there?" Reynolds asked.

"Five," Harris said.

Carver looked disappointed. "Only five?"

Harris shrugged. "The place was empty. At least I got five, though."

He realized he was stalling, unwilling to do the thing he had come out here to do.

A silent voice said within him, *Will you betray us again? Or will you keep faith this time?*

Carver was saying something to him. He did not hear it. Carver said again, "I asked you—were there any important documents there?"

"No," Harris said.

A cold wind swept in from the river. Harris felt a sudden chill.

He said to himself, *I will keep faith.*

He stepped back, out of the three-foot zone, and activated the subsonic generator in his hip.

"What—" Carver started to say, and fell. They all fell: Carver, Reynolds, Tompkins, McDermott, Patterson, slipped to the ground and lay in huddled heaps. Five Darruui wearing the skins of Earthmen. Five Servants of the Spirit.

He drew the disruptor.

It lay in his hand for a moment. Thoughtfully he released the safety guard and squeezed the trigger. A bolt of energy flicked out, bathing Carver. The man gave a convulsive quiver and was still.

Reynolds, Tompkins, McDermott, Patterson.

All dead.

Smiling oddly, Harris pocketed the disruptor again and started to walk away, walking uncertainly, as the nervous reaction started to swim through his body. He had killed five of his countrymen. He had come to Earth on a sacred mission and had turned worse than traitor, betraying not only Darruu but the entire future of the galaxy.

He had cast his lot with the Earthmen whose guise he wore, and with the smiling yellow-haired girl named Beth beneath whose full breasts beat a Medlin heart.

Well done, said the voice in his mind. *We were not deceived in you after all.*

Harris began to walk back toward the Medlin headquarters, slowly, measuredly, not looking back at the five corpses behind him. The police would be perplexed when they held autopsies on those five, and discovered the Darruui bodies beneath the Terran flesh.

He looked up at the stars.

Somewhere out there was Darruu, he thought. Wrapped in its crimson mist, circled by its seven moons—

He remembered the Mating of the Moons as he had last seen it: the long-awaited, mind-stunning display of beauty in the skies. He knew he would never see it again.

He could never return to Darruu now.

He would stay here, on Earth, serving a godlike race in its uncertain infancy. Perhaps he could forget that beneath the skin of Major Abner Harris lay the body and mind of Aar Khiilom.

Forget Darruu. Forget the fragrance of the jasaar trees and the radiance of the moons. Earth has trees that smell as sweet, it has a glorious pale moon that hangs high in the night sky. Put homesickness away. Forget Darruu.

It would not be easy. He looked up again at the stars as he reached the entrance to the Medlin headquarters. Earth was the name of his planet now.

Earth.

He took a last look at the speckled sky covered with stars, and for the last time wondered which of the dots of brightness was Darruu. Darruu no longer mattered now.

Smiling, Aar Khiilom turned his face away from the stars.

Spacerogue

Chapter One

They were selling a proteus in the public auction place at Borlaam when the stranger wandered by. The stranger's name was Barr Herndon, and he was a tall man with a proud, lonely face. It was not the face he had been born with, though his own had been equally proud, equally lonely.

He shouldered his way through the crowd. It was a warm and muggy day, and a number of idling passersby had stopped to watch the auction. The auctioneer was an Agozlid, squat and bull-voiced, and he held the squirming proteus at arm's length, squeezing it to make it perform.

"Observe, ladies and gentlemen—observe the shapes, the multitude of strange and exciting forms!"

The proteus now had the shape of an eight-limbed star, blue-green at its core, fiery red in each limb. Under the auctioneer's merciless prodding it began to change slowly as its molecules lost their hold on one another and sought a new conformation.

A snake, a tree, a hooded deathworm—

The Agozlid grinned triumphantly at the crowd, baring fifty inch-long yellow teeth. "What am I bid?" he demanded in the guttural Borlaamese language. "Who wants this creature from another sun's world?"

"Five stellors," said a bright-painted Borlaamese noblewoman down front.

"Five stellors! Ridiculous, milady. Who'll begin with fifty? A hundred?"

Barr Herndon squinted for a better view. He had seen proteus lifeforms before and knew something of them. They were strange, tormented creatures, living in agony from the moment they left their native world. Their flesh flowed endlessly from shape to shape, and each change was like the wrenching apart of limbs by the rack.

"Fifty stellors," chuckled a member of the court of Seigneur Krellig, absolute ruler of the vast world of Borlaam. "Fifty for the proteus."

"Who'll say seventy-five?" pleaded the Agozlid. "I brought this being here at the cost of three lives, slaves worth more than a hundred between them. Will you make me take a loss? Surely five thousand stellors—"

"Seventy-five," said a voice.

"Eighty," came an immediate response.

"One hundred," said the noblewoman in the front row.

The Agozlid's toothy face became mellow as the bidding rose spontaneously. The proteus wriggled, attempted to escape, altered itself wildly and pathetically. Herndon's lips compressed tightly. He knew something himself of what suffering meant.

"Two hundred," he said.

"A new voice!" crowed the auctioneer. "A voice from the back row! Five hundred, did you say?"

"Two hundred," Herndon repeated coldly.

"Two fifty," said a nearby noble promptly.

"And twenty-five more," a hitherto-silent circus proprietor said.

Herndon scowled. Now that he had entered into the situation, he was—as always—fully committed to it. He would not let the others get the proteus.

"Four hundred," he said.

For an instant there was silence in the auction ring, silence enough for the mocking cry of a low-swooping sea bird to be clearly audible. Then a quiet voice from the front said, "Four fifty."

"Five hundred," Herndon said.

"Five fifty."

Herndon did not immediately reply, and the Agozlid auctioneer craned his stubby neck, looking around for the next bidder. "I've heard five-fifty," he said crooningly. "That's good, but not good enough."

"Six hundred," Herndon said.

"Six twenty-five."

Herndon fought a savage impulse to draw his needler and gun down his bidding opponent. Instead he tightened his jaws and said, "Six-fifty."

The proteus squirmed and became a pain-smitten pseudo-cat on the auction stand. The crowd giggled in delight.

"Six-seventy-five," came the voice.

It had become a two-man contest now, with the others merely hanging on for the sport of it, waiting to see which one would weaken first. Herndon eyed his opponent: He was a courtier, a swarthy red-bearded man with blazing eyes and a double row of jewels around his doublet. He looked immeasurably wealthy. There was no hope of outbidding him.

"Seven hundred stellors," Herndon said. He glanced around hurriedly, found a small boy standing nearby, and called him over.

"Seven twenty-five," said the noble.

Herndon, whispered, "You see that man down front—the one who just spoke? Run down there and tell him his lady has sent for him and wants him at once."

He handed the boy a golden five-stellor piece. The boy stared at it popeyed a moment, grinned, and slid through the onlookers toward the front of the ring.

"Nine hundred," Herndon said.

It was considerably more than a proteus might be expected to bring at auction and possibly more than even the wealthy noble cared to spend. But Herndon was aware there was no way out for the noble except retreat, and he was giving him that avenue.

"Nine hundred is bid," the auctioneer said. "Lord Moaris, will you bid more?"

"I would," Moaris grunted. "But I am summoned and must leave." He looked blankly angry, but he did not question the boy's message. Herndon noted that down for possible future use. It had been a lucky guess, but Lord Moaris of the Seigneur's court came running when his lady bid him do so.

"Nine hundred is bid," the auctioneer repeated. "Do I hear more? Nine hundred for this fine proteus—who'll make it an even thousand?"

There was no one. Seconds ticked by, and no voice spoke. Herndon waited tensely at the edge of the crowd as the auctioneer chanted, "At nine hundred once, at nine hundred for two, at nine hundred ultimate—

"Yours for nine hundred, friend. Come forward with your cash. And I urge you all to return in ten minutes when we'll be offering some wonderful pink-hued maidens from Villidon." His hands described a feminine shape in the air with wonderfully obscene gusto.

Herndon came forward. The crowd had begun to dissipate, and the inner ring was deserted as he approached the auctioneer. The proteus had taken on a froglike shape and sat huddled in on itself like a statue of gelatin.

Herndon eyed the foul-smelling Agozlid and said, "I'm the one who bought the proteus. Who gets my money?"

"I do," croaked the auctioneer. "Nine hundred stellors gold, plus thirty stellors fee, and the beast's yours."

Herndon touched the money plate at his belt, and a coil of hundred-stellor links came popping forth. He counted off nine of them, broke the link, and laid them on the desk before the Agozlid. Then he drew six five-stellor pieces from his pocket and casually dropped them on the desk.

"Let's have your name for the registry," said the auctioneer after counting out the money and testing it with a soliscope.

"Barr Herndon."

"Home world?"

Herndon paused a moment. "Borlaam."

The Agozlid looked up. "You don't seem much like a Borlaamese to me. Pure-bred?"

"Does it matter to you? I am. I'm from the River Country of Zonnigog, and my money's good."

Painstakingly the Agozlid inscribed his name in the registry. Then he glanced up insolently and said, "Very well, Barr Herndon of Zonnigog. You now own a proteus. You'll be pleased to know that it's already indoctrinated and enslaved."

"This pleases me very much," said Herndon flatly.

The Agozlid handed Herndon a bright planchet of burnished copper with a nine-digit number inscribed on it. "This is the code key. In case you lose your slave, take this to Borlaam Central and they'll trace it for you." He took from his pocket a tiny projector and slid it across the desk. "And here's your resonator. It's tuned to a mesh network installed in the proteus on the submolecular level—it can't change to affect it. You don't like the way the beast behaves, just twitch the resonator. It's essential for proper discipline of slaves."

Herndon accepted the resonator. He said, "The proteus probably knows enough of pain without this instrument. But I'll take it."

The auctioneer seized the proteus and scooped it down from the auction stand, dropping it next to Herndon. "Here you are, friend. All yours now."

The marketplace had cleared somewhat; a crowd had gathered at the opposite end where some sort of jewel auction was going on, but as Herndon looked around, he saw he had a clear path over the cobbled square to the quay beyond.

He walked a few steps away from the auctioneer's booth. The auctioneer was getting ready for the next segment of his sale, and Herndon caught a glimpse of three frightened-looking naked Villidon girls behind the curtain being readied for display.

He stared seaward. Two hundred yards away was the quay, rimmed by the low sea wall, and beyond it was the bright green expanse of the Shining Ocean. For an instant his eyes roved beyond the ocean, to the far continent of Zonnigog where he had been born. Then he looked at the terrified little proteus, halfway through yet another change of shape.

Nine hundred and thirty-five stellors altogether for this proteus. Herndon scowled bitterly. It was a tremendous sum of money, far more than he could easily have afforded to throw away in one morning—particularly his first day back on Borlaam after his sojourn on the out-planets.

But there had been no help for it. He had allowed himself to be drawn into a situation, and he refused to back off halfway. Not anymore, he said to himself, thinking of the burned and gutted Zonnigog village plundered by the gay looters of Seigneur Krellig's army.

"Walk toward the sea wall," he ordered the proteus.

A half-formed mouth said blurredly, "M-master?"

"You understand me, don't you? Then walk toward the sea wall. Keep going and don't turn around."

He waited. The proteus formed feet and moved off in an uncertain shuffle over the well-worn cobbles. Nine hundred thirty-five stellors, he thought bitterly.

He drew his needler.

The proteus continued walking through the marketplace and toward the sea. Someone yelled, "Hey, that thing's going to fall in! We better stop it!"

"I own it," Herndon called coolly. "Keep away from it if you value your own lives."

He received several puzzled glances, but no one moved. The proteus had almost reached the edge of the sea wall now and paused indecisively. Not even the lowest of lifeforms will welcome its own self-destruction no matter what surcease from pain can be attained thereby.

"Mount the wall," Herndon called to it.

Blindly, the proteus obeyed. Herndon's finger caressed the firing knob of the needler. He watched the proteus atop the low wall staring down into the murky harbor water and counted to three.

On the third count he fired. The slim needle projectile sped brightly across the marketplace and buried itself in the back of the proteus' body. Death must have been instantaneous; the needle contained a nerve poison that was effective on all known forms of life.

Caught midway between changes, the creature stood frozen on the wall an instant, then toppled forward into the water. Herndon nodded and holstered his weapon. He saw people's heads nodding. He heard a murmured comment: "Just paid almost a thousand for it, and first thing he does is shoot it."

It had been a costly morning. Herndon turned as if to walk on, but he found his way blocked by a small wrinkle-faced man who had come out of the jewelry-auction crowd across the way.

"My name is Bollar Benjin," the little prune of a man said. His voice was a harsh croak. His body seemed withered and skimpy. He wore a tight gray tunic of shabby appearance. "I saw what you just did."

"What of it? It's not illegal to dispose of slaves in public," Herndon said.

"Only a special kind of man would do it, though," said Bollar Benjin. "A cruel man—or a foolhardy one. Which are you?"

"Both," Herndon said. "And now if you'll let me pass—"

"Just one moment." The croaking voice suddenly acquired the snap of a whip. "Talk to me a moment. If you can spare a thousand stellors to buy a slave you kill the next moment, you can spare me a few words."

"What do you want with me?"

"Your services," Benjin said. "I can use a man like you. Are you free and unbonded?"

Herndon thought of the thousand stellors—almost half his wealth—that he had thrown away just now. He thought of the Seigneur Krellig, whom he hated and whom he had vowed so implacably to kill. And he thought of the wrinkled man before him.

"I am unbonded," he said, "but my price is high. What do you want, and what can you offer?"

Benjin smiled obliquely and dipped into a hidden pocket of his tunic. When he drew forth his hand, it was bright with glittering jewels.

"I deal in these," he said. "I can pay well."

The jewels vanished into the pocket again. "If you're interested," Benjin said, "come with me."

Herndon nodded. "I'm interested."

Chapter Two

Herndon had been gone from Borlaam for a year before this day. A year before—the seventeenth of the reign of the Seigneur Krellig—a band of looters had roared through his home village in Zonnigog, destroying and killing. It had been a high score for the Herndon family—his father and mother killed in the first sally, his young brother stolen as a slave, his sister raped and ultimately put to death.

The village had been burned. And only Barr Herndon had escaped, taking with him twenty thousand stellors of his family's fortune and killing eight of the Seigneur's best men before departing.

He had left the system, gone to the nineteen-world complex of Meld, and on Meld XVII he had bought himself a new face that did not bear the telltale features of the Zonnigog aristocracy. Gone were the sharp, almost razorlike cheekbones, the pale skin, the wide-set black eyes, the nose jutting from the forehead.

For eight thousand stellors the surgeons of Meld had taken these things away and given him a new face: broad where the other had been high, tan-skinned, narrow-eyed, with a majestic hook of a nose quite unlike any of Zonnigog. He had come back wearing the guise of a spacerogue, a freebooter, an unemployed mercenary willing to sign on to the highest bidder.

The Meldian surgeons had changed his face, but they had not changed his heart. Herndon nurtured the desire for revenge against Krellig—Krellig the implacable, Krellig the invincible, who cowered behind the great stone walls of his fortress for fear of the people's hatred.

Herndon could be patient. But he swore death to Krellig, someday and somehow.

He stood now in a narrow street in the Avenue of Bronze, high in the winding complex of streets that formed the Ancient Quarter of the City of Borlaam, capital of the world of the same name. He had crossed the city silently, not bothering to speak to his gnomelike companion Benjin, brooding only on his inner thoughts and hatred.

Benjin indicated a black metal doorway to their left. "We go in here," he said. He touched his full hand to the metal of the door, and it jerked upward and out of sight. He stepped through.

Herndon followed, and it was as if a great hand had appeared and wrapped itself about him. He struggled for a moment against the stasis field.

"Damn you, Benjin, unwrap me!"

The stasis field held; calmly the little man bustled about Herndon, removing his needler, his four-chambered blaster, and the ceremonial sword at his side.

"Are you weaponless?" Benjin asked. "Yes; you must be. The field subsides."

Herndon scowled. "You might have warned me. When do I get my weapons back?"

"Later," Benjin said. "Restrain your temper and come within."

He was led to an inner room where three men and a woman sat around a wooden table. He eyed the four-some curiously. The men comprised an odd mixture: One had the unmistakable stamp of noble birth on his face, while the other two had the coarseness of clay. As for the woman, she was hardly worth a second look: Slovenly, big-breasted, and raw-faced, she was undoubtedly the mistress of one or more of the others.

Herndon stepped toward them.

Benjin said, "This is Barr Herndon, free spacerogue. I met him at the market. He had just bought a proteus at auction for nearly a thousand stellors. I watched him order the creature toward the sea wall and put a needle in its back."

"If he's that free with his money," remarked the noble-seeming one in a rich bass voice, "what need does he have of our employ?"

"Tell us why you killed your slave," Benjin said.

Herndon smiled grimly. "It pleased me to do so."

One of the leather-jerkined commoners shrugged and said, "These spacerogues don't act like normal men. Benjin, I'm not in favor of hiring him."

"We need him," the withered man retorted. To Herndon he said, "Was your act an advertisement, perhaps? To demonstrate your willingness to kill and your indifference to the moral codes of humanity?"

"Yes," Herndon lied. It would only hurt his own cause to explain that he had bought and then killed the proteus only to save it from a century-long life of endless agony. "It pleased me to kill the creature. And it served to draw your attention to me."

Benjin smiled and said, "Good. Let me explain who we are, then. First, names: This is Heitman Oversk, younger brother of the Lord Moaris."

Herndon stared at the noble. A second son—ah, yes. A familiar pattern. Second sons, propertyless but bearing within themselves the spark of nobility, frequently deviated into shadowy paths. "I had the pleasure of outbidding your brother this morning," he said.

"Outbidding Moaris? Impossible!"

Herndon shrugged. "His lady beckoned him in the middle of the auction, and he left. Otherwise the proteus would have been his, and I'd have nine hundred stellors more in my pocket right now."

"These two," Benjin said, indicating the commoners, "are named Dorgel and Razumod. They have full voice in our organization; we know no social distinctions. And this—" gesturing to the girl—"is Marya. She belongs to Dorgel, who does not object to making short-term loans."

Herndon said, "*I* object. But state your business with me, Benjin."

The dried little man said, "Fetch a sample, Razumod."

The burly commoner rose from his seat and moved into a dark corner of the poorly lit room; he fumbled at a drawer for a moment, then returned with a gem that sparkled brightly even through his fisted fingers. He tossed it down on the table where it gleamed coldly. Herndon noticed that neither Heitman Oversk nor Dorgel let their glance linger on the jewel more than a second, and he likewise turned his head aside.

"Pick it up," Benjin said.

The jewel was ice-cold. Herndon held it lightly and waited.

"Go ahead," Benjin urged. "Study it. Examine its depths. It's a lovely piece, believe me."

Hesitantly Herndon opened his cupped palm and stared at the gem. It was broad-faceted, with a luminous inner light and—he gasped—a face within the stone. A woman's face, languorous, beckoning, seeming to call to him as from the depths of the sea—

Sweat burst out all over him. With an effort he wrenched his gaze from the stone and cocked his arm; a moment later he had hurled the gem with all his force into the farthest corner of the room. He whirled, glared at Benjin, and leaped for him.

"Cheat! Betrayer!"

His hands sought Benjin's throat, but the little man jumped lithely back, and Dorgel and Razumod interposed themselves hastily between them. Herndon stared at Razumod's sweaty bulk a moment and gave ground, quivering with tension.

"You might have warned me," he said.

Benjin smiled apologetically. "It would have ruined the test. We must have strong men in our organization. Oversk, what do you think?"

"He threw down the stone," Heitman Oversk said heavily. "It's a good sign. I think I like him."

"Razumod?"

The commoner gave an assenting grunt, as did Dorgel. Herndon tapped the table and said, "So you're dealing in starstones? And you gave me one without warning? What if I'd succumbed?"

"We would have sold you the stone and let you leave," Benjin said.

"What sort of work would you have me do?"

Heitman Oversk said, "Our trade is to bring starstones in from the Rim worlds where they are mined and sell them to those who can afford our price. The price, incidentally, is fifty thousand stellors. We pay eight thousand for them and are responsible for shipping them ourselves. We need a supervisor to control the flow of starstones from our source world to Borlaam. We can handle the rest at this end."

"It pays well," Benjin added. "Your wage would be five thousand stellors per month, plus a full voice in the organization."

Herndon considered. The starstone trade was the most vicious in the galaxy; the hypnotic gems rapidly became compulsive, and within a year after being exposed to one constantly, a man lost his mind and became a drooling idiot, able only to contemplate the kaleidoscopic wonders locked within his stone.

The way to addiction was easy. Only a strong man could voluntarily rip his eyes from a starstone, once he had glimpsed it. Herndon had proved himself strong. The sort of man who could slay a newly purchased slave could look up from a starstone.

He said, "What are the terms?"

"Full bonding," Benjin said. "Including surgical implantation of a safety device."

"I don't like that."

"We all wear them," Oversk said. "Even myself."

"If all of you wear them," Herndon said, "to whom are you responsible?"

"There is joint control. I handle the out-world contacts; Oversk, here, locates prospective patrons. Dorgel and Razumod are expediters who deal in collection problems and protection. We control each other."

"But there must be somebody who has the master control for the safety devices," Herndon protested. "Who is that?"

"It rotates from month to month. I hold them this month," Benjin said. "Next month it is Oversk's turn."

Herndon paced agitatedly up and down in the darkened room. It was a tempting offer; five thousand a month could allow him to live on high scales. And Oversk was the brother of Lord Moaris, who was known to be the Seigneur's confidante.

And Lord Moaris' lady controlled Lord Moaris. Herndon saw a pattern taking shape, one that would ultimately put the Seigneur Krellig within his reach.

But he did not care to have his body invaded by safety devices. He knew how those worked; if he were to cheat the organization, betray it, attempt to leave it without due cause, whoever operated the master control could reduce him to a groveling pain-racked slave instantly. The safety device could only be removed by the surgeon who had installed it.

It meant accepting the yoke of this group of starstone smugglers. But there was a higher purpose in mind for Herndon.

"I conditionally accept," he said. "Tell me specifically what my duties will be."

Benjin said, "A consignment of starstones has been mined for us on our source world and is soon to be shipped. We want you to travel to that world and accompany the shipment through space to Borlaam. We lose much by way of thievery on each shipment—and there is no way of insuring starstones against loss."

"We know who our thief is," Oversk said. "You would be responsible for finding him in the act and killing him."

"I'm not a murderer," Herndon said quietly.

"You wear the garb of a spacerogue. That doesn't speak of a very high moral caliber," Oversk said.

"Besides, no one mentions murder," said Benjin. "Merely execution. Yes: execution."

Herndon locked his hands together before him and said, "I want two months' salary in advance. I want to see evidence that all of you are wearing neuronic mesh under your skins before I let the surgeon touch me."

"Agreed," Benjin said after a questioning glance around the room.

"Furthermore, I want as an outright gift the sum of nine hundred thirty golden stellors, which I spent this morning to attract the attention of a potential employer."

It was a lie, but there was cause for it. It made sense to establish a dominating relationship with these people as soon as possible. Then later concessions on their part would come easier.

"Agreed," Benjin said again, more reluctantly.

"In that case," Herndon said, "I consider myself in your employ. I'm ready to leave tonight. As soon as the conditions I state have been fulfilled to my complete satisfaction, I will submit my body to the hands of your surgeon."

Chapter Three

He bound himself over to the surgeon later that afternoon after money to the amount of ten thousand, nine hundred and thirty golden stellors had been deposited to his name in the Royal Borlaam Bank in Galaxy Square and after he had seen the neuronic mesh that was embedded in the bodies of Benjin, Oversk, Dorgel, and Razumod. Greater assurance of good faith than this he could not demand; he would have to risk the rest.

The surgeon's quarters were farther along the Avenue of Bronze, in a dilapidated old house that had no doubt been built in Third Empire days. The surgeon himself was a wiry fellow with a puckered ray slash across one cheek and a foreshortened left leg. A retired pirate-vessel medic, Herndon realized. No one else would perform such an operation unquestioningly. He hoped the man had skill.

The operation itself took an hour, during which time Herndon was under total anesthesia. He woke to find the copper operating dome lifting off him. He felt no different, even though he knew a network of metal had been blasted into his body on the submolecular level.

"Well? Is it finished?"

"It is," the surgeon said.

Herndon glanced at Benjin. The little man held a glinting metal object on his palm. "This is the control, Herndon. Let me demonstrate."

His hand closed, and instantaneously Herndon felt a bright bolt of pain shiver through the calf of his leg. A twitch of Benjin's finger and an arrow of red heat lanced Herndon's shoulder. Another twitch and a clammy hand seemed to squeeze his heart.

"Enough!" Herndon shouted. He realized he had signed away his liberty forever, if Benjin chose to exert control. But it did not matter to him. He had actually signed away his liberty the day he had vowed to watch the death of Seigneur Krellig.

Benjin reached into his tunic pocket and drew forth a little leather portfolio. "Your passport and other traveling necessities," he explained.

"I have my own passport," Herndon said.

Benjin shook his head. "This is a better one. It comes with a visa to Vyapore." To the surgeon he said, "How soon can he travel?"

"Tonight, if necessary."

"Good. Herndon, you'll leave tonight."

T he ship was the *Lord Nathiir*, a magnificent superliner bound on a thousand-light-year cruise to the Rim stars. Benjin had arranged for Herndon to travel outward on a luxury liner without cost as part of the entourage of Lord and Lady Moaris. Oversk had obtained the job for him— second steward to the noble couple, who were vacationing on the Rim pleasure planet of Molleccogg. Herndon had not objected when he learned that he was to travel in the company of Lord—and especially Lady—Moaris.

The ship was the greatest of the Borlaam luxury fleet. Even on Deck C, in his steward's quarters, Herndon rated a full-grav room with synthik drapery and built-in chromichron; he had never lived so well even at his parents' home, and they had been among the first people of Zonnigog at one time.

His duties called for him to pay court upon the nobles each evening so that they might seem more resplendent in comparison with the other aristocrats traveling aboard. The Moarises had brought the largest entourage with them, over a hundred people, including valets, stewards, cooks, and paid sycophants.

Alone in his room during the hour of blastoff, Herndon studied his papers. A visa to Vyapore. *So that* was where the starstones came from—! Vyapore, the jungle planet of the Rim where civilization barely had a toehold. No wonder the starstone trade was so difficult to control.

When the ship was safely aloft and the stasis generators had caused the translation into nullspace, Herndon dressed in the formal black and red court garments of Lord Moaris' entourage. Then, making his way up the broad companionway, he headed for the Grand Ballroom where Lord Moaris and his lady were holding court for the first night of the voyage outward.

The ballroom was festooned with ropes of living light. A dancing bear from Albireo XII cavorted clumsily near the entrance as Herndon entered. Borlaamese in uniforms identical to his own stood watch at the door and nodded to him when he identified himself as Second Steward.

He stood for a moment alone at the threshold of the ballroom watching the glittering display. The *Lord Nathiir* was the playground of the wealthy, and a goodly number of Borlaam's wealthiest were here, vying with the ranking nobles, the Moarises, for splendor.

Herndon felt a twinge of bitterness. His people were from beyond the sea, but by rank and preference he belonged in the bright lights of the ballroom, not standing here in the garment of a steward. He moved forward.

The noble couple sat on raised thrones at the far end, presiding over a dancing area in which the grav had been turned down; the dancers drifted gracefully, like figures out of fable, feet touching the ground only at intervals.

Herndon recognized Lord Moaris from the auction. A dour, short, thick-bodied individual he was, resplendent in his court robes, with a fierce little beard stained bright red after the current fashion. He sat stiffly upright on his throne, gripping the armrests of the carved chair as if he were afraid of floating off toward the ceiling. In the air before him shimmered the barely perceptible haze of a neutralizer field designed to protect him from the shots of a possible assassin.

By his side sat his Lady, supremely self-possessed and lovely. Herndon was astonished by her youth. No doubt the nobles had means of restoring lost freshness to a woman's face, but there was no way of recreating the youthful bloom so convincingly. The Lady Moaris could not have been more than twenty-three or twenty-five.

Her husband was several decades older. It was small wonder that he guarded her so jealously.

She smiled in sweet content at the scene before her. Herndon, too, smiled—at her beauty and at the use to which he hoped to put it. Her skin was soft pink; a wench of the bath Herndon had met below decks had told him she bathed in the cream of the ying apple twice daily. Her eyes were wide-set and clear, her nose finely made, her lips two red arching curves. She wore a dress studded with emeralds; it flowed from her like light. It was open at the throat, revealing a firm bosom and strong shoulders. She clutched a diamond-crusted scepter in one small hand.

Herndon looked around, found a lady of the court who was unoccupied at the moment, and asked her to dance. They danced silently, gliding in and out of the grav field; Herndon might have found it a pleasant experience, but he was not primarily in search of pleasant experiences now. He was concerned only with attracting the attention of the Lady Moaris.

He was successful. It took time, but he was by far the biggest and most conspicuous man of the court assembled there, and it was customary for Lord and Lady to leave their thrones, mingle with their courtiers, even dance with them. Herndon danced with lady after lady until finally he found himself face to face with the Lady Moaris.

"Will you dance with me?" she asked. Her voice was like liquid gossamer.

Herndon lowered himself in a courtly bow. "I would consider it the greatest of honors, milady."

They danced. She was easy to hold; he sensed her warmness near him, and he saw something in her eyes—a distant pinched look of pain, perhaps—that told him all was not well between Lord and Lady.

She said, "I don't recognize you. What's your name?"

"Barr Herndon, milady. Of Zonnigog."

"Zonnigog, indeed! And why have you crossed ten thousand miles of ocean to our city?"

Herndon smiled and gracefully dipped her through a whirling series of pirouettes. "To seek fame and fortune, milady. Zonnigog is well and good to live in, but the place to become known is the City of Borlaam. For this reason I petitioned the Heitman Oversk to have me added to the retinue of the Lord Moaris."

"You know Oversk, then? Well?"

"Not at all well. I served him a while; then I asked to move on."

"And so you go, climbing up and over your former masters until you scramble up the shoulders of the Lord Moaris to the feet of the Seigneur. Is that the plan?"

She smiled disarmingly, drawing any possible malice from the words she had uttered. Herndon nodded, saying in all sincerity, "I confess this is my aim. Forgive me, though, for saying that there are reasons that might cause me to remain in the service of the Lord Moaris longer than I had originally intended."

A flush crossed her face. She understood. In a half-whisper she said, "You are impertinent. I suppose it comes with good looks and a strong body."

"Thank you, milady."

"I wasn't complimenting you," she said as the dance came to an end and the musicians subsided. "I was criticizing. But what does it matter? Thank you for the dance."

"May I have the pleasure of milady's company once again soon?" Herndon asked.

"You may—but not too soon." She chuckled. "The Lord Moaris is highly possessive. He resents it when I dance twice the same evening with one member of the court."

Sadness darkened Herndon's face a moment. "Very well, then. But I will go to Viewplate A and stare at the stars a while. If the Lady seeks a companion, she will find one there."

She stared at him and flurried away without replying. But Herndon felt a glow of satisfaction. The pieces were dropping into place.

Viewplate A, on the uppermost deck of the vast liner, was reserved for the first-class passengers and the members of their retinues. It was an enormous room shrouded at all times in darkness, at one end of which a viewscreen opened out onto the glory of the heavens. In nullspace, a hyperbolic section of space was visible at all times, the stars in weird out-of-focus colors forming a breathtaking display. Geometry went awry. A blazing panorama illuminated the room.

The first-class viewing room was also known to be a trysting place. There, under cover of darkness, ladies might meet and make love to cooks, lords to scullery maids. An enterprising rogue with a nolight camera might make a fortune taking a quick shot of such a room and blackmailing his noble victims. But scanners at the door prevented such devices from entering.

Herndon stood staring at the fiery gold and green of the closest stars a while, his back to the door, until he heard a feminine voice whisper to him.

"Barr Herndon?"

He turned. In the darkness it was difficult to tell who spoke; he saw a girl about the height of the Lady Moaris, but in the dimness of the illumination of the plate he could see it was not the Lady. This girl's hair was dull red; the Lady's was golden. And he could see the pale whiteness of this girl's breasts; the Lady's garment, while revealing, had been somewhat more modest.

This was a lady of the court, then, perhaps enamored of Herndon, perhaps sent by the Lady Moaris as a test or as a messenger.

Herndon said, "I am here. What do you want?"

"I bring a message from—a noble lady," came the answering whisper.

Smiling in the darkness, Herndon said. "What does your mistress have to say to me?"

"It cannot be spoken. Hold me in a close embrace as if we were lovers, and I will give you what you need."

Shrugging, Herndon clasped the go-between in his arms with feigned passion. Their lips met; their bodies pressed tight. Herndon felt the girl's hand searching for his and slipping something cool, metallic into it. Her lips left his, traveled to his ear, and murmured:

"This is her key. Be there in half an hour."

They broke apart. Herndon nodded farewell to her and returned his attention to the glories of the viewplate. He did not glance at the object in his hand, but merely stored it in his pocket.

He counted out fifteen minutes in his mind, then left the viewing room and emerged on the main deck. The ball was still in progress, but he learned from a guard on duty that the Lord and Lady Moaris had already left for sleep and that the festivities were soon to end.

Herndon slipped into a washroom and examined the key, for a key it was. It was a radionic opener, and imprinted on it was the number 1160.

His throat felt suddenly dry. The Lady Moaris was inviting him to her room for the night—or was this a trap, and would Moaris and his court be waiting for him to gun him down and provide themselves with some amusement? It was not beyond these nobles to arrange such a thing.

But still—he remembered the clearness of her eyes and the beauty of her face. He could not believe she would be party to such a scheme.

He waited out the remaining fifteen minutes. Then, moving cautiously along the plush corridors, he found his way to Room 1160.

He listened a moment. Silence from within. His heart pounded frantically, irking him; this was his first major test, possibly the gateway to all his hopes, and it irritated him that he felt anxiety.

He touched the tip of the radionic opener to the door. The substance of the door blurred as the energy barricade that composed it was temporarily dissolved. Herndon stepped through quickly. Behind him the door returned to a state of solidity.

The light of the room was dim. The Lady Moaris awaited him, wearing a gauzy dressing gown. She smiled tensely at him; she seemed ill at ease.

"You came, then."

"Would I do otherwise?"

"I—wasn't sure. I'm not in the habit of doing things like this."

Herndon repressed a cynical smile. Such innocence was touching but highly improbable. He said nothing, and she went on: "I was caught by your face—something harsh and terrible about it struck me. I had to send for you to know you better."

Ironically Herndon said, "I feel honored. I hadn't expected such an invitation."

"You won't—think it's cheap of me, will you?" she said plaintively. It was hardly the thing Herndon expected from the lips of the noble Lady Moaris. But as he stared at her slim body revealed beneath the filmy robe, he understood that she might not be so noble after all once the gaudy pretense was stripped away. He saw her as perhaps she truly was: a young girl of great loveliness married to a domineering nobleman who valued her only for her use in public display. It might explain this bedchamber summons to a Second Steward.

He took her hand. "This is the height of my ambitions, milady. Beyond this room, where can I go?"

But it was empty flattery he spoke. He darkened the room illumination exultantly. *With your conquest, Lady Moaris,* he thought, *do I begin the conquest of the Seigneur Krellig!*

Chapter Four

The voyage to Molleccogg lasted a week, absolute time aboard ship. After their night together, Herndon had occasion to see the Lady Moaris only twice more, and on both occasions she averted her eyes from him, regarding him as if he were not there.

It was understandable. But Herndon held a promise from her that she would see him again in three months' time when she returned to Borlaam; and she had further promised that she would use her influence with her husband to have Herndon invited to the court of Seigneur.

The *Lord Nathiir* emerged from nullspace without difficulty and was snared by the landing field of Molleccogg Spacefield. Through the viewing screen on his own deck, Herndon saw the colorful splendor of the pleasure planet on which they were about to land growing larger now that they were in the final spiral.

But he did not intend to remain long on the world of Molleccogg.

He found the Chief Steward and applied for a leave of absence from Lord Moaris' service without pay.

"But you've just joined us," the Steward protested. "And now you want to leave?"

"Only for a while," Herndon said. "I'll be back on Borlaam before any of you are. I have business to attend to on another world in the Rim area, and then I promise to return to Borlaam at my own expense to rejoin the retinue of the Lord Moaris."

The Chief Steward grumbled and complained, but he could not find anything particularly objectionable in Herndon's intentions, and so finally he reluctantly granted the spacerogue permission to leave Lord Moaris' service temporarily. Herndon packed his court costume and clad himself in his old spacerogue garb; when the great liner ultimately put down in Danzibool Harbor on Molleccogg, Herndon was packed and ready, and he slipped off ship and into the thronged confusion of the terminal.

Bollar Benjin and Heitman Oversk had instructed him most carefully on what he was to do now. He pushed his way past a file of vile-smelling lily-faced green Nnobonn and searched for a ticket seller's window. He found one eventually and produced the prepaid travel vouchers Benjin had given him.

"I want a one-way passage to Vyapore," he said to the flat-featured, triple-eyed Guzmanno clerk who stared out from back of the wicker screen.

"You need a visa to get to Vyapore," the clerk said. "These visas are issued at infrequent intervals to certified personages. I don't see how you—"

"I have a visa," Herndon snapped, and produced it. The clerk blinked—one-two-three, in sequence—and his pale rose face flushed deep cerise.

"So you do," he remarked at length. "It seems to be in order. Passage will cost you eleven hundred sixty-five stellors of the realm."

"I'll take a third-class ship," Herndon said. "I have a paid voucher for such a voyage."

He handed it across. The clerk studied it for a long moment, then said: "You have planned this very well. I accept the voucher. Here."

Herndon found himself holding one paid passage to Vyapore aboard the freight ship *Zalasar*.

The *Zalasar* turned out to be very little like the *Lord Nathiir*. It was an old-fashioned unitube ship that rattled when it blasted off, shivered when it trans-lated to nullspace, and quivered all the week-long journey from Molleccogg to Vyapore. It was indeed a third-class ship. Its cargo was hardware: seventy-five thousand dry-strainers, eighty thousand pressors, sixty thousand multiple fuse screens, guarded by a supercargo team of eight taciturn Ludvuri. Herndon was the only human aboard. Humans did not often get visas to Vyapore.

They reached Vyapore seven days and a half after setting out from Molleccogg. Ground temperature as they disembarked was well over a hundred. Humidity was overpowering. Herndon knew about Vyapore: It held perhaps five hundred humans, one spaceport, infinite varieties of deadly local life, and several thousand nonhumans of all descriptions, some of them hiding, some of them doing business, some of them searching for starstones.

Herndon had been well briefed. He knew who his contact was, and he set about meeting him.

There was only one settled city on Vyapore, and because it was the only one, it was nameless. Herndon found a room in a cheap boardinghouse run by a swine-eared Dombruun and washed the sweat from his face with the unpleasantly acrid water of the tap.

Then he went downstairs into the bright noonday heat. The stench of rotting vegetation drifted in from the surrounding jungle on a faint breeze. Herndon said at the desk, "I'm looking for a Vonnimooro named Mardlin. Is he around?"

"Over there, " said the proprietor, pointing.

Mardlin the Vonnimooro was a small, weasely-like creature with the protu-berant snout, untrustworthy yellow eyes, and pebbly brown-purple fur of his people. He looked up when Herndon approached. When he spoke, it was in lingua spacia with a whistling, almost obscene inflection.

"You looking for me?"

"It depends," Herndon said. "Are you Mardlin?"

The jackal-like creature nodded. Herndon lowered himself to a nearby seat and said in a quiet voice, "Bollar Benjin sent me to meet you. Here are my credentials."

He tossed a milky-white clouded cube on the table between them. Mardlin snatched it up hastily in his leathery claws and nudged the activator. An image of Bollar Benjin appeared in the cloudy depths, and a soft voice said, "Benjin speaking. The bearer of this card is known to me, and I trust him fully in all matters. You are to do the same. He will accompany you to Borlaam with the consignment of goods."

The voice died away, and the image of Benjin vanished. The jackal scowled. He muttered, "If Benjin sent a man to convey his goods, why must I go?"

Herndon shrugged. "He wants both of us to make the trip, it seems. What do you care? You're getting paid, aren't you?"

"And so are you," snapped Mardlin. "It isn't like Benjin to pay two men to do the same job. And I don't like you, Rogue."

"Mutual," Herndon responded heartily. He stood up. "My orders say I'm to take the freighter *Dawnlight* back to Borlaam tomorrow evening. I'll meet you here one hour before to examine the merchandise."

H e made one other stop that day. It was a visit with Brennt, a jewel monger of Vyapore who served as the funnel between the native star-stone miners and Benjin's courier, Mardlin.

Herndon gave his identifying cube to Brennt and said, once he had satisfactorily proved himself, "I'd like to check your books on the last consignment."

Brennt glanced up sharply. "We keep no books on starstones, idiot. What do you want to know?"

Herndon frowned. "We suspect our courier of diverting some of our stones to his own pocket. We have no way of checking up on him since we can't ask for vouchers of any kind in starstone traffic."

The Vyaporan shrugged. "All couriers steal."

"Starstones cost us eight thousand stellors apiece," Herndon said. "We can't afford to lose any of them at that price. Tell me how many are being sent in the current shipment."

"I don't remember," Brennt said.

Scowling, Herndon said, "You and Mardlin are probably in league. We have to take his word for what he brings us—but always three or four of the stones are defective. We believe he buys, say, forty stones from you, pays the three hundred twenty thousand stellors over to you from the account we provide, and then takes three or four from the batch and replaces them with identical but defective stones worth a hundred stellors or so apiece. The profit to him is better than twenty thousand stellors a voyage.

"Or else," Herndon went on, "you deliberately sell him defective stones at eight thousand stellors. But Mardlin's no fool, and neither are we."

"What do you want to know?" the Vyaporan asked.

"How many functional starstones are included in the current consignment?"

Sweat poured from Brennt's face. "Thirty-nine," he said after a long pause.

"And did you also supply Mardlin with some blanks to substitute for any of these thirty-nine?"

"N-no," Brennt said.

"Very good," said Herndon. He smiled. "I'm sorry to have seemed so overbearing, but we had to find out this information. Will you accept my apologies and shake?"

He held out his hand. Brennt eyed it uncertainly, then took it. With a quick inward twitch Herndon jabbed a needle into the base of the other's thumb. The quick-acting truth drug took only seconds to operate.

"Now," Herndon said, "the preliminaries are over. You understand the details of our earlier conversation. Tell me, now, how many starstones is Mardlin paying you for?"

Brennt's fleshless lips curled angrily, but he was defenseless against the drug. "Thirty-nine," he said.

"At what total cost?"

"Three hundred twelve thousand stellors."

Herndon nodded. "How many of those thirty-nine are actually functional starstones?"

"Thirty-five," Brennt said reluctantly.

"The other four are duds?"

"Yes."

"A sweet little racket. Did you supply Mardlin with the duds?"

"Yes. At two hundred stellors each."

"And what happens to the genuine stones that we pay for but that never arrive on Borlaam?"

Brennt's eyes rolled despairingly. "Mardlin—Mardlin sells them to someone else and pockets the money. I get five hundred stellors per stone for keeping quiet."

"You've kept very quiet today," Herndon said. "Thanks very much for the information, Brennt. I really should kill you—but you're much too valuable to us for that. We'll let you live, but we're changing the terms of our agreement. From now on we pay you only for actual functioning starstones, not for an entire consignment. Do you like that setup?"

"No," Brennt said.

"At least you speak truthfully now. But you're stuck with it. Mardlin is no longer courier, by the way. We can't afford a man of his tastes in our organization. I don't advise you try to make any deals with his successor, whoever he is."

He turned and walked out of the shop.

Herndon knew that Brennt would probably notify Mardlin that the game was up immediately so the Vonnimooro could attempt to get away. Herndon was not particularly worried about Mardlin's escaping since he had a weapon that would work on the jackal-creature at any distance whatever.

But he had sworn an oath to safeguard the combine's interests, and Herndon was a man of his oath. Mardlin was in possession of thirty-nine starstones for which the combine had paid. He did not want the Vonnimooro to take those with him.

He legged it across town hurriedly to the house where the courier lived while at the Vyapore end of his route. It took him fifteen minutes from Brennt's to Mardlin's—more than enough time for a warning.

Mardlin's room was on the second story. Herndon drew his weapon from his pocket and knocked.

"Mardlin?"

There was no answer. Herndon said, "I know you're in there, jackal. The game's all over. You might as well open the door and let me in."

A needle came whistling through the door and embedded itself against the opposite wall after missing Herndon's head by inches. Herndon stepped out of range and glanced down at the object in his hand.

It was the master control for the neuronic network installed in Mardlin's body. It was quite carefully gradated; shifting the main switch to *six* would leave the Vonnimooro in no condition to fire a gun. Thoughtfully Herndon nudged the indicator up through the degrees of pain to *six* and left it there.

He heard a thud within.

Putting his shoulder to the door, he cracked it open with one quick heave. He stepped inside. Mardlin lay sprawled in the middle of the floor writhing in pain. Near him, but beyond his reach, lay the needler he had dropped.

A suitcase sat open and half-filled on the bed. He had evidently intended an immediate getaway.

"*Shut . . . that . . . thing . . . off . . .*" Mardlin muttered through pain-twisted lips.

"First some information," Herndon said cheerfully. "I just had a talk with Brennt. He says you've been doing some highly improper things with our starstones. Is this true?"

Mardlin quivered on the floor but said nothing. Herndon raised the control a quarter of a notch, intensifying the pain but not yet bringing it to the killing range.

"Is this true?" he repeated.

"Yes—yes! Damn you, shut it off."

"At the time you had the network installed in your body, it was with the understanding that you'd be loyal to the combine and so it would never need to be used. But you took advantage of circumstances and cheated us. Where's the current consignment of stones?"

". . . suitcase lining," Mardlin muttered.

"Good," Herndon said. He scooped up the needler, pocketed it, and shut off the master control switch. The pain subsided in the Vonnimooro's body, and he lay slumped, exhausted, too battered to rise.

Efficiently Herndon ripped away the suitcase lining and found the packet of starstones. He opened it. They were wrapped in shielding tissue that protected any accidental viewer. He counted through them; there were thirty-nine, as Brennt had said.

"Are any of these defective?" he asked.

Mardlin looked up from the floor with eyes yellow with pain and hatred. "Look through them and see."

Instead of answering, Herndon shifted the control switch past *six* again. Mardlin doubled up, clutching his head with clawlike hands. "Yes! Yes! Six defectives!"

"Which means you sold six good ones for forty-eight thousand stellors, less the three thousand you kicked back to Brennt to keep quiet. So there should be forty-five thousand stellors here that you owe us. Where are they?"

"Dresser drawer . . . top . . ."

Herndon found the money neatly stacked. A second time he shut off the control device, and Mardlin relaxed.

"Okay," Herndon said. "I have the cash and the stones. But there must be thousands of stellors that you've previously stolen from us."

"You can have that, too! Only don't turn that thing on again, please!"

Shrugging, Herndon said, "There isn't time for me to hunt down the other money you stole from us. But we can ensure against your doing it again."

He fulfilled the final part of Benjin's instructions by turning the control switch to *ten*, the limit of sentient endurance. Every molecule of Mardlin's wiry body felt unbearable pain; he screamed and danced on the floor, but only for a moment. Nerve cells unable to handle the overload of pain stimuli short-circuited. In seconds his brain was paralyzed. In less than a minute he was dead, though his tortured limbs still quivered with convulsive postmortuary jerks.

Herndon shut the device off. He had done his job. He felt neither revulsion nor glee.

He gathered up jewels and money and walked out.

Chapter Five

A month later he arrived on Borlaam via the freighter *Dawnlight* as scheduled and passed through customs without difficulty despite the fact that he was concealing more than three hundred thousand stellors' worth of proscribed starstones on his person.

His first stop was the Avenue of Bronze where he sought out Benjin and the Heitman Oversk.

He explained crisply and briefly his activities since leaving Borlaam, neglecting to mention the matter of the shipboard romance with the Lady Moaris. While he spoke, both Benjin and Oversk stared eagerly at him, and when he told of intimidating Brennt and killing the treacherous Mardlin, they beamed.

Herndon drew the packet of starstones from his cloak and laid them on the wooden table. "There," he said. "The starstones. There were some defectives, as you know, and I've brought back cash for them." He added forty-five thousand stellors to the pile.

Benjin quickly caught up the money and the stones and said, "You've done well, Herndon. Better than we expected. It was a lucky day when you killed that proteus."

"Will you have more work for me?"

Oversk said, "Of course. You'll take Mardlin's place as the courier. Didn't you realize that?"

Herndon had realized it, but it did not please him. He wanted to remain on Borlaam, now that he had made himself known to the Lady Moaris. He wanted to begin his climb toward Krellig. And if he were to shuttle between Vyapore and Borlaam, the all-important advantage he had attained would be lost.

But the Lady Moaris would not be back on Borlaam for nearly two months. He could make one more round trip for the combine without seriously endangering his position. After that he would have to find some means of leaving their service. Of course, if they preferred to keep him on, they could compel him, but—

244

"When do I make the next trip?" he asked.

Benjin shrugged lazily. "Tomorrow, next week, next month—who knows? We have plenty of stones on hand. There is no hurry for the next trip. You can take a vacation now while we sell these."

"No," Herndon said. "I want to leave immediately." Oversk frowned at him. "Is there some reason for the urgency?"

"I don't want to stay on Borlaam just now," Herndon said. "There's no need for me to explain further. It pleases me to make another trip to Vyapore."

"He's eager," Benjin said. "It's a good sign."

"Mardlin was eager at first, too," Oversk remarked balefully.

Herndon was out of his seat and at the nobleman's throat in an instant. His needler grazed the skin of Oversk's Adam's apple.

"If you intended by that comparison to imply—"

Benjin tugged at Herndon's arm. "Sit down, Rogue, and relax. The Heitman is tired tonight, and the words slipped out. We trust you. Put the needler away."

Reluctantly Herndon lowered the weapon. Oversk, white-faced despite his tan, fingered his throat where Herndon's weapon had touched it but said nothing. Herndon regretted his hasty action and decided not to demand an apology. Oversk still could be useful to him.

"A spacerogue's word is his bond," Herndon said. "I don't intend to cheat you. When can I leave?"

"Tomorrow, if you wish," Benjin said. "We'll cable Brennt to have another shipment ready for you."

This time he traveled to Vyapore aboard a transport freighter since there were no free tours with noblemen to be had at this season. He reached the jungle world a little less than a month later. Brennt had thirty-two jewels waiting for him. Thirty-two glittering little starstones, each in its protective sheath, each longing to rob some man's mind away with its beckoning dreams.

Herndon gathered them up and arranged a transfer of funds to the amount of two hundred fifty-six thousand stellors. Brennt eyed him bitterly throughout the whole transaction, but it was obvious that the Vyaporan was in fear for his life, and would not dare attempt duplicity. No word was said of Mardlin or his fate.

Bearing his precious burden, Herndon returned to Borlaam aboard a second-class liner out of Diirhav, a neighboring world of some considerable population. It was expensive, but he could not wait for the next freight ship. By the time he returned to Borlaam, the Lady Moaris would have been back several weeks. He had promised the Steward he would rejoin Moaris' service, and it was a promise he intended to keep.

It had become winter when he reached Borlaam again with his jewels. The daily sleet rains sliced across the cities and the plains, showering them with billions of icy knifelike particles. People huddled together, waiting for the wintry cold to end.

Herndon made his way through streets clogged with snow that glistened blue-white in the light of the glinting winter moon and delivered his gems to

Oversk in the Avenue of Bronze. Benjin, he learned, would be back shortly; he was engaged in an important transaction.

Herndon warmed himself by the heat wall and accepted cup after cup of Oversk's costly Thrucian blue wine to ease his inner chill. The commoner Dorgel entered after a while, followed by Marya and Razumod, and together they examined the new shipment of starstones Herndon had brought back, storing them with the rest of their stock.

At length Benjin entered. The little man was almost numb with cold, but his voice was warm as he said, "The deal is settled, Oversk! Oh—Herndon—you're back, I see. Was it a good trip?"

"Excellent," Herndon said.

Oversk remarked, "You saw the Secretary of State, I suppose. Not Krellig himself."

"Naturally. Would Krellig let someone like me into his presence?"

Herndon's ears rose at the mention of his enemy's name. He said, "What's this about the Seigneur?"

"A little deal," Benjin chortled. "I've been doing some very delicate negotiating while you were away. And I signed the contract today."

"*What* contract?" Herndon demanded.

"We have a royal patron now, it seems. The Seigneur Krellig has gone into the starstone business himself. Not in competition with us, though. He's bought a controlling interest in us."

Herndon felt as if his vital organs had been transmuted to lead. In a congealed voice he said, "And what are the terms of this agreement?"

"Simple. Krellig realized the starstone trade, though illegal, was unstoppable. Rather than alter the legislation and legalize the trade, which would be morally undesirable and which would also tend to lower the price of the gems, he asked the Lord Moaris to place him in contact with some group of smugglers who would work for the Crown. Moaris, naturally, suggested his brother. Oversk preferred to let me handle the negotiations, and for the past month I've been meeting secretly with Krellig's Secretary of State to work out a deal."

"The terms of which are?"

"Krellig guarantees us immunity from prosecution and at the same time promises to crack down heavily on our competition. He pledges us a starstone monopoly, in other words, and so we'll be able to lower our price to Brennt and jack up the selling price to whatever the traffic will bear. In return for this we turn over eight percent of our gross profits to the Seigneur and agree to supply him with six starstones annually, at cost, for the Seigneur to use as gifts to his enemies. Naturally we also transfer our fealties from the combine to the Seigneur himself. He holds our controls to assure loyal service."

Herndon sat as if stunned. His hands felt chilled; coldness rippled through his body. Loyalty to Krellig? His enemy, the person he had sworn to destroy?

The conflict seared through his mind and body. How could he fulfill his earlier vow, now that this diametrically opposed one was in effect? Transfer of fealty was a common thing. By the terms of Benjin's agreement, Herndon now was a sworn vassal of the Seigneur.

If he killed Krellig, that would violate his bond. If he served the Seigneur in all faith, he would break trust with himself and leave home and parents unavenged. It was an impossible dilemma. He quivered with the strain of resolving it.

"The spacerogue doesn't look happy about the deal," Oversk commented. "Or are you sick, Herndon?"

"I'm all right," Herndon said stonily. "It's the cold outside, that's all. Chills a man."

Fealty to Krellig! Behind his back they had sold themselves and him to the man he hated most. Herndon's ethical code was based entirely on the concept of loyalty and unswerving obedience, of the sacred nature of an oath. But now he found himself bound to two mutually exclusive oaths. He was caught between them, racked and drawn apart; the only escape from the torment was death.

He stood up. "Excuse me," he said. "I have an appointment elsewhere in the city. You can reach me at my usual address if you need me for anything."

It took him the better part of a day to get to see the Chief Steward of Moaris Keep and explain to him that he had been unavoidably detained in the far worlds, that he fully intended to re-enter the Moaris service and perform his duties loyally and faithfully. After quite some wrangling he was reinstated as one of the Second Stewards and given functions to carry out in the daily life of the sprawling residence that was Moaris Keep.

Several days passed before he caught as much as a glimpse of the Lady Moaris. That did not surprise him; the Keep covered fifteen acres of Borlaam City, and Lord and Lady occupied private quarters on the uppermost level, the rest of the huge place being devoted to libraries, ballrooms, art galleries, and other housings for the Moaris treasures, all of these rooms requiring a daily cleaning by the household staff.

He saw her finally as he was passing through the fifth-level hallway in search of the ramp that would take him to his next task, cataloguing the paintings of the sixth-level gallery: He heard a rustle of crinoline first, and then she proceeded down the hall, flanked on each side by copper-colored Toppidan giants and in front and back by glistening-gowned ladies in waiting.

The Lady Moaris herself wore sheer garments that limned the shapely lines of her body. Her face was sad; it seemed to Herndon, as he saw her from afar, that she was under some considerable strain.

He stepped to one side to let the procession go past; but she saw him and glanced quickly to the side at which he stood. Her eyes widened in surprise as she recognized him. He did not dare a smile. He waited until she had moved on, but inwardly he gloated. It was not difficult to read the expression in her eyes.

Later that day a blind Agozlid servant came up to him and silently handed him a sealed note. Herndon pocketed it, waiting until he was alone in a corridor that was safe from the Lord Moaris' spy rays. He knew it was safe; the spy ray in that corridor had been defective, and he himself had removed it that morning, meaning to replace it later in the day.

He broke the seal. The note said simply: *I have waited a month for you. Come to me tonight; M. is to spend the night at the Seigneur's palace. Karla will admit you.*

The photonically sensitized ink faded from sight in a moment; the paper was blank. Smiling, he thrust it in a disposal hatch.

He quietly made his way toward the eleventh-level chamber of the Lady Moaris when the Keep had darkened for the night. Her lady in waiting Karla, the bronze-haired one who had served as go-between aboard the *Lord Nathiir*, was on duty. Now she wore night robes of translucent silk; a test of his fidelity, no doubt. Herndon carefully kept his eyes from her body and said, "I am expected."

"Yes. Come with me."

It seemed to him that the look in her eyes was a strange one: desire, jealousy, hatred, perhaps? But she turned and led him within, down corridors lit only with a faint night glow. She nudged an opener; a door before him flickered and was momentarily nullified. He stepped through, and it returned to the solid state behind him.

The Lady Moaris was waiting.

She wore only the filmiest of gowns, and the longing was evident in her eyes. Herndon said, "Is this safe?"

"It is. Moaris is away at Krellig's." Her lip curled in a bitter scowl. "He spends half his nights there toying with the Seigneur's cast-off women. The room is sealed against spy rays. There's no way he can find out you've been here."

"And the girl—Karla? You trust her?"

"As much as I can trust anyone." Her arms sought his shoulders. "My rogue," she murmured, "why did you leave us at Molleccogg?"

"Business of my own, milady."

"I missed you. Molleccogg was a bore without you."

Herndon smiled gravely. "Believe me, I didn't choose to. But I had sworn to carry out duty elsewhere."

She pulled him urgently to her. Herndon felt pity for this lovely noble-woman, first in rank among the ladies of the court, condemned to seek lovers among the stewards and grooms.

"Anything I have is yours," she promised him. "Ask for anything! Anything!"

"There is one prize you might secure for me," Herndon said grimly.

"Name it. The cost doesn't matter."

"There is no cost," Herndon said. "I simply seek an invitation to the court of the Seigneur. You can secure this through your husband. Will you do it for me?"

"Of course," she whispered. She clung to him hungrily. "I'll speak to Moaris—tomorrow."

Chapter Six

At the end of the week Herndon visited the Avenue of Bronze and learned from Bollar Benjin that sales of the starstones proceeded well, that the arrangement under royal patronage was a happy one, and that they would soon be relieved of most of their stock. It would, therefore, be necessary for him to make another trip to Vyapore during the next several weeks. He agreed, but requested an advance of two months' salary.

"I don't see why not," Benjin agreed. "You're a valuable man, and we have the money to spare:'

He handed over a draft for ten thousand stellors. Herndon thanked him gravely, promised to contact him when it was time for him to make the journey to Vyapore, and left.

That night he departed for Meld XVII where he sought out the surgeon who had altered his features after his flight from sacked Zonnigog. He requested certain internal modifications. The surgeon was reluctant, saying the operation was a risky one, very difficult, and entailed a fifty percent chance of total failure, but Herndon was stubborn.

It cost him twenty-five thousand stellors, nearly all the money he had, but he considered the investment a worthy one. He returned to Borlaam the next day. A week had elapsed since his departure.

He presented himself at Moaris Keep, resumed his duties, and once again spent the night with the Lady Moaris. She told him that she had wangled a promise from her husband and that he was soon to be invited to court. Moaris had not questioned her motives, and she said the invitation was a certainty.

Some days later a message was delivered to Barr Herndon of Zonnigog. It was in the hand of the private secretary to Moaris, and it said that the Lord Moaris had chosen to exert his patronage in favor of Barr Herndon and that Herndon would be expected to pay his respects to the Seigneur Krellig.

The invitation from the Seigneur came later in the day, borne by a resplendent Toppidan footman, commanding him to present himself at the court reception the following evening on pain of displeasing the Seigneur. Herndon exulted. Now he had attained the pinnacle of Borlaamese success; he was to be allowed into the presence of the sovereign. This was the culmination of all his planning.

He dressed in the court robes that he had purchased weeks before for just such an event—robes that had cost him more than a thousand stellors, sumptuous with inlaid precious gems and rare metals. He visited a tonsorial parlor and had an artificial beard affixed in the fashion of many courtiers who disliked growing beards but who desired to wear them at ceremonial state functions. He was bathed and combed, perfumed, and otherwise prepared for his debut at court. He also made certain that the surgical modifications performed on him by the Meldian doctor would be effective when the time came.

The shadows of evening dropped. The moons of Borlaam rose, dancing brightly across the sky. The evening fireworks display cast brilliant light through the winter sky, signifying that this was the birth month of Borlaam's Seigneur.

Herndon sent for the carriage he had hired. It arrived, a magnificent four-tube model bright with gilt paint, and he left his shabby dwelling place. The carriage soared into the night sky; twelve minutes later it descended in the courtyard of the Grand Palace of Borlaam, that monstrous heap of masonry that glowered down at the capital city from the impregnable vantage point of the Hill of Fire.

Floodlights illuminated the Grand Palace. Another man might have been stirred by the imposing sight; Herndon merely felt an upwelling of anger. Once his family had lived in a palace, too—not of this size, to be sure, for the people of Zonnigog were modest and unpretentious in their desires. But it had been a palace all the same until the armies of Krellig razed it.

He dismounted from his carriage and presented his invitation to the haughty Seigneurial guards on duty. They admitted him after checking to see that he carried no concealed weapons, and he was conducted to an antechamber in which he found the Lord Moaris.

"So you're Herndon," Moaris said speculatively. He squinted and tugged at his beard.

Herndon compelled himself to kneel. "I thank you for the honor your Grace bestows upon me this night."

"You needn't thank me," Moaris grunted. "My wife asked for your name to be put on my invitation list. But I suppose you know all that. You look familiar, Herndon. Where have I seen you before?"

Presumably Moaris knew that Herndon had been employed in his own service. But he merely said, "I once had the honor of bidding against you for a captive proteus in the slave market, milord."

A flicker of recognition crossed Moaris's seamed face, and he smiled coldly. "I seem to remember," he said.

A gong sounded.

"We mustn't keep the Seigneur waiting," said Moaris. "Come."

Together they went forward to the Grand Chamber of the Seigneur of Borlaam.

Moaris entered first, as befitted his rank, and took his place to the left of the monarch, who sat on a raised throne decked with violet and gold. Herndon knew protocol; he knelt immediately.

"Rise," the Seigneur commanded. His voice was a dry whisper, feathery-sounding, barely audible and yet commanding all the same. Herndon rose and stared levelly at Krellig.

The monarch was a tiny man, dried and fleshless; he seemed almost to be a humpback. Two beady, terrifying eyes glittered from a wrinkled, world-weary face. Krellig's lips were thin and bloodless, his nose a savage slash, his chin wedge-shaped.

Herndon let his eyes rove. The hall was huge, as he had expected; vast pillars supported the ceiling, and rows of courtiers flanked the walls. There were women, dozens of them: the Seigneur's mistresses, no doubt.

In the middle of the hall hung suspended something that looked to be a giant cage completely cloaked in thick draperies of red velvet. Some pet of the Seigneur's probably lurked within: a vicious pet, Herndon theorized, possibly a Villidonian gyrfalcon with honed talons.

"Welcome to the court," the Seigneur murmured.

"You are the guest of my friend Moaris, eh?"

"I am, sire," Herndon said. In the quietness of the hall his voice echoed cracklingly.

"Moaris is to provide us all with some amusement this evening," remarked the monarch. The little man chuckled in anticipatory glee. "We are very grateful to your sponsor, the Lord Moaris, for the pleasure he is to bring to us this night."

Herndon frowned. He wondered obscurely whether he was to be the source of amusement. He stood his ground unafraid; before the evening had ended, he himself would be amused at the expense of the others.

"Raise the curtain," Krellig commanded.

Instantly two Toppidan slaves emerged from the corners of the throne room and jerked simultaneously on heavy cords that controlled the curtain over the cage. Slowly the thick folds of velvet lifted, revealing, as Herndon had suspected, a cage.

There was a girl in the cage.

She hung suspended by her wrists from a bar mounted at the roof of the cage. She was naked; the bar revolved, turning her like an animal trussed to a spit. Herndon froze, not daring to move, staring in sudden astonishment at the slim, bare body dangling there.

It was a body he knew well.

The girl in the cage was the Lady Moaris.

Seigneur Krellig smiled benignly; he murmured in a gentle voice, "Moaris, the show is yours, and the audience awaits. Don't keep us waiting."

Moaris slowly moved toward the center of the ballroom floor. The marble under his feet was brightly polished and reflected him; his boots thundered as he walked.

He turned, facing Krellig, and said in a calm, controlled tone, "Ladies and gentlemen of the Seigneur's court, I beg leave to transact a little of my domestic business before your eyes. The lady in the cage, as most of you, I believe, are aware, is my wife."

A ripple of hastily hushed comment was emitted by the men and women of the court. Moaris gestured, and a spotlight flashed upward, illuminating the woman in the cage.

Herndon saw that her wrists were cruelly pinioned and that the blue veins stood out in sharp relief against her pale arms. She swung in a small circle as the bar above her turned in its endless rotation. Beads of sweat trickled down her back and stomach, and the harsh, sobbing intake of her breath was audible in the silence.

Moaris said casually, "My wife has been unfaithful to me. A trusted servant informed me of this not long ago: she has cheated me several times with no less a personage than an obscure member of our household, a groom or a lackey or some other person. When I questioned her, she did not deny this accusation. The Seigneur"—Moaris bowed in a throneward direction—"has granted me permission to chastise her here, to provide me with greater satisfaction and you with a moment of amusement."

Herndon did not move. He watched as Moaris drew from his sash a glittering little heat gun. Calmly the nobleman adjusted the aperture to minimum. He gestured; a side of the cage slid upward, giving him free target.

He lifted the heat gun.

Flick!

A bright tongue of flame licked out, and the girl in the cage uttered a little moan as a pencil-thin line was seared across her flanks.

Flick!

Again the beam played across her body. Flick! Again. Lines of pain were traced across her breasts, her throat, her knees, her back. She revolved helplessly as Moaris amused himself, carving line after line along her body with the heat ray. It was only with an effort that Herndon held still. The members of the court chuckled as the Lady Moaris writhed and danced in an effort to escape the inexorable lash of the beam.

Moaris was an expert. He sketched patterns on her body, always taking care that the heat never penetrated below the upper surface of the flesh. It was a form of torture that might endure for hours, until the blood bubbled in her veins and she died.

Herndon realized the Seigneur was peering at him. "Do you find this courtly amusement to your taste, Herndon?" Krellig asked.

"Not quite, sire." A hum of surprise rose that such a newcomer to the court should dare to contradict the Seigneur. "I would prefer a quicker death for the lady."

"And rob us of our sport?" Krellig asked.

"I would indeed do that," said Herndon. Suddenly he thrust open his jeweled cloak; the Seigneur cowered back as if he expected a weapon to come forth, but Herndon merely touched a plate in his chest, activating the device that the Meldian had implanted in his body. The neuronic mesh functioned in reverse; gathering a charge of deadly force, it sent the bolt surging along Herndon's hand. A bright arc of fire leaped from Herndon's pointing finger and surrounded the girl in the cage.

"Barr!" she screamed, breaking her silence at last, and died.

Again Herndon discharged the neuronic force, and Moaris, his hands singed, dropped his heat gun.

"Allow me to introduce myself," Herndon said as Krellig stared white-faced at him and the nobles of the court huddled together in fright. "I am Barr Herndon, son of the First Earl of Zonnigog. Somewhat over a year ago a courtier's jest roused you to lay waste to your fief of Zonnigog and put my family to the sword. I have not forgotten that day."

"Seize him!" Krellig shrieked.

"Anyone who touches me will be blasted with the fire," Herndon said. "Any weapon directed at me will recoil upon its owner. Hold your peace and let me finish.

"I am also Barr Herndon, Second Steward to Lord Moaris, and the lover of the woman who died before you. It must comfort you, Moaris, to know that the man who cuckolded you was no mere groom but a noble of Zonnigog.

"I am also," Herndon went on in the dead silence, "Barr Herndon the spacerogue, driven to take up a mercenary's trade by the destruction of my household. In that capacity I became a smuggler of starstones, and"—he bowed—"through an ironic twist, found myself owing a debt of fealty to none other than you, Seigneur.

"I hereby revoke that oath of fealty, Krellig—and for the crime of breaking an oath to my monarch, I sentence myself to death. But also, Krellig, I order a sentence of death upon your head for the wanton attack upon my homeland. And you, Moaris—for your cruel and barbaric treatment of this woman whom you never loved, you must die, too.

"And all of you—you onlookers and sycophants, you courtiers and parasites, you, too, must die. And you, the court clowns, the dancing bears and captive lifeforms of far worlds, I will kill you, too, as once I killed a slave proteus—not out of hatred but simply to spare you from further torment."

He paused. The hall was terribly silent; then someone to the right of the throne shouted, "He's crazy! Let's get out of here!"

He dashed for the great doors, which had been closed. Herndon let him get within ten feet of safety, then blasted him down with a discharge of life force. The mechanism within his body recharged itself, drawing its power from the hatred within him and discharging through his fingertips.

Herndon smiled at Lord Moaris, pale now. He said, "I'll be more generous to you than you to your Lady. A quick death for you."

He hurled a bolt of force at the nobleman. Moaris recoiled, but there was no hiding possible; he stood bathed in light for a moment, and then the charred husk dropped to the ground.

A second bolt raked the crowd of courtiers. A third Herndon aimed at the throne; the costly hangings of the throne area caught first, and Krellig half-rose before the bolt of force caught him and hurled him back dead.

Herndon stood alone in the middle of the floor. His quest was at its end; he had achieved his vengeance. All but the last: on himself, for having broken the oath he had involuntarily sworn to the Seigneur.

Life held no further meaning for him. It was odious to consider returning to a spacerogue's career, and only death offered absolution from his oaths.

He directed a blazing beam of force at one of the great pillars that supported the throne room's ceiling. It blackened, then buckled. He blasted apart another of the pillars, and the third.

The roof groaned; after hundreds of years the tons of masonry were suddenly without support. Herndon waited, then smiled in triumph as the ceiling hurtled down at him.

About the Author

ROBERT SILVERBERG (1935–) began writing in the mid-1950s for science fiction magazines such as *Amazing Stories*, *Science Fiction Adventures*, and *Super-Science Fiction*. He has gone on to author more than one hundred science fiction and fantasy novels, including *A Time of Changes*, *Roma Eterna*, *The Last Song of Orpheus*, and the bestselling Majipoor cycle, and is widely regarded today as one of the all-time greatest science fiction and fantasy writers. He is also the author of more than sixty nonfiction works, in addition to editing or co-editing sixty-plus anthologies, including *The Science Fiction Hall of Fame, Volume One (1929-1964)*, *Legends I & II*, and *Far Horizons*. He has won five Nebula Awards, four Hugo Awards, and the Prix Tour-Apollo Award. In 1999, he was inducted into the Science Fiction Hall of Fame, and in 2004, the Science Fiction and Fantasy Writers of America presented him with the prestigious Damon Knight Memorial Grand Master Award.

Collect all of these exciting Planet Stories adventures!

THE WALRUS AND THE WARWOLF
BY HUGH COOK
INTRODUCTION BY CHINA MIÉVILLE

Sixteen-year-old Drake Duoay loves nothing more than wine, women, and getting into trouble. But when he's abducted by pirates and pursued by a new religion bent solely on his destruction, only the love of a red-skinned priestess will see him through the insectile terror of the Swarms.

ISBN: 978-1-60125-214-2

WHO FEARS THE DEVIL?
BY MANLY WADE WELLMAN
INTRODUCTION BY MIKE RESNICK

In the back woods of Appalachia, folk-singer and monster-hunter Silver John comes face to face with the ghosts and demons of rural Americana in this classic collection of eerie stories from Pulitzer Prize-nominee Manly Wade Wellman.

ISBN: 978-1-60125-188-6

THE SECRET OF SINHARAT
BY LEIGH BRACKETT
INTRODUCTION BY MICHAEL MOORCOCK

In the Martian Drylands, a criminal conspiracy leads wild man Eric John Stark to a secret that could shake the Red Planet to its core. In a bonus novel, *People of the Talisman*, Stark ventures to the polar ice cap of Mars to return a stolen talisman to an oppressed people.

ISBN: 978-1-60125-047-6

THE GINGER STAR
BY LEIGH BRACKETT
INTRODUCTION BY BEN BOVA

Eric John Stark journeys to the dying world of Skaith in search of his kidnapped foster father, only to find himself the subject of a revolutionary prophecy. In completing his mission, will he be forced to fulfill the prophecy as well?

ISBN: 978-1-60125-084-1

THE HOUNDS OF SKAITH
BY LEIGH BRACKETT
INTRODUCTION BY F. PAUL WILSON

Eric John Stark has destroyed the Citadel of the Lords Protector, but the war for Skaith's freedom is just beginning. Together with his foster father Simon Ashton, Stark will have to unite some of the strangest and most bloodthirsty peoples the galaxy has ever seen if he ever wants to return home.

ISBN: 978-1-60125-135-0

THE REAVERS OF SKAITH
BY LEIGH BRACKETT
INTRODUCTION BY GEORGE LUCAS

Betrayed and left to die on a savage planet, Eric John Stark and his foster-father Simon Ashton must ally with cannibals and feral warriors to topple an empire and bring an enslaved civilization to the stars. But in fulfilling the prophecy, will Stark sacrifice that which he values most?

ISBN: 978-1-60125-084-1

Collect all of these exciting Planet Stories adventures!

THE SWORD OF RHIANNON
BY LEIGH BRACKETT
INTRODUCTION BY NICOLA GRIFFITH

Captured by the cruel and beautiful princess of a degenerate empire, Martian archaeologist-turned-looter Matthew Carse must ally with the Red Planet's rebellious Sea Kings and their strange psychic allies to defeat the tyrannical people of the Serpent.

ISBN: 978-1-60125-152-7

INFERNAL SORCERESS
BY GARY GYGAX
INTRODUCTION BY ERIK MONA

When the shadowy Ferret and the broad-shouldered mercenary Raker are framed for the one crime they didn't commit, the scoundrels are faced with a choice: bring the true culprits to justice, or dance a gallows jig. Can even this canny, ruthless duo prevail against the beautiful witch that plots their downfall?

ISBN: 978-1-60125-117-6

STEPPE
BY PIERS ANTHONY
INTRODUCTION BY CHRIS ROBERSON

After facing a brutal death at the hands of enemy tribesmen upon the Eurasian steppe, the 9th-century warrior-chieftain Alp awakes fifteen hundred years in the future only to find himself a pawn in a ruthless game that spans the stars.

ISBN: 978-1-60125-182-4

WORLDS OF THEIR OWN
EDITED BY JAMES LOWDER

From R. A. Salvatore and Ed Greenwood to Michael A. Stackpole and Elaine Cunningham, shared-world books have launched the careers of some of science fiction and fantasy's biggest names. Yet what happens when these authors break out and write tales in worlds entirely of their own devising, in which they have absolute control over every word? Contains 18 creator-owned stories by the genre's most prominent authors.

ISBN: 978-1-60125-118-3

ALMURIC
BY ROBERT E. HOWARD
INTRODUCTION BY JOE R. LANSDALE

From the creator of Conan, Almuric is a savage planet of crumbling stone ruins and debased, near-human inhabitants. Into this world comes Esau Cairn—Earthman, swordsman, murderer. Can one man overthrow the terrible devils that enslave Almuric?

ISBN: 978-1-60125-043-8

SOS THE ROPE
BY PIERS ANTHONY
INTRODUCTION BY ROBERT E. VARDEMAN

In a post-apocalyptic future where duels to the death are everyday occurrences, the exiled warrior Sos sets out to rebuild civilization—or destroy it.

ISBN: 978-1-60125-194-7

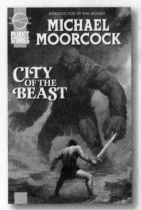

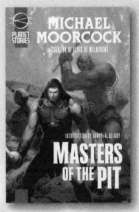
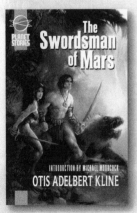

STRANGE ADVENTURES ON OTHER WORLDS

PLANET
stories

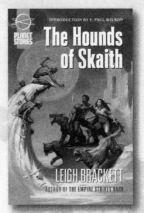
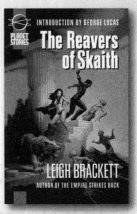

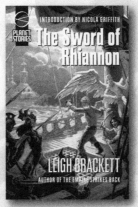

HIDDEN WORLDS AND ANCIENT MYSTERIES

PLANET
stories

SWORD & SORCERY LIVES!

Planet Stories is proud to present these classics of magic and perilous adventure from three unparalleled masters of heroic fantasy: Robert E. Howard, A. Merritt, and C. L. Moore.

···

"Howard's writing is so highly charged with energy that it nearly gives off sparks."

Stephen King

"[A. Merritt] has a subtle command of a unique type of strangeness which no one else has been able to parallel."

H. P. Lovecraft

"C. L. Moore's shimmering, highly colored prose is unique in science fiction."

Greg Bear

Can a single Earthman hope to overthrow the terrible devils that enslave the savage world of Almuric?
ISBN 978-1-60125-043-8
$12.99

A mysterious artifact from ancient Babylon hurtles amateur archaeologist John Kenton onto the seas of another dimension.
ISBN 978-1-60125-177-0
$14.99

Jirel of Joiry, the first-ever sword and sorcery heroine, takes up her greatsword against dark gods and monsters.
ISBN 978-1-60125-045-2
$12.99

Available now at quality bookstores and **paizo.com/planetstories**

EXPLORE THE WORLDS OF HENRY KUTTNER!

From brutal worlds of flashing swords and primal magic to futures portraying binge-drinking scientists and uncooperative robot assistants, Henry Kuttner's creations rank as some of the most influential in the entirety of the speculative fiction genre.

"A neglected master . . . a man who shaped science fiction and fantasy in its most important years."

Ray Bradbury

"I consider the work of Henry Kuttner to be the finest science-fantasy ever written."

Marion Zimmer Bradley

"The most imaginative, technically skilled and literarily adroit of science-fantasy authors."

The New York Herald Tribune

A scientist wakes from each drunken bender having created an amazing new invention—now if he could only remember how it worked!

ISBN 978-1-60125-153-4
$12.99

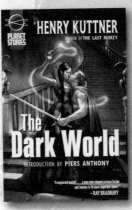

Edward Bond falls through a portal into an alternate dimension only to find himself trapped in the body of the evil wizard Ganelon.

ISBN 978-1-60125-136-7
$12.99

A dashing swordsman with a mysterious past battles his way through warriors and warlocks in the land of doomed Atlantis.

ISBN 978-1-60125-046-9
$12.99

Available now at quality bookstores and **paizo.com/planetstories**

PLANET
stories

MYTHIC HEROES!

From the pen of master fantasist and Pultizer Prize-nominee Manly Wade Wellman comes the complete and authorized collections of Silver John, the legendary balladeer and monster-hunter of back woods America, and Hok the Mighty, humanity's first hero!

....

"From pulp magazines to Arkham House to 'The Twilight Zone,' Manly Wade Wellman is a legend—and one of the finest regional fantasists of his day."
Greg Bear

"One of science fiction's few, legitimate artists."
Mike Resnick

"Just as J. R. R. Tolkien created a modern British myth cycle, so did Manly Wade Wellman give us an imaginary world of purely American fact, fantasy, and song."
Karl Edward Wagner

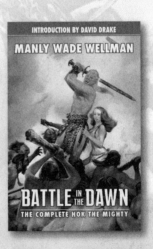

Folk-singer Silver John travels the back woods of Appalachia, facing off against the ghosts, devils, and monsters of rural America.
ISBN 978-1-60125-188-6
$15.99

A hero from humanity's past battles savage Neanderthals and journeys to lost Atlantis in this complete and authorized edition.
ISBN 978-1-60125-289-0
$15.99

Available now at quality bookstores and **paizo.com/planetstories**